color *the* sidewalk *for* me

W9-BYK-810

Also by Brandilyn Collins

Eyes of Elisha

color *the* sidewalk *for* me

BRANDILYN COLLINS

ZONDERVAN™

GRAND RAPIDS, MICHIGAN 49530

ZONDERVAN™

Color the Sidewalk for Me
Copyright © 2002 by Brandilyn Collins

Requests for information should be addressed to:

Zondervan, *Grand Rapids, Michigan 49530*

Library of Congress Cataloging-in-Publication Data

Collins, Brandilyn.
  Color the sidewalk for me / Brandilyn Collins.
    p. cm. — (Bradleyville series)
  ISBN 0-310-24242-8
  1. Parent and adult child—Fiction. 2. Mothers and
daughters—Fiction. 3. Kentucky—Fiction. I. Title.
  PS3553.O4747815 C65 2001
  813'.6—dc21
                                       2001006356

Interior design by Susan Ambs

Printed in the United States of America

---

02 03 04 05 06 07 08 /❖ DC/ 10 9 8 7 6 5 4 3 2 1

For my mother and father,
Ruth and J. T. Seamands,
who have colored the sidewalk for me
since the day of my birth.

Come unto me, all ye that labour and are heavy laden, and I will give you rest. Take my yoke upon you, and learn of me; for I am meek and lowly in heart: and ye shall find rest unto your souls.

—Matthew 11:28–29 KJV

Acknowledgments

Many thanks to Niwana Briggs for her insightful editorial comments as this story progressed.

To my agent, Jane Jordan Browne, who surely never sleeps, I send my utmost gratitude. We did it!

To my editor, Dave Lambert, and copy editor, Robin Schmitt, and to Sue Brower and Sherry Guzy and all the other terrific marketing and publicity folks at Zondervan—my deepest appreciation. Ron Huizenga, you're batting a thousand. Can't wait to see what you all have in store for me next.

~ *1997* ~

chapter 1

The boxes are heavy, their rough rope handles cutting into my palms. A frayed purse weights my weary shoulder. Heat shimmers from the fuel-spotted asphalt, stifling humidity wrapping greedy fingers around my throat. The squat, gray building seems so far away, and my legs are wobbling. Others move ahead of me as we file from the bus into the station. I breathe deeply, lungs filling with roiling air. My head feels light. Detaching itself from my body, it begins to float. Somewhere below are my arms, the boxes, my stumbling feet.

"Ye shall find rest unto your souls," I mumble, half dazed. "Ye shall find rest . . ."

And then the building looms before me. The door opens. My head drifts over the threshold. Distantly I survey the interior. Three people are in line to buy bus tickets; others dot plastic orange chairs as they wait. Two children are squabbling at a vending machine. I try to remember what I am looking for.

The door closes behind me. Air-conditioning slaps my cheeks. I shiver. Numbness chews away my feet, my legs. Vaguely I feel my fingers loosen, the boxes fall away. They hit the dusty tile floor with a clunk. Two women are watching me. I see the questions on their faces, feel their stares.

The world dims. My knees fold. For a time there is only blackness . . .

Muffled voices above me. Faces out of focus.

"Poor child, she's exhausted from the heat."

"And probably hasn't eaten."

"Go get her a candy bar."

Footsteps hurrying away.

The scene undulates, reshaping itself. I am in a cab, then a hotel room. So sterile, heartless. The bed beckons me. I stagger to it and collapse.

The walls close in. I suck air and my throat rattles. "Danny," I whisper. "Kevy."

After all the miles and all the running, the tears finally flow.

"Oh, Danny . . . Danny . . . Kevy . . ."

A gurgle in my throat yanked me to the present. My eyes blinked open. Morning sun sifted through my white lace curtains, dusting the bedcovers with flecks of gold. One of my cats stretched beside me, surveying me with lazy indifference.

Ye shall find rest unto your souls. God's promise to Granddad that he tried to pass on to me.

I lay very still, allowing my mind to adjust, as I always did after the dream. I forced myself to breath deeply until my tingling nerves settled.

Staring at the ceiling, I reflected that I'd not had the dream in a long time. Perhaps a year. Not that it mattered. Out of the many images from the past that capriciously filled my head at any given moment, this one was the least to bear.

I swallowed, passed a hand over my eyes. Glanced at the clock. Six-thirty. My alarm would go off any minute. I reached out to turn it off.

Not until I'd pulled myself from bed did I remember what day it was. Friday. My thirty-fifth birthday *and* my employment anniversary. Exactly ten years ago I had joined the creative team of Sammons Advertising Agency.

Ten years.

I stepped into the shower and stood under hot water, letting it wash away the residue of my dream as the scent of lavender soap flowed around me. If only it could wash away the stain on my soul as well. Fifteen minutes later I was dressing, still pushing away the memories, as I'd done countless times in the past seventeen years. It was a well-honed defense, this distancing from myself. On automatic, I donned a cornflower blue business suit that matched my eyes, brushing my shoulder-length blond hair. With smooth skin and a natural blush to my cheeks, I needed little makeup. I knew people thought me beautiful. Not that it mattered.

By the time I was ready, my thoughts were in place, wrenched from the tragic past and firmly wedged into the present. Mentally I went over my schedule for the day. As typical, it was overloaded with clients to please and coworkers to supervise. But the day did promise a new event, something I knew I'd never forget. My "surprise" party.

A few days before, I'd been walking down the hall toward the lobby when I overheard Monica, our young receptionist, scheming with our business manager about "how to keep Celia away from the conference room while it's being set up." I almost rounded the corner and asked, "Set up for what?" when I heard further discussion about a cake and whether it should have thirty-five candles for my age or ten for my years with the firm. I'd stopped in my tracks, scarcely believing it. They were planning a surprise birthday-anniversary party—for *me*. I'd never imagined anyone doing such a gracious thing. For a moment I'd just stood there as the realization sank in. Then I quickly faded back down the hall the way I'd come. Not for the world would I let them know that I'd overheard. Only later when I was again at my desk did I further realize whose idea the party must have been. Neither Monica nor our office manager had been around long enough to know when I started working with the firm. Only Quentin Sammons, owner of the agency, would have reason to remember that date. The thought that Quentin, busy as he was, would take time to honor me left me feeling all the more humbled. He was truly as much a friend as he was my boss, and our admiration for each other was mutual.

Quentin Sammons' agency was in its twenty-seventh year and was one of the most prestigious advertising firms in Little Rock. I had joined the firm as the lowliest of employees and had risen to an account executive. Not only was I more than capable at coming up with ideas and creating visuals; I also had a "way with words," as Quentin put it— a knack for painting a picture verbally. How ironic that the same glib tongue that had earned Mama's wrath so often when I was young would help earn my living now.

Mama.

Another thought to push away. I still had to eat breakfast, feed the cats, water a few plants before I left for work.

"Mamie! Daisy!" I called, opening a can of fishy-smelling cat food. They appeared from opposite directions, padding expectantly into the kitchen with tails raised high. I petted them both, then left them to their meals.

During the twenty-minute drive downtown, as hard as I tried to focus, scenes from my dream kept crowding into my head. Sighing, I stopped at the final red light before pulling into the parking lot of the Conart Building, the imposing six-story black glass structure that housed the exquisitely decorated offices of the agency. Forcefully then I shoved my haunting past aside. I would not think of it. This wasn't the time to deal with it anyway. It was never the time. I had too much work to do.

And a party to attend.

chapter 2

"Surprise!"

I froze in the doorway, mouth dropping open, eyes widening. Even though I'd known, I was still overwhelmed at the sight. Every Sammons employee was crowded into our conference room, grinning.

"Oh, you all," I breathed when I could find my voice. "This is *incredible.*"

"Well, come on in," Quentin cried. "Join the party!"

Chattering, the crew pushed me toward the long, polished cherry-wood table spread with presents and a multiflowered cake. Chairs had been pulled back to line the wall, some of them sporting sassily bright helium balloons. Streamers hung from the ceiling. Quentin shushed the small crowd and made a glowing speech about my importance to the firm, complete with humorous quips. Everyone laughed and applauded. When he was done, I tried to express my gratitude, but no words could have sufficed. Fortunately Quentin rescued me.

"You'd better start opening all these presents," he prodded.

A rare anticipation surged within me. "Oh well, if I *must.*" With growing gusto I tackled the first one. "Look at this!" I cried, holding up a T-shirt that read *When in doubt—go for it.* "Thank you, Jack." I hugged my colleague. He pecked me fondly on the cheek.

"Girl, I *love* this," Monica declared as she ogled the shirt. She put it down abruptly. "Here, do mine next."

Coming from Monica, it would have to be over the top. It was—a heart-bedecked coffee mug large enough to swim in.

"I'm not sure this thing will fit on my desk," I chuckled.

Before long I had an impressive pile of gifts and still had a few to open. A picture frame, two novels, a pen, a couple of CDs, and other thoughtful presents littered the table. I'd cut into the cake, and Marilyn and Wendy, two new graphic designers under my supervision, were passing out pieces. Monica was running in and out to answer the phone, indignant at each interruption. "I'm just taking messages," she announced as she returned after the third call. "After all, we'll probably have to wait ten years till we get another party."

But after she disappeared the fourth time, she stuck her head back in the conference room to look at me with trepidation. "I think you'd better take it," she said carefully. "It's your mother."

My coworkers were well aware of my business skills but knew little about my personal life. I never spoke about my childhood tragedies— the losses, the funeral attended. All my colleagues knew was that I was estranged from my family and spent holidays volunteering at Hillsdale Nursing Home. Undoubtedly they had speculated among themselves about the details.

At Monica's disquieting announcement, heads turned, curious. Discussions melted. Within seconds the ballooned and streamered room had fallen silent. A tingle shot through my chest as I clutched a present, my animation peeling away to lie, like the torn wrapping paper and ribbon, in tatters at my feet.

"She probably just wants to wish you a happy birthday." Monica forced a smile, her face raw with the awareness that she had brought the party to an abrupt halt.

Of their own accord my hands reached to drop my present on the conference table. "Of course." I glanced around the room. "Excuse me; I'll take it in my office."

As I exited, I heard the chitchat resume.

Behind my closed door I steeled myself to pick up the phone. Mama did not call often and never did she call at work. I spoke to my father more frequently, but even those conversations were stilted and shallow. There was far too much pain underneath the surface—pain that I had caused. I didn't know how to begin to address all the issues surrounding it and so had never tried.

Slowly now I lifted the receiver. "Mama?"

"Celia." Her voice sounded old. "It's your father."

Dread hit me in the pit of my stomach. I collapsed into my black leather swivel chair. "What happened?"

"He's had a stroke. Last week. I've been meanin' to call you, but I wanted to wait until I knew more. The doctors think he'll improve but it'll take a lot of work. They're sendin' him home and I'll be takin' care of him. Right now he can barely talk or use his left side."

A rush of air escaped my lips. I pictured my father—a Christian man, gentle, quiet. As meek under Mama's control as I had been contentious. And so loving to me, even after everything I had done. No one deserved this less than he. Tears bit my eyes.

"He needs you, Celia. He's been callin' your name over and over as best he can." Her voice hardened. "'Course, I told him you won't come; you're not done runnin' yet, and maybe you never will be."

The words slapped me in the face. They were so like Mama, accusing and cold.

"But he won't let up," she continued. "Celia, you need to come home."

Home?

It was too much to take in at once. A deep pain over the image of my father pitifully calling for me clashed with the dread of facing him and, far worse, facing my mother. I took a long breath, and in that instant the strangest succession of thoughts bombarded me. My eyes flitted waywardly over my desk, and I was struck by its sparseness. Most of my colleagues' desks were littered with pictures of children and spouses and siblings. Not so with mine. Between a basketed plant on either side was a meager grouping of three gold-framed photos. The first was of my cats cozily stretched across quilted pillow shams on my bed; the second, of me and a gap-toothed, brilliantly smiling old man at the nursing home; and the third, also of me, standing proudly in front of my little white house with its grass-lined sidewalk and muted blue shutters the day escrow closed five years ago. Gazing at that picture, I thought of how my Toyota just fit in the compact detached garage and how pretty the white wicker furniture looked on my back patio. I thought of the small second bedroom transformed into an office that conveniently beckoned with busyness when the ancient memories threatened. Raising my eyes to the off-white walls of Sammons, I focused on framed art from ad campaigns I had helped launch. Each one was a testament to the productive adult I had become.

You need to come home.

The words wrenched my thoughts from Little Rock to tiny Bradleyville, flung against the foothills of the Appalachian Mountains in eastern Kentucky. Bradleyville was a highly conservative town, founded by my great-grandfather upon Christian principles that I'd once held dear. I had fled Bradleyville at age eighteen, shedding not only my Kentucky accent but also my family, my friends, and ultimately God himself. Now I couldn't imagine finding a welcome among any of them.

Home? I *was* home.

chapter 3

Jerome's bustled with its suit-and-tie crowd at the plaza across the street from the Conart Building. Lush green ferns hung from beamed ceilings. Tables were spread with white paper, a coffee mug of crayons inviting doodles. Enticing scents of garlic and pasta filled the glass-walled rooms, the noise level a low buzz. Carrie Wells had insisted that I forgo my habit of working through lunch and meet her at Jerome's every other week. "You know what they say about all work and no play," she said, raising a plucked eyebrow. After Mama's phone call I'd almost canceled but knew Carrie wouldn't hear of it.

Three years previously I'd literally bumped into Carrie as I hustled into the Conart lobby elevator one day. She was clad in a dark green suit that gracefully fit her slim figure, strawberry blond hair layered and falling in gentle waves to her shoulders. Her makeup was subtly perfect. The poise she exuded was intimidating. And then she'd grinned at me, showing straight white teeth. "Whoa," she teased, "you're supposed to take the stairs in case of fire!"

I managed a smile. "Sorry. I just met with one of our advertising firm's new clients, and my mind's already on logos."

We chatted briefly on the way to the fifth floor, and she informed me she worked as a title officer for First United.

"Oh," I responded, "your company handled the purchase of my home five years ago. Were you there then?"

"No." Sadness flicked across her face. "I was mostly nursing my husband at that time. He died of cancer. I went back to work soon afterward."

"Oh, I'm sorry." I felt a sudden urge to watch the elevator numbers glow red in sequence. Her loss, too similar to mine in depth, had left me tongue-tied.

At that moment Carrie apparently chose to take me on as her personal mission, recognizing the pain in my eyes that reflected her own. As we became friends, she eventually managed to draw out information about my past that no one else had. And she was always bold in speaking about the importance of Christ in her life, gently prodding me to return to the faith of my childhood. She just couldn't understand that for me it was too late.

"Well," she breathed after the waitress at Jerome's had brought our salads, "I was all set to tell you my news, but you look like you've been hit by a truck. What happened?"

"Gee, thanks." I smiled weakly. "But I'm not ready to talk about it yet. You go first."

She looked at me askance. "You know I'm not going to let you wallow in whatever it is by yourself."

"I know, I know." Tiredness washed over me, and I leaned my head back against the booth cushion as a waitress refilled our water glasses. "I promise I'll talk. But what's going on with you?"

Her face lit up as she began to describe the new assistant pastor at her church. "Thirty-eight years old, dark hair, brown eyes, even a dimple in his cheek. And never married, can you believe that? His name is Andy. I'm so attracted to him, I hardly know how to act." She paused for a bite of salad topped with nonfat dressing. "I mean, the instant I saw him, I felt this ... *pull*. Isn't that amazing? And guess what? He feels it, too!"

Since her husband died, Carrie had not been interested in any other man. She had wanted to be, believing that an attraction would be a sign that her grief had finally begun to ebb. For all her vivaciousness—and selfless concern about me—I knew Carrie still mourned her husband. It was that time-seasoned pain that allowed her to understand mine.

I smiled, very glad for her. "Carrie, that's terrific."

"We went out to dinner last Saturday, and I had a great time," she babbled on, waving a red-nailed hand. "He's a wonderful man, so interested in his ministry at the church. His values and goals are the same as mine, and we just have this sort of ... *chemistry.*"

I speared a cherry tomato. "Like DuPont."

"Huh?"

"You know, the big company. Years ago their slogan was 'There's a lot of good chemistry between us.' Great play on words."

She rolled her eyes. "Celia, I'm talking to you about this incredible thing that's happened to me, and your mind's still on advertising?"

"No, no. I really am happy for you! But if he's so great, why hasn't he ever been married?"

"Well," she grinned, not thinking, "you're great and you've never been married."

Touché. I looked at my plate.

"Oh, Celia," she said quickly, "I didn't mean anything by that."

"I know."

All the same, I felt a solemnity descend between us. Seven years ago Roger had wanted to marry me. More recently so had Michael. Their love for me had felt good at first, very good, and there'd been a time in both relationships when I thought it just might work. I'd even allowed the thought that maybe God had forgiven me—at least that much. But I was twice wrong. My past loomed too large, age-old desires and guilt drowning out what might have been.

"Hey." Carrie tapped my plate. "Turtle. Your neck's disappearing."

I put my fork down. "Sorry."

"Okay, enough of me for now. Your turn."

Sighing, I told her about Mama's phone call. She listened, full of concern, her eyes never leaving my face.

"Your poor father. How sad," she said when I was done. She took a thoughtful drink of water. "Maybe God's giving you this chance, terrible as the situation is for your dad, to work on your relationship with your parents. When are you leaving?"

"Oh, Carrie, it's not that simple." I couldn't help but sound defensive; this was my mother's idea, not God's. "Mama's not asking me just to come for a few days. She'd probably expect me to stay three weeks, maybe more. I can't imagine being back in that town, in that house. My throat almost closes at the thought of it. I can't face her. I just *can't*."

"But how can you not help your father?"

"I don't know. I can't not help him."

"You must help him," she said gently, placing her hand on top of mine. "You can't let the fear of facing your mother keep you away."

The proximity of my half-eaten salad suddenly annoyed me, and I withdrew my hand from hers to push the plate away. I placed my clean knife across it, then my fork. Folded my napkin. Slid it beside the plate.

"Celia, listen to me. You need to do this. You need to deal with both of them."

I focused on the white paper between my elbows. "I *am* dealing with Mama. By staying away for seventeen years."

Silence. I sensed she was waiting for me to admit the ridiculousness of my statement. Fine. She could wait all day.

"Seventeen years," she said finally, "and emotionally you've just treaded water. Celia, please hear me. God wants to heal you. He *can* heal you. Remember that verse I like so much from Jeremiah? 'I am the LORD, the God of all mankind. Is anything too hard for me?' This is your chance. Take it. I know God can fix things between you and your mom. And that healing could in turn help break through the barrier of guilt you've built between yourself and God."

Carrie was rarely this confrontational with me. I stared at her, struck by her statements. *Emotionally you've just treaded water.* She had me pegged well, but at that moment admitting it was the last thing I'd do. Sometimes I felt so fractured, as if I were three or four people. I'd worked hard to become the cool, competent professional, but mere thoughts of Mama could turn me back into the emotional teenager of Bradleyville. At Hillsdale Nursing Home I could be cheerful and even humorous with patients, for that was the demeanor they so needed, yet these traits were sorely missing in the rest of my life.

I swung my eyes away. Reaching for a crayon, I spun it against the table, listlessly watching the swirl of red on white. "Carrie," I said, "if I can't even find my way back to God, you can be sure I'll never find it back to my mother's heart."

Carrie began to utter her disagreement, but I shook my head, silencing her. I'd had enough talk for the moment. The crayon stopped. I flicked it into motion again. A third time. And a fourth. Gazing through the crayon as it spun, as if into the distance, I felt a familiar emptiness as memories of Mama began to etch my thoughts.

Red on white, white under red.

Jerome's buzz of conversation, its clink of plates, began to fade. The crayon was smoothing into chalk, our table cover graining into cement. Walls and ferns melted into the enchantment of a certain spring day twenty-nine years ago, when the temperature so perfectly matched that of my own young body that I felt no separateness between myself and the air, both sun-washed and flowing with magic . . .

~ *1968* ~

chapter 4

The red chalk sputtered as I drew it over the concrete, outlining a large heart and filling it in. My hands bore the marks of a passionate artist in a fit of creativity, a pallet of pastel colors blended and sifting into the creases of my palm. My shoulders were tired from the scribbling, my knees pockmarked and scraped, but that didn't matter to a six-year-old trembling with excitement. Melissa Westerdahl, my petite best friend who lived two doors up the street, was kneeling behind me. Hearing her grunts, I pictured her tongue lolling as she labored over our dazzling designs on the short sidewalk that led from my house to the street. We were nearly finished, but time could run out at any moment with the much anticipated arrival of my newborn brother, Kevin Thomas Matthews. He was named after his two granddads—Kevin after my dad's father, who had died before my birth, and Thomas for my other granddad, who lived with us at 101 Minton.

An hour earlier I'd been bouncing anxiously around the worn carpet in front of our brand-new color TV, pestering Granddad with "How much longer? How much longer?" Daddy had left for the hospital to bring Kevin and Mama home, and even Saturday morning cartoons with the Pink Panther in his true pigment could barely hold my attention. "Jus' lookit how *pink* he is!" Granddad exclaimed numerous times in an effort to distract me. He was almost as proud of owning the first color television in Bradleyville as he was of his first grandson, since both helped fortify his place as town patriarch. Granddad cared not a whit that Mama had been beside herself with rage at his purchase, railing that too much television was "the Devil's tool." "Oh, cats-in-the-cornbread, daughter!" he'd retorted as the delivery men scurried out the door to escape Mama's wrath. "Our black-and-white one ain't done us no harm yet, so I don't see what a little color'll do!"

As *The Pink Panther* ended, with Granddad still humming the theme song and chasing me around the coffee table on his hands and knees, Melissa had called through our screen door. Melissa and I spent so much time together, Mama sometimes called us the Twins even though we looked nothing alike. My hair was blond and wavy, and hers was brown and straight as a stick. My eyes were blue; hers were brown. Melissa would bounce with energy, throwing her light frame into cartwheels, often bubbling with giggles. Sometimes she even made *me* tired.

Melissa and I both were dancing with anticipation. Granddad gave up trying to distract us, falling into the sofa to fan his face.

"Oh, I know," I cried, eyes widening. "Let's get some chalk and color the whole sidewalk for Mama and Kevin! It'll be a great present, and Mama will have a pretty carpet to walk on!"

"Yeah!" agreed Melissa.

We finished our masterpiece with only a moment to spare, the entire sidewalk covered with glorious pictures. God himself couldn't have made it any finer. No matter that my legs had fallen asleep and felt as if they were covered with biting ants.

As I was cleaning my hands against the grass, Daddy pulled up to the curb. You would have thought he was driving a chariot of gold for the care he took in stopping so Mama's door was perfectly aligned with the sidewalk. *My* sidewalk.

"They're here! They're here!" I yelled, jumping up and down. Melissa jumped too as I ran to our steps to call Granddad, who was already easing out the door, whistling the *Pink Panther* theme song through his teeth. "Be careful of the sidewalk, Granddad," I sang. "Don't scuff it!"

He stopped dead still, a veined hand on his chest as he admired our artistry. "That's so pretty, girls," he exclaimed. "The prettiest thing I ever did see!"

Daddy was opening Mama's car door with a mixture of grandiosity and awe. Mama rotated her legs slowly until her feet hit pavement, then rose with his help. The naturally smooth skin on her face was lined with fatigue, and she moved with the languidness of a hard day's housework. In her arms lay a yellow-blanketed bundle.

"Look, Mama!" I burst. "We colored the sidewalk for you!"

My cry tumbled over the pavement between us, ricocheting off the oak trees in our front yard to career around their breeze-ruffled leaves. The moment grew heavy with import as I sensed the jockeying of positions in our family now that I had a little brother. I needed Mama's breathless response, her embracing of me and my desperate desire to please. Silently I pleaded to God that she would still want me.

Granddad had not yet moved from the porch. I was still on the bottom step, Melissa frozen on the grass. Daddy's arms were steadying Mama; the yellow blanket was silent. I lifted my eyes to Mama's face and the afternoon stood still.

Her expression was one of utter dismay. It reminded me of the time I spilled a bottle of vegetable oil on her newly cleaned kitchen floor, or when a neighbor's dog left a steaming pile among her rosebushes. She stared at the sidewalk, then at Melissa and me. Daddy remained anxiously at her side, his face shuttered, awaiting her pronouncement. Time spun itself out and I held my breath.

"Well, William," Mama uttered finally, "I guess we won't spank her, since she was tryin' to give me a present."

Relief spilled from Daddy. "I think you did a right fine job, girls," he ventured, smiling at me with reassurance.

"They worked a long time on it, Estelle." Granddad's voice behind me held more than a tinge of disapproval. Mama shot him a look.

Mama and I had volleyed our share of heated words in the past. But for once I had no retort. Mouth gaping, throat tight, I let my eyes fall to the sidewalk, sweeping them over its glory-filled length, searching its decorations for a clue to her reproach. Not to save my own right hand, not for the life of me, could I understand how she could view this heartfelt gift as a mess. How could she even think of spanking me; how could she not grasp that I had lovingly prepared this for her, that I'd worked hard on it, that I was so proud?

The magic of the afternoon melted away, and I shivered as a chilling realization washed over me, coating me with desolation. It was a knowledge that I'd somehow sensed from my earliest memories but had not quite grasped hold of, like a deep, festering splinter that finally works its way to the surface.

For all her Christian charity, my mama could not love me.

~ *1997* ~

chapter 5

After my lunch with Carrie, the rest of the day saw a whirlwind of meetings. Our campaign for Cellway Phone Systems was gearing up, and three assistants were reporting to me as they drafted and redrafted the script for a local TV commercial and copy for supporting newspaper ads. The Southern Bank account had just landed unexpectedly in our laps after four years of pursuit by Quentin Sammons. Southern Bank was redefining its stodgy image into one with which high-tech, younger entrepreneurs would identify. This involved devising a campaign from the ground up—new colors, new logo and slogan—to be incorporated into everything from brochures, radio spots, a series of television commercials, and full-page newspaper ads to the large signs on the sides of metro buses. Quentin Sammons would personally oversee the account but looked to me to lead the creative process and organize logistics.

On the other end of our new client spectrum was a young company that managed the personal finances of entrepreneurs who were bootstrapping their high-potential, high-risk business ventures while still needing to make mortgage payments. The principal of Partners Corporation, Gary Stelt, was driving my poor coworker Matt crazy, rejecting one creative idea after another. At 3:00 p.m. a rumpled-looking Matt stuck his head in my office and pleaded for help. He was meeting with Stelt—again—and getting nowhere. He was afraid he'd lose the account.

"Sure. Okay." I pushed aside my scribbling for Southern Bank and followed him into the conference room, wishing I could as easily cast aside my tumultuous emotions over Mama's phone call. In light of my father's needs, I was amazed at my own selfishness and fear. How ironic that I, who had helped many a stroke victim while volunteering at the nursing home, would think twice about caring for my own daddy. Lunch with Carrie hadn't helped one bit. I was still smarting over her response.

"Look, we want something *catchy*," Gary Stelt declared after brief introductions. He was leaning back in his chair with a make-my-day expression, his suit coat unbuttoned to reveal a middle-aged paunch. His face was round, the corners of his mouth turned down. As he spoke, he hit pudgy knuckles together for emphasis.

I smiled indulgently. *Catchy*. How many times had I heard that term? What did our clients think, that Sammons prided itself on being dull? The catch was, *catchy* meant different things to different people. Over the years I had honed my observation skills until I was adroit at discerning what clients would and would not like. I listened to Gary Stelt's lengthy explanation of how efficiently his company managed its clients' money, putting them on a budget, paying bills, helping them save. "We take care of their personal business so they can concentrate on building their new companies," he continued. "Without us a lot of them would go under."

Unobtrusively I glanced at my watch. My Cellway meeting was scheduled for 3:45. For the next ten minutes I spoke softly but decisively to Gary Stelt, soothing his frustrated feathers, complimenting him on adhering to his vision for his company's image, assuring him that Matt and I would come up with the right words to summarize the essence of his business—a catchy, memorable phrase. He was, for the moment, placated as Matt ushered him out. Feeling drained, I returned to my office to gather the Cellway files, my mind on Daddy.

By 7:00 p.m. my head was pounding and my back muscles tight. I was gathering some files to stuff into my briefcase for work at home when Quentin Sammons appeared in my doorway. Inwardly I braced myself. He was my boss, but he and his wife, Edna, were also parental figures, and I'd known that sooner or later he'd want to talk about the phone call that had stalled our rare office party.

"Congratulations again on ten years," he said, gracefully lowering his angular frame into a leather chair across from my desk.

"Thanks. They've been good ones."

Fleetingly I thought of what my career could have been like had I remained at Grayland Advertising, which offered me my first job after I'd earned a degree in graphic arts through the University of Arkansas. Grayland Advertising had been a flailing mom-and-pop affair that could not keep its clients, due to Ed Grayland's ineptitude and Dorris Grayland's constantly simmering argument with life. But it was work, and I gained experience that year until Quentin "discovered" me, as he liked to say. Alvin Kepler, the owner of Kepler Electronics, a chain of local computer stores, made good on threats to pull his account from Grayland and huffed over to the offices of Quentin Sammons' agency. Kepler didn't have enough derogatory words to describe Grayland, making exception only for "the lovely young blond gal" that created their logo and newspaper ad copy. "She's sure wasting her time with that pair!" he'd declared to Quentin, who promptly called me for an interview after ushering his new client out the double mahogany doors.

Quentin Sammons was fifty when I met him, a tall, lanky figure with the most graceful, spindly fingers I'd ever seen on a man. He'd steepled them above the stacks of paper on his desk as we talked. Obviously impressed with my portfolio, he'd questioned me about my goals in "the business." His thick hair was beginning to gray. I was struck by the aura of his agency—an insistent hum of associates hurrying to meetings, sketch pads and draft copy thrust under their arms.

"I've never sought out anyone to work for me before," he'd said. "In fact, I've turned down many. But you show promise. If you stay at Grayland, you'll soon be out of a job. Work here and you'll earn a higher salary, plus I'll be around to help you really learn the ropes. That's my part of the bargain. Yours is—and I don't mind telling you— that you'll work like crazy. Nights, weekends. You'll spend hours to come up with a brilliant advertising campaign only to hear that the client's girlfriend thinks it's too cute or not cute enough, and the opinion of a layperson will send you back to the drawing board. You have to possess both talent and a high degree of diplomacy in leading clients to accept what you know is right. If you can manage that, you'll do well here."

The talent I'd possessed. But diplomacy? I'd spent the previous seven years drifting away from people, swimming in my grief and guilt. Then again, I thought, the promised hours were appealing. I figured I could lose myself in the work's hectic pace and have little time left to mourn all that my life was lacking.

"I'll manage it," I'd declared, holding out my hand. We shook on it.

Now, ten years later, after a few minutes of chitchat as he sat in front of my desk, Quentin Sammons artfully steered our conversation to the morning's event. Matter-of-factly I told him of Mama's request. "I need to go but I don't see how I can. I've got two new big accounts, plus now I've been pulled in on Partners, not to mention all my old clients." I dropped my head and rubbed my temples.

Quentin was silent. I heard his chair creak, knew he was leaning back to gaze absently out my window, chin puckered, hands clasped across his chest. After Carrie's words I now found myself waiting for his response like a child pleading for a benevolent uncle to whisk away a daunting burden. At least he wouldn't preach.

The chair squeaked again as he leaned forward to place both elbows on my desk. He cleared his throat, his words careful. "I don't think work is the real reason you're reluctant to go."

I stared at him, a denial dying on my lips.

"Celia," he said gently, "I'm about to say some things that until this moment I've kept to myself. In all the time I've known you, you've never once talked of your parents except in grudging answers to Edna's prying questions. You've never taken a real vacation. Your holidays are spent nursing old folks and working on accounts at home. We're like family here, and you're one of the most liked and respected of all my employees. You have such a giving spirit—yet you only allow your friendships to go so deep. I don't know what happened to you in that little town where you came from, but I think you fear facing it. Your parents won't be around forever. So go. We can handle the work while you're gone, and with all your accrued vacation time, it'll be a paid leave. Take care of your personal business. Then come back and get on with your life. I think you'll be happier for it."

Echoes of Carrie. Once again I was betrayed.

After Quentin left, I gazed unseeing out my window, wishing he'd minded his own business. My thoughts tumbled from our conversation to Southern Bank, from lunch with Carrie to Partners and Mama. *Partners.* My eyes narrowed. Out of nowhere a catchy phrase for Gary Stelt began forming in my head. With sudden inspiration I reached for the phone to dial Matt's extension.

"Still here, huh? Look, I've got an idea for a slogan for Partners. How's this: 'When you *want* someone minding your business.'"

He repeated it, rolling it over his tongue. Thought it had promise. "Hey, thanks!"

"Anytime," I replied.

Mamie rubbed against my hand as I sat on the patio Friday night, head tilted toward reluctant stars, a mug of tea balanced on my lap. My irritation with Quentin Sammons and Carrie had seeped away, leaving me with the old emptiness and longing.

The neighborhood was quiet, children gone to bed, their bikes and balls stored in overfilled garages. I was the only single homeowner on my tree-lined street, the helpful person who could always be counted on to feed my neighbors' animals and watch over their homes while they were on vacation. I occasionally spent time with Carrie or other friends, went to movies, sometimes hosted dinners in my small dining room. But Quentin was right—Celia Matthews' friendships merely skimmed the surface. Like the purring of the cat at my feet, Quentin's words rolled over me in undulating waves. I'd learned so well to gloss over my loneliness, filling my time with busyness. And for years a lulling "there's still time" thread had woven through the tapestry of my estrangement from my parents. Now with one phone call that thread was rippling apart.

How could I return to Bradleyville and face Mama?

The day I'd fled Bradleyville, clutching every penny I owned, I took a cab to the Albertsville bus station, prepared to catch the next bus for anywhere. The next one turned out to be an overnighter to Little Rock. I remembered that ride so well—the countless stops, people getting on and off, tepid yellow lights washing over fuel-stained parking lots at midnight and 3:00 a.m. I remembered how I focused gritty eyes out the window, inviting no conversation, wondering at the sun's audacity as it rose. I could not cry. There is a pain that finds release in tears. There is a pain so deep, so enmeshed within the very core of your being, that tears cannot touch it, and so do not fall.

I landed in Little Rock and fainted in the bus station. For days afterward, as I stayed in a hotel, I remained in a state of near catatonia.

In time I pulled myself together enough to find an apartment and land two jobs—providing maid service at a hotel by day and stocking shelves at a grocery store by night. I didn't care that the work was hard; I needed to be busy every moment so I wouldn't have time to think. In the fall of the following year I enrolled in the University of Arkansas, keeping the grocery store job. For five years I worked to earn my degree in graphic arts. I did not date, had no friends. Like a beaten dog skulking into the forest to lick her wounds, I kept to myself. I merely studied, worked at the store, and practiced art projects over and over, defining and refining my skills. I kept telling myself I'd call my parents, let them know where I was, but every time I picked up the phone, my heart would race, my hands shake. What could I possibly say to Mama? Would she even want to hear my voice? And how to apologize to Daddy? The longer I waited, the harder it became.

It took six years to make the call.

By that time I was working at Grayland Advertising. The company had shut down between Christmas and the new year, and, desperate with boredom and loneliness, I found myself propelled almost unwittingly to the phone, heart pounding.

"Mama, it's Celia."

A long pause, a sharp breath inhaled. *"Celia!"*

I heard background noise—footsteps, the receiver being pulled away—and Daddy was on the line, voice shaking, asking where had I been. Didn't I realize their worry? Didn't I know they'd been trying to find me? Would I come home? My throat was tight as I answered his questions, saying I was sorry I'd had to leave, that I couldn't bear to face Mama, then or now, that even hearing her voice brought it all back. My quiet daddy talked for a long time, urging me to "let God forgive you so you can forgive." I found myself softening. But then Mama returned to the phone, her tone reserved, cold, the way I remembered her. "Thank you for the call," she said stiffly, as if I were a distant relation. "I hope you'll stay in touch." And I knew afresh that the wounds between us would never be healed.

All the same, during that call the guilt I already bore was deepened by the hurt in Daddy's voice. After I hung up, I simply could not deal with it, and it was a long time before I brought myself to phone again. Eventually I told my parents where I was, gave them contact information. "Sometime I'll see you," I promised Daddy, "when I'm ready and Mama's ready."

There were numerous ways I could describe my guilt, each symbolizing one of its different facets. Sometimes it was a glacial lake in a yawning cave, with a sucking whirlpool at its center. Sometimes it was a steel rod through my heart, red-hot from the constant blaze of regret. Most times it was a huge movie screen that forever replayed that instant of momentous decision, the camera whirring as it rolled, the horrific consequences of my wrong choice unfolding in slow motion, the audio a raucous blare. Over and over again, a million times in the past seventeen years, those scenes had played in my head. Sometimes the reason for the screen's appearance was obvious. Other times the memories came from nowhere. I could be in a meeting with a client or combing the hair of an elderly patient at Hillsdale. I could be driving. Showering. Falling asleep. Waking up.

Soon after that initial call to my parents I began volunteering at the nursing home, both in penance and in dread of facing future holidays alone. There I found a bottomless need for extra hands and compassion. Now, years later, I still spent two to three evenings a week plus Sundays and holidays with my aged friends, reading to them, helping them from bed to wheelchair, listening to life stories, rubbing lotion on dry, spindly arms. I loved making them happy. And I'd benefited as much as they— both from feeling needed and by filling what free time work left me. Keeping busy precluded me from thinking too much.

Sometime I'll see you, Daddy. Sometime . . . .

Staring at the brightening stars, I reflected on Quentin Sammons' words about my returning home. *You'll be happier for it.* How easy for him to say. I'd long imagined that any chance for my happiness would be as impalpable as a milkweed seed drifting by. And that, preoccupied as I was with the past, even if it should appear I would lack the keen-eyed delicacy to pluck it. A return to Bradleyville was anything but a weightless milkweed seed. The mere thought of it was heavier than lead. There were too many people there I did not want to face, too many wrongs to make right. And as for Carrie's talk of God giving me a chance to heal, I knew better. Even if my past didn't stand in his way, my mama certainly did.

Still, one fact remained. Daddy needed me. He was calling for me, perhaps even at that moment. How could I live with myself if I didn't help him? Hadn't I made enough mistakes for one lifetime?

Mamie's hair tickled my legs. I took a long drink of tea, now cold, and shivered suddenly despite the warmth of the spring night.

chapter 6

Quentin was hanging up the phone when I appeared in his office doorway Monday morning. His coat was off and dangling from a hook in the corner, his desk spread with an associate's draft designs for a car dealership. A mug of coffee had been set on the credenza behind him, where it could not spill on the artwork.

Taking a deep breath, I made my commitment. "I need to talk to you about that leave of absence."

That day and the next were a blur. I met with one coworker after another, going over accounts, calling clients to explain that due to a family emergency, I was placing them in the capable hands of a colleague. I wondered about taking my computer, what it would require to set up a fax line in Mama's house. When I began asking assistants to copy files for me, Quentin quietly intervened.

"Remember what I told you?" he said. "Take care of your business at home. Call maybe, help with ideas, counsel us when we run into a snag. But leave the rest until you return."

His gentle chastisement only heightened my anxiety. How could I stay in Bradleyville without work to occupy my thoughts?

I also had to say good-bye to every patient at Hillsdale, plus figure out what to do with my home and cats. Fortunately, Monica came to my rescue. The day I left she moved into my house, nodding patiently at my harried plant-watering instructions and petting Mamie and Daisy under their upraised chins.

"You're wonderful," I panted as we lugged in her things. "Don't worry, I won't be gone too long."

"Are you kidding?" she said, grinning. "A cute place and no roommate! Take your time!"

The insouciance of the young.

I forced down half a sandwich for lunch and left. I drove all after-noon, fighting my memories and losing the battle. The farther I got from Little Rock, the more my dread increased. It was as if I rode a time machine, the familiar present unraveling into an inhospitable past. When I could pull my thoughts back to Little Rock, it was only to remember what the consequences of Bradleyville had cost me there.

In seventeen years I'd had only two relationships with men. Roger, an attorney, had asked me out numerous times before I said yes. After three months of dating, he finally broke through my barriers enough to convince me to tell him all about my troubled past. And like all armchair counselors, once I capitulated, he knew exactly what steps I needed to take in order to heal.

For all his good intentions, he got nowhere.

"You have to get past that guilt of yours," he told me with exasperation four months later over dinner at an expensive restaurant. "You need to see a therapist."

I bristled beneath my red silk dress. "No, I don't. I'm handling it just fine on my own."

"You call sobbing before a lighted candle all night handling it just fine?"

"That's none of your business," I retorted. "It's only once a year. I told you to go home."

"I wanted to help you."

"I didn't want your help. You can't help!"

He reached for my hand. "But I want to. Please let me. You keep it all bottled up, but it's got to go somewhere. And where it's gone is right here, sitting between us, getting in the way of what we could have."

Three years later Michael could do no better with me. I'd learned from the heartbreak with Roger and so had told Michael nothing. "You're so remote," he said one evening at dinner after we'd been seeing each other for ten months. Frustrated hurt poured from him. "You just won't trust me with who you really are."

On I drove. Around dinnertime I crossed the state line. "Welcome to Kentucky, the Bluegrass State," read the large sign.

Soon afterward I left the interstate, heading east through familiar winding hills. After an hour darkness began to fall. The evening air breezed through my window and swirled my hair in floating spiderwebs around my face. Cicadas were singing among the darkened hills that cradled the narrow road. Massive, gnarled oaks jutted from those hills, their dignity heightened by their blackness against a clouded sky.

Tomorrow it may rain, I thought.

Turning the wheel, I rounded a long, sly bend that curved like the crook of a beckoning finger. Bradleyville was now less than ten miles away. Childhood memories rushed me like the shadowed road leaping to life at the wash of my headlights. For some reason I thought of a day twenty-five years before, when I'd dared the biggest jump ever out of the tree swing hanging from a thick branch of a wizened oak in our backyard. I remembered pushing away hard, scraping my fingers against the scratchy rope, the smooth board pulling from my thighs. The air had been warm then also. It whizzed past my ears and shot up my nose, snatching away all breath. Or perhaps my breathing had stopped amid the ecstasy, the sheer freedom, of flying. For a moment I, at ten years of age, was suspended above the world. The idea had flashed through my head that I could conquer anything, that I, who had the courage to launch into space, could transcend it all. I was giddy with elation. Grandiose. All-powerful.

Then I began to lose momentum, saw the ground rush up to meet me. Gathering my legs, I fell, tumbled, and immediately thrust to my feet, grinning like a warrior who'd just slain her fiercest dragon. "Did you see that?" I cried to Kevy, then four. "Did you see how high I got?"

His eyes were huge. "Wow! That was great!" He ran on short legs to throw his arms around my waist in unabashed worship. We giggled and fell over, rolling and victory-punching each other like two playful bear cubs. I was only vaguely aware of the window dully screeching open above us.

"Celia? *Celia!*" My mother's voice dampened the warm afternoon. Kevy and I ceased our scuffling. "Celia Marie, you do that again and I'll get a switch! Likely to break both your legs, you are, and with your brother watchin'!"

Kevy sat up, legs splayed, casting me a baleful stare. I was still on my back, raised up on one elbow. I tilted my head and squinted up at my brown-haired mama, registering the whiteness of her bare forearms, the natural blush in her cheeks. Something shifted inside me, like a stream's current backing up to flow around a sudden rock.

"You hear?"

I pursed my lips. "Okay, Mama."

"All right, then." She withdrew from the sill and disappeared.

With the budding awareness of a child, I'd sensed the incongruity of my mother's reaction. Now, cruising quietly through the night, I still found it illogical: to prevent hurt, she would inflict it.

I crested a long grade, the hills on either side melting away, and slowed at the sight before me. Bradleyville spread demurely in the valley below, its lights a tiny silver bracelet against the flesh of the shadowed hills. Winding through a bordering forest were the glimmering waters of the river. The buildings and machinery of the lumber mill built by my great-grandfather jutted into the sky above the riverbank, boldly silent against a scrim of nascent stars.

The otherworldliness of the scene was too much to absorb. Something was missing, something important. The squall of the town seemed so removed from that vista, the pulses of its rhythm fading long before they reached me. Yet for so many years the town's effect on me had been so strong. Looking down on Bradleyville, I wondered at its seeming insignificance.

Ten minutes later, trembling, I entered the town through the back way of Route 347. All was dark and quiet. Yellow streetlights, green lawns, old wooden houses. Everything I could see looked just the same. I pictured the outlay of the town, doubting that much progress had come to any of it. I imagined it still had only two stoplights, both on Main Street. Between them would be the post office. Past the second light would be the one-block downtown area with a few stores, the doctor's office, a tiny police station, and the town bank.

I turned onto Minton, our street. *There.* Long before I was ready, I saw our house. I wiped a tear away and passed it by, eyes straight ahead. It was a peripheral blur, white and boding, a porch light on—Mama's signal that she was waiting for me. Then I was at the first stoplight at Minton and Main, my mind snapping back in time as the pictures in my head began to roll. Their vividness left me nauseous.

The light turned green. I gathered myself, then turned right.

Even as I told myself not to go, I knew where I was drawn. After a few blocks I turned off Main and wound up Maple toward our old church. Easing up to the curb, I parked the car and stiffly got out. Beside the building, in a grassy cemetery dotted with gnarled trees and wildflowers, I found the grave. I stared at the headstone, barely able to breathe, then sank to my knees. My hesitant fingers traced the letters blurring through tears. The stone was so cold, sterile, void of life. *Dear God, how did we ever come from a colored sidewalk to this?*

Moments later I tore myself away, unable to look at the inscription any longer. Numbly I sank behind the wheel of my car, driving on automatic, my head filling with memories of my childhood after I'd decorated the sidewalk for Mama. How many times had I yearned for Mama's affection, even while she loved my sweet little brother easily?

I turned off Maple back onto Main, the pain of those years washing over me. As a chalk-fingered child of six, I had worn my craving for Mama's love on my sleeve. But as I grew, that craving became cloaked in excuses and denial until slowly it sank beneath my skin to lie unheeded but vital, like the sinews of my framework. By the time I became a teenager, I thought the gap between Mama and me could not be wider.

And then Danny came along. . . .

~ 1977 ~

chapter 7

I want to go into Albertsville, Mama. Why won't you let me? There's nothing to do here!"

"Celia, I said no and I mean no. Now hush up about it."

Sunlight filtered dustily through the living room window, the lazy buzz of honeybees drifting from the roses lining our lawn. A neighbor's dog was barking. It was a beautiful day in May, school was almost out for summer, and I couldn't think of one thing right with the world.

"Bradleyville's so boring!" I threw out my hands. "Fifteen years old and I can't even go to the next town. I might lay eyes on a boy, God forbid, or see the outside of a movie theater. My very soul would be tainted!"

"Celia, stop it!" Mama spat, face flushing. "I'm tired of fightin' about this every Saturday. Your friends' mamas wouldn't let them go, either."

"Mary Lee can take me. She's my friend and she's got her own car at *sixteen*, for heaven's sake! She even goes on dates."

"Mary Lee wasn't raised in this town."

"Isn't that the truth!" I paced furiously, lips pressed. "So what am I supposed to do—hang out at Tull's? Go swimmin' in the river? Big deal!"

"Celia, enough!" Mama said, throwing down a mended sock. "You are not going into that town. You'll stay right here like the rest of your friends. You will not drive all over tarnation in that fancy green car of Mary Lee's, and you will stop yelling at me!"

"Why? You're yelling at me!"

"That's it. Go to your room!"

I huffed away, slammed my bedroom door for effect, and flung myself across the wedding ring quilt on my bed. Narrow-eyed, I hissed words at Mama, wishing I could be like Mary Lee. The lucky girl lived in Bradleyville but attended a private school in Albertsville. More important, she wasn't slave to all the rules heaped on my head. If I thought it would do any good, I'd have begged Daddy to intercede for me, but he always just said, "Ask Mama." Heaving a sigh, I pounded my pillow in frustration.

A tentative knock sounded at my door. "Can I come in, Celia?"

Wearily I pulled Cubby, the teddy bear I'd had since I was a baby, to my chest. "Yeah, Kevy, it's okay."

He slipped into my blue-walled room and closed the door, absently pulling at his T-shirt. Fixing upon my desk, he took in the bright watercolor I'd painted of ocean waves and sand. "I like your new picture," he ventured.

Gazing at his round Charley Brown face with the sprinkle of freckles across its cheeks, I felt a familiar burst of affection. I had watched over Kevy since his birth, and he'd certainly needed it at times. He was bold and daring in his play, as if his sweet naïveté precluded all thought of nature harming him.

"Well, you're in, Kevy. What do you want?"

I knew what he wanted, deep down in his sensitive being—he wanted peace in the house. Like Daddy, he craved mellow understanding, a light banter around the supper table. Kevy's heart was generous. He was the first to comfort anyone who was sad, the last to say a negative word. Sometimes, I thought, living in our family was hardest for him. Rarely in trouble himself, he was continually in the maelstrom of Mama's arguments with me and Granddad.

He shrugged. "Just wanted to see if you're okay, I guess."

"Yeah, sure, I'm great."

Wandering over to the dresser, he picked up my silver brush and pulled a hair from its bristles, absently watching it drift to the floor.

"What do you *want*, Kevy?"

He straightened his shoulders with purpose. "I wanna go fishin'."

"So go with Reid." Reid Barth was Kevy's best friend, and they were seldom apart.

"He's busy. And so are all my other friends; I already tried." He waited. "And Mama won't let me go alone. She says the water's too high."

"Well, you're wastin' your time here. I don't want to go fishin'. Have to walk all the way down there," I grumbled. "Have to buy worms."

"Please," he begged, clasping his hands in supplication. "Never know who you'll meet along the way. Maybe some kids from school. Maybe some boys." He flashed me a dopey grin.

"Come on, Celia!" Happily toting his fishing pole, Kevy skittered over pebbles at the water's edge until he hit a group of idly scattered boulders. Sunlight glittered off the water as it flowed briskly, fed by mountain runoff from the long winter's melting snow. The water would be icy cold.

"Keep up the shoutin', Kevy. Let those fish know we're comin'." I picked my way across the rocks toward our usual spot, carrying my pole and a bucket halfheartedly. Nobody interesting had been downtown or in the hardware store, where we picked up a can of night crawlers. I'd waved to a couple of younger girls hanging out at Tull's Drugstore, who turned up their noses at Kevy. When I was their age, I hadn't cared for boys, either. Then suddenly after my thirteenth birthday something had fallen away from my senses, like ice slithering down a warmed windowpane.

In all of ninth grade Melissa had giggled about how Bobby Delham, whose daddy ran the bank, was in love with me. At first I'd tossed my head at the notion. Bobby was short for his age and his full mouth a little too large for his oval face. His hair was black and his eyes brown and big like a doe's. I hadn't been interested; nevertheless I began carefully choosing clothes that best reflected my blue eyes. Let him suffer for his affection, having to watch me from afar, cool and collected. But lately I'd begun to dream of going on dates with him or sitting beside him on a moonlit beach.

Kevy was prying off the top of the worm can with stubby fingers. "Ooh, nice fat ones!" he exclaimed. He stuck a hand inside and drew out a wriggling night crawler spotted with dirt. "This is gonna get me a nice trout." I gazed at it absently. Granddad had taught me to fish before Kevy was born, hauling me down here and patiently demonstrating how to hook the worm and cast the line into the river. I'd screwed up my face in disgust the first time but had been determined not to let Granddad down. Now I could bait a fishhook while chewing on a sandwich. Kevy was an expert in his own right. In no time his line was in the water. We leaned side by side against one of the large boulders. "Aren't you gonna fish?"

"Maybe later."

As he waited in silence for a bite, I listened to the faint rush of the rapids downstream. Typically they couldn't be heard from here, but the water was deeper and swifter with the spring runoff. "Be careful of that water," Granddad had warned.

I thought of Granddad as I tipped my head back against the rock and closed my eyes, seeing the black-red of my lids, smelling the rich scent of earthworms. Granddad was seventy-four now and slow-moving. Sometimes he needed to rest during our walks downtown to Tull's, where he and his old friends Jake Lewellyn and Hank Jenkins would yak the afternoon away in their chairs under the green awning, cold drinks sweating in their hands. On Saturdays he could drive down if Daddy or Mama didn't need the car, but he didn't like to. Much as he wouldn't admit it, I think he was scared of having one of his "heart flares" behind the wheel. I used to love driving into Albertsville with him when I was little; he'd fly over the hills, pretending we were chasing the Germans out of Paris. But those days were gone. Even the lifelong besting feud between Granddad and Mr. Lewellyn, once energetic and conniving, had recently been reduced to playing checkers at our dining room table, crabbing over who was cheating.

Mama was forever fussing over Granddad's health until his ears turned red with annoyance. "I ain't dead yet, Estelle!" he'd holler at her, and she'd back off. But when he bragged of his battles in the war, she'd turn a deaf ear. As for Granddad, it seemed the less he could do, the more he wanted to talk about those battles, clinging to the days when he was gallant and strong. Over the years the whole town had heard how he'd earned the three Bronze Star Medals that lay upon gold velvet in dark blue rectangle boxes on his bookcase. Visitors were always invited to view the famed stars hanging from their patriotically striped ribbons, along with the military insignia Granddad kept in a sandalwood box. The details of his first medal constituted his favorite story, about when he stealthily crossed the Volturno River in Italy under heavy enemy surveillance to scout out a German camp. He earned his second medal also in World War II by single-handedly shooting seven German soldiers before they could surround his ragtag group of men in a lethal "pocket." And the third one he earned in Korea after risking his life to drag numerous wounded American soldiers from a perilous knoll to safety.

My granddad was a wonderful Christian man, full of integrity. But he wasn't afraid of confrontation if God led him to it. "Choose your battles carefully," he always told me. "Then if you gotta fight, fight like the angel Michael."

The afternoon sun was making me drowsy. Abandoning the boulder, I sat on a log, leaning against an ancient tree. Kevy hadn't gotten a single nibble. It was shortly after four o'clock—time to leave soon, but I couldn't summon the energy. I was beginning to think I could curl up for a nap right there on the rocky riverbank. My head dipped and my jaw slackened. The world began to fall away . . .

A sudden splash jerked my head up. Automatically I checked for Kevy. He was knee-deep in the river, holding his fishing pole high, his shoes on the riverbank, each one stuffed with a sock.

"What are you doin'! Get back here right now!" I jumped to my feet.

"I'm wadin' over to Jake's Rock," he called. "Bet there's plenty of fish around it."

Jake's Rock had been named for Mr. Lewellyn years ago when he and Granddad, at age twelve, had held a spur-of-the-moment fishing contest, the loser having to sing a serenade under the window of an ugly girl chosen by the winner. Granddad had fished from the bank; Mr. Lewellyn had decided to sit on the huge boulder in the middle of the river. It was a perfect seat for fishing. Upstream its slope was gentle, offering an easy climb to the top, which was good and flat for sitting. The downstream side fell off abruptly—a great spot to hang your knees over and cast. According to Granddad, he'd have won the contest fair and square if Jake Lewellyn hadn't stolen two of Granddad's fish and thrown them in his own bucket once he was back on the bank.

"The water's too cold, Kevy! Another minute and you won't even feel your legs!"

He threw me a grin. "I can't feel 'em now!"

"Well, get back, idgit! You're gonna be chest-deep by the time you reach the rock." I strode as close to the water as I could without getting my feet wet. "Besides, the current's too strong. Look at it!"

He was up to his thighs now, fighting to stay even with the rock as the current swirled. "I don't have to look at it; I can feel it." His voice drifted over one shoulder.

"Drat it, Kevy," I breathed, putting my hands on my hips as I watched in silence, willing him to make it to the boulder. "Go, Kevy, go," I urged under my breath. He seemed to be making no progress. "Kevy!" I yelled. *"Move!"*

"My legs won't work, Celia!" His voice was tinged with fear.

I resisted the urge to declare I'd told him so. "Just try harder, Kevy!" I cried, pacing along the water. "You're almost there."

And miraculously he did. One step, then another. A third and a fourth, and he was pulling himself up on the rock. "See! Told you I could do it!" He lay breathing hard near the bottom of the slope, watching his hand in fascination as he tried vainly to move his fingers.

I exhaled loudly, feeling the clutch in my chest release. "Well, on your way back," I hollered, "if you drown, don't come runnin' to me. I'm not about to go in that water after you!"

"Whew!" a voice exclaimed behind me. "I was sweatin' for a minute there."

With a start I spun around to see the jean-clad figure of Danny Cander, an old white T-shirt turned lengthwise and tied around his hips, his chest bare. He held a fishing pole in one hand and a rusty tackle box in the other. A strand of his thick brown hair was hanging into one vivid green eye, and he absently tossed it away. "Sorry," he said, embarrassed. "Didn't mean to scare you."

My mouth dropped open, then snapped shut. "Oh . . . oh no," I managed. "It's okay." Our eyes met and held; then I looked down, seeing his gaze slip away at the same time. I was suddenly aware of the old beige shorts and faded blue T-shirt I was wearing. My hair had to be in tangles and my skin was too pale. I shifted from one foot to the other during the awkward pause, feeling a flush rise in my cheeks, hoping he'd say something. But the only noise I heard from Danny was the sound of his swallowing. I put a hand to the nape of my neck and turned back toward the river to look at Kevy. "My silly brother. Thought the fishin' would be better out there."

He exhaled. "Probably is."

I watched Kevy climb up the rock, dragging his pole along with him, a worm writhing on its hook. "Guess he's warmin' up."

"What?"

I turned back to face Danny. "I said I guess he's warmin' up."

He nodded. "Oh. Yeah."

Funny thing about Danny Cander. He'd always held a certain mildly threatening fascination for me, ever since I'd met him at the wedding of his father's handsome first cousin, Lee Harding, who was assistant manager at the lumber mill. Danny was seven then and I was six, and I'd been jealous when Granddad had enthralled him at the reception with a recounting of how his Volturno River medal was earned. "Stay away from him," Mona Tesch had warned me later at school with a sniff. "His daddy drinks."

Brazen and tough in fights when he was younger, Danny was also amazingly shy when cornered for a mere chat by a girl. He'd always been one of the school's best athletes, hitting a baseball with grace, running races with the keen edge of competitiveness flashing under those dark eyebrows. Choosing teams on the playground, any one of us at school would pick him first. But that was his only point of popularity. His daddy's alcoholism in a town where liquor wasn't even sold set him apart.

At school there were plenty of other farm kids with chores, but nobody else dragged in late as often as he did, rubbing a hand across his forehead as he stumbled past the door of my first-period class. Sometimes I'd hear whispers about the bruises on Danny's face, and I'd go out of my way between classes to check them out for myself. If I happened to catch his eye, he'd always glance away. When he arrived at school on time, I'd often see his mama dropping him off in their ancient pickup truck, hair hanging around her face in wisps. As Melissa and I walked home in the afternoons, we'd see Danny headed in the opposite direction, cutting across town to go over the tracks. Most times he was alone. Occasionally he'd walk with Bart Rhorer, a boy who lived on the farm next to his. Younger boys would sometimes try to tag along with Danny, punching at him playfully to show they were as tough as he was, and he'd usually go along good-naturedly enough. But sometimes for no apparent reason he'd holler "Git!" and they'd skim away like water bugs in a stirred-up pond.

"The bigger problem is," I heard myself saying, "he's gonna have to come back across. He'll get to walk home wet." I shook my head and looked Danny daringly in the eye. "Why do boys do such stupid things?"

A faint surprise flicked across his face. "Well," he said, clearing his throat, his gaze sliding away again. "I suppose we like to do things now and think later."

I laughed, feeling a twisted enjoyment at his discomfort. A strange sense of power, fresh and tingling, washed through me at the thought that I could cause a reaction in someone as rough as Danny Cander. I flashed back to a perfume ad I'd seen in a magazine at Tull's, the beautiful model, red-lipped and narrow-eyed, pulling a man toward her by his tie, an electrified apprehension on his face. Thinking of that picture, suddenly I understood it. Here at the riverbank, with the rocks under my sneakers, the sun on my face, and my chilled little brother fishing, I felt as if I'd just tapped into an age-old secret bursting to be discovered. My mouth opened for another laugh, but at that moment Danny's face hardened and he stared straight back at me. The sound died in my throat.

We looked at each other in silence.

Had I ever noticed how big he was for his age? He must have been a good head taller than me, and his chest was broad compared with the skinny boys in my class. His voice had deepened long ago, when the rest of the boys were still squeaking. Maybe that's why he didn't fight anymore, I thought. Nobody was willing to take him on.

Danny turned away. "I better be goin'," he said, suddenly shy again.

"No, wait." Impulsively I stepped forward to lay a hand on his arm. He shot a glance at my fingers and I took it away.

"What is it?" He wouldn't look at me.

My courage was crumbling. "You came here to fish, didn't you?"

"I can go down the bank a ways."

No, I thought. "Stay here, Danny. I didn't mean to run you off."

He swiveled toward me, a challenge glimmering in his eye. "You weren't runnin' me off."

I smiled up at him through my lashes. "Then stay."

Our eyes locked. His eyebrows relaxed, his jaw softened. I could have sworn I saw a flicker of delight play around his mouth; then it was gone.

"Sure," he shrugged.

chapter 8

Danny and I had a heck of a time carrying on a normal conversation. I trailed him as he walked over to the large rocks to set his tackle box down. Seeing our can of worms, he made the mistake of offering to bait my hook. Huffily I replied that if I cared to fish, I could do it myself. A minute later I tried to make amends by inquiring about his parents, to which he answered stiffly that they were just fine. Then when Kevy waved to him, I shouted across the water teasingly, "Look what the cat drug in!" only to reap a black look from Danny as if he'd taken me seriously.

Good grief, I thought. Getting along with him was almost as bad as trying to get along with Mama.

Danny was frowning at Kevy. "Hey! Ain't you got a catch on your line?"

"Yeah! It's pullin'!" Kevy started reeling in slowly. "Told you, Celia!"

"It'll be the last fish he catches, he keeps makin' so much noise," I grumbled.

"You started it," Danny said.

"Celia, look how big it is!" The fish was out of the water, scales sparkling as it flopped fiercely on the hook. Kevy was standing at the edge of the boulder, leaning forward precariously as he tried to grab the line.

"Kevin, watch out!" Danny shouted.

It happened so fast. One minute Kevy was on the rock, jabbering about his catch, and the next minute he was tumbling headfirst in the air. His pole flew upward, the reel spinning from the weight of the fish, then sailed down into the current. My brother hit the frigid water six feet below with a loud splash, then disappeared.

"Kevy, you idgit!" I leaped up and watched anxiously for him to appear. *Stupid boy, he never should have gone out there in the first place.* "Where is he?" I scanned the river, shading my eyes. "You see him?"

Danny was on his feet, too, squinting. "There he is!"

A good five feet downstream from where he'd plunged in, Kevy surfaced, his face blanched against the dark water.

"Come on, Kevy, swim!" I cried. "Forget your pole!"

My brother and I had both learned to swim at a young age, Granddad often walking us to the swimming hole below the rapids. Under his watchful eye I'd first learned how to roll onto my back and float, then mastered the forward crawl, and finally perfected the powerful arm and leg movements of the breaststroke. Years later I stood a few feet away from Granddad, helping him teach Kevy, backing up a little at a time, calling, "You're doin' great!" as I urged my brother longer distances.

I trotted toward the water. "Would you come on!"

Kevy gasped air in a terrorized rattle. Frantically he flailed his arms. "Kevy? Kevy! Swim!" I yelled. But something was wrong. He could only slap erratically at the water, coughing ferociously. While I froze in fear on the riverbank, my brother went under for the second time. A trapdoor opened in my stomach. "Kevy!" I wailed.

"I'll git him." Danny was throwing off his shoes and socks, jerking the T-shirt from his waist. He ran into the river, dove shallowly, then lunged into a powerful swim.

"Please, God," I prayed aloud, watching the current flow, desperately looking for Kevy—an arm, a head rising above the water. The river was so cold; falling into it must have shocked him something terrible. I should never have let him wade out to that rock. Mama would not forgive me for this. I ran down the bank, watching Danny slice through the current, but Kevy had popped up far ahead, spluttering. "Kevy! Swim to Danny!"

He splashed crazily for another second, then disappeared for the third time.

"*Kevy!*" I sprang into the frigid water only to feel my spine pull away in terror, my calf muscles melting. I stumbled and fell, hands plunging into the river, unseen rocks cutting into my palms and knees. As the water soaked my shirt, I struggled to raise my head. Kevy had surfaced again but wasn't moving, Danny swimming toward him with all his might. Somehow I pulled myself to my feet and lurched through knee-deep water, shoes saturated and pulling off my heels. I could taste blood from a cut in my hand as I pressed it against my mouth. Breathing another prayer, I watched Danny as he fought to close the gap. They neared a bend in the river, and suddenly I jerked to a stop, hearing the rapids far too loudly. The gorge ahead would be swollen to capacity, the icy water churning in its headlong plunge over heavy rocks.

Kevy slipped out of sight around the curve. A moment later Danny was gone, too.

I heaved myself out of the water and ran down the bank, tripping over rocks and logs, calling their names. I reached the bend and rounded it, the roar of the rapids hitting me in the face, and saw the water's hue lighten as it began to spiral into a surging white. There I saw Danny Cander throw an arm around my brother, pause a moment to change course, then begin to swim toward shore with one hand, face taut with effort.

"Swim!" I screamed. "*Swim!*" I fell over sun-bleached wood, pulling up immediately. Danny was sliding with the current faster than he could reach the shore, eyes bulging with the knowledge that he could not make it. I watched him falter, then slow, losing precious headway as the current strengthened. They were so close, twenty feet from me now, but the river was beginning to funnel, plowing them back into its center. "Danny!" He lifted his head and caught my eye. "Swim!"

In three steps I'd jumped back into the water, diving into a shock that snatched my breath away. Then I was stroking toward Danny. Seeing me, he struggled harder, pulling against the current. *Yes*, I cried inside. *Yes!* In another minute our fingertips were touching, and then my arm was around his shoulder, straining toward shore as he pulled my brother. The rapids rose to a scream in my ears, my eyes blinded by foaming water. Then Danny's arm fell away and he floated aimlessly, eyes half closed, his other hand loosening its grip around Kevy. "No!" I kicked, connecting with Danny's thigh, and dazedly he shook his head. His eyes opened, filling with fear. With a final effort he strengthened his fingers around Kevy and began to swim. I felt us both lift slightly, then surge forward.

The shore stretched before us, rugged and unreachable. *Close the gap, close the gap*, I chanted in my head, the frigid water numbing my senses. Kevy's dead weight was like a giant stone around our necks. *Get to shore, close the gap.* Would the bank ever grow near? Stroke, kick, stroke, kick. *Hold Danny tight. Danny, hold Kevy tight.* Stroke, kick. The rest of the world ceased to exist. I was in a dazzling white, cold place, no sound as loud in my ears as our gasps for breath. Then a thought spun across my mind with sudden, brilliant clarity. Our own choking was louder than the rapids' roar.

We were going to make it.

The knowledge lent me a burst of speed. We moved faster through the water, the gathering sweep of current behind us. Two more strokes and I let my legs sink, touching bottom. I stood, shaking ferociously, and pulled Danny and Kevy toward me. Danny dragged himself to his feet, bent over and heaving, gripping my brother so tightly that I had to forcibly unclench his fingers. "It's okay, Danny," I gasped. "We made it."

We huddled, filling our aching lungs. I glanced at Kevy. He was still, his eyelids and lips cold and blue. "Come on, we gotta get him out of the water." Still gasping, we floated Kevy to shore and dragged him up the rocky bank, his head rolling listlessly, arms limp. Kneeling over his body, we slapped his cheeks. "Kevy! Kevy!" My voice sounded tinny. His wet, cold face stung my fingers. "Kevy! Wake up!" I gripped his wrist, checking for a pulse, his skin like frozen wax. It was there, faintly. "His heart's beatin'!"

Danny leaned close to his face. "He's not breathin'."

Willfully I calmed myself, summoning my knowledge. Hadn't we studied it enough in P.E.? Hadn't we practiced dozens of times on dummies and teased our classmates about being mouth-to-mouth? "Tilt his head," I said.

Kevy's chin jutted into the air. Danny pulled open my brother's mouth, looking inside; then I took over. Pinch the nose closed. Cover the victim's entire mouth. Exhale forcefully. And again. How many times in a row? I couldn't remember. Danny pushed me aside for another look. Nothing. I repeated the steps and pulled back. Still no movement. "Turn him over," Danny commanded.

Panic rose within me and I fought to push it away. We flopped Kevy like a fish, ignoring the sharp discomfort on which he lay. Danny turned his head to one side and pushed on his back. "Lord in heaven," Danny prayed aloud, "please save him." Brown water trickled out of Kevy's mouth. Danny pushed again. Another trickle. On the third push Kevy's lips convulsed, his legs smacking against the rocks. He coughed violently, then retched. His eyeballs rolled under their closed lids, his throat gurgling. Danny flipped Kevy over to his back again and tilted his head. I bent down to cover my brother's mouth with my own once more, feeling the slick coldness of Kevy's skin on my lips. After three breaths I pulled away. "Come on, Kevy, *breathe.*"

I started to bend down again but Danny caught my arm. "No, wait." My brother's chest began to rise, air whining in his throat. "Yes, Kevy." I rubbed his forehead hard. "Come on." His chest fell with a moan.

"Thank you, Jesus!" Danny cried excitedly. "Come on, Kevin!"

Kevy sucked in air again, his white face turning a slight pink, eyes fluttering open. "Celia." His lips barely moved. Danny and I shot each other a victorious glance.

"Yes, Kevy, I'm here."

For no reason a sob rose suddenly in my throat. I hadn't cried the whole time; now was an odd moment to start. "Oh," I moaned, voice breaking. I tried to push the emotions away but could not. Kevy was all right; my brother was going to be fine. "Thank God!"

"Don't cry, Celia," Kevy whispered.

I brought both hands to my mouth, overwhelmed with exhaustion and relief. Dear Kevy, nearly drowned, and he was worried about me. I felt the chilly touch of his fingers on my forearms, which made me cry all the more. "It's okay, Kevin," I heard Danny say. And then I stood up and Danny was standing, too, saying my brother was going to be all right. I nodded fiercely but still I sobbed, turning away so he wouldn't see my face. After a minute I felt a tentative touch on my shoulder and was embarrassed to find him right behind me. "Please don't cry, Celia; he's okay now."

"I know."

"Then why're you cryin'?"

"I can't help it; I'm just glad he's all right. He's the only brother I've got."

"Oh." I could sense him shifting uncomfortably. "Are you through yet?"

I tried to breathe evenly but the tears kept coming. "No. I'm sorry."

"That's okay. You don't have to apologize."

I turned toward him, the ground blurry beneath my feet. "I just w–want," I stuttered, covering my mouth so he wouldn't see my lips pull, "to thank you for s–savin' my brother."

"It's all right; I couldn't a done it without you. And God helped us both."

"No, if you hadn't jumped in—"

"Celia." He put a hand on each of my shoulders. "You got to stop now; we still need to help Kevin. He's shiverin' somethin' awful."

"Okay, I w–will. Sorry I'm bein' so stupid."

"You're not bein' stupid."

Danny's unexpected empathy pulled another sob from me. I tried to apologize for the third time but couldn't talk, so I just shook my head.

"Oh, brother," Danny said, sighing. He put his hands halfway around my back and we stood awkwardly for a minute. "Come on, stop now." He patted the back of my head as he would a whimpering puppy.

"Okay." Swallowing hard, I raised my head to look at him, hiccuping. His hair was plastered against his forehead, droplets of water still on his neck, green irises vivid against chilled skin. Our eyes met and held, an unreadable expression flickering across his face. As the last cry died in my throat, something changed inside me. I was suddenly, acutely aware of Danny Cander's arm warming my shoulders and how close we were. A tingle ran through my nerves. Blinking hard, I stepped back quickly, his arms falling away and his cheeks flushing a deep red. "I'm sorry. I'm okay now." I dropped my eyes, turning to lean down at Kevy's side. My brother's eyes were not quite focused. "Kevy. You okay?"

He nodded, reaching for my hand. I grasped him tightly, my fingers turning white. A shiver shook his body. "I'm c–cold."

"I know, Kevy. We'll get you warm." I turned to catch Danny staring at me. Flustered, he glanced away. *It's okay*, I wanted to assure him. *Don't worry about it.* "Danny, your T-shirt. It's still dry, remember?"

For a moment his face was blank. "Oh. Yeah."

"Can you run get it?"

His brow knit with concern. "Yeah. Sure."

I smiled at him briefly. Slowly he smiled back. Then he was off, loping barefoot over the rocks upstream.

"Celia." Kevy rubbed my hand. I turned toward him.

"Yes, little brother. What is it?"

"Did you get my fishin' pole?"

chapter 9

With Danny's shirt reaching to his knees, Kevy lay on the ground, still shivering. I wished girls could go shirtless as Danny was; my bra chafed and my damp shirt was smeared with dirt and blood. *I must look a sight*, I thought.

"Kevy, can you walk?" I squatted beside him.

He rolled his head, teeth chattering. "I'm s–so cold." His cheeks were still unnaturally white, each freckle a dark contrast. I shot Danny a concerned look.

He nodded. "We gotta git him somewhere quick, git him warm."

I was tired enough to lie beside Kevy and go to sleep. I tried to think of the closest place to take him, but my brain wouldn't work. "What should we do?"

Rubbing his forehead, Danny looked across the field that bordered the riverbank. His hair was half dry and looked good in a messed-up way. I took in his strong profile and the length of his black lashes. One hand was on the hip of his wet jeans, the other dangling, his muscles well defined. He'd been wearing his shoes and socks when he returned, and he'd picked up Kevy's shoes as well. He must have hurt his feet on his way up the riverbank, but he wasn't complaining. I glanced at the cuts on my palms and knees. They had stopped bleeding, although they stung a little.

Danny and I were keeping our distance. I knew he was thinking about our hug, too, was probably even more embarrassed than I. It wasn't his fault any more than mine; it just happened. The whole thing was almost funny. If anybody had told me I'd end up clinging to Danny Cander today, sobbing on his shoulder, I'd have laughed myself silly. He shifted awkwardly under my gaze, our eyes meeting. I made sure not to glance away, lest he think I still had that particular moment in mind.

"We should take him to my house."

I tried to hide my surprise but it was too late.

"It's closest," he explained quickly, pointing across the field. "We cut through there, it's only about a half mile."

"Are you sure it's okay?"

"Why shouldn't it be okay?" he said sharply.

Suddenly it was the same old Danny, with a challenge in his eye and a chip on his shoulder. It startled me, his acting like that now. Not that our hug meant we liked each other or anything, but I certainly didn't deserve his school-yard-fight cockiness. I opened my mouth to retort, but he looked away, neck stiffened, and in a flash I was back on the school playground in fifth grade, gaping with my friends at his balled fists and blood-spattered shirt.

"This is a stinkin' town," Danny had leered at me that day, "and when I'm old enough, I'm gittin' out of it."

"It's not this town that's stinkin', Danny Cander!" Gerald Henley had huffed. "It's the smell a your daddy, 'cause he's always drunk!"

Gerald was short and stout and known for his clumsiness. He was an idiot to spout off to Danny like that, and the minute he shouted the words, his pasty face blanched with fear. Like a bolt of lightning Danny's fist shot out and smashed him in the nose. Gerald yelled in pain, blood spurting through his splayed fingers. Danny stood his ground, glaring down at him.

"Don't you ever say a word about my daddy again."

It was the tone of his voice—quiet, shaking—that caused me to ignore Gerald's howls and gaze wide-eyed at Danny. Suddenly I saw him differently. It wasn't hatred or anger that had made him hit sissy Gerald, I realized; it was shame.

That same expression was now narrowing his mouth and eyes. If you didn't recognize its essence, you'd think he was angry. I supposed in a way he was—angry that for all his life he'd had to battle for the honor of a drunken father. Guilt flushed through me as I realized how hard it was for Danny to invite us to his house. I wasn't thrilled about going, either, but I would never let him know that.

Brushing wet dirt off my shorts, I said, "Let's get started, then."

Kevy protested having to move but I pushed him to his feet. "Danny, can you get under his other arm? I don't think he's good for much, are you, Kevy?"

"N–no." He managed a teeth-chattering smile. "Not m–much."

It's amazing how long a half mile can seem under such circumstances. Danny offered to carry Kevy, but I said, "No, you're already exhausted;

if you fall over, what am I supposed to do, carry you both?" I spoke lightly, smiling at him, hoping he understood the message beneath my words. He shrugged but I saw in his eyes that he'd heard me.

We moved on either side of Kevy, Danny's arm around my brother's back, brushing against my side as we began to half drag him along.

"Just go upriver," Danny pointed with his chin, "back to where we were fishin'. There's a path there that cuts through the field to my house."

In a few minutes we reached the spot where Kevy had fallen from Jake's Rock. "What about our stuff?" I asked, spotting the tackle box, bucket, and poles.

"I'll git it later." Danny urged us toward the path through the daisy-covered field. It seemed to stretch endlessly.

All those years, I marveled, I'd been fishing near the path that led to Danny Cander's house. I couldn't explain why that made me feel so strange. Maybe it was because our worlds had always seemed so far apart, when they really weren't at all. Yet in one sense they would always be far apart, Danny's daddy being the target of town gossip while my family was respected. What did it matter that I was Thomas Bradley's grandgirl and Danny was a Cander? Shouldn't people be judged by their own actions? And didn't God tell us not to judge at all?

We trudged in silence for another ten minutes, the path leading us toward a grove of trees. "My house isn't too far from the other side," Danny told Kevy. My brother was panting hard but at least his lungs were working. My hands ached from supporting him, and I knew Danny's arms must be terribly tired after his hard swimming. Finally we reached the cool shade of the trees. When we emerged on the other side, Danny announced, "See, Kevin, there it is."

It was still a hundred feet away, but Kevy's spirits picked up at the sight of the ramshackle white wood house. To its left rose an old red barn, paint peeling, separating the yard from a cornfield and pasture. In the barn's shadow chickens clucked in a lean-to henhouse. As we approached Danny's house, I could see that its long front porch was scattered with dozens of tools, a wound-up rope, battered shoes, a couple of sweat-stained hats, and three rusted, saggy-bottomed iron chairs, their cushions a faded red. The front door was open. We reached the porch steps, and through the screen door I could just make out a bare hallway and staircase, its banister scratched and worn. Exhaling my relief, I felt a rush of sympathy for Danny.

"Just sit here for a second. I'll get Mama." Gently Danny pushed Kevy into a chair, his eyes drifting nervously through the door. I sank wearily next to my brother, unsure if my worry about seeing Danny's daddy was for my sake or Danny's. "Thank you so much," I said, my eyes closing.

Not a minute later Danny's mama was hustling toward us, worry lines in her forehead, her brown hair falling astray from a bun as she wrapped her arms around Kevy. Her voice was soft as a cotton ball as she murmured his name, her face sun-weathered, cheeks gently rounded. Full of concern, her large eyes were green like Danny's. Something within me twinged as I imagined Mama looking at me the way she fussed over my brother. Efficiently she helped him to a front bedroom and began to undress him. I followed, wondering where her husband was and jumping when Danny appeared, carrying a cup of hot chicken broth.

"Thank you, honey." Mrs. Cander had fluffed three pillows for Kevy to lie against, his face pale against their dark blue cases. "Drink this, Kevin; it'll warm you up." She glanced at me. "You better call your mama. The phone's in the kitchen."

I held her eyes for a moment, my insides stirring. I wanted to capture the scene as she turned back to Kevy, one roughened hand sliding gently under his neck, the other holding the dirt brown mug, a small chip showing white at its base. She was wearing a green-and-white checked, long nubby skirt with a plain blouse half untucked. "Come now, Kevin, take a drink," she urged.

If I'd had any doubts about my brother's welfare, they spun away as I watched her nurse him. Quietly I slipped from the room.

As I reached for the phone on the yellowed counter, I was struck by what I was about to do. Perched in a metal chair with a green vinyl cushion gaping at the seam, Danny watched me pensively. He hadn't changed from his still-damp jeans, although he'd obeyed his mama's hurried whisper to "be proper and get a shirt on."

"What's the matter?" he asked.

I met his gaze, my hand on the receiver. How to answer him, when I was unsure of my own thoughts? It was . . . awkward, our two families about to mix like this. I was afraid of what Mama would say. Would she ask what Danny Cander had been doing with us at the river? Trekking through that daisy-laden field, I'd begun to question Bradleyville's seeming prejudice. God was loving and forgiving, judging each person individually. At least that's what I'd come to understand, from teachings both at home and in our church. No one had a right to judge Danny just because he'd been a troublemaker as a young kid. Who wouldn't be, in his situation?

And there was another problem. I fretted about Mama blaming me for Kevy's accident. Would she carry her anger to Danny's house, its blaze licking around the long skirt of Danny's mama, who was so tenderly taking care of my brother? I dreaded Mama's comparison with Mrs. Cander, didn't want Danny to know what was lacking in my own home. And then I realized I was cringing at the smallest inkling of what he must have felt all these years about his daddy.

"I'm afraid she'll blame me."

His look was quizzical. "You helped save him."

"Yes, but Mama . . . loves Kevy a lot. And she and I don't get along so well."

He searched my face. "That's not really why, is it?"

That weight on his shoulder was more than a chip. "Danny," I said, "don't."

Firmly I picked up the receiver.

Daddy's car scattered gravel as it scratched to a stop in Danny's driveway. Mama spilled out of it first to hasten up the porch steps, followed by Daddy and Granddad. In her arms was a bundle of dry clothing for Kevy. "Where is he?" she demanded breathlessly as Danny opened the door.

"In there with Mama." He pointed toward the bedroom, sliding me a look as she brushed past.

Mrs. Cander stood aside as Mama sank down on the edge of the bed, leaning over to hug Kevy, fingers smoothing his forehead. Granddad clasped Mrs. Cander's hand, thanking her profusely and proclaiming Danny's bravery. I had made it very clear during my phone call that it was Danny who had saved Kevy from the rapids, with my help only at the end. Daddy started to shake Danny's hand, then embraced him awkwardly, mumbling that God himself had placed him at the river in time. Mama gently began helping Kevy into his dry clothes.

After a few minutes Dr. Richardson's long gray car slid behind ours in the driveway, throwing up dust. Mama hovered at the foot of the bed, hands pressed against her lips, as Doc Richardson listened to Kevy's chest. Putting a cheek to Mama's, Mrs. Cander murmured how glad she was that Kevy seemed all right, and slipped from the room. Danny turned to leave as well but Granddad laid a hand on his arm.

"I think he'll be fine, Estelle," the doctor said quietly, removing the stethoscope. "But I want to keep him in the hospital for a day or two just to make sure his lungs stay clear. Otherwise pneumonia could set in."

I stood back and watched it all, stealing glances at Danny, imagining the feel of Mama's caresses upon Kevy as she motioned for Daddy to pick him up. We all followed as Kevy was carried to our car, Mama finally thanking Danny. She could not find the words, she breathed, to tell him of her gratitude. He had saved her son's life and she would never forget it. Danny accepted her thanks humbly, repeating, as he had to Granddad and Daddy, that he could not have done it alone. They'd have both died, he declared, if I hadn't rescued them at the last minute. Only then—and after Kevy had been tenderly deposited in the backseat of the car—did Mama turn to me.

"Celia," she said, her hands alighting on my shoulders, "you did a brave, wonderful thing today...." The words trailed away, her chin quivering.

My throat tightened. I could not remember feeling so close to her. I wanted to throw my arms around her, wanted us to bask in each other's relieved comfort. But all I could manage was the smallest of nods. Abruptly her hands pulled away, leaving spots of warmth on my shoulders.

"We need to be going." Her voice was gruff. "We'll be followin' Doc Richardson to the hospital."

Climbing into the backseat, she put an arm around Kevy and drew his head to her chest.

chapter 10

By Sunday the whole town was chattering about Kevy's near drowning, no doubt fueled by magpie Eva Bellingham, who ran the post office and knew everything about everybody. Mrs. B. was known in town as a godly "prayer warrior," but I harbored my own opinions of her. Unfortunately—and inexplicably—she was Mama's closest friend, even though Mrs. B. was a good twenty years older. Worse, she had an indirect connection with Danny. Miss Jessie, the orphaned niece whom Mr. and Mrs. B. had raised, was married to Lee Harding. Miss Jessie owned a sewing shop down by Tull's, and everyone loved her. I often baby-sat her three kids.

Monday morning Danny and I were the talk of school. Kevy was still in the hospital; we hoped he would be released that afternoon. Daddy had taken a rare day off his accounting job at Sledges' Farm Equipment in Albertsville to stay with him and Mama at the hospital.

Students and teachers alike inquired about Kevy's health, all saying that they were praying for his full recovery. Then my friends' expressions would change, announcing a new path of thought. Depending upon how close our friendship, the questions varied somewhat. On the way to school Melissa had demanded every titillating detail, assuming that being my best friend gave her the right. Melissa was still very much the same as when we were six—small for her age, constantly moving, fun-loving, bubbly. She often made me laugh yet was the first person I'd turn to if I needed a good cry. My fights with Mama were a repeated topic of our conversations. Melissa in turn would mourn about her worries over being so short and small-figured. "The boys look at me like I'm their little sister," she'd breathe in disgust, tossing brown hair out of her eyes. Then she'd laugh, lest she sound too morose.

But that morning her giggling invitation to gossip, her pixie face tilted toward me, was suddenly irritating. Just last Friday she'd whispered in similar stance about Bobby, her eyebrows arched, and I'd responded, breathless with feigned rapture. Then we'd laughed and laughed, delight sailing over our shoulders toward Randy and Bobby walking behind us. But I had no desire to giggle about Danny with anyone; what had happened between us was too personal, too real.

Mona Tesch caught me at my locker between classes. "Goodness, Celia, *Danny Cander*," she said, brown eyes round behind thick lenses. Because of her short, squat figure, the boys called her Stump behind her back. Her report cards were always full of A's, and she prided herself on an extensive vocabulary. "What was it like pullin' *him* out of the water? You must have been apoplectic."

I slid my math book onto the shelf and took out a history text. "He pulled himself out, Mona; he's the one who rescued Kevy."

"Yeah, but I heard he was so exhausted, you had to save them both."

Mona tended to stick out her tongue like a panting dog when she was excited. That and her curly white-blond head reminded me more of a distressed poodle than a stump.

"Did you have to do mouth-to-mouth on Danny too?"

I was getting tired of these conversations. Banging shut my locker door, I tried to keep my voice neutral. "No. He was fine. I just took care of Kevy."

"So nothin' happened?"

"Nothin' happened? Danny saved my brother's life. I don't call that nothin'."

"I know, but—"

"I gotta get to class, Mona."

Not five minutes later, before history started, a hawkeyed Miss Fleming was remarking, "Isn't it wonderful that Danny happened to come along at just the right time." She was much relieved when I said, "Yes, it is." Heaven forbid, Miss Fleming, that Danny and I had actually been talking on the riverbank *before* Kevy needed our help.

The boys in my class—Lyle, Randy, Kenneth, and especially Gerald, with his pudgy cheeks and know-it-all attitude—were looking at me askance, mouths twisted as they shared their viewpoints in low tones. Bobby was so jealous that he wouldn't talk to me, knitting his thick eyebrows and staring woodenly at the floor when I walked by.

By third hour it was hard to concentrate as Mr. Leam diagrammed sentences on the board. Doodling flower petals on my paper, I worried about Danny. If I was catching this much flak, what about him? Were teachers praising him with their mouths while their eyes accused, "Just why *were* you hangin' around the river, watchin' Celia Matthews?" When the bell finally rang, I hurried for the door, intent on talking to Danny even if it meant appearing obvious.

My math teacher, Mr. Rose, stopped me in the hall, students chattering as they flowed around us. "Hey, Celia, I heard about Kevin. Hope he's all right."

"Thank you. He'll be fine. Probably come home soon."

"That's good news."

I waited for the inevitable question, clasping my books and peering up at Mr. Rose, who was well over six feet. He had worked at the school as long as I could remember, his hair turning gray in the process. Amid the slamming of locker doors and thumping of feet, I flashed again to that playground scene five years ago when Gerald Henley's blood sprayed across Danny's white shirt. Mr. Rose had broken up the fight and was gunning for Danny when I heard myself protest, "It wasn't all his fault; Gerald called his daddy a drunk." Compassion had flicked across Mr. Rose's face, and he'd hauled both boys into the office for three-day suspensions. My friends had been incensed at me.

"It's only because of Danny," I blurted now. "Kevy would've gone through the rapids if it hadn't been for him." My cheeks flushed as the defensive remark rang in my ears, and I knew Mr. Rose understood more than I'd uttered. But he only smiled.

"God used him. I'm glad he was there," he said simply and was gone.

It was too late to find Danny.

Carrying my lunch tray, I spied Danny across the cafeteria, watching me as he stood in line. I threw him an experimental smile and he smiled back. With the warm plastic in my fingers and the smell of meat loaf in the clatter-filled room, I felt a wash of relief. He seemed okay. For a moment I actually entertained the notion of inviting him to sit with me.

"Celia," Miss Hemington called as I passed her third-grade tables. "Tell Kevy we miss him and we hope he's back soon."

Kevy's best friend, Reid, gave me a rueful smile, nodding his agreement. "He'll be okay," I reassured him. I knew he and Kevy were two of Miss Hemington's favorites, partially due to their good grades.

Kevy's studious attitude in school earned him as much fondness from teachers as his loyalty earned him friends. "Thanks," I responded to Miss Hemington. "We hope this afternoon."

"That's wonderful." Her lips spread wide beneath her upturned nose. "And how fortunate Danny appeared just in time."

Over her shoulder I could see Barbara Dawson, Shirley Clangerlee, and Melissa at our table gesturing at me, overflowing with more pesky questions. Melissa and Shirley were like David next to Goliath, Melissa's dainty ballerina hands fluttering against Shirley's meaty shoulder. The Clangerlees ran the town's IGA grocery store, and Shirley's entire family was big-boned and overweight. Gerald was mean enough to say that was because they ate half the produce on their shelves. Barbara appeared polished as always, her thick brown hair meticulously brushed, a crisp white blouse tucked smoothly into her pleated navy skirt. While Shirley beckoned with abandon, Barbara was raising one eyebrow as if to say, "My, my, aren't we slow." Fingers tightening around my tray, I felt indignation bubble up in my throat. Except for Mr. Rose, I'd had it with everyone.

"He didn't appear just in time," I declared to Miss Hemington firmly. "He was there with me before. Talking. Okay?"

Her smile congealed. I wasn't sure if that was due more to my rudeness or to the information I'd imparted. "Well. Lucky for you it turned out." She swiveled purposefully back to her students.

My eyes slipped shut. What on earth was wrong with me, arguing with teachers, disgusted with my friends? I walked to my usual table with dread.

"Come on, Celia, I've been dyin' to hear all about it." Barbara leaned toward me, nearly pressing her blouse into cinnamon apples. I slumped into my chair with a sigh. "So." Her alto voice was conspiratorial. "First off, what was Danny doin' there anyway?"

Last period we were supposed to be answering review questions in our world geography book. Gazing absently at a picture of the Amazon River, I couldn't help but remember Kevy's frantic cries in the current. *Kevy.* A pang of guilt shot through me. I'd been thinking of nothing but Danny all day while my own brother was still in the hospital. Tapping pencil against paper, I wondered if he'd be able to come home that afternoon.

An idea flitted warmly across my mind. Suddenly I had the perfect excuse to talk to Danny after school. He'd want to hear about Kevy. When the bell rang, I was ready to spring, books gathered in my arms.

"Celia!" Bobby Delham called as I sped for the door. "Wait up, I gotta ask you somethin'."

"Later, Bobby," I said over my shoulder. "I'm in a hurry."

He hurried to catch up. "I just wanted t—"

"Not now, Bobby." We passed through the door and into the hall side by side.

"But I was just wonderin'—"

I pivoted abruptly in exasperation, which sent an eavesdropping Randy colliding into me. "Oh, sorry," he mumbled sheepishly, fading toward the lockers along the wall.

I gave him a look, then glowered at Bobby. He clutched a notebook against his side, his chocolate eyes apprehensive. "What's wrong with you?" I asked. "What is wrong with everybody today? I don't have time right now; can't you hear?" Flouncing away, I left him watching me with a mixture of confusion and indignation. He didn't deserve it, and word about my treatment of him wouldn't set kindly. Everyone liked Bobby. *I don't care*, I told myself. *I do not care.* Reaching my locker, I jerked out the books I needed for homework, started down the hall, then changed my mind. Spinning around, I headed for the back door, traipsed around the outside of the building, and managed to reach the street without running into anyone.

I looked up the sidewalk. No Danny yet. With a deep breath I tried to settle myself, consciously relaxing my shoulders and tossing hair out of my eyes. Students were beginning to spill out of the building onto its wide steps, some glancing at me with curiosity. Most of us had our daily habits; mine was to leave school out the side door, cutting across the yard with Melissa. I was most conspicuous here. "Hi," I said to them with nonchalance.

"Who you waitin' for?" Bart Rhorer asked, the sun reflecting in his carrot red hair.

I hesitated. "Danny. He promised to fetch my fishin' pole, and I need to talk to him about gettin' it back."

Bart raised his chin and let it sink again. "Oh. Well, see ya." He sauntered up the sidewalk, looking back with a knowing grin.

I pressed my lips together, swinging my head away from him, and caught sight of Danny easing down the steps. For no reason at all my heart started to beat harder. He saw me and reacted, then tried to cover it up by kicking a small rock out of his path.

"Hi, Danny." I kept my voice light.

"Hi." His eyes were green like a cat's as he squinted in the sun.

"I just wanted you to know that Kevy's goin' to be okay. And that he'll probably be comin' home today."

His gaze glided across my face to my hair and back again. "That's great."

Watching him shift from one foot to the other, a couple of books under one arm, I found it hard to believe he'd hugged me less than forty-eight hours ago. We weren't but four feet apart now, but the distance was a canyon.

"Did you get the poles and stuff?" I asked.

"Yeah."

"Good. I'll have to get mine back sometime." I managed a laugh. "I guess Kevy'll be gettin' a new one."

He smiled. "Guess so."

"Well." I glanced down the street to see Melissa following our every move with eyeball-popping interest. "I suppose I'd better go."

He tilted his head in understanding, a shock of hair falling across his right eyebrow. For some reason I imagined myself pushing it back into place. "See you tomorrow," I said, not moving.

"Sure." Starting to step around me, he faltered. "Maybe I could give them back to you this Saturday," he blurted. "I mean, if you happened to be at the river. I might see you. If I'm done with my work and everything."

I smiled slowly. "That's an idea. If I can go, I'll be there."

"Good." His face was a mask that ill-concealed his anticipation. "See you then."

"Okay."

He headed his way and I headed mine, rehearsing what I'd tell Melissa.

"Hi, Celia," Kevy called as I banged through the screen door.

"Hey, Kevy!" I threw my books down and headed to the couch where he lay. Sinking to my knees, I hugged him hard.

"Ow, I can't breathe," he protested in a muffled voice.

Laughing, I eased away. "That'd be funny, huh? Save you from drownin' only to hug you to death."

He grinned at me winningly. I examined his face, counting the freckles. His skin had returned to its normal, healthy pink. Smoothing hair from his forehead, I pictured the blanched cheeks and blue lips of Saturday, unmoving and cold. The rush of the rapids echoed through my head. "Don't ever, ever scare me like that again, Kevy," I whispered.

He nodded solemnly. "I won't. I'm sorry."

Sensing a shift in our house's atmosphere at supper, I wondered if it was real or if *I* had changed. A quiet joy simmered within me at the sight of our family together again, and for once I wasn't fighting with Mama. She hadn't blamed me for Kevy's accident after all and had almost hugged me for helping to save him. The feel of her hands on my shoulders had been wonderful. And she'd told Danny we owed him a debt we couldn't repay. Last night we had returned from the hospital to a hastily heated bowl of Mama's vegetable soup and thick slices of her wheat bread. I'd been starved, but the food couldn't fill the hole in my stomach, for Kevy's seat was empty. His near death, our family's teetering escape from tragedy, had lent that vacancy a heaviness, as if the very air around it were weighted with grim relief. Now, watching him happily chew fried chicken, I felt a wholeness flow through me, warm and sweet.

Granddad was in high form, chuckling over his old story of how he'd tricked Jake Lewellyn into trading his favorite marble for a toadstool when they were nine years old. That cunning victory had touched off their lifelong besting competition, with Mr. Lewellyn scheming unsuccessfully ever since to get the marble back. "Yep," he went on, "that black and silver marble a Jake's gave me the favorite story for tellin' in foxholes. I remember one time in Korea we were hunkered down, tryin' to git over a knoll, and our boys was feelin' low. I figured it was time to dust off that story, tellin' about my wiliness and Jake's carryin' on. Halfway through it we heard a mighty whistlin'. Our heads jerked up, eyeballs showin' white. We knew we was about to be hit bad. That was the day—"

"Daddy! Please give us one night. Kevin's just come home."

Even amid her inevitable protest Mama's voice was different. Usually it was sharp, impatient when she interrupted Granddad, signaling half a dozen things with the mere word *Daddy*. That this was her home, her table. That her life's burden was bearing his animated war stories. That for some unfathomable reason she despised these tales with a tight-lipped, hard-eyed passion, and therefore he was not to mention the subject of battle—an expectation he failed daily. So the cycle began again. But tonight, because of Kevy, Mama's interruption was more of a quiet pleading. And Granddad, instead of making a display of snapping his mouth shut, simply let the subject drop.

"Well, Son," Daddy said to clear the air, "I guess we owe you a new fishin' pole for comin' home so soon."

"Yep. Guess so."

"Gee, Kevy," I put in, "how could you want to even go near water again?"

He shrugged, swishing iced tea around his mouth, then swallowed. "It don't bother me none. I still wanna go with Reid. Guess I'll stay on the bank, though."

It don't bother me none. I sneaked a look at Mama but she didn't blink an eye. She may not have been able to control Granddad's grammar but was typically unwavering when it came to Kevy and me.

"That's a good idea, Kevin." Granddad smacked the table for emphasis. "Jake's Rock's meant nothing but trouble to our family for years. Best keep away from it."

We all laughed.

"What about your pole, Celia?" asked Kevy. "And Granddad's bucket?"

I sprinkled pepper on some potatoes, keeping my eyes down. "I'm gonna get them this weekend. Danny Cander said he'll bring them to the river on Saturday." I finished my peppering and set down the shaker. Reached for my iced tea and drank.

Silence.

"Well, that's as good a way as any," Granddad declared after a moment. "Right nice of him to fetch your pole."

"Uh-huh." My fork slid under my peas. Mama had ceased all motion, a knife halfway through cutting her roll. After a second bite of peas I couldn't stand it anymore and shot her a glance. She was looking at Daddy and he was looking straight back. I decided my potatoes needed a little more salt.

"Celia." Mama's voice was quiet.

My arm froze, then moved again, fingers closing around the shaker. Events of the school day raced through my mind. My determination to be Danny's friend could end right here and now, I thought, with Mama declaring I couldn't meet him on Saturday because it wasn't fitting, no matter how much we owed him. "Ma'am?"

She hesitated. I could almost hear her thoughts churn. She didn't like the idea yet demurred at appearing ungrateful after what Danny had done. Daddy was eating quietly; this was Mama's call, his actions said. I wished he'd say what he thought for once. I was willing to bet he didn't agree with half her decisions.

Mama finished cutting her roll. Her voice was mild when she finally spoke. "Don't be goin' in the water now, hear?"

chapter 11

Saturday dawned overcast, with flat gray clouds lurking the skies like the battleships in Granddad's stories. All morning I prayed it wouldn't rain, although after waiting all week, straining for glimpses of Danny between classes, I probably would have walked to the river in a hurricane. I kept an eye on the weather while we ate lunch, thankful for the unusual peace between me and Mama. It was the first Saturday in weeks that we hadn't argued about my going into Albertsville.

"You goin' to Melissa's house this afternoon?" Mama asked as she set down Daddy's plate.

My chest went cold. Daddy met my eye for a moment, then looked away. Granddad busied himself pouring iced tea into Kevy's already full glass. "No. I promised Granddad to get his bucket back, remember?"

"Oh, that's right." The lightness in Mama's voice was heavier than lead. She hadn't forgotten, not for a minute. She'd probably lain awake the past five nights wondering why on earth she was letting me go. Glancing at the menacing clouds, she remarked, "You may be sorry you went."

She was talking about more than just rain. "Don't worry. I'll be fine." I finished my sandwich and did the dishes in silence.

By one o'clock the skies were still threatening, but not a drop had yet fallen as I brushed my long hair until it rippled down my back and examined my face in the mirror. A couple of months ago in a moment of gushing unself-consciousness, Bobby had told me I was the prettiest girl in school. I wondered if Danny thought so. Backing away from the dresser, I looked at my full-length reflection, turning sideways to critically eye my figure. I'd made a point of sitting in the sun after school that week, and my skin had already turned a light tan. A bright blue knit shirt set off my eyes. As Granddad would say, it wore me well.

"Bye, Mama. Bye, Daddy." The screen door banged as I left.

"Bye, Celia. Don't stay too long," Mama said.

Walking the block toward Main Street, I could have sworn I felt her peering through the door, watching me go.

Danny was already at the river when I arrived, casually looking through his tackle box, that piece of hair hanging over his eye. Something in his manner was too cool, too collected, and I knew he'd affected it. Wordlessly I approached, crunching over rocks.

"Oh, hi," he said.

"Hi back."

Danny never fished that day. When the rain started just moments later, plinking in fat drops across the river, we gathered our things quickly.

"Come on," he urged. "There's a place upstream where the trees are extra thick."

We ran carrying our belongings, rain pelting us with fury. So much for brushed hair, I thought, then started to laugh. Danny looked at me curiously before breaking into a grin. "We can't get any wetter than we were last week!" I called above the hiss of rain against rock.

"At least it's warm!"

After a few minutes Danny swerved away from the riverbank and I followed, swishing through wild grass. Breathlessly we reached the trees, throwing down the poles and bucket and tackle box before dropping to the ground. The leaves of two giant oaks formed a dense canopy, dancing in the splattering downpour but shielding us from the water.

"Whew!" I gasped, drawing an arm across my face and whipping back my hair. I glanced at Danny. "You're soaked."

"So are you."

I examined my clothes in exasperation. "I can't seem to run into you without lookin' like a drowned rat."

"It don't matter; you're still beautiful."

My eyes jerked to his face, but he was already in profile, keenly aware of crossing a line. A splinter dug at my chest as he flushed with embarrassment as if he'd done something wrong. Why did I keep going back to when he'd punched Gerald Henley in the nose? I felt now as I did then—wanting to put my arm around Danny and tell him to relax, everything would be all right.

"Thank you," I said quietly. And that was that.

Lying in bed that night, gazing at the gleam across my ceiling cast from the corner streetlight, I played that moment over and over again in my head. *It don't matter; you're still beautiful.* The window was open a little, emitting a humid breeze that smelled of rain. Fingering the tiny stitches on my Appalachian quilt, I remembered the warm clasp of Danny's hand when he'd pulled me up after the torrent had passed. As soon as I was on my feet, he'd quickly let go, busy with gathering his pole and tackle box.

How long had we been under the trees? It seemed five minutes but it must have been more like forty-five. We talked about Kevy. I told him about my brother's return from the hospital and what I'd felt when he was missing from our supper table. I thanked Danny again for what he did. He responded that if it hadn't been for me, both he and Kevy would have drowned. We also talked about school, teachers we liked, teachers we hated. I said Mr. Rose was someone I respected but didn't explain why. As for Miss Hemington, no wonder she still wasn't married; she was a witch underneath that perky little face. He laughed at that.

"I threw mashed potatoes on her once," he said.

"No, you didn't. You slung 'em at the ceilin' and they fell back down on her nose."

He was sitting with arms wrapped around his knees. "You remember that?"

"Of course, Danny. Everybody does. We remember lots of things you did."

He let a hand fall to pluck an acorn from the grass. "I'll bet."

There we were, hitting that wall of his again. I'd been thinking of his antics and victories on the baseball field; he was remembering the fights over his daddy.

Neither of us had wanted to leave but I didn't dare push it with Mama. I casually mentioned I might go fishing again next Saturday if she allowed it. Danny shrugged, saying he might mosey on back if his chores were done.

I rubbed my quilt, wondering if Mama would let me go. Surely she'd guess Danny would be there. And I'd have no excuse this time; I'd brought the bucket and pole home.

Mama did let me go the following week, but only with Kevy as chaperone. He didn't mind cutting into his play hours with Reid Barth; to Kevy, time alone with his sister was a treat. However, he was, as Mama ordered emphatically, to stay on the bank. She also instructed him not to leave my side. Kevy shrugged at this further directive, unaware of her pointed look at me as she proclaimed it.

Shortly after we arrived at the river, Danny showed up "unexpectedly." Kevy was thrilled, carelessly tossing down his new pole to hug his rescuer with unabashed adoration.

"Danny and I are going to sit under some shade around that bend for a little while," I told Kevy, pointing upstream.

His eyes widened. "But I'm supposed to stay with you."

"You'll be all right." I ruffled his hair. "You're not goin' in the water, are you?"

"No way."

"All right, then. It'll be our secret. You can't tell Mama."

Guilt flicked across his forehead, dusted his freckled cheeks, then was gone. He shrugged. "Okay. I'm big enough to fish by myself anyhow."

"School's out in two weeks," Danny remarked once we were beneath the oak canopy, a blade of wild grass in his mouth. "What're you gonna do this summer?"

I shrugged. "Not much, I guess. How about you?"

He spat out the grass and picked another blade. "I always just stay around here. Got lots of work at home."

"Do you ever wish you had a brother or sister?"

"Sometimes. Why?"

"Well, I just wondered what it would be like not to have any."

"You're real close to Kevy, ain't you?"

I resisted the temptation to tell him not to say *ain't*. "Yeah."

He looked into the distance at nothing. "Almost had me a brother or sister once."

"What happened?"

"The baby died."

His face held that drawn, Gerald's-blood expression again, defining his jaw with pencil strokes of sadness. "Before it was born, you mean?"

"Yeah."

Gazing across the rocky bank, I watched a redbird flit across the water, its wings a brilliant sheen in the sun. I'd slipped out of my sneakers and socks, the thick, shaded grass cool between my curled toes. "How?"

I shouldn't have asked. Clearly, Danny wished he hadn't brought up the subject. There was so much about him I didn't know, and I sensed that his detachment from me, from the rest of Bradleyville, ran as deep and cold as a mountain river current. The barrier I kept being swept against was the wall of the dam that held it back, rock solid and fortified by an inner pain I couldn't reach. I wanted to break through it, but I was far too clumsy, asking my nosy questions. The truth was, the barrier would never come down unless Danny wanted it to. *It couldn't be comfortable, living with something like that inside you,* I thought. Gazing at his lowering eyes, the narrow slant of filtered sunlight that danced across his shoulder, I thought that maybe he'd hidden behind that barricade so long, he didn't know how to live without it.

"Mama had an accident."

"Oh. I'm sorry." I was imagining the details he'd left out.

"Yeah." He looked thoughtful, as if making a decision. "It was a couple years back. Anyway, I . . . changed after that."

"What do you mean?"

He smiled wanly. "I started listenin' to Mama. She has a strong faith in Christ, you know, even through everything. I don't know why I changed then; you'd think somethin' that awful would make me shake a fist at God. But for some reason I realized I really needed Jesus in my life. One night, with Mama's help, I turned my life over to him. And I felt different inside. I didn't get in trouble no more after that."

I searched for words, amazed that he'd said this much. "I'm a Christian, too. I went to the altar at church when I was nine."

He nodded. "And all your family? Well, I know your granddad is; everybody knows that."

"I don't know about Mama," I said slowly. "She talks the talk and everything, but she doesn't always . . ." The thought died away. "She has this thing with Granddad and me. She's so harsh sometimes and I've never known why. As for Daddy, he's pretty quiet about his faith but he sure lives it. Granddad talks to me about it quite a bit, though."

Danny chuckled. "Your granddad and Mr. Lewellyn sure do have their fights."

"Yeah, but that's just for fun; people know that. It's entertainment for them and the town. Goodness knows, nothin' else happens here."

Enough had been said. Our conversation veered away from personal issues after that, and we both worked at making small talk. After traipsing back downriver, we congratulated Kevy on his four trout. "Think you can do any better next week?" I asked him, making sure not to look at Danny.

chapter 12

Except for Saturdays, once school was out, I was encumbered with boredom. When I wasn't baby-sitting Miss Jessie's kids, I'd go over to Melissa's or Barbara's house, where talk of boys was the highlight of our social agenda. I remained quiet during much of the slumber party chatter, amused that details of my afternoons with Danny would have set off the biggest squeals of dismay and delight. He and I had fallen into a ritual of meeting at the river once a week while Kevy fished for our family's supper. I still could not bring myself to talk about him, however.

"Why're you so quiet?" Barbara asked during a sleep-over at her house in mid-July. She was wearing pink baby-doll pajamas that flounced over her voluptuous figure, an inquisitive finger against her cream-petaled cheek. Her brown hair hung genie-like down one shoulder from a ponytail on the top of her head.

"She hasn't seen Bobby enough lately to add anything to the conversation," Melissa teased. I played along, raising my eyebrows. Bobby. I hadn't thought of him in weeks. "Oh, look at her; she *does* have something!" Melissa pointed her hairbrush at me, rosebud mouth pursed. "Out with it, Celia."

"Well," I said slowly, "actually, I did run into him at the IGA last week. Mama had sent me down to pick up some things, and I was rummaging around in the frozen section when he came up behind me and squeezed my neck."

"What did you do?" asked Mona. She pushed her glasses up her sweaty nose with one finger, then played with a curly pigtail.

I shrugged. Feigned interest was a hard thing to sustain. "Just talked awhile, that's all. He did walk me home."

"Whatdja talk about?" Melissa was brushing her hair again as she pranced about the room. She could never keep still for very long.

Remembering the affected bravado in Bobby's voice, the courtly precision with which he'd offered to carry my grocery bags, I couldn't help but chuckle. Poor Bobby. "He made a point of telling me that when he turns sixteen next year, he'll be allowed to drive his daddy's car around town."

Barbara's hazel eyes grew wide. "Ooh, he wants you along. Before you know it, he'll be askin' if he can take you out."

"For what it's worth. That's a lifetime away."

"Wouldn't you want him to?"

I grabbed a pillow and hugged it to my chest. "My mama's not goin' to let me date until I'm seventeen anyway."

Melissa sighed. "Mine either."

The magic age in Bradleyville. When a girl was seventeen, a boy could formally ask her parents for permission to date their daughter, or "come to call," as older folks termed it. Asking permission was an anxiety-filled event for the boy standing before the parents of his heart's desire. If he was approved, he could take her on dates to Albertsville, to the bowling alley maybe, or to sit in the park. But their behavior had to be impeccable.

My friends were moaning that they'd never even be kissed before marriage if their mamas had their way. Lying on Barbara's bed, I found my thoughts drifting to Danny. Mona's breathy voice ran the gamut of inflection as she went on and on about Wendell Roberts, her new heartthrob in eleventh grade. Danny and I had met seven times now, not counting when Kevy almost drowned. Mama knew I was meeting him, although we never talked about it directly. She'd quiz Kevy but I'd trained him well. "They just talk," he'd answer, not bothering to add that we'd typically walk upriver to our shade trees. Things were so much better between Mama and me that I think she was relieved that the only price she had to pay for peace was letting me out to fish once a week. At least we weren't fighting about Albertsville anymore. Now I lived for Saturdays.

After about a month Danny and I had settled into an amicable ease. He smiled more often and I'd tease him gently. We still didn't talk about his home life, however, and by some implicit understanding neither did we talk of mine, lest the comparison plunk us too close to forbidden territory. School was out; Bradleyville was eventless. So we spoke of the future.

"I want to travel," he'd declared two weeks ago, his profile lighting up at the thought. The river's current was slow and the weather hot and dank.

"So do I. Where do you want to go?"

He wore jean shorts cut off in a fringe and a plain gold T-shirt that matched the hairs on his tanned arms. "The ocean. I want to sit on the beach. Run the sand through my fingers, watch the waves. I bet I could do that for hours."

My intake of breath turned his head. "Me too," I whispered. "I'm always drawing something, and lately I've been drawing nothin' but oceans—you should see all the pictures on my bedroom walls. And so many times I've dreamed of sitting on the sand at night, wrapped in a blanket, seeing the moon's reflection on the water."

I didn't tell him the dreams once included Bobby Delham.

Danny had gazed at me with those green eyes, a faraway expression softening his mouth. How many people yearned to see the ocean? Thousands, millions, yet the discovery of our shared desire brought a glow to his face as if he'd just unearthed the world's most precious jewel. Perhaps it was because we had so little in common. Or perhaps my desire somehow validated his own.

Then there was last Saturday. Just thinking about it now made me hug Barbara's pillow tighter. We'd been talking of traveling again, Danny saying he was praying that God would allow his future work to take him sailing around the world.

"What would the job be?" We were leaning against one of the wide oaks under our canopy, legs stretched out, my right shoulder touching his left as we gazed dreamily at the river.

"I don't know. I'm good with fixin' things, since I always had to work on equipment and stuff on the farm."

"A sailin' janitor," I said, giggling.

His muscles tensed. "You think that's all I can be, a janitor?"

There was that chip again. Why did he always have to be so sensitive? "No." I rolled my head in his direction against the tree, its bark catching my hair. "I think you can be anything you want, because you're Danny Cander. And you can have whatever you want. For the same reason."

He rolled his head toward me, chin practically touching his collarbone. His eyes were so green, like velvet emeralds. I'd never been that close to them before, had never noticed the golden-tinged ring around his irises. He was staring at me with such intensity that I felt heat rise in my chest. The shy Danny I knew would not look away, his eyes searching mine with a longing that captured my breath. I could smell his skin, rich and musky, like Granddad's sandalwood box. His hands rested on his stomach. I was clutching my elbows. *Kiss me.* The thought wafted through my head, leaving a clamor in its path like a sudden breeze through wind chimes. He swallowed, his gaze traveling to my mouth and up again. In the last second his eyes fell away. Neither of us moved.

"Danny," I said quietly, letting go of my elbows. He would not look up. Before I lost my nerve, I reached out to take his hand. He shot me a startled glance, then slowly and solemnly entwined his fingers through mine. It was too embarrassing to look at each other anymore, so we gazed at the sunlight dancing across the river.

Remembering it now in Barbara's room, my friends chattering on, I could re-create the scene—the roughness of his palm, his smell, the black fringe of his lashes when he'd glanced away. A long sigh escaped me. This was only Tuesday night. How could I possibly wait until the weekend to see him again?

"Ooh, look at her." Barbara's voice drifted over my thoughts.

"She's gone, y'all, totally gone," Melissa piped, nudging me with her brush. "Hey! You dreamin' about bein' in that car with Bobby?"

I just smiled.

chapter 13

After staying up half the night at Barbara's, I could hardly keep my eyes open as I watched Miss Jessie's kids. Busy making bridesmaid dresses for a couple over in Albertsville, Miss Jessie had lately been requesting my help often during the week. I didn't mind; it gave me something to do and the extra money was good. And we were all proud Miss Jessie had gained such a reputation as a seamstress that people were beginning to come from Albertsville just for her services.

"It's good for local business," Mr. Tull had remarked in his reedy voice a few days ago after the bride-to-be and her mother had bought numerous articles in his store. Granddad and I were standing at the counter, having just brought our glasses, sticky and rose-colored from our strawberry milk shakes, back inside. Jake Lewellyn and Hank Jenkins were still ensconced under the awning in their usual chairs.

Wayne Tull had run the town's drugstore for twenty years, having inherited it from his father. He was now forty-five. The whole town knew his age due to his unabashed announcing of his birthday every year, complete with balloons and a colorful sign in his large front window. This naturally prompted the competitive ladies of the Methodist church and the Baptist church to bake him their fanciest cakes. He would gush and sigh over every flower decorating those cakes, privately declaring to each woman, "Now don't tell Mrs. So-and-so, but I do believe your petals are the prettiest." I used to think Mr. Tull announced his birthdays for the attention. Now I realized he just loved a party.

Mr. Tull was short with a round, spectacled face and sparse tufts of brown hair. He looked and moved like a fussy bird, flitting around his store with unending energy, now filling a prescription, now making sodas. Jake Lewellyn and Hank Jenkins were two of his favorite patrons, but Granddad walked on water. Mr. Tull would titter unendingly at the shenanigans of Granddad and Mr. Lewellyn, telling the latest exploit to all his customers. He was Granddad's public relations dream.

"Sure is," Granddad had replied. "Miss Jessie's just plain good for this town. Not bad to look at, either." He winked at Mr. Tull, who gave him the expected mock-disapproving huff. Mr. Tull couldn't disagree, however. Miss Jessie had wavy brown hair, a smooth complexion, trim waist, and an equally beautiful disposition.

I left her neatly kept house and dragged home in the afternoon sun to find Mr. Lewellyn hobbling up our porch steps, his white Buick carefully parked at the curb. Two years ago he'd traded in his old car and had immediately driven by to show off his new chariot to Granddad. "He's just tryin' to best me," Granddad had grumbled that night at supper. "Just 'cause he got hisself a new car and I got rid a mine years ago." Granddad stabbed forcefully at some ice cubes stuck together in his tea. "Well, he's got car payments and I ain't, so who's bestin' who?"

Jake Lewellyn reminded me of the old bulldog that used to live on our street before it got run over. His mottled jowls hung fat and red, and they shook with righteous indignation when he argued with Granddad. His legs were short and bent, his chest wide. He used to scare me to death. In the last few years he'd slowed considerably, the veins in his beefy arms popping out beneath thinning skin, an omnipresent black cane in his hand.

"Hi, Mr. Lewellyn," I called, summoning the energy to run up the steps and open the screen door for him.

"Hello, Celia." He bumped across our wooden porch. "Your granddad home?"

"I imagine so."

"Sure as I'm livin'," he said to himself with a wheeze. "Where else would the old goat be?"

"You okay?" I asked, pressing against the door frame to let him pass. "Sounds like you got a cough there."

"It's nothin'. Don't go squealin' it to Thomas now; he'll be lookin' for me to keel over, a gleam in his eye."

I laughed. "Don't worry, I won't."

In the hallway he stopped, both hands resting on his cane, which was smudged with a multiplicity of fingerprints. "Thomas Bradley, where are you!" He picked his way toward the dining room table and our box of checkers while I pulled out his usual chair.

"Want some iced tea?"

"Yes, pretty girl, and I thank you." He smacked the table with an open palm. "Thomas! Where is everybody around here?"

"Mama's probably at the store," I called over my shoulder as I entered the kitchen. "And Kevy's playin' with Reid, I guess. Maybe Granddad's takin' a nap; I'll check."

"Humph," I heard him mutter. "Naps're for old men."

When Granddad appeared, looking as spry as possible, he made sure to inform Mr. Lewellyn he'd been reading, not napping. Gray as Granddad's face could become when his heart suffered palpitations, he always managed to exude energy around Jake Lewellyn. Their lifelong competition hadn't abated, I mused as I set Mr. Lewellyn's tea before him; it had simply adapted to the limitations of their seventy-four years. I was pleased that Granddad looked the younger one, and often made a point of telling him so.

"No games yet, my girl," Mr. Lewellyn said when I pushed the checkers toward him. His chair creaked as he leaned back, easing out his leg and rolling slightly to one side so he could dig in his pants pocket. "I came to show you this, Thomas." Pulling out a newspaper article and unfolding it, he suppressed a cough.

Granddad accepted the piece of paper, eyeing his friend curiously. "You all right, Jake? Where'd you git that cough?"

"See what I tol' you?" Mr. Lewellyn stuck his chin out at me. "One little catch in my throat and I made his day."

Ignoring the comment, Granddad adjusted the article a certain distance from his face and began to read, lips moving. Once or twice he glanced up in surprise. When he was through, he studied the other side of the paper, eyeing a portion of an ad for a storewide clearance sale, then flipped it back over. "You expect me to believe this, Jake Lewellyn? Where'd you git it?"

"What is it, Granddad?" I reached for the paper.

"The *Lexington Herald*, see right there." Mr. Lewellyn stopped my hand, pointing to the small print above the headline. "Page A-4, that's what it says."

"I don't believe it; it ain't real," Granddad declared. "This is another one a your tricks. And a poor one at that, I might add."

"Pshaw." Mr. Lewellyn shook his head. "I come all the way over here to bring you this, and you end up callin' me a liar."

"Well, ya are one."

"Oh, get off it, Thomas!"

"Get off it yourself!" Granddad shot back. "What do ya think I am, some acorn-spittin' idiot?"

"You ain't got no cause to shout!"

"I got cause when you try to trick my medals away from me!"

"Aagh!" Mr. Lewellyn banged the table with his cane. "Never mind, then; I'll just take it on home. You can forgit the whole thing." His jowls sprayed pink.

Unable to read in the midst of their arguing, I headed for the kitchen, wincing as Granddad pronounced his friend jealous and yellow-bellied—remaining behind in two wars while Granddad had volunteered to fight.

"Well, *somebody* had to stay here and protect the town, not to mention your wife and daughter, while you ran around makin' a monkey a yourself!"

"Monkey! You think that's what those medals I got're for? You gone teched in the head, Jake Lewellyn!"

I plopped into a kitchen chair, set the newspaper article in front of me, and stuck a finger in each ear. "Governor Honors War Heroes," the title read.

Lexington—On Veteran's Day in November, the *Lexington Herald*, aided by Governor Julian Carroll, will honor medal-bearing veterans now living in Kentucky, in a special ceremony on the steps of the governor's Frankfort mansion.

"There are many heroes living in our state," Governor Carroll said, "and I'm proud to accept the *Herald*'s invitation to recognize their valiant sacrifices for our country."

Veterans who wish to participate in the ceremony are urged to send their medals as proof of their accomplishments to reporter Lawrence Tremaine at the *Lexington Herald* by August 11, with a completed registration form explaining the circumstances under which the medals were earned. The medals will then be re-awarded during the ceremony, which Vice President Mondale has been asked to attend.

"We know these medals are precious," Bradley Gottenheim, editor of the *Herald*, noted, addressing the concern that some may be reluctant to part with them even temporarily. "My staff will hold them with the utmost care, and we will see that each is returned to its rightful owner—with all the pomp and circumstance the Blue-grass State and our illustrious governor can muster."

For a registration form please call Lawrence Tremaine at (606) 555-2822. All honorees' travel expenses relating to the ceremony will be paid by the *Lexington Herald*.

Fingers still in my ears, I read the article a second time. Oh boy. Mama would be more than a little perturbed at having to drive Granddad all the way to Lexington for a war medal ceremony. Suddenly it occurred to me that Granddad hadn't been telling his battle stories lately and that this could be as much the cause for the recent calm in our house as my not arguing with Mama. I'd been thinking so much of Danny, I hadn't been paying attention. But how strange, Granddad's inexplicable silence regarding his favorite subject.

By the time I left the kitchen, Mr. Lewellyn had pulled to his feet and was heading for the door, his right hand shaking as he clutched his cane, fat cheeks a vibrant red. "That's the last time I try to help you, Thomas Bradley!" he stormed, sliding into a fit of wheezing. "Just tryin' to help a friend . . . and all I git . . . is more a your crab-edged . . . ill-tempered, cantankerous, dim-witted accusations. . . ."

"Wait, Mr. Lewell—"

"You tell that ol' coot granddad a yours"—he jerked his head in my direction—"I ain't talkin' to him no more, ya hear?" Hacking and sputtering, he plodded to the screen door and threw it open. I ran to hold it for him, costing him the pleasure of banging it on his way out.

"Land sakes," Granddad muttered as we listened to him pound his cane down our porch steps. "What a temper."

"You mailin' your medals tomorrow, Granddad?" Kevy asked that night at supper. "I can't wait to see you at the ceremony; I'll be right proud."

"Daddy," Mama said, casting him a warning look.

He met her eye, glanced at me, then continued smearing butter on his potato with gusto. "Thank you, Kevy, but I ain't sayin' nothin' about my illustrious service in the wars now, hear? So don't be talkin' about it at the table."

I raised inquisitive eyebrows at Daddy and he shrugged. Something was going on. Granddad had not talked of battles since about the time Kevy fell into the river—a feat to this day unequaled for Granddad.

And he'd certainly never been this accommodating with Mama before. His intestines must have kinked just hearing his own words. But whatever was happening between them, Daddy wasn't in on it.

I did know Granddad had called about that article before Mama arrived home. Once Mr. Lewellyn had huffed off, he'd wasted no time running down the *Lexington Herald* reporter. "Lawrence Tremaine, please," he'd snapped, expecting to hear there was no such man. But Lawrence Tremaine had come on the line and verified that he'd written the article and yes, he could mail a registration form to 101 Minton Street in Bradleyville. "And congratulations, sir," he'd added politely, according to Granddad.

I'd given him a look. "Sounds like you owe Mr. Lewellyn an apology."

"Humph." He'd wandered down the hall toward his bedroom, the newspaper clipping in his hand.

I went to bed early that night, exhausted from Barbara's slumber party. Before disappearing into my bedroom, I hesitated, then tiptoed over to Mama, who was sewing in her favorite chair. "Good night," I whispered, kissing her cheek. "I love you."

"Good night, Celia." She did not look up.

Pulling back quickly, I told myself she needn't say more. Even so, when she called my name I turned, breath catching. "Yes, Mama?"

"That basket of clothes needs mending. You'll need to do that tomorrow."

My eyes closed. "Okay."

I shut my bedroom door softly.

chapter 14

On that hot, muggy Saturday, by the time Kevy and I reached the river, our faces were running with sweat. We'd beaten Danny, and I was grateful for the time to rinse my face and run fingers through my hair. I'd never before been this anxious to see him. Sinking onto a boulder as Kevy cast off a ways downstream, I dreamed of the moments we'd soon have. Things were different now. We'd stepped over a boundary and would no longer be satisfied with just sitting and talking. I wanted to hold his hand again, longed to brush that strand of hair from his forehead. The thought of being close to him sent a quivering through my chest. "Hurry up, Danny," I whispered.

I waited. Time ticked slowly by. Kevy caught a fish. After twenty minutes I stood up to stretch, my rear end numb.

"Where's Danny?" Kevy called.

I shrugged. "Who knows?"

What if Danny was watching me from afar, enjoying the sight of my impatience? Imagining that, I managed a laborious yawn, wandering a few steps as if I hadn't a care in the world. When he didn't appear after a few minutes, I dropped my pretense, daring a glance at the field, then swept my eyes up and down the riverbank. No Danny.

He just has extra chores, I told myself. *He'll be here.* I sat down again, absently picking up a handful of pebbles to drop one by one with a light click on the ground. When my hand was empty, I picked them back up. Dropped them one by one again.

Something swished at the field's edge and I jerked up my head, smiling with anticipation. But it was only a squirrel staring at me, mouth working, before it frisked away. My smile faded.

With a dull pain growing in my lungs, I repeated to myself that he would come. I knew he wanted to see me, too, that he'd probably dreamed all week about our last time together, as I had. He would not stand me up without very good reason.

No, I chided myself five minutes later, not true. I'd gone too far in taking his hand; I'd scared him away. He was unsure of himself and now he was embarrassed. Or maybe he didn't like girls behaving so boldly. Why had I done it? I asked, sighing at the river. Why had I frightened him off just when I couldn't stand not being with him again?

Ten more minutes. I'd give him that.

When ten minutes had passed, I told myself five more.

Even then I couldn't give up on him. It was an eternity since last Saturday; I couldn't stand to wait another week. And what if he didn't show up then? After another excruciating seven days, I couldn't bear it. He had extra chores, that was all. Maybe he'd finished and was now on his way. If I took the path through the field to his house, I could meet him. We could walk back to the river holding hands.

"Kevy!" I called. "I'm gonna walk toward Danny's house. We'll be back soon."

"Okay!"

I crunched over the rocks and onto the path. Entering the field, I searched for him in the distance. It hadn't rained for a while, and the trail was dusty and simmering with heat. The longer I walked without spotting him, the more anxious I grew, until I knew I'd jump happily at the first sign of Danny Cander, even if I did appear too anxious.

Far ahead the thick grove of trees at the outskirts of the field signaled Danny's property on the other side. I envisioned Danny the day he'd saved Kevy, his jeans damp and his chest bare. Expanding each detail of his hugging me, wet and shivering, I watched the trees grow closer until they were only a stone's throw away. I stopped for a moment to gather my hair and swish it up and down, fanning my neck. When I started up again, I dawdled, willing Danny to appear through the trees before I reached them. He didn't.

A few moments later I'd entered the grove, relative coolness surrounding me. I paused to wipe sweat from my face. Following the weaving path, I listened for Danny but heard only the sound of my own footsteps. *He's not coming*, I taunted myself. *He doesn't want me.* Leaning against the last tree, I berated my impetuousness. What now? I certainly couldn't appear on Danny's front lawn. Once he saw me, there would be no way to explain myself, no way to slip gracefully from the scruffy grass and the memory of his hand grasping mine. I was no more than a hundred feet from his house. I could almost feel him.

I prayed for him to appear but knew I'd already waited too long. I needed to get back to Kevy. My chest sank. Turning to retrace my steps, I tossed a strand of hair from my face, telling myself it didn't matter; I didn't need Danny Cander anyway. Who did he think he was, trying to hurt me? I emerged from the trees, blinking in the sunlight, repeating that I didn't need Danny, I did *not*.

Then the sound came from Danny's house, a muffled stridence through the grove.

I halted, skin tingling. Cocked my head. There it was again. A man argued vehemently. A woman's voice pleaded. I held my breath. The pleading escalated, then abruptly stopped.

Silence.

My eyes danced across the field as I waited, muscles tense.

The woman screamed. My heart revved, thudded against my chest. *Mrs. Cander.*

I spun toward Danny's house and raced back through the trees. The pleading welled up again, deep from within a woman's throat constricted with fear. The man's bellowed words garbled as they hurled over the Cander's lawn and split against the tree trunks around which I ran. Nearing the edge of the grove, I heard banging and scuffling, as if someone were fighting inside Danny's house. The picture of Mrs. Cander's worn face, her gentle hands holding a cracked cup of chicken broth to my brother's lips, flashed through my head. I veered around the last tree, terrified. The sun's glare slapped my forehead as I burst into the clearing.

I tripped on a small rise in the trail, then caught myself with both hands, grunting as I pushed away from the dirt. I raised my head toward Danny's house as the sounds grew more distinct, the bellows forming into threats that surged through the Cander's screen door. In the next instant the door jerked open and Mrs. Cander flailed through it, careening across the rickety front porch and down the steps. Her flowered housedress swished between her knees as she ran barefoot, her long brown hair flying. One hand swept up against the side of her mouth, blood oozing down her chin to splatter across her dress.

Before the door could slam, Mr. Cander lunged after his wife. He was barefoot and shirtless, his face purple with rage. "Don't you be runnin' away from me, woman!" he hollered. He banged drunkenly into the porch rail, reeled backward, then scuffled down the steps. "I ain't through with you yet!"

I froze, ashamed to see a man undressed like that but unable to tear my eyes away from the thick dark hair on his shoulders. I remembered him years ago at Miss Jessie's wedding, dressed up and sipping punch. Now he looked like a madman. Standing shakily at the edge of the field, palms pressed against my lips, I stared in horror as he chased Danny's panicked mama.

"No!" she was crying. *"No!"*

Mrs. Cander lost her footing as her housedress wrapped around her legs. Sprawling headfirst onto the patchy lawn, she quickly flipped over in self-defense, aghast to see her crazed husband so close behind. She scuttled backward on all fours, her backside dragging the ground. As he rushed for her, she keened, praying for him to stop.

He'll kill her, I thought. And still I could not move.

"Mama!"

I heard Danny's cry a split second before I saw him. Bare-chested, he exploded around the side of the house to sprint toward his parents, dropping a bucket that sprayed his jeaned legs with the dregs of brown food scraps as it bounced against the dirt. Mr. Cander jerked his head toward Danny and stumbled, giving his wife the chance to scramble from his grasp.

"Daddy, no!" Danny screamed, his face contorting into hard-edged fury as he raced toward his father, slamming into him with a force that shoved him backward. Looking shocked at his own violence, Danny immediately jumped away.

Mr. Cander staggered, then lurched to a stop, his chest expanding as he turned his murderous glance from his wife onto Danny. "I'll git you, boy," he spat through twisted lips. "This ain't none a your affair, hear? None!"

On her hands and knees now, dirt puffing around her wrists, Mrs. Cander skittered away from them and back toward the porch, a long strand of hair stuck to the blood on the side of her chin.

Shoulders heaving, Danny faced his father, legs apart, hands curling. A sneer crossed his face, narrowing his eyes. "Come on, then," he challenged, his voice catching. "Come on then, Mr. Big Man."

I'd seen a young Danny in many a fight at school, seen him take on boys near twice his size. Watching at playground's edge with my friends, biting my lower lip, I'd seen the anger etched across his face, knew the swell of his cheekbones and the hardened line of his jaw. I could vividly remember his looming over Gerald, dark brows jammed together over slit eyes. But I had never, ever seen him look like this.

About the same height, Danny and his father hulked in semiprofile to me, Danny's face three-quarters visible. The wrath that poured from him, sloshing off his shoulders and over his tightly muscled arms, swept like a wave across the yard to smash against my own stomach. I could almost reach out and touch its vengeance. It was more than anger; it was a loathing, cold and pure, that frothed from him. Seeing Danny that way turned my lungs to ice.

"I said come on!" he shouted through clenched teeth. Danny's voice dripped with disgust. "You a big man, ain'tcha! Big enough to hit a *woman.*"

Mr. Cander's rib cage pulsed. He opened his mouth and his upper lip disappeared. "I'll kill you, boy." The promise was gravel in his throat. I sucked in air, heart congealing, as he gathered his strength, then plunged toward Danny with a roar, head lowered.

"Danny!" Mrs. Cander screamed, pushing to her feet to help her son.

Danny faced the attack straight on; then at the last second he pivoted, pulling a knee up high to slam it under his daddy's chin. I could hear the teeth snap at impact. Mr. Cander's head jerked up and he stumbled. He fell forward with a dull thud, then rolled over on his back. In an instant Danny was astride him, hands pummeling, a torrent of words hurling from his mouth. The blows landed with wet smacks across his daddy's chest and head, like the sound of my mama tenderizing meat.

Mrs. Cander shrank away, knuckles blanching as she gripped the skirt of her dress.

With a sudden bellow Mr. Cander brought both arms up and encircled his son in a bear hug. Danny's yells ceased as he struggled to break free. His daddy slid a knee up, straining to dig into the ground with his heel, then pushed with a loud grunt. He raised his hip and rolled, trapping Danny underneath.

I thought my heart would stop.

"Anthony, don't!" Danny's mama raced to her husband, sank fingers into his wrist and yanked with all her might.

Mr. Cander let go of Danny with one hand and flung out his elbow. It caught her in the waist and knocked her aside, breathless. I flinched as my own ribs imagined the blow. Danny dragged his arm out from under his daddy, curled his fingers, and smashed his fist into Mr. Cander's left eye.

"Aagh!" Mr. Cander slapped a hand over the wound. Danny snarled and pushed his daddy off his chest, then spun over and leaped up to kick his attacker's ear with the heel of his shoe. Mr. Cander cried out again, protecting his head with an arm as he tossed to his side, away from the blows. Danny closed in on his father.

"I hate you!" he cried thickly, kicking Mr. Cander's head once more. "God help me, I hate you!" He aimed his foot again and again at his daddy's ribs and back and spine, the words spewing from his mouth with each violent stroke. "I . . . hate . . . you, . . . you . . . stinkin' . . . drunk!"

"Stop!" Mrs. Cander reached for Danny, her fingers stiff as she tried to grab his upper arm. His movements were so erratic, she couldn't find a hold. "Danny! Danny, stop. *Stop it!*" Wrists fluttering, she snatched at him until she finally caught him with both hands.

"Lemme be!" Danny jerked away, still kicking viciously. Mr. Cander's arms slid noiselessly away from his face and splayed, dirt-covered and still, upon the ground.

My fingers pressed against my lips.

"Danny!" His mama gained hold of him again, her grip firm. "Don't kill him!"

"I don't care!"

Her fingers tightened. *"No!"*

The fear in her voice finally pierced him. I watched, a lump in my throat, as Danny's vehemence drained away, his blows ebbing until, with a halfhearted kick, he stopped. He turned to face his mama, gusts of breath popping his ribs in and out. Spittle flecked his lips, and his mouth hung open. His eyes were hazed.

"That's it," Mrs. Cander soothed, holding him by the shoulders and urging him toward her. Briefly she looked past him at her unconscious husband. "Come on, now." He stiffened, then slumped. "Come on, Danny." His eyes closed with exhaustion.

Quietly he dropped his bruised hands and sank against her side, letting her draw him away from the figure at his feet. His mama put an arm around his waist, casting another anxious glance at the motionless Mr. Cander, then led Danny slowly across the yard. After they'd walked a few steps, Danny brought his left hand up, examining it idly, then halted, reaching over to turn his mother's face fully toward him. She flinched and he took his hand away.

"It's nothin'," she said quickly. "It doesn't hurt."

With a shaking finger he touched the drying blood on his mama's chin. He started to say something, then choked on the words. A quiver rippled across his cheekbones, crumpling his face. His legs started to wobble and he dropped to his knees, pressing his head against her waist. Her arms slipped around him as a wrenching sob racked its way through his lungs and up his throat.

"I'm sorry," he blurted into her dress. "Lord forgive me for hatin'; I'm sorry! But I just can't *stand* it anymore."

His shoulders and back heaved as he began to cry, clutching her. Between sobs he said other things but I couldn't understand the words. Nor could I hear what she said to him as she smoothed his hair, tears tumbling down her cheeks and dropping onto her neck. Not in my life had I heard a boy cry like that. My own chest was tight, my hands still clasped against my mouth. I was trembling all over, a daisy tickling my ankle. I knew I shouldn't be there, that I should walk away while I had the chance, but I couldn't summon the strength. Only because of the intensity of the fight had they not seen me yet, standing in plain view at the edge of the field.

Leave now, a voice whispered in my head. But I could only watch Danny's anguish. I hurt deep inside, for the first time really understanding what he'd lived with all these years, the cause for the shame written across his features when he'd bloodied Gerald Henley's nose. I wanted to run to him, to comfort him as he'd once comforted me. But it was not my place.

Leave, the voice repeated. And I would have obeyed, had Danny's mama not seen me at that moment.

Who can say why she lifted her head just then and turned toward me? Perhaps from the corner of her vision she'd caught a glimpse of my blue shirt against the yellow-white field, her gaze absently finding its source as she murmured to her son. When she realized what it was, her hand stilled against the back of Danny's head. Our eyes locked. Then she looked back down, fingers moving once more. "Danny," she said.

He quieted slowly, his gasps diminishing until he no longer shuddered. Mrs. Cander slipped her hand to his shoulder in a gentle grasp. He must have sensed the change in her because he pulled away, shooting a distrustful glance at his daddy. But the man remained motionless. Tipping his head back, Danny searched his mama's face, following her eyes as they traveled in my direction. His head swiveled. When he looked at me, I couldn't breathe.

"Celia?"

The startled tone told me what I already knew. I should not have let him see me.

He sprang to his feet in an awkward two-step, backing in embarrassment away from his mama. "What're ya doin' here?" He headed toward me, sweeping an arm self-consciously under his nose. "What're ya *doin'* here?"

I tried to swallow the lump in my throat as I lowered my hands from my lips, searching for an explanation. If I'd been caught peeping in his window, I couldn't have felt more ashamed.

"Celia, why are ya here?" His voice rose with accusation and he picked up speed. His features were pinched, angry. A vein stood out on his right arm.

"Danny!" Mrs. Cander's voice was sharp.

"Just . . . ," I stammered. "I didn't . . ."

He swiped at his face again with his hand, flushed with indignation. He was ten feet away from me, his mouth twisting, a deep red mottling his neck.

I rocked backward, eyes stinging. "Please."

"Came to see for yourself, didn't ya?" He wiped his hand against his jeans.

"Danny," his mama called again, "don't!"

"Came to see, huh?" He stopped abruptly in front of me, close enough for me to see the etch of tears through his dust-covered cheeks. I could smell the dankness of his sweat. "Well, you seen it. Now git home."

His voice was sludge, and he threw the words in my face with all the force of his mortification. I reached for him, shaking my head. My mouth opened, then closed, the denials dying in my throat.

"Go, Celia!" he commanded.

"Danny, *please*—"

"Git outta here!"

"But I—"

Swiftly he lurched forward, grabbed my arm and shoved. I stumbled back, staring at him in disbelief.

"You don't belong here," he whispered fiercely, eyes glittering with tears.

"*Danny!*" His mama's harsh reprimand brought no response.

"I didn't mean—"

"Git." He slashed a hand toward the river.

Once more I tried to touch him, brushing his arm before he jerked it away.

"Git home, Celia Matthews!" he shouted, choking on my name. "Git on back to where you belong!"

The rage on his face sent me spinning toward the field. Before I knew it, my legs were pumping up the trail and into the grove of trees, away from Danny Cander. He yelled at my retreating back, but I couldn't make out the words over my own ragged breaths. I heard his mama call him again, and then their voices faded in the distance.

I ran through the trees and then into sunshine, gulping air that whined through the tightness in my chest. Flowers and weeds smacked my legs; my hair slapped up and down against my back. Blurry-eyed, I focused on the path before me. I did not slow until a wave of nausea roiled through my stomach, sending goose pimples popping down both arms. I was going to be sick. A cold sweat flushed over me and I stopped abruptly, tossing my head to one side as my throat bulged. The acid in my mouth reminded me of Kevy, wax-lipped and throwing up on the riverbank. In the next instant I pictured Danny later walking this same trail, seeing the mess and knowing it had come from me. I would not give him the satisfaction. Swerving, I staggered off the path and through daisies while my intestines crimped, then bloated. Sourness tumbled up my gullet.

Sinking down, palms crushing into the ground, eyes watering, I retched until my stomach held no more.

~ *1997* ~

chapter 15

She looks so old.
    The thought paralyzed me as I faced Mama on the front porch. Rays from an overhead light spilled over our shoulders, casting us in a pallid sheen. I had not needed to knock; she apparently had heard the crunch of my tires on the gravel driveway, the trunk lid opening and closing. In each of my hands was a large suitcase.

"Celia."

She breathed my name, holding the screen door open as we studied each other's face. Her hair, swept back in a bun, was dull and gray-streaked, silver at the temples. Her once translucent skin now matched that dullness, with wrinkles cut deeply from her nose to the turned-down corners of her mouth, around the eyes, across her forehead. She looked heavier, a pink robe tied at her waist.

She did not move. I supposed she was waiting for me to make the first gesture, since I'd been the one to leave so long ago. Or maybe it was because she didn't want me there; after all, it was Daddy who called for me. On my way from the cemetery, the imagined sight of him had sliced like a knife through my self-centeredness, reminding me that I had come for his sake and that my emotional pain would have to be pushed aside. For pain required energy, and my energy was to be spent on him. Waiting now for a hint of welcome from Mama, I told myself I must get along with her; fighting too would only sap my strength.

"Hello, Mama." I set down the suitcases and put my arms around her awkwardly. Feeling her stiffen beneath them, I pulled away.

I found busyness in my bags then, bringing them inside while she held the door. Toting them into the hallway, I scanned the living room. They had replaced Granddad's old color TV. The couch also was new. Mama's chair remained where it had always been, but with new solid-blue upholstery. I looked back toward the formal dining area, to the oak table dusted and empty, and a pang shot through me. How often

when I was a teenager had Granddad and Jake Lewellyn played checkers there. The phone remained on its little stand by the wall that separated the dining area and kitchen. The carpet was the same as I
remembered. The same off-white paint on the walls was dingy.

A sudden shiver ran through me and was gone. It was the air, I
thought. The very air in this house was dull like my mama's hair, barren
like the dining table. Laden with sadness.

"Your daddy's already asleep." Her voice was accusing. "He waited
for you as long as he could, but you were too late. He's been so excited
about you comin'. He seemed so much better today, like the happiness
alone was healing him. He was smiling for the first time since his
stroke. He smiles crooked, you know, 'cause his left side's not working,
but at least he was smiling, hearin' your name."

She stopped abruptly, a hand on her neck, staring vacantly at my suitcases, as if surprised at her own flow of words. I was surprised as well,
wondering at the spillage from this woman who had always kept her
feelings inside until they burst forth in a torrent of anger. A stunning
realization hit me.

She had been as anxious about this moment as I.

"I . . . I'm sorry it took me so long. It was a long trip."

No response. Her eyes had risen to the height of my knees beneath
my long casual skirt. Automatically I leaned over to brush off any
remaining dirt. Then she was studying my face for the second time,
noticing the red puffiness of my eyes. "Where you been, Celia?"

I could not meet her gaze. "I made a quick stop on the way. It didn't
take long."

She swallowed, nodding. "It's a nice marker, isn't it?"

I couldn't respond. Would she feel vindicated, I wondered, to hear
of the guilt I carried? Suddenly I was filled with the strong knowledge
that I should speak of it at that moment, and that I should plead with
Mama for the cancer between us to be removed so together we could
help Daddy heal. *This is the time, Celia,* declared a voice in my head. *Do
it now.*

I froze, marveling at the voice. I had not heard it in a very long time.
I opened my mouth, summoning the words from across a chasm of
seventeen years. But they would not come.

"Yes," I whispered. "It's very nice."

A curtain of silence draped between us, heavy and black.

"Well." Her tone turned unnaturally light. "You must be exhausted. Go on and rest now; you'll be in your old room. Tomorrow is soon enough to see your daddy. I'm goin' off to bed myself. I'm tired." Swiftly she left me on soundless, slippered feet. I blinked at her abrupt departure, feeling terribly alone in the house of my childhood.

Before the weight of it could settle upon me, before I berated myself for letting the moment pass, I forced myself into action, carrying my suitcases down the hall and into my darkened bedroom, flicking on the light. I sucked in a breath. Nothing had changed. There was my bed, my old wedding ring quilt upon it. My desk, with the same books and lamp. My dresser, the silver brush and mirror on its center. Open closet doors displayed the remnants of a teenager's wardrobe. The baby blue walls were empty, my pictures of oceans having long ago been ripped to shreds as I sobbed. I could see dozens of marks left by the thumbtacks.

Pulled by an unseen hand, I backed out and crossed the hall toward the two empty bedrooms. They beckoned and mocked me with their memories, and I felt a sudden urge to give them their heed. View them and be done with it. Granddad's door was closed and I opened it furtively, reaching to turn on the light. The room was spare, silent, the furniture gathering dust, like my heart. I stared at Granddad's bed; then my eyes trailed to his bookcase. I pictured it as it used to be, polished and sporting his medals in a meticulously straight row on the top. Next to them had rested his sandalwood box, which held sleeve patches from his uniforms, his unit crests, and a few military pay certificates. One shelf down, a little cracked blue cup from an ancient play tea set had held Jake Lewellyn's black and silver marble. A German canteen that Granddad had plucked from the enemy camp at the Volturno River had been slung over his straight-backed chair.

I could stand no more. Quickly I turned and left.

Feet gliding, I watched Kevy's room draw near. The knob smooth in my palm, I pushed the door back. Expecting to find it preserved like mine, I gaped at the stripped room, no trace of him remaining. I couldn't bear the sterility of that vacuum, as if my little brother had never lived here. How could Mama have done this to her darling Kevy, I wondered, and left my room untouched?

Closing the door, I asked myself bitterly what I was doing in that house, whose very walls held memories that threatened to crush me. A deep tiredness washed over me as I returned to my room. The day's long drive had me spent and I felt my senses dulling. For a short while

I busied myself unpacking by rote, hanging up shirts, opening drawers. Besides clothes, I'd brought the same few precious items that had been so carefully packed in my boxes when I fled Bradleyville. First, Granddad's three war medals in their velvet containers, plus his battered sandalwood box. These I placed in the bottom of my dresser, where Mama could not see them. Second, my ancient teddy bear, Cubby, whose face had once reminded me of baby Kevy. I set him on the desk. And third, I'd brought the letters that held my life, tied in a stack with blue ribbon. Even as I hid the letters under clothes in my dresser, I wondered at my own morbidity in bringing them. As if simply being in that room wasn't enough reminder of the pain.

I heaved a deep sigh. At the moment, Little Rock and ad campaigns and my house seemed very far away. Suddenly longing for the familiar, I tried to recapture the pulse of my hectic pace at Sammons, but the beats were already feeble beneath the hushed rhythm of my old room.

In bed I fingered the familiar stitches on my quilt, gazing out my window at Minton Street bathed by the corner light. How often in my teenage years had I lain there looking at that light, wishing . . . waiting . . . regretting . . .

Forcefully I pushed the thoughts aside, reminding myself that I had to get up early the following morning to see Daddy. Remorse washed over me as I pictured him waiting that evening, fighting his own weakness. I wanted to focus my energy on him; he was the one who needed healing. I had no right to steep in my own past hurts. But I wondered if rest would come; my mind was teeming with emotion. Mentally I tried to prepare myself for a restless night, even as exhaustion began to weight my eyelids and blanket my limbs.

Sleep was a smothering black velvet.

chapter 16

The next morning I clicked open Daddy's bedroom door to see early sunlight spilling weakly across his bed. He was already awake and propped against pillows. I moved quickly to his side. "Daddy!"

His drawn face, that of a man ten years his senior, jumped to life. "Saaaa." I hugged him gently, feeling his slightness. His left arm did not move; his right one slipped around my back. "Saaa." The sound was low in his throat, followed by a chest-deep bark of sad laughter. "Saaa."

Mama stood in the doorway. "He's tryin' to say your name," she explained. "That's very good, William."

I frowned at her. My volunteer work at the nursing home had taught me never to speak to a stroke victim as if he were a child. "Daddy. Let me look at you!" I placed palms on his cheeks, drinking in the wrinkles and lines, concealing my dismay. The right side of his face held animation, while the left could only attempt it, pulling to no avail at the sag from his eye to his lips. His eyes were bright with happiness as he gazed at me, but I could see a well of sadness beneath the sheen. I blinked at tears. "You look wonderful."

His mouth trembled, eyes filling. "Saaaaa." My ill-formed name ended in a choke.

"Oh, Daddy, don't." I pressed his head against my chest, stroking the fully grayed hair. "Don't cry. You're going to be fine. I'm here to help you now."

The guttural sounds turned high as he sobbed, the fingers of his right hand pressing into my arm. "Saaaa. Saaaa. Maas aaa."

I was cut to the heart. I hadn't expected this. What I had expected I couldn't say, but it wasn't my daddy crying as I never knew he could. Helplessly I looked to Mama.

"'I missed you.' That's what he's sayin'." The accusation in her voice was unmistakable.

My eyes squeezed shut as I realized he was crying not over his sickness but over my absence. Could I have broken his heart more than the stroke had broken his body? "I missed you, too, Daddy. So much. But I'm here now." I swallowed hard. "And I'm not going anytime soon, I promise." I held him until the tears ebbed and he fell against the pillows, exhausted.

Mama still had not moved from the doorway.

"Tell me everything, Mama. What's going on with his therapy? Can he get out of bed yet? What does the doctor say?" After seeing Daddy, I was still beside myself over his condition.

She was in profile at the kitchen sink, her waist-length hair pulled into a scraggly low ponytail. "It depends on how hard William works at it. He's got to have physical therapy for movement and speech. I haven't started any of that yet; he's only been home two days. I figured you'd talk to the doctor about it. He's supposed to stop by this mornin'."

The response angered me. It seemed to me she had taken the easy way out, waiting to place on me all responsibility for finding a therapist. Not that I was sorry to take it on, for a hot determination to help Daddy was already bubbling within me like lava. I didn't know how to fix the emotional pain I had caused him, but his weak arm and leg and his tattered speech were tangible challenges. It was not the work that angered me; it was Mama's undertone. While I may have viewed nursing Daddy as my due penance, Mama's alleging it was something else again. I kept my voice steady. "Is Dr. Richardson still around?"

"Land sakes, no, he retired," she replied. "You remember John Forkes, Mona Tesch's cousin? He went to the University of Kentucky when you were about eleven. Married a Lexington girl and settled there, but she died of a brain aneurysm after they'd only been together a few years. When Doc Richardson retired, John moved back here and took over the practice. He's engaged now to a teacher in Albertsville, a real sweet Christian girl."

I stared out the kitchen window at our old oak tree, the swing from which I used to jump long gone. Briefly I wondered what had happened to Mona, Melissa, Barbara, Mary Lee, and all my other friends. What had ever happened to Bobby? In the conversations I'd had with Mama and Daddy over the years, I hadn't found the courage to ask, the very thought of hearing their names stirring up memories I'd tried to avoid.

The scent of homemade strawberry jelly rose from my toast, and I pushed the plate aside. "Well, I hope he can lead us to a good therapist. We've got to get that started right away. Plus we've got to get Daddy out of bed. I don't think he needs to wear those awful diapers; I'll bet you could get him to the bathroom."

"It might take two of us to get him up. Besides, I haven't wanted to push him."

She, who'd pushed him around all their married life. "He needs to be pushed, Mama; it's the only way he'll get better. I've volunteered with enough patients over the years to know that."

The dishwater gurgled out of the sink. "You've volunteered to help people?"

I ignored her obvious surprise. "For over ten years now I've worked at a nursing home, even longer than I've worked at the ad agency. The patients there are so grateful for anything you do; they just need their days brightened a little."

"Does it make you feel better?"

Her simple question was laden with such complexity that for a moment I couldn't respond. Did she fully grasp my guilt; was that it? Was she accusing me of coming home only to help myself "feel better"? Or was she saying, "Celia, you've never done a thing in your life for anyone but yourself, so why should your volunteer work be any different?"

"Sure," I said evenly. "It makes me happy to see them happy, and it makes me feel . . . useful."

"Mm." She sniffed. "Speakin' of old folk, Eva and Frank want to see you."

Oh great. I searched for something pleasant to say. Seeing Mr. B. would be a pleasure, but I cringed at the thought of his wife.

"How are they?" I asked.

"Pretty good for their age. She's eighty and he's eighty-two. He's fairly spry and still drives. Eva can walk all right, but she can't drive 'cause her hands are terrible with arthritis. Frank does most of the cookin' and housework."

"All the more time for her to stick her nose in other people's business," I commented snidely. The moment the words were out of my mouth, I could have kicked myself. Some way to try to get along with Mama. "Sorry, I didn't mean that."

Mama looked disgusted. "I can't understand why you never liked her; she's been my support all these years."

"What do you mean, your support?" The edge in my tone matched hers. "What about your own family? Why wasn't Daddy your support?"

Her eyes drifted to the window, a dishwater-red hand against her hip. "He was the reason I needed her support," she said quietly.

As I stared at her, incapable of summoning a response, she picked up a dish towel and began to dry a plate.

chapter 17

After reading the newspaper to Daddy, I placed a lengthy call to the ad agency, discussing Cellway, Southern Bank, and the other accounts in progress. Not much had happened since I left, but then I'd only been gone a day. It seemed more like a week. I did hear good news about Partners, however.

"Celia," Matt cried, "Gary Stelt loves your slogan! You're a gem for helping me out."

"That's great," I said, a warmth spreading through me. Matt's appreciation was a wonderful reminder that I was still needed. "Wish it worked that easily all the time."

After dealing with the client issues, I checked with Monica, who said my cats were faring well, but how often was she supposed to water that fern in the kitchen? By the time I hung up, I felt renewed by the call, basking in the familiarity of my colleagues' voices and their daily problems, picturing my desk at Sammons, my house and patio. For a moment I lingered by the phone, my hand still on the receiver and my throat tight with longing.

My thoughts were cut short when I gazed through the living room curtains to see a man striding up our sidewalk, black bag in hand. It had to be Dr. Forkes. I looked at him more closely, not sure I would have recognized him. He was surprisingly tall and broad-chested, with a straight nose and rugged jaw, exuding masculinity even from a distance. Although he was wearing a suit, I could easily have imagined him in jeans and a T-shirt, chopping wood for a campfire. His hair was salt-and-pepper, wavy. I crossed the room to open the door before he knocked. Our eyes met, his a light hazel, almost opaque, against tanned skin. Briefly we studied each other.

"You must be Celia." He held out a hand.

"I remember you, John. Though I suppose I should call you Dr. Forkes now."

He smiled, his fingers in mine across the threshold. "John is fine."

While Dr. Forkes examined Daddy in the bedroom, I watched his hands, struck by their gentleness and strength. There was a certain grace to them as he listened to Daddy's heart, pulled a blood pressure cuff from his bag and placed it around Daddy's arm. When he was finished with the examination, he tapped Daddy on the cheek with affection. My heart tugged at the gesture.

Afterward he took the time to sit with Mama and me at the dining table, patiently answering my nonstop questions, his suit coat hanging from the back of his chair. Daddy's bedroom door was closed so he could rest. Dr. Forkes' manner was easy as he leaned his arms on the table, hands clasped, watching me attentively. With therapy Daddy could recover, he told me, but he wasn't sure to what extent. Only time would tell if the recovery would be complete enough for Daddy to return to work.

"That's taken care of," Mama said casually. "William's sixty-two, only three years from retirement. His boss, Mr. Sledge, said they're thinkin' of replacin' him."

"Replacing him," I repeated in wonderment. "Just like that?"

"It's not just like that, Celia," Mama retorted. "He had the stroke over two weeks ago. Someone has to do their books. Business goes on, you know."

"But he worked there all his life." My voice rose. "How can they just throw him away so quickly?"

"They haven't thrown him away," she insisted. "For now the job is there. Mr. Sledge has hired a temporary in the meantime. But he said they could only hold your daddy's job for eight weeks, and if he can't return by then, they'll give him an excellent package for early retirement, plus their medical insurance will continue for the next three years."

The old tension between us fizzed. "Does Daddy know this?"

"Of course not." Her tone was edgy. "It would only upset him, and there's nothin' he could do about it anyway."

Indignation blazed within me. "Maybe he can't but you certainly could! You could fight for him! You could remind Mr. Sledge that he's never had a more loyal worker and that your husband deserves better!"

"I can't do that, Celia; it's Mr. Sledge's company." Mama threw an embarrassed glance at the doctor.

"You'd do it if you wanted to," I pressed, accusation on my face. As long as I could remember, she hadn't liked the idea of people leaving

apter 18

ng down at Daddy's hopelessly crooked face, I
[H]is eyes were bleary.
I summoned a grin.
[l]opsidedly.
[p]ulled a chair near his bed and plopped into it.
I'd glued to my features had been well honed
[vo]lunteer service. Patients didn't need melancholy;
[l]aughter. It had to be balanced, however, with
struggles. More than once I'd cried with them
[e]s. One thing was certain—I could empathize
[ha]ving carried my own for so long.
small TV in here, maybe on your dresser? It
[ng]ing to do."
[f]ace, then shook his head slowly.
[l]ike me to read to you, then? I could buy some

[s]miling. "Then what am I supposed to do with
[hel]ping with your therapy, that is?"
[po]inted at me.
announced. "You're looking at your therapist.
[m]y cat too, so you'd better do what I say."
[t]he covers in a one-handed clap.
[mo]ve," I said, raising an eyebrow. "Tell you the
[kn]ow how much the doc likes it. But we'll prove
[W]e'll show him up good!"
[la]ughed. I watched as he struggled to say more, then
[wa]ved his right hand in the air, thumb against
[mo]ment to understand.
[so]mething?"

her. I was convinced she just wanted to keep Daddy home for her sake.
"When do you plan to tell him? When he's on his way out the door to
go back to work?"

"That's enough; we'll talk about this later." Mama turned to the
doctor, color mottling her cheeks. "Please forgive my daughter," she
said tightly. "She's still tired from her trip."

I clenched my teeth. I was tired all right, tired of her never ending
need to control our lives. I couldn't imagine someone snatching my
job out from under me. To think of Daddy losing his, when he'd
worked at Sledge's since before I was born ... I could easily imagine
his enjoying at work the appreciation and respect he never got from
Mama at home. I knew I was breathing too rapidly. I knew John Forkes
was beginning to wish he were anywhere other than between us at the
moment. Still, I could barely rein in my disgust. Swallowing hard, I
forced my eyes from Mama back to him.

"You were talking about therapy," I said with utmost control.

"Right." He cleared his throat, probably wishing he could clear the
air as well. "I was going to say that a therapist should come daily to work
with his left arm and leg and to work on speech. In time the therapist
can help him relearn things like getting himself dressed. There's a
woman in Albertsville who's very good. I've already mentioned your
father to her, and she's able to fit him into her schedule."

"No," I heard myself declare.

He hesitated. "Is there someone else you'd rather have?"

Angry as I was with Mama, I didn't think twice. "I mean no to
anybody," I said firmly. "I'll do his therapy myself. Now that I find
we're working under a deadline"—I emphasized the word with a tight
smile—"I can't trust his therapy to anyone else. Eight weeks hardly
seems like enough time, does it?"

"Well." Dr. Forkes seemed nonplussed. "Even so, I don't know if
I'd advise your trying it. The regimen must be followed closely, and
you have to know what you're doing. You need to understand speech
patterns too. It would be better for a trained professional to handle it."

"I'm not a professional but I've worked with stroke patients before."

"Then you know that the therapy should be consistent." He paused.
"Forgive me for asking but William is my patient. Are you going to
stay long enough to see this through?"

My first thought was ridiculously beside the point. Under the
circumstances it was a question the doctor was entitled to ask, but for

some reason I sensed that John Forkes, the man, was posing it. Then, as the realization of what I'd just committed myself to do set in, the thought vanished.

Eight weeks. I cringed. As I'd driven away from my house and work—my life—I couldn't have imagined being in Bradleyville for so long. Yet when I really thought about it, how could I have expected Daddy to recover quickly after such a serious stroke? Just what had I expected—that Daddy's problems would magically disappear at my return? That after a week or so I could leave once again without looking back, filled with piety over having performed my filial duty?

But still. Eight weeks. What was I doing? How could I ever be in that house and around Mama for so many days? How could Sammons Advertising manage without me for so long?

Worse, what if they did?

Without looking at Mama, I could feel her cool appraisal as my mind raced. *She'll back out,* I could hear her thinking. *She's far more concerned with her own life than with her daddy.* I ignored her, trying to imagine Daddy recovering in time to return to work without my support. But I couldn't imagine it. Mama would never push some therapist to make it happen. No way around it; I was Daddy's only chance.

I took a silent, slow breath and focused on Dr. Forkes. "You must know enough about the therapy to teach me," I said with quiet determination. "I'd like you to do that."

He held my eyes. "Are you sure? It's a big commitment, Celia; you don't have to do this."

I drew myself up, mouth firm. "Yes, I do. Because I'll do a better job than anybody else. And that's because I care more than anybody about getting him back to work."

Mama was silent, but I knew she understood that my statement included her. Dr. Forkes undoubtedly understood it as well. I gazed at him challengingly but he seemed almost amused. "Estelle?" He turned to Mama. "What do you think?"

She spread her hands. "What does it matter? Celia always gets her way."

"Look." His expression darkened. He'd had enough of us both. "Ordinarily any argument between the two of you would be none of my business, but I repeat, William is my patient. In order to agree to this, I have to believe you're both going to do your part to make it work. So. What do you think about Celia's offer, Estelle?"

Mama slid me
so insistent. One t
mind to somethin

Her words hit
my chair.

"All right, ther
at any time. And
insist on it. Unde

I met his eyes
rough, and I was

"Good." He d
last patient out
things. Okay?"

"Sounds good

"We'll see yo
our meeting wi
spectacle of us
nized the smug
she hadn't orch

C

An hour later, gaz
wanted to cry.
"Have a nice nap?
"Yaaa." He smiled
Feigning energy, I
The cheerful attitude
through my years of v
they needed humor,
understanding of thei
over their tragic stor
with another's pain, h
"Would you like a
would give you somet
He screwed up his
"Okay. Would you
books."
"Naaa."
I shrugged at him,
you? When I'm not he
Questioningly he p
"Yeah, that's right,"
And I'm mean as an al
His right palm beat
"I'm glad you appr
truth, though, I don't k
him wrong, won't we?
"Uh huh!" he exhale
finally gave up. He wa
fingers. It took me a m
"You want to write s

"Yaaa."

"Really?" My eyes grew round. "I didn't know you thought you could do that. Mama's at the grocery store; have you told her?"

His head rolled back and forth.

"So what then, you been practicing while she's asleep?" I teased. "You been doing cartwheels too?" My eyes traveled around the room. "Is there some paper in here? We'll just have to give this a try."

He pointed to Mama's dresser.

I walked over and began opening its drawers, feeling uncomfortable at such intimacy with Mama's possessions. In the bottom left drawer I saw a stash of cards, pens, and spiral notebooks of lined paper. "Perfect." I picked up a notebook and opened it to a bare page, placing it on his lap and putting a pen in his hand. He began to print laboriously. "Amazing," I whispered. After a moment he stopped, turning the notebook toward me.

I want you to talk to me.

Within the core of me I felt a sudden chill. "Of course I'll talk to you," I replied lightly. "Haven't I been chattering enough already?"

He shook his head and printed again.

I mean talk to me. What have you been doing all these years?

I smiled ruefully at the earnestness on his sagging face, hiding my dismay. This could go no further. "But Daddy, I came here to help you, not talk about myself. It's not very exciting anyway."

You talk. That will help me.

He'd laid the trap perfectly and I felt myself falling in. It was too much, too fast. I'd not yet recovered from pledging to handle his therapy; now this. My work at Sammons Advertising, my volunteer duty, Roger, Michael—all were in one way or another connected to my past. How could I tell Daddy about my life without dwelling on the emotions that undergirded it?

"Oh, I see what you mean," I said, pretending to understand. "You just want to hear lots of words so you can practice imitating the sounds. It would probably just be easier if I read to you."

He bounced the pen against the paper with impatience, as if he saw right through me. Writing again, he pressed deeply into the page.

I want to know about you. We never talked much before. It's not too late. Please.

His fingers gripped the pen, frustration at his slowness shooting across his brow. I placed my hand over his. "Okay, Daddy. Okay. I'll tell you what I've been doing."

My weak promise failed to satisfy him. He went back to writing, then turned the paper toward me.

Start when you left B.

"B? Bradleyville?" The very thought rooted me to my chair. I never wanted to relive that trip again. "No, Daddy, I can't. Surely you don't want me to start on *that* day."

His eyes held mine until it was all I could do not to drop my gaze. Then he reached for the notebook again, his movements deliberate. When he swiveled the paper back to me, he lay the pen down.

Yes, I do. That's when you left me.

The last word shot through my heart like an arrow. I'd hurt Daddy terribly when I left, far more than I'd realized. Without a word, without a backward glance, I'd disappeared from his life. How could I have done that to him?

For a moment I could not find my voice.

"I wasn't leaving *you,*" I finally breathed. "Please believe me, it wasn't you! I was running from Mama and the town and everything I'd done. I never meant to hurt you, Daddy! I was in so much pain myself, I didn't think."

The words were true, but they couldn't explain years of absence and sporadic phone calls. "Oh, Daddy, I'm sorry. I'm so sorry." I gripped his hand, my own trembling. He held on to me, tears springing into his eyes. Mine filled also. Love such as I had not felt in a long, long time flowed between our fingers. I tried to say more but couldn't. After some time he released me, then carefully picked up his pen. His one good eyebrow raised as if to indicate that what he was about to write was only half in jest.

If you talk, I'll forgive you.

Somehow I managed a wan smile. "Well then, I guess you've got me where you want me."

We sat silently for a moment.

"Yuu kaaa?" he asked.

I shook my head, overwhelmed by his selflessness. "Oh, Daddy, I'm okay. You shouldn't be worrying about me. I'm here to fix you."

His smile was lopsided. Once again he picked up the pen.

God will fix us both.

Late in the afternoon I sat at the dining table, files for various Sammons accounts spread before me, my pen tapping against white paper. Languidly I gazed at the gnarled oak tree in the backyard, its green leaves lightly swaying in a shy spring breeze. Mama was in the bedroom with Daddy, making one-sided small talk. The awkwardness of their constantly being together was already apparent. Reality is often far removed from desire, I reflected. Mama may have wanted him home all day after he recovered, but I doubted she'd know what to do with him. Once he could talk again, I imagined the conversation remaining every bit as stilted.

I too was filled with the awkwardness of being there. Emotions drifted around me like the smell of Mama's casserole in the oven. Again I longed for my old frenetic pace. The blank paper lay before me, waiting for me to doodle logo ideas for Partners. But I could not begin to concentrate. Instead I thought of Daddy's written pleas to me, of the lingering pain in his eyes that my running away had caused. Then I thought of Mama and the accusation on her face. Daddy's response to my selfishness had been to close the gap; Mama had only moved further away.

Through sheer willpower I dragged my thoughts back to Partners, picturing Gary Stelt. That morning, Matt had reminded me that Gary would expect a catchy symbol to go with his catchy slogan. I groaned at the task. Sometimes if a company's name was short, it could be the basis for a symbol, but the word *Partners* was too long. Tilting my head, I wrote a *P*, vaguely wondering what I could do with that. *Partners* in this case implied working alongside others in business, helping, supporting. I considered links. Crisscrossed lines. Dollar signs.

Nothing worked.

Memories pulled at me.

Dropping my pen, I rubbed my forehead, wondering what on earth I would do in this house for eight weeks. What was it about returning that had swept my mind so far from Little Rock? I told myself that I had just arrived, that I had to allow time for settling in. But I wasn't convinced.

Bradleyville, my parents, the past, seemed to be settling into *me*.

John Forkes arrived as we were finishing supper. It had been anything but a family meal. Mama had taken a plate into the bedroom for Daddy after standing at the kitchen sink picking at her own food. Sitting alone in the kitchen, I'd managed only a few bites. When the doctor knocked on our door, Mama appeared immediately, ever the hostess.

"Would you like some chicken casserole?" she offered. "We have plenty left."

"No thanks. I've got to be getting into Albertsville. Probably pick up some dinner there."

"Taking that pretty gal of yours out, are you?" Mama said it lightly, painting it as an offhand remark, but I knew better. The comment was for my sake, a reminder of my past sins. A message that John Forkes had a life that needed no interference from me.

The doctor threw me a glance. Had he caught Mama's meaning as well? Surely not. All the same, I fleetingly calculated the personal knowledge of me that such understanding would have required, and felt a wash of vulnerability. The town must have been talking since folks heard of my return. I imagined all the patients John Forkes saw in a day, waiting room gossip riding on their tongues into his office.

"Afraid not," he smiled. "I have a patient to visit at the hospital."

"Well." I jumped in, all business. "Let's get to it so you can be on your way."

He prepared for the task, taking off his suit coat and rolling up the sleeves of his white shirt. The hair on his arms was golden against brown skin. I wondered how he'd managed such a tan in April. Mama hung around until he and I went into the bedroom to see Daddy; then she drifted toward the kitchen, mumbling that the dishes needed washing. Clearly, she would shoulder no part of Daddy's therapy.

At Daddy's bedside Dr. Forkes explained with clinical precision the arm lifts, leg lifts, and other motions I was to push Daddy to attempt twice a day. "We don't expect much at first, William," he said, patting Daddy's arm, "but you've got to start somewhere." Reaching into his bag, he extracted a red rubber ball, which he placed under Daddy's left hand. "Here's a little present for you. Make you feel young again." Daddy attempted a smile. "Keep it with you at all times," Dr. Forkes told him. "Try to squeeze it every time you think about it. It'll strengthen your fingers."

Diligently I listened to explanations of the various muscles, of why certain speech sounds presented more problems than others, of the expected lag time between the brain's ability to process its desires and the nerves' ability to respond. Mama had reappeared, which surprised me, and was sitting in a corner chair, observing. She spoke no words, but Mama always had a way of saying a great deal without talking. Her facial expression, the tap of her heel against the carpet, announced her protest that such medical realities be stated in front of Daddy. Her overprotective attitude annoyed me. "Daddy's not a child," I wanted to tell her. "He has a right to know these things."

When my lengthy training session was finished, I announced, as Daddy and I had planned, that he had a surprise. With a flourish I placed the spiral notebook before him and put a pen in his hand. Mama rose from her chair, eyes widening. The three of us watched in expectant silence as Daddy labored, the doctor's eyes flitting to me in wonder. Daddy put down the pen and held the notebook up, pride in his crooked face.

Hi, folks. Guess what I can do.

"See! How about that!" I cried joyously, looking to John for approval like a first-grade student.

Mama sucked in her breath. "William. That's wonderful."

Later I stepped out onto the porch to see the doctor off. "I have plenty of hope that your father will heal," he told me. "But helping him will take lots of patience, Celia. Don't get down if things go slowly. Just keep doing the exercises. And in time you can help him with the occupational therapy of dressing, brushing his teeth, and the rest. As for his medication, will you or Estelle see to that?"

Daddy had been on blood thinners since the stroke. "I imagine our work will be clearly delineated," I replied carefully. "As you've noticed, Mama and I tend to step on each other's toes. She'll dress him, see to his bath; I'll handle his therapy, talk and read to him. They don't talk all that much, although she was trying this afternoon." I sighed. "I guess after living with someone so long, you can just . . . coexist." Abruptly I shut my mouth, wondering why I'd said so much.

"I suppose that can happen."

Something in his tone pulsed. I could have kicked myself, suddenly remembering that his own wife had died so early in their marriage. I scrambled to place us back on track. "So when do I start getting Daddy up?"

"Right away." He glanced toward the street. "That's right, I've got a wheelchair for him in the car. Almost forgot to bring it in." He turned toward me. "But just be sure you can support him. He's bound to be dizzy at first, and the last thing we want is for him to fall."

"I'm pretty strong."

His smile was quick. "I can see that. Let me get the chair."

I gazed down our sidewalk as he pulled it easily from the trunk of his gray Buick and returned to the porch. "I suppose you've worked with these," he said, unfolding it. "You know to make sure the brakes are on." I leaned down unnecessarily as he pointed, my hair brushing his neck.

"Sure."

"Well." He straightened. "Good night, then. And good luck. I'll be back to check on him in a few days. If you have any questions, call me."

He returned to his car, looking back at me over the top. "And by the way, I'm glad you're here for him."

His eyes were warm. I couldn't help but smile at his kindness. "Thanks," I called. "I'm glad I'm here, too."

"Good night, Daddy."

My first full day in Bradleyville was nearly over. I kissed him on his sagging cheek, arranging the covers over his shoulders. "You get a good sleep, you hear, 'cause tomorrow your therapy starts. And we're gonna fight like the angel Michael."

He smiled tiredly. "Yaaaa."

"Okay. See you in the morning." I left the darkened room feeling out of kilter, the child tucking her parent into bed.

Afterward I waited two hours in my room, trying to read, until Mama finally went to bed. I longed to hear Carrie's familiar voice but could have no privacy on the phone with Mama in the living room. At the click of her door I pattered out to place the call.

Carrie answered grouchily.

"Well, hello to you too."

"Oh, Celia!" she cried. "I'm sorry. I couldn't imagine who'd be calling me this late."

I glanced at my watch. It was past eleven, and Carrie tended to go to bed with the chickens. "Oh no, I'm sorry," I returned. "This is my parents' only phone, and of course it's not a cordless. It's hard to get a chance to call without Mama around."

"I forgive you. Tell me how it's going."

Where to begin? The day's events spilled from me in broken fragments. Mama. Our argument. Daddy. Dr. Forkes. Therapy.

"Sounds even rougher than I thought." Carrie didn't hide her concern. "I've been praying for you every time I think about it; I want you to know that. I still believe God is in this."

"Well, thank you." I sighed. "Maybe he is."

I did not want the conversation to continue in that direction, and apparently she sensed it. We were silent for a moment.

"How's DuPont?" I asked.

She laughed. "Great! More chemistry now than ever. We've had another date. I think it could really go somewhere. It's been a long spell," she added almost wistfully. "It feels so good now, having someone to be with."

My heart tugged at the thought. "I'm glad for you."

We talked about her relationship with Andy for another five minutes or so. I warned her to be cautious, remembering the pain that Michael and Roger had ultimately brought in my life. She was the last person I wanted to be hurt.

"Don't worry," she responded softly. "It's in God's hands."

How I envied her trust.

Before we hung up, Carrie demanded that I call every few days, even if it had to be late. "You're going to need someone to talk to," she said. "I'm proud of you for calling tonight, for not retreating like you usually do. So promise me."

I shrugged in resignation. What else could I do? Usually I had work and clients and the nursing home and my house—all sorts of distractions. Here I was completely exposed. "I promise."

I replaced the receiver quietly, wondering what to do with myself. I wasn't yet ready to sleep. Wandering over to the television, I turned it on to a late-night talk show, keeping the volume low. Then I stretched out on the couch, fussily arranging a pillow under my head. In the darkened room the flickering pictures cast a haunting gray glow. The front window was slightly open, and a humid breeze, heavy with the scent of rain, played with Mama's curtains. My thoughts drifted from Carrie and Andy to Mama . . . Daddy . . . Dr. Forkes . . .

When the patter of rain awakened me well past midnight, I shut the window and went to bed.

chapter 19

After breakfast the following morning, Mama informed me with ill timing that Mr. and Mrs. B. were coming over to visit in an hour. It was all I needed at the moment. I was trying to gather energy for Daddy's first therapy session after a fitful night's sleep. Besides, visitors—any visitors, but especially Mrs. B.—meant conversation for which I was hardly ready. I could imagine the questions about my life in Little Rock, the careful sidestepping of delicate topics from the past. *Sure*, I thought, *let's all have a delightful conversation as we ignore the elephant in the living room.* It would have been different had I expected any sensitivity from Mama. Instead I was convinced that she relished the opportunity to see me put on the spot, just as she'd secretly relished my volunteering as Daddy's physical therapist. From her point of view these events were merely the beginning of many required acts of contrition. Problem was, I kept adding to my sins. She still hadn't forgiven me for arguing with her in front of Dr. Forkes.

Mama made her announcement as I was pushing the empty wheel-chair into Daddy's room. For the first time since he'd come home from the hospital, he would be getting out of bed. "They're coming already?" I turned to her with impatience. "You should have asked me first. I've got to start things with Daddy."

"Well, you know Eva." Mama wouldn't back down. "She's dyin' to see you. Besides, you should be done with your daddy by then. I don't want you overworking him the first day."

I bit my tongue at a retort, then said evenly, "I'll keep that in mind."

Her eyes flicked to my face, searching for the unspoken sarcasm. She compressed her lips. "Eva and I visit about every other day, you know, so you might as well get used to it."

I had no polite response to this further piece of news. With a sigh I resumed pushing the wheelchair.

"Do you want me to help get him out of bed?" she asked.

"No, thank you, I can do it."

I had exactly ten steps to put my irritation behind me. By the time I reached the master bedroom doorway, I'd pulled my cheery face from my pocket.

"Okay!" I sang to Daddy. "Time to get you up. You ready?"

"Yaaa."

I placed the chair by the bed so it was near his left side, and locked the wheels. Earlier I had pulled him to a more upright position against his pillows so he wouldn't feel so dizzy when he stood. "Okay. First I'm going to raise you up completely straight. Then we'll swing your legs over." My arm slid between him and the pillows and lifted. Carefully I eased his left leg over the side of the bed. He was able to follow with his right leg. I let him get used to the position for a moment. "All right. Here goes." Bracing myself, I pulled him to a standing position, turned him, and eased him into the chair almost before he knew it. "Ha!" I cried. "You didn't know I was that strong, did you? I've done this lots of times."

"Uh. Guh."

"Yes, it is good; it put me in practice for you. Now let me put some pillows behind your back." I fussed about, getting him comfortable and pulling his left leg onto the footrest. "Here, you can do your right one, can't you? That's great." I moved to his side. "Now, the best part is first."

For the next ten minutes I gently massaged his left side from shoulder to ankle. His eyes, clearly adoring, never left my face. Under their gaze I felt both self-conscious and bathed in love. It had been years since someone had looked at me like that.

"Okay, Daddy," I said, standing up. "Enough spoiling. Time for your exercises."

"Kaaa."

His agreeableness panged my heart. I pushed his wheelchair to the center of the room, aware that Mama had appeared in the doorway. "Haaa," Daddy called, but I did not acknowledge her presence. Following Dr. Forkes' instructions, we began at the top, looking for the smallest of movements. A shrug of Daddy's shoulder, a lift of his elbow, a rotation of the wrist, a flex in the fingers. All these things he could do to some extent, and I praised him at each accomplishment. At some point during our work Mama disappeared, but Daddy and I were concentrating too hard to notice. Whatever Daddy could do, I had him repeat five times. For some reason his forefinger could wiggle more than the others, and I commented that this was so he could point the way to the door if Mrs. B. stayed too long. He laughed gutturally. Next I placed the red ball on his lap beneath the palm of his left hand. "Show me what you can do with this."

He focused on it like a good pupil, willing his fingers and thumb inward. They curved, but not enough to touch the ball. He stopped, then tried again with no better success. Air whooshed from his nose and his eyes closed in frustration.

"That's okay," I soothed. "You've got some movement; it'll get better. We have lots of time." I had not told him of our eight-week deadline.

He gazed at me like a child seeking assurance.

"It's true. I told you I'm not going anywhere, didn't I?"

One side of his mouth smiled.

Next we struggled through leg exercises as I urged him to lift his foot, rotate his ankle, flex his toes, with five repetitions. When we were finally through with that, Daddy was tiring, but I pushed him to do everything once more, starting back at his shoulder. Then we turned to speech.

"Let's try the vowels first," I suggested. "Now, we know you can say 'ah.' How about 'ee'? Don't worry about moving your tongue; make the sound at the back of your mouth."

He tried, the sound closer to that of a short *i*.

"That's very good. Now make an 'ah,' then an 'ee.'"

He obeyed.

"Good."

We continued through vowel sounds, then progressed slowly through the alphabet. Consonants like *b* and *m* that required the lips to meet were impossible; others like *t* or *s* were muddled but understandable. By the time we reached *z*, Daddy was exhausted, holding up his right hand to gesture, "Enough."

"You've done great." I bent down to hug him. "I'll put you back to bed so you can rest now, but eventually you'll have to learn to sit up. And"—I tapped his nose with a finger—"we get to do this all over again once more today."

He affected a convincing groan.

chapter 20

Celia!" Mrs. B. clasped her misshapen hands as she greeted me. "I'm so glad to see ya!"

Her appearance shocked me. Her red hair had turned completely white, her freckles faded to near nonexistence. Her nose had widened, small blue veins at the end, and I couldn't help but notice the dentures. Her fingers were awkwardly bent, their joints gnarled like an ancient dwarf tree. I thought of her years of processing mail and was sorry for her crippling.

"Hi, Mrs. B." My smile was wide enough to satisfy both her and Mama. I had willed myself to be gracious. "Mr. B." I took his outstretched hand with pleasure. Even now, years after he'd retired as foreman at the sawmill, his fingers showed the wear of hard physical labor. "It's really good to see you."

His watery eyes traveled over my face, the expanse of years in their trail. He had aged, too, but not as dramatically as Mrs. B. His jowls had fattened and hung below his chin, reminding me of Jake Lewellyn. The rounding of his shoulders lent him a stooped, worn stance. Patches of scalp shone through thin gray hair.

"Lord love ya, chil'," he said in a trembling voice, "it's wonderful a you to come back. Your daddy was so happy to hear it."

"Thank you." I released his hand, feeling suddenly exposed. It occurred to me that Mr. B. would understand the pain of a man who had lost his children, for he and Mrs. B. had lost their only son, Henry, in the Korean War. I had heard little of the story. I did know that Henry had just turned eighteen when he and Granddad enlisted together. Henry, I'd imagined, must have had dreams of glory in his head as he was ushered out of Bradleyville by Granddad, who'd already been decorated twice for his bravery. If Henry had lived, he wouldn't be much older than Mama.

Hiding my self-consciousness, I busied myself playing hostess, serving iced tea, explaining to Mr. B. that Daddy was too tired to visit at the moment. At Mrs. B.'s insistence I went over in detail our exercise and speech routine. She oohed and aahed numerous times, shaking her head. "How wonderful. Ain't you a sweet thing." Once we finished that topic of conversation, I longed for a reason to excuse myself but could think of none. I answered a few questions from Mrs. B. about my work in Little Rock, but my responses were brief and did not invite further investigation. With a little sigh she gave up and launched into talk of the town. We heard all about old Mrs. Zimmerman's hernia operation and how a teacher at school planned to marry a man from the mill. "But they're Baptists," she added, "so the weddin' won't be at our church." The IGA had the biggest tomatoes she'd ever seen. And did I remember Mrs. Pennyweather? That lady who used to sing so loud in church? Well, she died years ago, of course, but her daughter in Albertsville was still living and she'd up and left her husband.

"Mrs. B.," I prompted, "tell me about Jessie and Lee."

"Oh, they're fine, fine." She waved a hand. "Kids all married, and with kids a their own. Gretchen and Grant live in Albertsville. Gretchen stays home with her two little ones, a course, and Grant works in construction. Kim's here in town. She's got three children, and when the littlest starts first grade next year, Kim's gonna start workin' in her mama's sewing shop. Right good seamstress she is herself."

"Who did she marry?" I wondered. "Someone from town?"

"Why yes! You remember Reid Brown, don't you?"

Reid Brown. Kevy's best childhood friend. Married to Kim Harding. I wanted time to sift this information as it deserved, to mentally separate the pleasant from the lost potential. But Mrs. B. rattled on, bragging about Miss Jessie's grandchildren, how one sang like an angel and another was bound to be an artist. And did I know that Lee's younger sister, Connie, had three children and two grandchildren? Thanks to God that he'd provided Connie with a husband so soon after the birth of her first child. Jason had been such a wonderful husband to her all these years. As for Lee, he was still managing the mill, and the owner, Dustin Taylor, still lived in that mansion out on Route 347. And speaking of houses, did I see them flimflam things on Route 622? "Some a those pretty farms between us and Albertsville are gone," she sighed. "And we got outsiders livin' in those tiny houses—with a bad influence on our town. Our kids're runnin' around, boys and girls together; it's just awful."

"No more comin' to call?" I'd hoped to suppress the bitterness in my voice but did not completely succeed.

Mama threw me a sharp glance. "No, not much of that anymore, Celia," she said tightly.

Mrs. B. looked uncomfortable. She'd wandered too close to things no one wanted to discuss. "Well," she muttered, "let's see. I s'pose you heared the sad news about Melissa. Sometimes it's just hard to understand the grief Christians go through. Her family lives next door to us, you know, have ever since she got married. The oldest is such a sweet thing, looks just like her mama at that age. She takes good care a her siblin's, plus has supper waitin' for her poor daddy every night."

A shift had occurred in the air around Mama, and I flicked my eyes to search her face. "What about Melissa?" I pressed.

Mama hesitated. "I haven't had a chance to tell you, Celia."

"Oh my," Mrs. B. exclaimed as if she'd jumped out of the frying pan into the fire. "I didn't mean to be the bearer of bad news!"

"What about Melissa?" I said again, my voice tightening. No one wanted to answer. "Is something wrong with her? Is she sick?"

"She died of stomach cancer six months ago," Mama said finally. "She went in less than a year."

The unexpected news weighted me to the couch. *No,* I thought. *Not Melissa.* Dainty Melissa, bubbly, full of life and giggles and motion. How could such animation be stilled? When I found my voice, I could only ask more questions. "And she left three children?"

Mrs. B. cast me a funny look. "That's right. Jackie's fifteen now, Robert's eleven, and Clarissa's eight."

Fifteen. That had been my age during my first summer with Danny. For a moment I tried to imagine myself on the other side of the fence. The mother of a fifteen-year-old, fighting with her daughter over a boyfriend. Then I realized Melissa would have had to marry soon after I left Bradleyville to have a daughter that old. "Who's her husband?" I looked from Mrs. B. to Mama.

"Land sakes, chil', you don't know that either? Estelle?" Mrs. B. looked to Mama with accusation, searching to displace the blame for the wrong turn the conversation had taken.

Mama glanced at her sternly, her mouth set. Mrs. B. continued to ogle me. Mr. B. was examining his fingernails.

"Melissa married Bobby Delham, Celia," Mama said quietly. "Just like she wanted."

A bubble of air escaped my throat. It was too much to grasp at once. Melissa and Bobby, married so quickly after I left. Together all those years during which I berated myself for destroying them both. For me, the news brought joy and enormous relief. But now she was dead. I searched for meaning in that, wondering how God could ever let such a thing happen after he'd kept them together. How unfair that Melissa, a wife and mother of three children, should die while I lived, childless.

"I . . . I'm sorry," I stuttered. "I didn't know."

Suddenly I had to escape the cloying Mrs. B., who scrutinized my every reaction. Nothing I could say at that moment would satisfy her. Before I knew it, I had risen, mumbling, "Excuse me" with a tight smile as I hurried across the worn carpet to my bedroom.

"Why didn't you tell me?" I accosted Mama when the Bellinghams had gone.

"There wasn't time." She was pulling meat out of the freezer to defrost for dinner. "I was goin' to tell you."

"I don't believe that!" I paced the kitchen, smoldering. "I swear, Mama, I think you wanted me to find out the hardest way, and I sure did, with Mrs. B. hanging on my every response."

She plunked a package of pork chops on the tile counter and placed her hands on her hips. "That's not true and you know it. I didn't bring you here to hurt you; I brought you here for your daddy—who, by the way, will hear you if you don't keep your voice down."

I stopped, gathering control. "I just don't understand why you didn't tell me." My voice caught. "How could you not remember something as big as that?"

She regarded me coolly. "Are you talking about Melissa dyin', or are you talking about her having a happy life with Bobby after you threw him away?"

I reeled from her words, reaching toward the counter for support. "I'm talking about Melissa, Mama." The words shook. "She was my best friend."

Mama's eyes narrowed. "You didn't treat her like a best friend, did you? And after you dragged her in the dirt, you ran away from her, just like you ran away from the rest of us."

There it was, the anger that had been threatening to boil over on me since I returned. Apparently, it had been simmering for seventeen years. No matter that we'd been speaking of Melissa's death; somehow she had twisted the conversation. "Yes, Mama," I managed, "I ran away. Now I'm back because you asked me to come. It wasn't easy coming back, believe me; I spent a lot of time while driving here thinking about the people I would have to face, including Melissa. Now I'll never have the chance to tell her I'm sorry. Or that I'm happy she married Bobby."

She eyed me as if my words held not one kernel of truth. "Why do you always have to think everything is about you?" she burst. "Your first thought about Melissa's death is that you can't ease your own guilt. There's more to life than you, Celia, and as much as this town's never forgotten the things you did, there's more to Bradleyville than you!"

"I don't think everything's about me!" I retorted, flinging out my hands. "I'm sorry for Bobby; I'm sorry for her children and her parents. Why can't you believe that? Why can't you believe I have hurts and feelings like everybody else?"

Her voice flattened. "Why couldn't you ever believe the same about me?"

I stared at her. She had once again changed courses midstream, this time riding a current I couldn't begin to follow. I felt my anger drain away, replaced with sadness, an emptiness that bore testimony to the chasm separating mother and daughter. How could two people live together for eighteen years, I wondered, and not know each other? Why were the cycles of life so immense that years, sometimes entire lifetimes, passed by before events rotated back to where they should have been in the first place? I had lived with my daddy until I was grown yet had never really talked to him. I'd lived with Mama all that time yet had never heard her confront me with such vulnerability. I knew I had done horrible things. But I'd always sensed that the rift between Mama and me had been firmly in place before I was ever born and that what was fractured I had neither broken nor could mend.

For the second time since I returned, I heard God's confident but quiet voice within me urge a gentle response to Mama's obvious hurt. I wanted to listen to it. Really I did. Briefly I thought of Carrie, what she would have done. But I wasn't Carrie. And after the emotions of thirty-five years, after the past two days, I couldn't begin to do what God asked.

"Because, Mama," I threw back at her coldly, "if you ever showed any feeling at all, it certainly wasn't to me."

I retreated to my room, shut the door, and heaved myself upon my bed, just as I had done as a teenager. A childish part of me never wanted to see Mama's face again. Another part listened for her knock on the door, wished for her to come after me just this once. I dropped my face in my hands, knowing I was foolish to even imagine such a thing.

Twenty years ago I'd sobbed on this very bed, cut to the core over Danny's harsh treatment. How I had needed a mother's love and consolation. But Mama never once knocked on my door. It was Granddad, as usual, who had reached out to help. . . .

~ *1977* ~

chapter 21

For three days after I witnessed Danny's fight with his daddy, I sat in my room, barely eating, refusing to take phone calls from my friends. "Tell 'em I'm sick," I'd mumble to Granddad through the door when he knocked with a message. On the second day he stuck his head in my room and cast a surprised look at the bare walls. My ocean drawings, their hues recently growing ever deeper, had practically covered the walls until the day before, when I'd ripped them down in sobbing fury.

"I got tired of 'em," I explained with a shrug.

Granddad regarded me intently, then stepped inside and closed the door. "Can an ol' man set down?"

I was sitting cross-legged on my bed, absently rubbing one of Cubby's ragged ears. His fur was worn to a smooth velvet beneath my finger. "Sure," I replied, scooting over and patting the quilt beside me.

Granddad settled himself with a sigh, palms flattened over his bony knees. "Been missin' you at mealtime," he said. "Just finished a good lunch."

The memory of my retching was still vivid in my mind. A wash in the river after I stumbled in from the field hadn't seemed to rid me of the bad taste in my mouth. I suppressed a shudder. "I haven't been very hungry."

"You should eat; you're a growin' girl," he said with feigned lightness.

His comment sank like a stone into my blue carpet. Silently I rubbed Cubby's ear.

Granddad cleared his throat. "You want to tell me what's wrong?" He lifted a blue-veined hand to rest it on my knee. "Never been a problem I couldn't solve for my best grandgirl."

"You can't solve this one," I said quietly.

"Try me."

I wanted to spill the whole story, but the words thickened in my throat. I wasn't a kid anymore. He couldn't dispel the hurt with a promise to walk me to Tull's for a milk shake.

"It's Danny, isn't it?"

Cubby's button nose blurred. "How'd you know?"

He blew air lightly out of his nose. "I ain't that old."

I blinked away sudden tears to stare across the room at the blue baseboard that disappeared behind my desk. Maybe I should paint my room a different color. Move the furniture around.

"Your mama's worried about you, you know."

I rolled my eyes. "She sure has a way of showin' it. Why isn't she in here tryin' to talk to me?" I was surprised by the hurt in my voice.

Granddad studied the weave of his brown pant leg. "Well, your mama's been hurt enough that sometimes she can't find the words to say. That's my fault, I guess, and I ain't never been able to make up for it."

I could find no response to such an incomprehensible remark.

With more gentle wheedling, Granddad managed to extract from me the story about Danny. I couldn't tell him everything, but I did explain that we'd become friends and that I didn't care if people talked. I told Granddad about going to Danny's house, like an idiot, and about my ambivalent feelings of anger over the way he'd treated me, and about my fear for his welfare. What if his daddy woke up after I'd left, and seriously hurt him? I'd begged God on my knees to protect him.

Granddad's face pinched with sadness. "God has protected him, missy. He's answered my prayers for years to protect both Danny and his mama. But I don't think even his daddy could hurt him as bad as you did."

I stared at him. His cheeks had sunk during the last few years, and I could see the white stubble of his shave. He took my hand in his paper-dry palms.

"Seems to me Danny likes you right much. But he don't think you'll find him good enough. Put yourself in his place. Imagine tryin' to impress someone, only to have them see you at your worst moment."

Fresh tears bit my eyes. "If I'm so important, then why wasn't he at the river?"

"I don't know. Maybe he had work to do; maybe his mama told him he couldn't go."

"Maybe he just didn't want to see me."

"No, that ain't possible. You're too purty a girl."

A rueful smile flitted across my lips.

"You need to go back next Saturday and try again."

"He won't come." My chin trembled. "You didn't see his face. You didn't hear what he sounded like when he yelled at me. Even if you're right, he'll never forgive me for bein' there, never."

"Well," Granddad said matter-of-factly, "if you don't try, you'll never know. I bet Danny'll be there and he'll explain his reason for not showin' up. He's an honest boy; he won't lie to you. But be easy with him, Celia. Any pride he has'll be lyin' in the dust."

After Granddad left my room, I lay upon my bed, hugging Cubby, wondering at his words about Danny and Mama. *Mama*. I'd been so wrapped up in thoughts of Danny, I had barely considered why she was letting me go to the river at all. Particularly since her legendary unwillingness to let me go to Albertsville was due to her fear that I'd meet boys. "Well, you did it!" I'd yelled at her once. "You met Daddy in Albertsville, and it didn't seem to hurt you any!"

"Celia," she'd shot back, her lips tight, "I was twenty-five years old."

When I finally rejoined the family for meals, Granddad continued his mystifying silence about his war escapades. And he didn't seem to be doing anything about sending his medals in for the ceremony, either.

"When are you goin' to mail 'em?" I asked on Friday as I placed a stack of folded clothes on his dresser.

"Soon. But I cain't get your mama all riled up about it."

"You don't have to say anything; just mail them quietly. The ceremony's not until November. That leaves us lots of time to work on Mama."

He picked at a spot of hardened skin on his hand. "Well, I got a few days yet. I don't wanna part with 'em any longer'n I have to. They may not seem like much to anybody else, but I'll tell ya, when you seen men and boys blown apart, those medals mean the world. They mean you fought hard to save a few a those dyin' souls, and the Good Lord saw fit to let you come home to your family."

I gazed at his medals. As respected as Granddad was in Bradleyville, I sometimes thought he'd left the greatest respect behind in the battlefields of Europe and Korea and now lived his life trying to regain it. Being honored in his own state as a triple hero would mean the world to him.

"I got to get on it, though," he declared. "Like Jake was remindin' me, the deadline is August 11. That's only a week and a half away."

I raised my eyebrows. "Oh, really. I thought Mr. Lewellyn wasn't talkin' to you."

He chuckled. "Jake Lewellyn ain't been talkin' to me for near sixty-five years now, and he's said plenty."

"Is his cough any better?"

"Sure, all gone," Granddad replied with a sniff. "Fat as that man is and with as much hot air as he has in his lungs, he'll probably outlive me ten years."

I patted his arm, feeling the bones of his wrist. "You couldn't let him do that, Granddad. That'd be bestin' you for sure."

"Yep," he said, crimping his jaw. "That it would."

His expression changed. "You goin' to see Danny tomorrow at the river?"

I nodded. How could I not go? Since my talk with Granddad, I'd thought of little else. The idea of seeing Danny again set my heart pounding with anticipation; the threat of his not showing up terrified me.

Kevy and I played a quiet game of Monopoly that evening while Mama sewed and Daddy read the paper. Granddad was in his room, most likely mulling over sending in his medals. I had said nothing to Mama about going back to the river, afraid of her answer in light of my recent attitude. On the other hand, she hadn't told me I couldn't go. I'd decided to assume I could as on any other Saturday. If she balked at the last moment, I'd deal with it then.

Friday night I fell asleep holding Cubby, something I hadn't done in years. Saturday morning I thought the hours would never pass until one o'clock. After lunch was finally over, I retreated to my room, carefully choosing my clothes and brushing my hair. Kevy had gone to the garage to fetch the fishing poles and bucket. We met in the living room, Mama appearing in the kitchen doorway, a dish towel in her hands. Casually I told her we were leaving and headed for the front door, feeling her eyes on me. They bore into my back as Kevy and I neared the screen door, our flower-lined sidewalk beckoning me from beyond. *Please*, I prayed. *Please*.

I reached for the door, my fingers touching the smooth wood. Holding my breath, I pressed it open. At the last moment Mama spoke up.

"Celia."

With one foot on the porch I froze. "Yes ma'am?"

"Don't stay long. Understand?"

I looked over my shoulder, our eyes meeting. Something told me she wanted to say more.

A breath escaped me. "Okay."

I hastened Kevy out the door before she could change her mind.

The sun bore down on us with fury. It had been days since Bradleyville had seen rain. *So far, so good*, I thought, wiping sweat off my forehead as we turned onto Main Street. Mama had proved accommodating. Now if only Danny would be there. I ached inside, anticipating his nearness once again, our exchanged apologies. Surely our first kiss would follow. Passing Tull's, crossing the tracks, cutting into the field that led to our fishing spot, I practiced what to say, how to behave. My dignity must be preserved; I could not appear overly anxious for our visit. Yet I should appear pleased enough by his presence to assuage any lingering anger.

But all my rehearsing would prove futile. He wasn't at the river. Kevy fished happily in the hot sun, catching five trout, as I sat woodenly on the bank, waiting in vain.

After two hours I picked up my pole and the bucket and told Kevy it was time to go.

chapter 22

I couldn't stand the pity in Granddad's eyes when he saw me drag home. "It doesn't matter," I insisted. My throat was so tight, it ached. "I don't care; I'm through with Danny Cander. He's just a stupid farm boy anyway. And I hate him."

I tried to pray and couldn't. God didn't seem to want to hear from me. Finally I got mad at him, accusing him of giving me Danny only to take him away.

For the rest of the day I stormed around the house, picking arguments with Mama and fighting with Kevy over the toy soldiers he'd left on the floor just so I could step on one of them barefoot. "Get 'em out of here!" I snarled, hurling it at my brother.

"Celia," Mama said sharply, "you got no cause to act like that! Go to your room."

"That's just fine!" I retorted, kicking at the rest of Kevy's toys. "I'll go to my room and never come out!" And I stomped down the hall, railing at myself that she was right—I had no cause at all. Danny Cander wasn't worth it. Slamming my door, I flung myself across the bed to sob into my pillow, fingers digging into Cubby's soft brown belly.

Sunday I sat in church stonily, splotchy-faced and exhausted from crying half the night. Pastor Frasier's sermon was, of all things, about letting God heal your worst hurts. I closed my ears. I managed to beg off supper that evening, slinking to my bedroom to cry some more. *The Cumberland River's got nothing on me*, I thought, pressing a hand to my pounding head.

Both Barbara and Melissa called during the next two days, asking me to spend the night. I couldn't bear the thought—sitting around yakking about boys. Who cared? The town held nothing for me except empty days in which to miss Danny, a dull pain in my heart. Worse, school would start next month. What would I do when I saw him again?

Then, fate clearly against me, things grew even worse. It happened Wednesday afternoon, when Granddad persuaded me to walk him to Tull's, which he hadn't done in quite a while.

"It's too hot; you'll faint," Mama clucked, trying to convince him to call Jake Lewellyn for a ride.

"Land sakes, woman, you'd think I up and died!" he snapped, heading for the bedroom to fetch his hat.

We stopped a couple times along the way, Granddad gratefully sinking into chairs on the Wedleys' and Smallbachers' porches as he declared how he'd been meaning to call on them for some time. When we finally arrived at Tull's, Mr. Lewellyn and Mr. Jenkins were already sitting outside, the former taking one look at Granddad's sweaty face and asking just what in tarnation had taken him so long.

"I walked," Granddad said as he lowered himself slowly into his seat, giving Mr. Lewellyn's parked car a meaningful glance.

Mr. Jenkins grinned, showing crooked yellow teeth, his two older friends' fights his favorite amusement. As long as I could remember, Hank Jenkins had owned just two pairs of pants, one brown and one blue. Both were faded and tight, riding above bony ankles when he sat. His shirts weren't plentiful, either, today's being the loud, gold-flowered short sleeve with a coffee stain at the third button. A grimy baseball cap hugged his forehead, making his ears stick out.

I went inside to order a strawberry shake and a Coke, returning to hear the three of them discussing the governor's medal ceremony. "How'd you hear about that article anyway?" Granddad was asking Mr. Lewellyn. "You don't get the Lexington paper."

"I'll tell you how. You remember ol' Mrs. Pennyweather."

Granddad chortled, Mr. Jenkins joining in. "Who could forget."

Mrs. Pennyweather had attended our church for years and always sang the hymns louder—and with more vibrato—than anybody. Granddad used to say she waddled around a note like a duck waddles around a riverbank.

"Well, you know she's livin' with her daughter in Albertsville now, and I met their neighbor when I was over to visit after her gallbladder operation. He was bragging about his brother in Lexington who'd been talkin' to the staff a Governor Julian Carroll hisself about some ceremony to honor Kentucky war heroes. 'Well,' I said, 'I been friends all my life with one a the biggest heroes the state's got; maybe you should tell me about it.'"

Granddad was watching Mr. Lewellyn intently, his tongue behind his upper lip.

"So a few days later," Mr. Lewellyn continued, "he sent me the article. Then, thinkin' about you, Thomas Bradley"—he fixed Granddad with a heavy-browed stare—"I took the time to take it by your house."

Granddad sucked his milk shake in silence. I could practically see the wheels turning in his head.

"I'd like to go with you to the ceremony," Mr. Jenkins said. "I'd be right proud to be there ..."

His voice faded, like the drone of a teacher when you're daydreaming in school. Because at that moment as I leaned against Tull's big glass window under the awning, chewing on a piece of ice, I caught sight of Danny parking his daddy's rusted pickup in front of the hardware store. A bolt of lightning shot through me. I watched as he climbed out, my chest sizzling. Slamming the door shut, he saw me, his arm going motionless. Our eyes held.

In the second that we stared at each other, downtown Bradleyville stood still. My first thought was, *Thank you, Jesus; he's okay.* I wanted to surreptitiously gesture my relief, but even as my arm began to lift, the burning in my lungs turned to sudden indignation. *Well, Danny Cander,* I thought, *if you're doing so great, why did you stand me up at the river again? Especially after yelling at me and pushing me, when I'd only been trying to help.*

I stared at him, unmoving.

Danny's eyes slipped to the ground. Slowly he took his arm off the truck door, then turned away. He stepped up onto the curb, crossed the sidewalk, and was gone, vanishing into the shadows of the hardware store. My legs went weak. Sliding down against Tull's window, I sat on the sidewalk, knees bent. I was aware of Mr. Lewellyn rambling on about the medals ceremony. Glancing at Granddad, I saw him focusing on the empty doorway across the street and knew he'd witnessed the whole thing. Dear Granddad. So intent on his conversation, but he'd tuned out at first sign of my troubles.

Leaning my head against the wall, I turned my gaze toward the street. Danny would reappear soon, and I wasn't about to let him know he'd hurt me. I tossed a swig of soda down my throat, crunching ice. As the minutes ticked by, I crushed more ice chips and glared at that empty doorway, telling myself I didn't care, I did not care. *This is how it will be at school,* I thought, *catching glimpses of him only to watch him ignore me*. And then without warning Danny's familiar form crystallized from the store's darkened entry. All anger drained down my gullet like the ice on my tongue.

Look at me, Danny.

His head seemed to turn of its own accord, and he fixed upon me a gaze, question-filled and smoldering. I couldn't breathe. For a second I thought he would cross the street. But once again he turned away, climbing back into his truck and placing his bag of goods beside him. He started the engine, slid out of his parking spot, made the U-turn to drive down Main and across the tracks. He did not look at me again.

That evening I was slipping out of my bedroom to take an early bath, a yellow cotton robe over my arm, when I heard the telephone ring. "Oh, hi, Eva," Mama said. "How are your hands?" I made a face. Mrs. B. sure seemed proud of her arthritic fingers.

"No," Mama said with a sigh, "no better at all. She's givin' us all fits."

I was immediately incensed. How dare Mama talk to old Mrs. B. about me. Granddad was watching the news, and Daddy was playing a game with Kevy at the kitchen table. With an effort I screened out the unwanted noise and faded against the hallway wall to listen.

"It's like livin' with a storm. She cries buckets one minute and thunders around the house the next." A pause. "Well, of course I worry. She won't eat; I know she's lost weight. I should never have let this thing get started. Has Patricia said anything more to Jessie?"

Patricia. *Danny's mama.* I sucked in a breath. I should have realized she would talk to the Hardings. How embarrassed I'd feel next time I baby-sat Miss Jessie's kids.

"Is she all right?" A long silence. Mrs. B. was probably talking a blue streak. "That man belongs in jail." Mama's voice was hard. "How she's lived with him all these years. And how's Danny?"

This was terrible; now they were discussing him. I felt a catch in my throat.

"Poor boy. And hardly more than a child himself."

I pictured Danny driving his daddy's truck, fighting for his mama, swimming with all his might to save Kevy. He wasn't a child. And neither was I. Children didn't feel the things we felt for each other. Neither Mama nor Mrs. B. nor any adult, save for maybe Granddad, could possibly understand.

"I know I shouldn't have let her see him," Mama was saying. "I compromised my standards by setting that bargain with Dad, just to enjoy a little peace in my own house. And now we're all paying for it."

I jerked my head toward Granddad on the couch. What was she talking about? Her inflection told me she wanted him to hear. The memory of their secretive glances across the table whirled through my head.

"I will say"—Mama's tone lightened—"I'm sorry to lose my clout with Dad. I imagine he'll be spoutin' war talk like mad now, makin' up for lost time."

There it was! I couldn't believe it. Right in front of me and I hadn't seen it. I leaned my head against the wall. My throat caught again, my eyes stinging. I wouldn't have thought this, even of Mama. How dare she use me and Danny in her shameful games! What kind of a Christian mother was she? She didn't care about me. What she cared about was ruling her house, being queen of her little domain. She'd already had her thumb over me and Kevy and Daddy all our lives; now she'd finally found a way to control Granddad too, with me as her pawn. Well, I hoped she was satisfied. And to think she was laughing to Mrs. B. about it, my pain nothing to her.

Yanking myself from the wall, I stalked down the hallway toward Mama, balling up my robe in both hands. At the threshold I ground to a halt, fixing her with a narrow-eyed stare. She caught sight of me mid-sentence and abruptly told Mrs. B. she had to go. I turned from her in disgust. "Don't worry, Granddad!" I called over the television. "You go right ahead and tell all the war stories you want. And send in your medals, too. You don't have to bargain for me anymore!" Bursting into tears, I flung my robe against the wall, ran into my room, and slammed the door.

chapter 23

Come on, Celia, let's go!" Mary Lee Taylor called over the roof of her green Cougar.

"I'm comin', I'm comin'!" I banged out our screen door, trotted down the sidewalk, then pulled to a gape-mouthed halt as I got a better look at Mary Lee. "What did you do to your hair?"

She laughed merrily, sifting a frizzy strand through her fingers. "Like it? Cost me a bunch, not to mention sittin' under a steamin'-hot dryer in curlers."

We slid into our seats while I examined her head warily. She'd cut her long dark tresses to shoulder length, and they stuck straight out like an overused mop, kinky waves running around her head. Mary Lee was a beautiful girl, big brown eyes, tall and slim. And she got to wear makeup, unlike me and my friends. But goodness, what she'd done now.

"It's the style, Celia," she declared, fluffing it again. I could only nod. "So, you wanna go somewhere?" The Cougar's engine purred to life.

"You know I can't go outside Bradleyville."

She shrugged. "Well, we can just ride around town for a while, I guess."

"Okay."

The breeze through our open windows was hot, whipping my hair around my face until I gathered it up and held it. Even driving around Bradleyville was a glorious escape from home; I'd not been able to stand looking at Mama since I overheard her phone conversation the night before. She'd probably allowed me to go to Mary Lee's just to get rid of me for a while, things were so tense between us.

"So where ya been? Every time I called lately, seems like you were sick." Mary Lee shifted into low gear for a stop sign.

"I haven't been feelin' too good lately."

She slid me a meaningful look. "So who is he?"

A strand of hair stuck in the corner of my mouth. I pulled it free. "Nobody."

"Come on, Celia, I know that expression. Happens to me every time I change boyfriends."

"Is that somethin' you do a lot?"

Her laugh was carefree. "Every now and then. When I get fed up with one, I just find another."

We'd circled the block and were coming back down Minton. At the corner she turned right on Main, headed downtown. I managed a smile. "Well, I couldn't do that if I tried. There's not that many boys in Bradleyville."

And only one I cared about, I thought. Gazing out the windshield, I mulled over the previous night. After I'd retreated into my bedroom, slamming the door, I could not be consoled. Kevy had tried his best, hugging me and fetching tissues as I slumped crying on my bed. Daddy had talked to me for a long time, telling me Mama hadn't meant to hurt me and that, bad as I felt right then, I'd get over Danny; there were other fish in the sea. I knew he hurt for me and meant well, but his words were so trite. He couldn't understand my torment, and he would never understand my anger at Mama's manipulations, he being so placid to her face. Kevy was the same way with Mama, malleable and meek. Granddad and I were the only ones who bucked and kicked against her reign, until even he had gone soft with her—for my sake.

"Now, don't be so judgmental," Granddad had chided. "That's not the Christian thing to do. You're not seein' how much your mama's tried to bend things your way."

"That's not true," I'd retorted. "She's never gone out of her way to make me happy. You're the one who wanted me to talk to Danny, weren't you, and she used that against you. Your war stories for her permission—how clever. It kept me from fightin' with her and you from talkin'. Two flies with one blow."

He'd squeezed my knee gently. "The bargain was my idea, missy. I was afraid she might not let you go to the river after that first time, and it seemed you were strikin' up a right good friendship with Danny. He mighta needed it more'n you. Ever since Jessie's wedding years ago I sorta kept an eye on that boy. There's something in him that speaks to my heart. So when I got a chance, I figured I'd help him out and pacify your mama at the same time. 'Cause I've been prayin' for God to heal things between me and your mama even longer than I been prayin' for Danny. Lord knows I done enough in my life to give her trouble."

"You have not." I'd been indignant.

"Celia! Hello!" Mary Lee waved a hand in front of my face.

I jumped. "Sorry. What?"

"I said Mona Tesch told me you're sweet on Bobby Delham, but you've been actin' kinda strange to him lately."

I rolled my eyes. "Bobby Delham. Right."

Two blocks down I could see the flag fluttering limply over the post office, where Mrs. B. worked. We cruised through downtown, crossed the railroad tracks, and made a U-turn. I looked longingly down Wilder Road, which ran parallel with the tracks. One mile and a left turn would take us past Danny's house. I thought about urging Mary Lee in that direction but didn't have the nerve. "We better go to your house now," I told her.

The stairs in Mary Lee's large pillared home were carpeted in lush white that sank scrumptiously beneath my bare feet. My sandals lay near the front door. The mansion spread majestically on ten acres just outside town on Route 347, custom built for Mary Lee's family when they moved from Lexington to buy the lumber mill.

Mary Lee led me to her room, proudly showing her canopied brass bed. "I got new furniture and everything since the last time you were here. And look." She crossed the large room to a record player and tall speakers. "This is new, too. What group do you like?" She began flipping through a stack of albums.

I squatted beside her, hiding my exasperation. Mary Lee had a way of pretending to assume things she knew weren't true. She was different from the other kids in Bradleyville, even went to an exclusive private school in Albertsville. Just being with her reminded me of everything I lacked. "I don't have a radio," I told her. "So I don't really know."

"I suppose your parents think listenin' to rock music is a sin."

"Well, lots of parents in Bradleyville don't want their kids hearin' it."

"And why, exactly?"

I sighed. "Same reason we don't watch much TV, I guess, other than the news—and cartoons when I was a kid. Supposedly, there's too much bad stuff in it."

She widened her eyes dramatically. "So tell me. You ever get tired of followin' all those rules?"

I knew that Mary Lee wasn't a Christian, that she couldn't understand how the rules in Bradleyville were founded on Christian principles. Hidden beneath my simmering rebellion was an indomitable awareness of that fact, even though I was growing to hate the rules more each day. My conscience twinged, prompting an explanation to Mary Lee and a witness of what God could do in her own life. And then a voice inside me said, *How hypocritical you are.* Lately I'd been pushing God away, convinced that he simply could not repair the gaping holes in my life. Not with Danny and certainly not with Mama. Watching the cynicism crease Mary Lee's face now, I felt tongue-tied. At that moment a shift occurred around me, like the slight temperature drop when one crosses the threshold of a poorly heated room. It struck me that unencumbered Mary Lee seemed to enjoy life more than the rest of my friends. "Yes," I declared, surprised at my cynical tone. "Mostly because Mama won't let me go anywhere or have a boyfriend."

She exhaled loudly. "What's the matter with this town anyway? How do you stand it?"

"Well . . ." I weighed my response. "Maybe I won't much longer."

"Is there somethin' you're not tellin' me?"

I pressed my lips together.

"Come on, Celia. The way you pooh-poohed Bobby Delham and all. You been sneakin' out with somebody behind your mother's back?"

"No." As if I could get away with such a thing.

"She's been lettin' you see somebody?"

"Not really."

"I know who you like," she drawled. "That country boy who saved your brother." She couldn't miss my flitting expression. "Ha! I knew it! Come on, tell me."

"It's kind of a secret."

She sucked in air. "That's the best kind."

When I hesitated further, she grabbed my hands to pull me across the room and onto the middle of her bed, climbing next to me. "Wait a minute," she said, shuffling on her knees to each brass corner, where she untied the lace that held back frothy rose curtains. Swishing down around the bed, they filtered the natural light, tinting our skin a dusky pink. "There." She faced me, cross-legged. "Now. Tell me."

After hiding my feelings for Danny, it was a relief to gush to Mary Lee. I couldn't bring myself to shame him by telling her about his fight with his daddy. But I did speak of my growing feelings for him despite his reputation. "He doesn't fight at school anymore," I added. "He's really different now. And around girls he's real shy."

"Well, you can get him over that."

I sighed, sudden tears clawing my eyes. Everything seemed so easy with Mary Lee, as if she could snap her fingers and creation would fall at her feet. That cavalier expression, the nuance of her lifted shoulder, only reminded me of skills I didn't possess. Nor could I imagine unleashing them on Danny. I'd been afraid to even take his hand, for goodness' sake.

Not that it mattered now.

"What is it?" Mary Lee tugged on my sleeve.

My legs were blurry against her white coverlet. "We had a fight and now he won't speak to me. Yesterday I saw him across the street but he just turned his back."

"Oh." Her voice dropped. "Did you try to talk to him?"

In front of Mr. Jenkins and hawk-eyed Jake Lewellyn? "No, I just . . . stared. He's the one who turned away."

"Yeah, Celia, but sometimes you gotta make the first move."

I started to shake my head.

"Well, you want him back, don't you? So call him, ask if you can meet somewhere."

"I *can't*, Mary Lee. I have no privacy on our phone; somebody's always around. Plus what if his daddy answered, or his mama?"

"Hang up!"

Absently I rubbed a finger over her lacy bedspread. There was no way to explain to Mary Lee the serene exhilaration I'd felt while being with Danny. It was like the time I marveled at a large butterfly that had alighted on my hand. Danny wasn't someone I could recapture with a net of feminine wiles. He had to want to come back to me. "I just can't go runnin' after him, Mary Lee." Blowing out air, I pulled aside a bed curtain, willing my face to brighten. "I'm sick of talkin' about him right now. Why don't you show me your new records?"

"Sure. We're gettin' too morose here anyway." Thrusting open the curtains, she jumped off the bed and padded across the sun-drenched carpet. "You've heard of *Saturday Night Fever*, haven't you?"

"Yeah, but I don't know that much about it."

Her mouth hung open. "You don't know much about *Saturday Night Fever*? It's only the biggest movie anywhere. And the Bee Gees? And disco?"

I raised my hands, palms up.

"Well, come on!" she cried happily. "I'll teach you how to do the Latin Hustle!"

Dancing. I managed a smile. Wouldn't Mama have a fit.

chapter 24

"William, I need the use a your car fer a spell, if you don't mind," Granddad announced as he rose from the supper table.

My hands were in soapsuds, scrubbing Mama's black roasting pan while she put food away. Our tacit agreement of silence wafted between us like winter air seeping underneath a weather-beaten door. Scraping mashed potatoes into a plastic container, Mama stopped with the bowl in midair when she heard Granddad's request. I kept my head down, scouring, blowing strands of hair away from the sides of my mouth. But my ears were pricked.

"Where ya goin', Granddad?" Kevy asked.

"Just need to run an errand, that's all. Won't be gone long."

"Can I go?"

"Nope." Granddad was pushing in his chair. "Got to take care a this on my own, Master Kevin."

I figured I knew where he was going—to the store for the packaging he needed to mail his medals.

"Daddy," Mama said, "you know you shouldn't be drivin'."

He headed out of the kitchen, muttering that he knew nothing of the sort.

"William," Mama hissed. "Do somethin'."

Daddy shrugged. "Like what?"

"Go with him!" She set down the bowl of mashed potatoes with a bang. "What if he has one of his heart spells on the way?"

"He can't be goin' far, Estelle. He'll be all right."

"Oh, William, you're no help at all."

My mouth moved before I thought. "Maybe he'll let me go."

I could feel Mama's glare at my back. I scrubbed the pan harder, smugly satisfied over her ambivalence at my suggestion. Sending me off with a secretive Granddad would only strengthen our bond against her. But at least I'd keep an eye on him.

"Well, you can ask." Her voice was grudging.

But Granddad eased off in Daddy's car on his own, headed toward town. When I turned from our living room window, Mama gave me a look. Daddy settled into his chair with a book while Kevy banged out the back door to play on the swing. I escaped to my room.

At Granddad's request I walked him to the post office the next day, after the worst heat had passed. The medals on his bookcase had disappeared, and a large manila envelope, painstakingly packaged with protective stuffing and addressed to Lawrence Tremaine at the *Lexington Herald*, was now clutched in his hand.

"Did you remember to fill out the form that reporter sent you?" I asked, holding his arm as he negotiated the porch steps.

"Don't you worry none," he chuckled. "I done this up right." He'd spent some time on the phone before lunch, while Mama and Kevy were out. "I need some privacy now, missy," he'd said as he picked up the receiver. I'd managed to look indignant. Eavesdropping on Mama was one thing but I wouldn't do that to Granddad.

"You must be excited," I remarked after we'd walked a block and a half down Main. About five blocks ahead the post office flagpole thrust into the hazy blue sky. Granddad was walking slower already. Fortunately, we weren't going all the way to Tull's. There was a bench under the shade of a maple tree outside the post office where he could rest awhile before we started back.

"Yep."

I was not looking forward to seeing Mrs. B. Loose-mouthed old hen. Sure enough, the minute Granddad and I stepped into the building, she started clucking. "Well, look who's here," she said ever so sweetly, patting her red-haired bun. "Good to see you, Thomas. Celia. Out helpin' your granddad, are you?"

I smiled tightly. I could well imagine what she was thinking, looking at me. She and Mama had probably yakked a blue streak since Wednesday night.

"Afternoon, Eva," Granddad replied, leaning tiredly against the counter. "Your hands treatin' you fair today?"

She held out freckled fingers. "They're okay today, thank you. Still, I used to think I'd be workin' for ages after Frank retires, but now I'm not so sure." Mr. B. had been made manager of the lumber mill immediately following the strike that occurred when I was six years old. "Oh, well." She sighed. "So whatcha got for me, Thomas?"

Granddad placed his envelope on the counter. "I'm sendin' this here package to Governor Julian Carroll hisself," he declared, "by way of a reporter in Lexington. But before I do, I need to know you'll take good care of it."

"Well, of course I will."

Granddad's eyes narrowed. "Ya ain't in on no funny stuff with Jake Lewellyn at my expense, are ya?"

"I don't know what you mean."

"I mean, you're not fixin' to take this after I done mailed it and give it to him?"

She inhaled slowly, drawing to her full height and spreading a hand across her chest. "Certainly not, Thomas Bradley," she retorted huffily. "This is the U.S. mail. It's my job to send it and receive it, not tamper with it!"

Granddad's mouth twitched. I turned away, pretending to gaze out the window so she wouldn't see my amusement.

"Well then, see that it gits there." The envelope scraped softly over the counter.

I contained my giggles until Granddad and I were parked on the bench outside Mrs. B.'s little kingdom. "You sure gave her a hard time."

"Yep." Granddad braced himself against the back slats of the green bench, his legs spraddled, hands on his thighs. He looked highly pleased with himself. He hadn't really been concerned about Mrs. B.'s working in cahoots with Mr. Lewellyn. He'd just given her a little grief on my account, and I could have hugged him for it.

"I've never liked her," I commented.

Granddad gazed across the street. "She's a fine woman, missy, just talkative, that's all. She has to watch her words sometimes; I have to watch my pride. We all got our own weaknesses. But Eva, she's had to face a lot a things. When her son, Henry, was alive, that boy was her life. He was only two years older'n your mama, you know. And a fine young man. Fine indeed. His dyin' broke our hearts."

Vainly I sought a response, struck by the unexpected sorrow flickering across Granddad's features. His eyes remained focused afar, and the specter of something ancient and forlorn brushed my shoulders. I shook it away. "I know November's a long time to wait to see your medals again," I ventured softly, "but it'll be worth it, with the whole family goin' to watch. I hope."

He knew what I meant. Grinning suddenly, he jutted out his chin. "It sure will."

"Well, Celia," Granddad said when we were two blocks from home, "tomorrow's Saturday. You'll be goin' to the river, I expect."

His feigned casualness didn't fool me for a minute. *He's been waiting our entire outing to say this*, I thought as a rock fell into my stomach. Danny was not a subject I wanted to discuss. "Why, Granddad? Danny doesn't want to see me."

"You don't know that."

"He stood me up twice."

"That don't mean he don't want to see you. It just means he's afraid."

"Afraid of what? That I'll scream at him and push him like he did me?"

"No, missy. Afraid a bein' his real self. You see, I know. When I was Danny's age, I was head over heels in love."

We had reached a corner, and I took his arm to help him step down. "With Grandmama, you mean."

"Nope. This was but a slip of a girl, only fourteen years old." He laughed lightly. "I knew I didn't dare touch her, she was so young. Her daddy'd be after me with a shotgun, sure's you're livin'. About all I could do was pine away. Then, afore I got the nerve to tell her how things was, I found myself eighteen and signin' up for the army, yammerin' to everybody about how I was finally goin' to see the world. That was the first time I served in the military, way before World War II. Anyway, by the time I got back four years later, she'd done married and gone."

The thought of Danny with anyone else turned my insides to ice. "But you got married to Grandmama eventually."

"Yep. And I loved Adele somethin' fierce, once I got over that little girl. But I was lucky. Love like that don't always come knockin' twice." He patted my hand. "What I'm tryin' to tell you is, you need to go back and give it one more chance."

My throat tightened at the thought of waiting futilely for Danny, hope drifting away with the river's current. "I just can't go through that again, Granddad."

We were at the corner of Minton and Main, an overhanging willow tree dancing shadows across his eyes. "You givin' up already?" he asked gently. "I thought Danny Cander was worth fightin' for."

I scuffed my shoe against a crack in the cement. "He is."

"Then go at it like the angel Michael, missy."

"I can't. I'm too tired of it all."

Granddad grunted in acknowledgment. "I remember thinkin' that many a time on the battlefield. When my heart was like a ball a lead, aching for the dead all around me, thinking I was goin' to lose an arm or a leg any minute. Those times I just wanted to give up and let 'em kill me.

"And then I'd git up and fight."

chapter 25

The heavens still decried no sign of rain as Kevy and I walked down Main Street. Lawns were turning brown and folks moved like slugs in the heat. When I passed Tull's, I tried not to think of Danny but failed miserably. His actions that day should have convinced me we could not surmount our differences. Crossing the tracks, veering into the field, I told myself I was merely taking Kevy fishing, that Danny wouldn't be there and I didn't care. When school started, I'd float right by him, trailing in my wake a half dozen boys who wanted me. I'd flirt with Bobby, make eyes at Randy or Lyle, maybe even sneak off to Albertsville in Mary Lee's car to meet boys.

I just about had myself convinced, too, when I glimpsed a figure perched on the highest boulder on the riverbank.

I've sometimes thought that life's essence is a series of pictures emblazoned on the walls of my mind, each capturing the passion of a certain time. My mother's face after I colored the sidewalk for her. Baby Kevy's first smile. Granddad's animated expression as he perched in his chair at Tull's, Jake Lewellyn's bulldog jowls reddened and Hank Jenkins' mouth in a wide guffaw. My brother's panic-stricken eyes as he bobbed helplessly in the swift current. And now Danny, seated on the rock in one-quarter profile, elbows resting on bent knees, fingers idly linked, the curve of his spine trailing down his green shirt. He was looking across the water, his figure cut out and pasted against the cloudless sky.

Kevy called a joyous greeting and Danny's head jerked around. I felt my mouth open to form some witty remark as we approached. "Hi," I said.

His smile was tentative as he jumped down. "Hi back."

My heart scudded as he playfully traded punches with Kevy. "Hey, fisherman of Bradleyville, mind if your sister and I git under some shade while you set to work?"

"Okay," Kevy replied, disappointed, "but will you talk to me later, too?"

Danny promised he would.

We walked upriver in awkward silence. *He's come to say he won't be seeing me anymore*, I thought. By the time we reached our oak canopy, I had steeled myself, and I boldly sat facing him when he sank cross-legged into the soft grass. Our knees were an inch apart, my hands a mere movement from his. I wasn't about to make it easy by sitting beside him where he wouldn't have to look at me.

He focused for a while on his own lap. The silence was uncomfortable but I refused to break it. "I'm sorry," he said quietly. "I'm real sorry for the way I done you."

Similar words rose to my lips but I held them back.

"It's just . . ." He exhaled slowly, picking at a loose fiber on his beige shorts. "He's not always like that, my daddy. I can't tell you how I felt, knowin' you . . ." His voice trailed away. "Most a the time he just drinks at night, 'specially on weekends, then sleeps it off. But once in a while he gets mean. I had to watch out for that all my life, 'cause we never knew when it was comin'." He swallowed, his throat clicking.

Little Danny Cander, I thought, *a chip on his shoulder and wariness in his eyes.*

"Anyway, that's how he was two weeks ago, grumbling around, touchy as a hornet." Danny's eyes flicked up at me, then away. "I wanted to see you real bad, Celia. Only I couldn't leave Mama with him actin' like that. I thought a you waiting for me and I felt miserable. I figured maybe I could sneak a call to you that night, explain what happened, tell you I was right sorry." Danny smoothed the thread against his shorts. "So I was just doin' some chores in the barn, keeping an ear out. Then I heard Mama yell, and I set off runnin' so fast, I forgot to drop the feed bucket I was carrying; it was like my hand was froze to it. Until I saw her on the ground. And then I just . . . busted apart."

I'd begun to portion my breathing, afraid that if I made one sound, I'd break the spell and Danny's words would trickle to nothingness.

"Celia, I ain't never done that before. I always had to watch my mama get beat, waitin' for the day I'd be big enough to take my daddy on. I feel guilty over it and I've prayed for forgiveness, but at least me finally standing up to him worked. It ain't been easy the last two weeks, but one thing's clear between us—he won't touch my mama again as long as I'm around." His fingers twisted the thread. "You can't understand what it's been like, Celia, livin' like that all the time."

No, I could not understand. I could barely imagine it. Picturing my own household, I was suddenly filled with shame at my constant complaints. All my troubles with Mama disintegrated into dust at the mere comparison.

"You're the last person on this earth I ever woulda wanted there, Celia. When I looked up, I couldn't believe it was you. And I was so hurt deep inside that I just took everything out on you. I didn't mean to."

My hands slid out of my lap to cover his, stop him from tormenting the thread. He grasped them and held on. "I'm sorry," I blurted. "I didn't know. I just wanted to see you so much. And I thought that if I walked through the field, maybe I'd meet you on the way."

"I had no right hurtin' you like that. I never raised my hand to a girl before, never. There I was, acting as bad as my daddy. I was stunned at what I'd done. My mama liked to die a shame after you run away. She ain't let me forget it yet."

I almost smiled, picturing Danny's mama scolding him in fury. "Then why didn't you come last week?"

"I couldn't imagine you bein' here. I figured after all that, you'd never want to talk to me again. And even if you was here, I didn't know how I'd face you."

"I *was* mad. Because of the way you treated me. I thought you never wanted to see me again. But I still came, just in case. I was willin' to face you." I hadn't meant to sound so challenging but it couldn't be helped. He'd beaten his daddy unconscious, yet he couldn't even talk to me? "Do you know what these two weeks have been like?"

"They been awful for me, Celia, more'n you'll ever know. I thought about you every minute, wondering what you was doin'. Wondering if you hated me. Hating myself for losin' the thing I'd pined after for so long."

A vague anticipation seeped through my chest. "What do you mean?"

Rubbing my thumb, he watched the brown skin whiten under his touch. "This is real hard for me."

"I know. But it's okay."

He concentrated on my thumb. The skin blanched, faded back to brown. "I always knew that 'cause of my daddy I was different," he said finally. "So I fought a lot as a kid 'cause I thought I had somethin' to prove. Then one time when I was eleven years old—you probably don't even remember it—I had a fight with Gerald Henley on the playground. I busted his nose."

"I remember that."

"Oh. Well, Gerald had said somethin' about my daddy. But you stood up for me. Nobody had ever done that before." He was back to the fascination of my thumb.

"Go on."

"Well, I just couldn't forgit it. And I started carin' about you. Right then."

The feeling in my chest crystallized. Right then? Right then was five years ago. I couldn't comprehend that. All the times I'd seen him in the hallway at school only for him to look at his feet. All the times Kevy and I had fished at the river in our spot, Danny's spot, a half mile from his house. A thought flashed through my head. "Were you ever at the river when I was; I mean before Kevy almost drowned?"

"Yeah." He smiled ruefully. "Lots a times. I took to lookin' for you but I never dared show my face. I figured you'd just run off."

No, this could not be true. The Danny I knew now, feeling like this since I was ten? While I giggled like an idiot with my friends over Bobby and Randy and Lyle? "Then why did you show your face in May?"

He raised a shoulder. "Your brother looked like he was in trouble, tryin' to cross that current. Watchin' him made me forgit myself. And after that I just couldn't believe I was talkin' to you every week. It made me real happy, but I was scared silly that one day you'd think, 'Now just what'm I doin' with a boy like that?' and you'd quit comin'. So when I saw you at my house the very day I took my daddy on, I was so ashamed. What I'm tryin' to say is, what I done wasn't right. But I only done it 'cause I was so afraid I'd lost you. Then afterward I just knew you'd hate me."

I shook my head. "I couldn't hate you. I came last week, hopin' you'd be here."

I thought my fingers would break beneath his grip. "You're sure what you saw don't matter? It don't change your mind about me?"

"No." My voice cracked. "I mean, it matters 'cause it's hard for you. But I want to be with you, not your daddy. Besides," I said, sniffing, "you should see my mama sometimes; she can be a real bear." Drat it, I did not want to cry; my nose would run and I'd look terrible. But I couldn't swallow the lump in my throat. "I'm sorry for hurtin' you."

"It don't matter now." He caught a strand of my hair and pressed it wonderingly between his fingers. "What matters is what you're sayin'.

And hearin' you say it, I just can't keep it back no more; I got to let you know how I feel. I love you, Celia. I've loved you for years."

The word burst through my chest like silver ashes, warm and shimmering.

Then he looked at me the way he'd done three weeks ago, and suddenly I understood the longing in his eyes when I'd so flippantly remarked that he could have anything he wanted. How stupid I'd been not to see it before.

In all my dreams of kissing Danny, I hadn't counted on the salty taste of tears on my lips or the way we leaned awkwardly toward each other over crossed legs, back muscles pulling. Still, it was better than all imagining. His mouth was softer than I'd expected, and there was a warm rush followed by a coolness as he breathed. Our heads tilted naturally, moving in rhythm. At some point I slipped a hand around his neck and he wound fingers in my hair. I think he was shaking. I know I was. If only I could tell Barbara, I thought. And Melissa. And Mona.

It was wonderful.

chapter 26

When Kevy and I got home, Daddy was reading the newspaper in his chair, groaning to Granddad over an article about gasoline prices. Daddy looked settled, but I had the distinct impression Granddad had just plopped down on the couch after prowling at the window, watching for our return. Kevy lugged his bucket of smelly fish into the kitchen, then headed for Reid's house. I hugged Daddy and dropped a kiss on Granddad's balding head. "Where's Mama?"

"At the IGA."

"Mm." I crossed my arms and eyed him. Chagrin flicked across his face, and he reached for a section of the paper. Daddy watched us curiously.

"Well, what's on your mind, missy?" Granddad drawled.

"You knew he'd be there."

His cheeks wrinkled into a smile. "He was, was he? That's wonderful, missy. You two talk out your troubles?"

"Granddad," I said. "You went to see him, didn't you?"

"Thomas," Daddy exclaimed, "what have you been up to now!"

"Daddy, you won't tell, will you?" I asked hastily, just as I'd done with Kevy. If Mama only knew how we all plotted behind her back.

"Scout's honor." Daddy raised his palm.

If ever a man could summon innocence across his features, it was Thomas Bradley. "Well, I ain't got a clue what either a you is talkin' about."

"Thursday night, Granddad? Your little errand? You had to have the car, nobody could go with you?"

He shook his head with mock wonder. "You still stewin' over that? I declare—"

"Granddad."

"—cain't an ol' man have a minute to hisself once in a while—"

"*Granddad.*"

"—without the whole durned family breathin' down his neck?"

My eyes rolled. "What Danny must have thought, you showin' up at his house. He probably figured you had a loaded pistol under your shirt."

Daddy laughed. A smile tugged at Granddad's lips.

"In case you're wondering"—I sat beside him, shoving away the newspaper—"he didn't tell me your little secret; I figured it out on my own. Thank you, Granddad. If you hadn't gone, he wouldn't have been there."

He reflected on that, staring at the floor. When he raised his eyes to me, they glimmered. "You got to give the ol' man credit for knowin' a thing or two."

With a rush of gratitude I hugged him, feeling the jut of his shoulder blades beneath my arms. Chuckling, he patted me on the back.

"You took a chance goin' out there, Thomas," Daddy said. "How'd you explain to Anthony you wanted to talk to his boy?"

Granddad scoffed. "Anthony ain't gonna hurt me; we git along just fine. I just chatted awhile with him and Patricia, sayin' I'd had a mind to visit for some time. Danny hung around the kitchen like a nervous puppy. So after a bit I says, 'Well, Danny, I ain't had the chance to talk to you since Lee and Jessie's weddin', and you were a right bit smaller. How about you and me takin' a walk afore I git on back home? I'll tell you about the time in Korea I earned my third medal.'"

"What did his daddy do?" I pressed.

"He was suspicious but he waved us on. Patricia knew but she'd never say."

"Do you think he knows?" The thought of Mr. Cander finding out about Danny and me struck fear in my chest. "'Cause I'm afraid of what he might do to Danny."

"Don't you worry none; I don't think he's any the wiser."

"Thomas," Daddy declared, "you are an amazing man."

"Oh, Granddad." I hugged him again. "Thank you so much. For everything."

Making amends with Mama would be harder; my feelings toward her remained ambivalent. Dealing with her had been as easy as biscuits and gravy compared with Danny's living with his daddy, but I still couldn't help balancing my mama against his. Mrs. Cander seemed saturated with the tenderness that had slipped away from Mama long ago, had she ever possessed it. Except for Kevy; Mama did have a soft spot for him. All the same, I asked God's forgiveness for the fierce arguments I'd hurled at her, even if she had given me good cause. With the exhilaration of the moment, I was prepared in turn to graciously forgive Mama her worst ills. I had little choice, for I would be at the mercy of her petulance if she decided my sudden happiness signaled danger and cut off my contact with Danny. Not trusting my own failing courage, I made a point to talk with her as soon as she got home.

"I'll get the rest of the food," I offered when she came panting up the back kitchen steps, a brown grocery bag in each arm. Her eyes traveled across my face before she brushed past me.

"Thank you," she said shortly, putting the bags on the counter.

I finished the job hastily, then plunged. "Mama, thank you for lettin' me go today."

She was too busy folding a bag to look up. "You're welcome."

I hesitated, a bunch of celery cool in my hands. "I'm sorry for the way I've acted."

The rustling of the paper bag ceased. "You're gettin' along with Danny again, is that it? So now you can be civil to your own family?"

I cringed at her tone but my face remained placid. "We're gettin' along but it's a lot more than that. Seein' the way his daddy is and what he's had to live with, I—"

"You see now that your own witch of a mother isn't half as bad."

"No, Mama, I just—"

"Celia." She faced me, a hand on her hip, her voice low with anger. "You've been *awful*. You've whirled around this house like nobody mattered but Danny. You've moped in your room, makin' people come to you like you're some kind of princess. You've screamed at your brother, not seemin' to care he almost died two months ago."

The last sentence hit my chest like a bullet. "And he would have," I retorted, "if Danny hadn't saved him."

"Yes. And I'll be forever grateful to him for that. But I hadn't thought I'd be payin' for it with my own daughter."

Paying for it? My mouth hung open as I searched for a worthy reply.

"Look, Celia." Mama put her hands on my shoulders. "You're growin' up. But you're still too young to have a boy come callin'."

"I'm not askin'—"

"Just listen. For once in your life, just listen to me." Her hold on me tightened. "There's one thing I've got that you don't. I've been your age. But you've never been mine. There are things you can't possibly understand yet. When I was fifteen, I liked a boy, too. Now I'm your mama and I have to worry about what's right for you."

Danny is what's right for me, I thought.

"I can't control your feelin's. But I can control what you do, whether you like it or not. So let's get some things clear. First, I have a right to know as much as I can about whatever boy you like, for your own protection. And second, I have a right to peace in my own house—from you and from Dad's battle stories too, by the way, which I will detest to my dyin' day. Do you understand?"

I gazed at her, fervently wishing that my answer could be yes, remembering the revelation of a wretchedly disappointed six-year-old on a colored sidewalk. I hadn't understood my mama then and I could not understand her now. True to character, she had spoken of *her* rights. And I could only view her "protection" of me, lacking the loving touches that should have bolstered it, as control. As for Granddad, he gave me everything she did not, and in return she denied him his utmost, harmless enjoyment.

"Celia. Do you understand?"

I nodded.

"All right then." She turned back to the counter.

A picture of Danny's mama floated through my head—her arms wrapped around him, smoothing his hair, comforting him as he cried. The only time I could remember half as much gentleness from my mother was when she'd almost hugged me after I helped save Kevy from drowning. The grocery bags rustled as Mama slid them into the cabinet below the sink, bumping the door shut.

"And about Danny," she continued as she put milk in the refrigerator. "If it'll keep peace in this house a few more weeks, I'm willin' to let you go to the river on Saturdays until school starts. With Kevin right beside you, hear? Once summer's over, that'll stop; you can see Danny at school."

Slowly I placed a box of rice in a cabinet. Seeing Danny at school was all I'd do. We wouldn't have a moment to ourselves, with the whole school watching. Didn't Mama realize how merely eating lunch with him would send gossip rippling through town? Not that I'd care, but Mama spent so much time keeping me "proper," I couldn't believe she'd stand for it.

"That's fair, isn't it?" she challenged.

Maybe it was the tilt of her head or that hint of amusement playing around her mouth. Whatever it was, it spoke volumes—*They're just kids; they'll get over it.* What I felt for Danny was nothing more to her than timorous fascination, a summer pastime that, come the fall, would dissipate like cheap perfume in the wind. Handing her the celery, I marveled at our peevish circle of misunderstandings.

"Sure," I said, "that's fair."

chapter 27

I may have calmed down in the house, but Granddad prowled around it with the alacrity of a three-year-old waiting to open presents, his worries about me replaced with impatience over his medals. "Good grief," I teased Sunday morning as I picked up my purse, "you gonna be like this all the way till November?" At church Jake Lewellyn yakked about the ceremony until one person after another congratulated Granddad.

"Gonna be honored by the governor, I heard!" Lee Harding declared jovially, pumping his hand. He cut an imposing figure in his Sunday suit, thick black hair matching his full mustache, eyes like giant coffee beans. His large hands were callused from years at the mill.

"Yep," was all Granddad could say. But his eyes sparkled.

Mr. Harding turned from Granddad to nod at me. *He's heard*, I thought. *Danny's mama probably called Miss Jessie last night.*

"Celia," Miss Jessie offered, taking my hand, "you're lookin' a bit more chipper than the last time you were at our house."

I squeezed her willowy fingers, grateful for her support. "I am." I glanced from her to Mr. Harding. "Thank you."

"Thomas!" Pastor Frasier boomed, approaching Granddad with an outstretched hand. "Jake's told me about your medals!"

I noticed Mama had positioned herself clear across the sanctuary, as far from Granddad's conversations as she could get.

All week long both Granddad and I were on tenterhooks—I waiting for Saturday and he apparently trying to acclimate to daily life without his medals. On Friday I reminded Kevy of our usual fishing date the following afternoon, casually adding that he remain quiet about Danny and I not staying beside him every minute at the river. He wasn't thrilled to be between me and Mama, history telling him that wasn't the most pleasant of locations.

"I don't want to lie," he protested.

"I'm not askin' you to lie. I'm just askin' you to fish and not worry about anything else."

"And if she asks me where y'all are? If you've gone upriver?"

"She doesn't know about us ever goin' upriver, so she won't ask."

"And if she does?"

"She *won't*, Kevy."

He sighed loudly, frowning until I teasingly said, "Don't smile." Then he couldn't keep a straight face. We both laughed.

"What're you kids cacklin' about?" Granddad asked as he stumped through the living room.

"Nothin'," I replied, rolling my eyes at Kevy. Granddad must have cut a path through our carpet the past few days, wandering in and out of his bedroom, sinking onto the couch only to roust himself again, muttering under his breath the entire time.

"Whatsa matter, Granddad?" Kevy asked, suppressing a giggle.

"Nothin'," he said back, meandering toward the kitchen.

When the phone rang, Granddad jumped, then veered to answer it. Mr. Lewellyn was calling, gallantly inviting us all to Tull's tomorrow morning; the milk shakes were on him.

"Sure thing, Jake," Granddad replied heartily. "We'll be there. Ten o'clock."

He hung up the phone, shaking his head with a chuckle until he caught our curious stares. "And just what're you two lookin' at?"

"Nothin'," we said in stereo.

Saturday morning Daddy balked at going with us. "This is more for you and the kids, isn't it?" he said to Granddad.

"No sir, not today," Granddad replied. "You been workin' hard all week; it's time you had a break with the family. Besides, I want you there with us."

Daddy would never deny Granddad a request. He graciously accepted the invitation. Mama proved a different story.

"Estelle," Granddad called into the kitchen, "come on outta there and go with us."

Daddy and I exchanged surprised glances. Mama never went to Tull's except to buy necessities.

"No, thank you, Dad," her voice lilted around the kitchen door. "I got some cannin' I want to do today."

"It's too hot to can."

"It's too hot to sit out at Tull's, too."

I hadn't seen Granddad so peeved in a long time. He gripped his hat, set it on his head hard, then snatched it off again. "Come on, Estelle, keep an ol' man company."

I felt a pang in my heart. He was only trying to make amends, simply trying to orchestrate a rare family outing. She appeared in the doorway, wiping a stray hair off her damp forehead, a kitchen towel hanging limply from her hand. "Thanks, Dad, but I got work to do. You go ahead now. And have a good time." She threw him a consolation smile.

Without another word Granddad turned from her, mouth set, pain in his eyes. I'd been trying my best to get along with Mama, but I couldn't help giving her a look. "Well, come on, children." Granddad put his hat back on. "And I thank you, William, for the pleasure of your company."

Daddy nodded solemnly, eyes sliding toward the kitchen doorway. Mama had already disappeared.

"Wow," Kevy commented as we pulled up to the curb by Tull's. "There's a whole bunch of people here. Look, there's Mr. Harding and Mr. B. and Policeman Scutch."

"Mm. Mr. Tull's gonna run out of chairs." Not that I cared if I had to sit on the sidewalk. I checked my watch, thinking that in less than three hours I would be on my way to see Danny. As I opened the car door, my thoughts flitted to Melissa and Barbara and Mona. I'd avoided them all week, not sure how and just exactly what to tell them. But I couldn't put it off much longer. They'd each called a couple of times, asking nosy questions. They already knew something was up.

"Well, hello there, Thomas! Brought near the whole family, I see." Jake Lewellyn was in fine form, lolling in his chair, fat legs spraddled and jowls pink with heat.

"Howdy, Jake. Hank." Granddad gave Mr. Jenkins' knees a friendly smack before settling in his chair. Mr. Jenkins was wearing his brown pants today and the wrinkled blue polyester shirt with a hole in its worn collar. "Afternoon, Frank," Granddad said to Mr. B. "Lee, you leavin'

Jessie adrift with your three young'uns?" Rotating to the left, Granddad smartly saluted Policeman Scutch, who leaned against the drugstore window, fanning his face with a hand. He stopped fanning to salute back.

Daddy shook hands all around. "Looks like we got ourselves a party here."

"What's the occasion?" Granddad wondered.

Mr. Lewellyn shrugged. "Ain't no occasion, Thomas, other than you comin' down on a Saturday, when these fine folk're outta work, so I suggested they mosey on over."

Granddad seemed disappointed.

There was a bit of settling to do, with Kevy and me fetching chairs from the store's back room, Mr. Tull flitting about filling orders for sodas and shakes, mopping his head with a hanky. I pictured Mama joining the group and thought she could have had a decent enough time. Looking around at our little gathering, I felt an unusual contentment. So much of my life was right there at that moment, I reflected—our family's closest friends, Granddad and his cronies, Tull's Drugstore, the frosty glass of a strawberry shake in my hands. Only Danny's presence would complete the picture. I tried to imagine him next to me, feeling at ease, but could not. His life in many ways was so far removed from mine.

"Aw, Thomas, what're you talkin' about?" Jake Lewellyn's voice broke through my thoughts. "You're as mean today as when you stole my marble over sixty years ago."

"I didn't steal your marble, you ol' coot; I won it fair and square!"

"Won it! You call gyppin' your best friend fair and square? Nobody but you would fall that low."

Granddad slushed his straw around his drink, animation spreading across his face. "Huh. That's a right good story; I wonder if everybody here's heard it."

"They heared it a dozen times, Thomas; you got no cause bringin' it up."

"I didn't bring it up; *you* did."

Mr. Lewellyn snorted. "Don't matter anyhow. We ain't gonna talk about it."

The tale of the marble was a Bradleyville legend. Seeing the man's huffiness now was all Granddad needed to launch into it, setting his milk shake between his legs so he could gesture. Mr. Lewellyn twiddled his thumbs with purpose, glancing down the street as if he'd be bored silly.

"Well, this favorite marble a his was black and silver, see, spectacularly beautiful. Jake got it from his daddy when we were both seven, and it took two years, but I was determined to git it for myself. Then one day I got me a fantabulous idea. The past Christmas my daddy had bought a box a glass balls for our tree. They was glorious, all colors a the rainbow, bright and shiny. They catch the sun just right, they'd send a spark a light clear through your eye. And one fine spring day I remembered those balls whilst thinkin' about Jake Lewellyn's marble."

Knowing what was coming, Mr. Jenkins began laughing already. I had to giggle just watching him.

"I had me an idea, but I knew if my mama found out, she'd tan my hide good. After that Daddy would set in and, tell you what, I'd be in real trouble. So I was right careful when I snuck into the closet and stole one a them Christmas balls. I took it way out past our house into the field"—Granddad waved his hand in the air—"just about where we're sittin' right now in lovely downtown Bradleyville. Then I broke it into pieces, about a quarter inch long, and trucked 'em home in my pocket. But before I come home"—his eyes sparkled—"I picked me a toadstool, a cute little thing with a button cap."

Mr. Jenkins laughed again, others joining in. Lee Harding exchanged an amused smile with Mr. B. I caught his eye next and he winked at me.

"Well, Mama always had a bowl a biscuit dough sittin' around before supper, so I slithered my fingers through it and used it to stick some a those colored glass pieces to the top a that toadstool. Then I broke the stem off it, placed it in the middle a some ol' cloth, put the whole thing in a box, and closed the lid. Then I was ready for Jake."

The laughter had attracted attention and our little group was growing. Mr. Tull perched in the doorway, keeping a steely eye on a few customers in the store. Mr. Delham had wandered out of the hardware store and looked at our bunch curiously before being waved over by Lee Harding.

Granddad nodded gleefully at the newcomers, chuckling. "Jake, you was such a trustin' soul back then."

Mr. Lewellyn humphed, tapping a foot.

"So anyhow, I paid Jake a visit, tellin' him all excited-like how my daddy had just come back from ridin' ol' Paddington—that was our horse—over to Albertsville. And there, I said, he'd bought me the shiniest, beautifulest marble anybody ever saw, brought over from the jungles a Africa."

"Jungles of Africa, for gracious' sake!" Policeman Scutch's shoulders shook.

Granddad's words caught on his own chortles. "So I says, 'Jake, I want you to see this here marble, but my daddy said whatever I do, I ain't to git it in the sun, else the colors'll fade.' So I told him I'd open the box just a smidgen and give him a peek, makin' sure I opened it toward the sun. Ol' Jake stuck his nose in that box and near died when that colored glass glinted off his eye. Then I closed the lid right quick."

Everyone laughed except Mr. Lewellyn. "Born liar, that's what ya are, Thomas Bradley," he muttered.

"Well, afore you knowed it," Granddad said, ignoring him, "Jake was declarin' he *had* to have that marble. 'No,' I says, 'yours is much better; leastways you can play with it outside. This one you got to be so careful with and all.' And he says it don't matter, he'd stay inside his house as long as he lived if he could just have that marble. He begged to see it one more time, so I obliged—right neighborly of me, wouldn't you say? Then I clamped that box lid shut and informed him we'd have to go inside if we was to play with it, no more foolin' around. That was when he offered to trade marbles."

"Oh my." Lee Harding slapped his thigh. "Thomas, you was downright mean."

"Still is," mumbled Jake Lewellyn, but that only made us laugh all the harder.

By this time I pressed close to Kevy, making room for more Bradleyville folk who had wandered over—Mrs. Clangerlee from the IGA; Mr. Peterson, an English teacher from school; and Jason King from the mill. Mr. King was married to Lee Harding's younger sister, Connie.

"I tried to talk ya out of it, ya idgit." Granddad pointed a gnarled finger at his friend. "But Jake insisted. So after two years a scheming, I had his marble and he was carting that box home like it was full a gold. I just couldn't help myself; I had to hang around, listenin' for when he finally got inside." Granddad laughed heartily, crossing his arms over his stomach, eyes squeezed shut. "You shoulda heared him when he opened that box! He done wailed like a polecat bein' skinned alive, I swear!"

"He's been wailin' ever since, too, Thomas!" Hank Jenkins hooted.

"Why didn't he just tell his daddy and git it back?" Bill Scutch wondered.

Granddad cast him a look. "Are you kiddin'? Tell his daddy what—that he'd traded in his best marble for some African wonder that was no more'n a smelly ol' toadstool? His daddy woulda kicked his behind for bein' such a fool."

I thought Mr. B. would fall out of his chair, he was laughing so hard.

"I wouldn't a put it past him to steal it back, though," Granddad added, "so I hid that marble down in the toe of an ol' sock for years. That was the danged thing about it; I'd worked so hard to git it but then I couldn't even play with it."

"The wages a sin, Thomas," Mr. Jenkins chortled.

Granddad ignored the comment. "Then when I was growed up and my mama passed away, I took a little teacup from a play set she had as a girl and put that marble in it." Granddad glanced around the group, his grin wide. "And that's where I've kept it all these years, on my bookcase along with my war medals."

"Except now your medals ain't there, are they, Thomas?" Mr. Lewellyn threw Granddad a feisty look.

"Nope, Jake, they ain't," he said proudly. "They's awaitin' till November, when I git 'em back from the governor hisself."

Mr. Lewellyn grew still as Mr. B. wiped tears away. Bill Scutch leaned over to Lee Harding with a remark that set them both off again. "Well," Mr. Lewellyn pronounced loudly, smacking his palms on the arms of his chair, "sixty-five years it's been. And look at all these fine people around us today. Now, I guess, is as good a time as any to git my marble back." He turned to Kevy and commanded, "Help me up, son."

Laughter scuttled from our group like a flock of startled quail. My brother and I exchanged puzzled glances as he rose to aid Mr. Lewellyn, pulling him up under the arm and handing him his cane.

"What in tarnation you up to now?" Granddad slurped purposefully at his shake.

Mr. Lewellyn waved a hand in the air. "You just wait, ol' man. You'll see."

Apprehension curled around my shoulders as I watched him plod to the curb, open his car door, and lean in carefully, extracting a brown IGA bag with a grunt. His jowls no longer shook; no righteous indignation lit his eyes. He was too calm now, his steps too confident. Watching closely, I could make out a slight tremor in the hand that held his cane and another around the edges of his mouth. But they weren't from anger; they were from excitement. I recognized that all too well from my own glowing anticipation the moment before Danny kissed me. Suddenly I was afraid for Granddad.

We all watched Mr. Lewellyn return to his chair, clutching the bag. *It's time to git my marble back.* Everyone knew that no matter what glowing victories Jake Lewellyn may have enjoyed in the besting feud over the years, they boasted little more significance than fireflies against a summer sun. Because Granddad still had the marble.

Only Granddad appeared unconcerned, stirring his milk shake and still laughing over his youthful victory. But I knew him too well. He'd sniffed in the air that something was coming, and he was bracing himself.

"Come on, Jake, you got us all on pins and needles," Mr. B. complained. "What's in the bag?"

"Ain't nothin' in that bag, Frank." Granddad's tone tinged with irritation. "He's just mad 'cause we all had our laughs at him; look at that red face."

"I don't know." Mr. Jenkins straightened in his chair. "He looks pretty sure a hisself."

"He sure does." Lee Harding was pulling at his black mustache.

"Will y'all quit talkin' about me like I wasn't even here!" Mr. Lewellyn eased himself into his seat, still gripping the bag as if his life depended on it. "Oof. There now!" Laying the bag in his lap, he looked around the group, drinking in our expectant attention like a puppy lapping milk. "Folks," he announced, "this here's a momentous occasion, and I'm glad each one a you's a part of it. Sixty-five years. Hank, you been friends with me and Thomas since we was kids; you know more'n anybody what this means."

I turned widening eyes to Granddad, hardly daring to breathe. Nobody really expected Mr. Lewellyn to ever get his marble back. In their feud Thomas Bradley reigned, had always reigned. Thomas Bradley, battlefield hero and Bradleyville wit. Granddad had enjoyed the latter reputation almost as much as the former. Studying him now, unable to quell the tightening in my chest, I saw my fear reflected not in his purposely blank face or even his eyes, but in the deliberate tapping of a single finger against the arm of his chair. I glanced at Daddy. He watched the same finger, his mouth set.

"Celia—," Kevy whispered.

"Hush."

With much fanfare Mr. Lewellyn opened the grocery bag and pulled out a flat brown package. "Ooh, looky what I got here, Thomas." He turned it over. Held it up on display. "The envelope with your medals that you mailed off to the newspaper."

"Oh my," whispered Mr. Tull, slapping a hand to his sunken chest.

My breath sucked in audibly. I felt Kevy grab my arm and out the corner of my eye saw Daddy's head fall back in dismay. Granddad's face paled. Everyone else broke into exclamations, Mr. B. bursting, "How in tarnation did you get that?" and Hank Jenkins groaning, "Oh, my heart."

Jake Lewellyn laughed merrily, waving the envelope in the air. "I got it from the newspaper reporter. There *ain't* no ceremony; I planned the whole thing, article and all! Oh, ho, ho, Thomas," he gloated. "You fell for it, too, right down to showin' up here today!"

"But—," Mr. Jenkins interrupted.

"I just couldn't resist it! When ol' Mrs. Pennyweather's neighbor told me his son worked at the paper, I knew there was an angle in there somewhere. He did a right good job, too, mockin' up this article. Even printed it with a real advertisement on the back to make it look official. Didn't charge me much, either." Mr. Lewellyn leaned back to pull a copy of the article from his pocket, passing it to Mr. B. "Read it; you'll see. It's good. Doggone good."

Daddy shook his head dazedly. I thought mine would rocket right off my shoulders, I was so mad. I wanted to stalk over to Mr. Lewellyn and strangle his red, bloated, good-for-nothing neck.

"So be it, Jake." Granddad's voice strained, his chest caving a little more with each taunting wave of the envelope that bore his life's greatest achievements. "Just give me back my medals."

"Oh no! Not till you give me back my marble."

Silence. Hank Jenkins' eyes slid back and forth between the two men. Mr. B. brought a hand to his neck, waiting. Lee Harding leaned forward in his chair, one heel off the cement.

Granddad examined his fingers, jaw working. He'd never been in such a spot before. Finally he inhaled deeply. "Well," he declared, looking Mr. Lewellyn squarely in the eye, "tell you what. You keep 'em. I earned 'em; you cain't take that away from me."

Astonishment rolled across Mr. Lewellyn's forehead and was gone. "Aw, Thomas, who you think you're kiddin'? If you cain't look at these dang medals every day, you'll drive the whole town crazy."

"Well, I done just fine this week, ain't I?"

I thought of Granddad popping around the house like a water droplet in a hot skillet. And he'd only thought his medals were in the mail. He'd never last a day knowing they were sitting in Jake Lewellyn's house.

Mr. Lewellyn's eyes narrowed. "I know you too well, Thomas."

Granddad shrugged. "I'll manage." Drumming his fingers on one knee, he looked around at everyone's stricken faces.

"Sorry, Thomas," Mr. Delham consoled. Mr. Tull was so upset, he couldn't utter a word. His head shook back and forth, back and forth.

"I thank you." Granddad nodded. Then he looked to Daddy. "Well, William. I guess that's that. Ready to head on home?"

"Anytime, sir."

"Hold on there just a second." Mr. Lewellyn would have none of it. "Afore you turn tail and run home, let's just have a look at what you'll be missin'." His smile turned treacherous. "That nice reporter," he said casually, running a finger across the envelope, "forwarded this to me unopened, just the way you packed it. He even added a great idea of his own. Once I saw how carefully you'd padded each of these medals, I figured I'd do like the reporter suggested and leave 'em be. That way you'd suffer through watchin' me undo your own wrappin'." He slid a hand into the envelope. "Now, Thomas, I'd just like to show you what you'll be missin'."

"No need, Jake." Granddad slid forward in his chair, preparing to rise. Bill Scutch leaned over to pat him on the arm.

"No, now, this'll just take a minute. Besides, how long has it been since all these people actually seen these adornments a yours, all shiny and spiffed like you keep 'em?"

"Fine, Jake." Granddad's eyes slipped shut as he slumped, awaiting the inevitable. All the fight was clean knocked out of him. Only Granddad, I thought, could manage to walk away with dignity when this was all over.

"Let's go, Daddy," I whispered loudly.

"Hold on there, Celia." Mr. Lewellyn pulled out the envelope's contents. "We got to do this up right."

I could see a bulky outline of the three rectangular boxes, wrapped carefully in newspaper. First he cut through the heavy tape with a pocketknife and meticulously unraveled the paper. After that came an old red-and-white striped dish towel, frayed at the ends. Finally the three dark blue boxes lay exposed to the whole world on top of his heavy legs.

By the time the disparaging show was done, Granddad had scooted back in his chair, breathing hard. "Doggone it, Jake, that's enough!" Sticking out a leg, he rooted in his pocket and, amid numerous gasps, pulled out the infamous black and silver piece that had started the whole mess. "Here!" he said, holding it up between his thumb and forefinger. "Here's your danged marble!"

Mr. Lewellyn puckered his chin. "Carrying it with you these days, are ya?"

Granddad's voice was tight. "I like the feel of it in my pocket."

"*Liked*, you mean. 'Cause you ain't gonna feel it no more. Gimme it." Mr. Lewellyn threw out his hand, palm up.

With disdain Granddad eyed him. Then he slowly obeyed, his stately movements worthy of the moment. But first he held up that swirled marble, two-toned and sparkling, for us all to admire. Every one of us was taken by it because of the history it represented, the decades it spanned. I hadn't even been thought of when that marble last changed hands; Tull's Drugstore was just a field. The mill was only a few years old, and Albertsville was still thumbing its nose at the foolhardiness of my great-granddad, who'd moved into the country with the grandiose notion of building a town that eschewed sinful ways.

Finally, reaching over to Mr. Lewellyn, Granddad prepared to drop that marble in the beefy, sweating palm. In the last second he stopped. Drew back. "Wait a minute. I ain't actually seen my medals yet."

Mr. Lewellyn dropped his arm, making a face. "Heaven's sake, Thomas, you know they're in there. What would I do with 'em?"

"So lemme see 'em."

"Danged stubborn ol' man," Mr. Lewellyn muttered as he rummaged through the boxes, picked one up and opened it, thrusting its contents toward Granddad. "Here."

My eyes perceived it faster than my brain. For a split second my mind flashed pure white as it scrambled to process. Then discernment burst like fireworks, showering colors of meaning over my shoulders.

I heard the staccato of a laugh and realized it was my own. Then other sounds—astonished chuckles, quickly tumbling into the deep guffaws of men and the higher laughter of women; the slapping of hands against metal; the scraping of a chair on cement; Kevy's giggles. We all gaped at the box in Mr. Lewellyn's hand, pointing, elbowing each other, while Granddad remained stock-still.

Except for the slow smile spreading across his face.

For in the gold velvet lining of the box, taped securely and now blackened with mildew, lay a long-stemmed, button-cap toadstool.

Mr. Lewellyn recoiled, yanking the box around to view its contents. An expression of abject horror crossed his face. "No," he breathed, jowls trembling. "It cain't be." Dropping the box like a glowing coal, he snatched a second, yanked it open.

"Ha!" Hank Jenkins cried, tipping back his chair. "It's another one!"

Our laughter swelled louder, echoing off the hardware store across the street, bouncing back against our own gleaming foreheads.

"Aagh!" Mr. Lewellyn's breath rattled in his throat. He snapped up the last box, hope shining through sudden wateriness in his eyes—a rarefied, last-dying-breath hope that all three medals would be there, stuffed into one box.

And for all his pains he uncovered a third toadstool.

Mr. B. and Lee Harding were out of their seats, bent over with hoots and howls, slapping Granddad on the back. Kevy and I hugged each other. Daddy hit his knee so hard, I thought his hand would break. Everyone else carried on like starlings on a phone line. Jake Lewellyn melted into his chair, mumbling incoherently.

Taking his time, Granddad pulled to his feet and stood at attention, like the straightest of soldiers. Then with solemn grandeur he held up that marble one last time between his thumb and finger, arcing it slowly through the air for us all to admire. After we'd all oohed and aahed, he opened his pocket with the other hand and delicately dropped it inside, bringing up his empty hands palms-out like a magician performing a disappearing act. After which his face broke into an all-consuming grin.

Our applause was resounding.

chapter 28

Granddad's only regret about his victory at Tull's was that Mama had not been there to witness it.

"William, I sure am glad you were there," Granddad exclaimed as he clambered into the car to go home. "Ya know, it was that cough a Jake's what first got me thinkin'. He just wouldn't a visited while he was like that unless he couldn't wait to git one over on me!" He grinned jubilantly, pounding the dashboard.

Wily as Granddad was, he'd noticed the date of that advertisement on the back of the news clipping. He'd called the store and discovered that the ad had run two days before the supposed date of the article. Then he phoned the reporter, using the utmost of his wiliness. "Play things my way," he wheedled, "and I'll pay you twice what Jake Lewellyn did." The reporter had happily obliged, right down to convincing Mr. Lewellyn not to open that package until he was in front of Granddad.

When we got home, Granddad told Mama the whole story, prancing about the kitchen in crowing detail as she ladled tomatoes into boiled jars, far too busy to listen with her eyes.

I wished Danny had been at Tull's as well. That afternoon I related the story as he laughed with delight. I also spilled to him my disgust over Mama's indifference about it. My openness seemed to lend Danny the courage to talk, and for the next two Saturdays his years of loneliness and dammed-up emotions flooded over our entwined arms in a torrent of disclosures as we sat side by side under our canopy, our backs against one of the oak trees.

His gentle kisses gained fervency as summer ran its course. Just before school started, I delivered the practiced revelation of my love for Danny to Mona, Barbara, and Melissa amid their round, anticipating eyes. They wanted details. I gave them none.

As expected, school proved a terrible frustration, but not for the reasons we'd anticipated. Yes, the whispering fairly echoed against the cafeteria walls the first day Danny and I sat together at lunch. The titillating word raced through town like brushfire—*Celia and Danny are sweet on each other!* My closest friends stuck by me but I was shunned by the rest. Randy and Gerald and their gang were appalled that a farm boy could move in on their territory. Bobby Delham was furious at first; then a slow sadness crept over him and stayed. He couldn't look at Danny.

Everywhere folks raised their eyebrows. Not that they were being judgmental, my mother claimed. The whole town knew Patricia Cander was a fine Christian woman and prayed for her continued strength and protection, even as they prayed for Anthony Cander's soul. And they rejoiced that Danny was apparently settling down. All the same, he'd been known most of his life as a troublemaker, and it was common knowledge that alcoholism tended to run in families. His reputation made him a poor match for any young girl until he really proved himself. No one wanted to see me take up with someone who might decide to hit the bottle. "Danny's not like that," I'd retort. "He's as good a Christian as you or me." *Better*, I'd think to myself.

It took a long time, but even in Bradleyville life goes on, and the talk did eventually lessen. My belief that God had put Danny and me together led me to think that folks were seeing the good in him. In my cynical moments I thought we simply proved disappointing gossip fare. The town's standards precluded us from touching at our age, and we had a long time—an eternity, in my eyes—to wait before we could really date. In Bradleyville no young couple got away with much, but we were different and we knew it. We sensed that the town was giving Danny just one chance. If he behaved himself and if my feelings for him did not lower me to unsightly actions, in the end we might be accepted. And so we were on our best behavior.

But we longed for private moments together. Instead we whispered I-love-you's in the hallway, kidded around at our lunch table with the friends who eventually joined us, took five minutes after school to talk before we walked our separate ways. And that was that. Over time the stress began to wear on Danny. He'd carried so much on his shoulders already. The crops had been poor that summer, thanks to little rain, and he and his family were barely eking out an existence. The worse things became, the more his daddy drank. Danny kept a watchful eye on his mama while staying out of trouble at school, lest he damage his tenuous reputation. He worked night and day on the farm while pushing himself for better grades. And he was near me five days a week, loving me with everything he possessed but unable even to hold my hand.

Until March. Wonderful March, when Mary Lee Taylor had her seventeenth birthday party and I convinced Mama after much begging to let me go. "We'll be chaperoned," I claimed, "and there won't be any dancing." I felt a stab of guilt for lying but pushed it from my mind. Danny's mama, well aware of his difficulties, managed to see that he had the truck to drive to Mary Lee's that Saturday night. And from somewhere she scraped up money to buy him a new outfit. The excitement we felt, waiting for that party! Mary Lee nearly died when Danny walked in, eyes reflecting off a fitted green satin shirt tucked into white pants. He was by far the best-looking guy there, and I was so proud. We didn't know how to dance, but when Mary Lee put on the Bee Gees in her large basement game room, we held each other as the words of "How Deep Is Your Love?" spoke to us alone.

Afterward we slipped out the back door into the shadows against the house and stole a long kiss. Melissa and Mona, my only friends who were allowed to go, were too busy ogling the boys from Albertsville to notice our absence. But Mary Lee was most envious.

Fortunately, Mama never found out, and she and I managed to temporarily lay down our arms. I simply gave her no cause to find fault with me, although I suppose if she hadn't let me attend Mary Lee's party, I'd have thrown a fit.

Mama still argued with Granddad about his war stories, even as he began to weaken, his straight back drawing to a stoop and his features wizening. Once Jake Lewellyn had started talking to him again, they played checkers at our dining room table during the cold winter. Come springtime they lolled in our porch furniture, ragging on each other with fire in their eyes and blankets across their knees. By the time summer arrived again, a walk to Tull's was unthinkable for Granddad. He was stricken with dizzy spells and more frequent heart palpitations. The cardiologist in Albertsville ran numerous tests but found nothing that he thought surgery could improve. Granddad was simply aging and his heart was wearing down. The doctor doled out little blue pills and told Granddad to take it easy.

At the time I believed it was Granddad who was responsible for my again being able to see Danny on summer Saturdays when I was sixteen, with Kevy along as chaperone. When Mama acquiesced at my pleading, I imagined he'd somehow talked her into it.

Not until years later did I learn that she had reasons of her own.

~ 1997 ~

chapter 29

After my argument with Mama, I spent two hours in my bedroom, wallowing in regret over how I'd treated Melissa when we were teenagers. I still could barely assimilate the news of her death. Finally my own morbidity sickened me, and I had to think about something else. Marching past Mama, I made a beeline for the phone, hoping that a call to Sammons Advertising would refocus me.

At best it gave me only a short reprieve. Through conversations with numerous colleagues, I learned that my accounts were proceeding at various paces. Matt had met again with Gary Stelt to get a clearer indication of exactly what a "catchy symbol" meant. I told Matt about my futile attempts at doodling for Partners. "It was late at night, though," I added, "and my brain wouldn't work."

"Yeah," he said. "Happens to me all the time. Days too."

Quentin Sammons was spending most of his time on Southern Bank and had become mired in the process—conceptual meetings being held regarding the bank's intended new image, board members arguing, secretaries calling, and faxes flying back and forth. As he spoke, I sat at the dining room table imagining the discussions, the diplomacy. I closed my eyes to picture my office, files spread across my desk. Remembering the energy of the challenge, I tried to evoke it to let it course through me, hum in my veins. But I could not find it.

By the time I had spoken to colleagues about Cellway and my other, smaller projects, I felt an emptiness never before associated with work. The people, the designs and creative concentration, seemed too far away for me to viscerally connect. Sammons Advertising may have filled the void while I was in Little Rock, but in Bradleyville it was failing miserably. By the time I hung up, I felt as though one of the foundations of my life were crumbling away.

I checked on Daddy. It was time to get him out of bed, have him sit in the wheelchair for a while. After supper we would embark on our second therapy session of the day. When he was settled in the wheelchair, I pushed him out to the living room to watch TV. "Will you be okay here for a while?" I asked. "I need to go back in my bedroom and work on a logo."

His eyes pierced mine. "Taaawkk," he reminded.

As if I'd forgotten. "We will, I promise. Just ... give me this little bit of time."

An hour later supper time was approaching. Mama worked in the kitchen, frying the pork chops, which I wasn't sure I could eat. In Little Rock I never touched fried food anymore. I knew she did not want my help cooking.

I had put off the dreaded talk with Daddy as long as I could. He sat in his wheelchair, pretending to watch television while he waited. His patience—and determination—shot remorse through me. Inwardly I chided myself. I was making too big a deal out of this.

I went back to the living room, turned off the television, and pushed him into their bedroom, out of Mama's earshot. Relating to him about the day I left Bradleyville would be hard enough; I could not stand the thought of her listening, too. No telling in what tortuous new ways she would use the information against me. I sat on my parents' bed, parking Daddy in front of me. "Well, here goes," I said with a shrug.

He smiled crookedly in reassurance. "Guuud."

As factually as possible I told him about leaving Bradleyville—the cab ride to Albertsville, the bus, the hotel room, eventually finding an apartment. Once that part was over, the story became easier. I told him about my attending college, my first disastrous job at Grayland, meeting Quentin Sammons. I explained to him what I did at work; I talked about my house, my cats and neighbors. Briefly I mentioned Roger and Michael. Daddy drank in my words, enthralled, as though he were living with me all the events of our separation. I had the sense that I was pouring forth my life and filling hollow places deep within him. But I never would have guessed how well he understood what I *hadn't* said. When my words finally trickled to a stop, he gestured for his notebook and pen. I waited in silence while he wrote.

You left God behind.

I raised my eyes to him in surprise. My immediate desire was to deny it, but his gaze told me he would not be fooled.

"Yes," I whispered.

He wrote again.

Must be lonely.

I knew that he meant lonely without God, but I didn't want to dwell on that. "Yes, Daddy, I missed you. But it's been far worse for you; I see that now." I placed a hand on his knee. "I'm so sorry I left you. I can't say that enough. I shouldn't have hurt you. Or Mama. But I just couldn't face things. She hated me after what I'd done."

"Naaa." His voice was strong.

I closed my eyes. "Sorry. I shouldn't have said that."

He shook his head, then wrote again.

Mama doesn't hate you.

"Okay, all right. I didn't mean it anyway."

You did mean it. She does not.

"Daddy, I believe you; it's *okay.*"

Why do you think she hates you?

I couldn't help but frown at him. "I don't want to talk about this."

He tapped the question with his pen. I looked at him helplessly. Daddy, passive all his life. Now stroke-ridden and displaying such resolve. I steeled myself. Might as well go all the way with this.

"All right, Daddy, if that's what you want. She's never liked me, period. She's always been cold. She hardly ever hugged me when I was little, and I can't remember one time hearing her say 'I love you.' Not one time in my whole life. There. Are you satisfied?"

"Naaa." The pen met paper.

I'm very sorry about these things. But you're thinking of something else.

His single-mindedness was exasperating. "Well, maybe I am."

He waited.

I blew out air. "You *know*, Daddy; why are you making me talk about this? It's . . . what I did."

What?

I rose from the bed and paced toward the door, hands on my hips. "Daddy, this isn't fair! Why are you doing this to me? This wasn't part of my promise!"

I stayed behind him purposely, knowing he could not turn in his wheelchair to face me. I leaned against the wall, arms crossed. Breathing hard, I watched the slump of his shoulder as he once again began to write, slowly, firmly. When he was finished, he held up the pad and waited until I reluctantly crossed the room to take it from him.

Mama doesn't hate you for anything. And God wants you back. When will you let go of the past and see the truth in the present?

chapter 30

When will you let go of the past?
My conversation with Daddy weighted my thoughts. When supper time rolled around, I still smarted from his words.

"I'm going to go for a little drive this evening," I told Mama after we'd eaten. She was at the kitchen sink, her back to me. She did not turn around.

"Fine. Go ahead right now, if you want; I'll clean up."

I didn't argue. My need to get out of the house was too urgent.

I drove up Minton, away from Main Street and Bradleyville, and turned right on Route 347. I chose that road thinking it was the least likely to stir up thoughts of the past, but in spite of myself I found my car slowing as I neared the Taylor's mansion.

The memories that house held for me.

Tears bit my eyes as I gazed at the house. Daddy was right; I couldn't let go of the past. It seemed to loom before me no matter which way I turned. Pulling to a stop on the side of the road, I waited for the old emotions about Danny to pass.

"You *can* love again, you know," Carrie once said to me after I'd finally told her about Danny. I'd shaken my head in despondence. That conversation had been two years ago, fifteen years since I'd lost Danny. Roger and Michael had entered and faded out of my life. Michael was now married; his recent wedding had been a large social event. Roger also was married, and his wife was pregnant, I'd heard. Carrie had now met Andy, her man of instant chemistry. People got hurt, they loved and lost, but they moved on. Why couldn't I?

I sat in my car, willing the swell of old pain to subside. When it finally passed, I chided myself for being so self-centered while my own daddy was at home, unable to even turn around in his wheelchair.

Too much free time to think—that was my problem. I had to find some project to keep me busy between Daddy's therapy sessions.

I pulled back onto the country road, wondering what that project could be.

An hour later I pulled into my parents' driveway with renewed determination to hold my emotions in check and focus on Daddy's health. Just as I reached the front porch, John Forkes rolled up to our curb.

"Hi, Celia." He stepped out of his car, carrying his black bag. "I was on my way home and thought I'd take an extra look at William. How's he doing?"

"Pretty good," I said, nodding. The setting sun behind Dr. Forkes threw a halo of light around his hair. "I'm pushing him to do the exercises and he's willing."

Dr. Forkes crossed our short sidewalk and halted before me, the elongated shadow of an oak dancing across his shoulders. He waited for me to continue. In the momentary silence something shimmered between us. I raised my eyebrows and tried to shrug it off.

"Guess that's about it."

He studied me. "You look like something's worrying you."

Was I that transparent? Quickly I sorted through my observations of Daddy, searching for a safe response. "Not really. But Daddy's sort of . . . different."

"What do you mean?"

Immediately I wished I hadn't opened my mouth. Explaining what I sensed in Daddy involved explaining how he had been in the past. How our household had always been run. But the memory of my argument with Mama in front of Dr. Forkes compelled me to continue. At the least he deserved some sort of context for that little altercation.

"When I was young," I said slowly, "Mama was always the dominant parent, and Daddy just went along with whatever she wanted. Now he's had a stroke yet he seems stronger. He's pushing himself, and he's pushing *me* like never before. He's downright demanding."

John Forkes smiled. "Well, you're certainly not telling me any bad news."

"Oh no, I didn't meant to say it was bad. Just surprising."

"Sure, I can see that." His gaze grew intense, as though he were trying to see deep within me. "So," he prompted, "what is he pushing you to do?"

I eyed him back squarely. That same barest hint of amusement that I'd seen yesterday played around his mouth. His question was no doctor's need-to-know. It was merely a man's curiosity about a woman. I felt the familiar guards rise inside me. Then, inexplicably, they melted away.

"He's pushing me to face some things that I don't want to face," I replied.

"I see." He processed the answer as if surprised I'd answered at all. Then the amusement faded, his professional manner returning. "Well. What you're noticing is not uncommon. Many times when people are struck by physical trauma, their inner strength rises to the surface. That's the wonder of being human. We don't know what we're made of until the going gets roughest."

Some of us perhaps, I thought. When my going got roughest, I had run away. I glanced at the shadow of the oak leaves on John's shoulder, and suddenly the picture reminded me of Danny under our tree canopy. Once again pain shot through my chest. My eyes slid to the sidewalk.

"We'd better go check on Daddy," I said, turning away.

chapter 31

Friday night I slept poorly. The next morning I felt groggy and tired, having to work much harder than I had the previous day to summon an energetic, cheerful face. Daddy performed his exercises with grim determination but was upset that his abilities were even less than they had been the day before. "It's okay," I told him glibly. "This is to be expected. Your muscles are just tired."

The speech lesson, however, went faster than it had before. Daddy had quickly learned the routine. I began prompting him to put sounds together in short words.

"Say 'sat.'"

"Ssaa."

"Uh-uh, no good. You can say that *t*."

"Ssaaathh."

"Better. Say the *t* by itself."

"Thh."

"Raise that tongue of yours a little bit."

"Tss."

"Better. Now make it short. 'Tuh.'"

"Tuh."

"Yes! Put it all together. 'Sat.'"

"Ssaaatuh."

"Great!" I raised a fist in the air. "That was so good, let's do another one. 'Day.'"

After ten minutes Daddy grew impatient and I allowed him to stop, wheeling him to the living room to sit with Mama. She and I had continued to keep our distance, our conversations strained.

"Well, William," she remarked, "sounds like your daughter just about did you in."

"Yaaa." He affected a pained expression and she laughed, pecking him on the cheek.

"Want me to read you the paper?" she asked.

"Kaaa."

My heart softened a little at her gentleness toward him. It seemed a good time to take care of other business I had to attend to. "I'm going out again for a while," I announced. "Daddy, don't forget your red ball."

Mama didn't respond, too busy reaching for the newspaper. Daddy produced the sigh of a martyr. "Yaaa."

The day was cloudless and sported daffodils—quintessential Kentucky spring before summer's humidity. I walked the short distance to Melissa's old house, thinking of the countless times my small footsteps had crossed that sidewalk. How many times had we spent the night together, watched Saturday morning cartoons, caught fireflies at twilight? I could still see her small figure on the porch, hear her calling me. Who would have guessed that her last words to me would have been full of such bitterness?

As I rang the doorbell I faltered, not knowing what I would say. I should have apologized years ago for what I'd done to Bobby and Melissa, but couldn't imagine bringing that up now.

"Why, Celia Matthews!"

Melissa's mother recognized me at once and graciously invited me inside, calling for her husband. "Would you like some iced tea?" she offered.

"No, thank you. I'm fine."

"Where is that man, anyway?" Mrs. Westerdahl said under her breath. "Excuse me, Celia. I'll just go fetch him."

I found myself standing before their fireplace, sweaty hands behind my back, gazing at photographs of Melissa, Bobby, and their children. Looking so happy and alive. Melissa's brown hair was cut to her shoulders, parted on one side, straight as always. Her face, a little fuller than I remembered, looked so content. She was sitting with Bobby standing behind her, a hand on her shoulder, their children around them. The smallest sat on her lap. The proud look on Bobby's face made my heart clutch.

"That picture was taken before she got sick. It's our favorite."

I started at Mr. Westerdahl's voice. Turning from the photo, I pulled my thoughts back to the present. "It's lovely," I murmured. "She looks wonderful."

"Celia." He took my hand. "It's good to see you. Please sit down."

I searched for words to express my sorrow over Melissa's death but found only triteness. "I can't tell you how sorry I am. I'd have written or called if I'd known, but I didn't hear until just last night. I had no idea she was even sick."

Mr. Westerdahl smiled grimly. "She went fast and was in a lot of pain. Lost a lot of weight. But she was strong to the end emotionally. Physically . . . well, it wasn't easy. But she praised God till the end. She always had such a strong faith."

Did she? I thought of how I'd practically cut Melissa and my other friends out of my life while I was with Danny. Hearing her father's words, I was struck by what I'd done. How loyal a friend she'd been, and I'd turned her away.

"Yes," I replied lamely, "she had a lot of faith."

The Westerdahls told me about their grandchildren—how Robert Jr. loved baseball and how Clarissa was a talented artist. They worried about Jackie, once so vivacious, now taking on with such joyless determination the responsibilities of housekeeper, cook, and mother to her younger siblings. "Melissa was a good mother, so close to her children," Mrs. Westerdahl was saying. "Now they're like little lost lambs."

I knew the pain of loss so well and my heart broke for them. "How is Bobby doing?"

Mrs. Westerdahl looked at me sharply, as though I had treaded on sacred ground. "He's heartbroken but he's managin'," she said with curtness. "God's seein' him through it. He's got a good job at Farmers Bank in Albertsville, and they've been real understandin'."

I nodded, unsettled by her reaction. I'd planned to tell them I would stop by and see Bobby, but it no longer seemed appropriate. "Are his parents still here?"

"Yes," Mr. Westerdahl said, nodding. "His father's still at the bank and his mama helps a lot with the kids."

"I'm glad to hear that."

An awkward silence followed, the three of us gazing with feigned preoccupation around the room. The conversation turned to Daddy, Mr. Westerdahl posing polite questions, their smiles polite as I

answered. I told them about Daddy's exercises, my hopes for him, my
determination to see him improve. And Mama? Yes, I declared, she was
handling it just fine.

"I'm so glad," they remarked in stereo.

The conversation lagged once again, their straight backs beginning
to slump. I wanted desperately to leave and finally made my excuse,
saying I needed to get back to Daddy. We all rose and they held out
their hands once more, thanking me for coming, thanking me for my
kind words, apprehension at the thought of my seeing Bobby written
all over their polite faces. I stepped out their door into the spring
morning, went down their porch steps, turned to wave one last time as
I smiled. Eyes on the sidewalk as I walked away, I marveled that after
all these years and after Melissa's death, the Westerdahls would worry
that I'd do anything to hurt Bobby Delham.

chapter 32

Rain washed the streets of Bradleyville for the next week, the historically fickle month of April erasing blue skies with thunderheads. I settled into a routine of caring for Daddy and making lengthy calls to the ad agency. Daddy could now get to the bathroom with Mama's help and continued to approach his therapy with gusto. His speech progressed as we worked on sounds, the rain against his bedroom window a constant patter. Slowly his tongue was beginning to gain control of its own thickened motion. Improvements in his muscles were slight by comparison, but we rejoiced at the smallest accomplishment.

While Daddy and I grew into the "dynamic duo," as John Forkes labeled us, the fracture between Mama and me continued to widen. It wasn't easy for two people in the same small house to avoid each other, but we managed. Meals were a challenge, Daddy in his wheelchair between us at the kitchen table, watching with grave intensity as we labored at chitchat, as if he saw right through us.

My questions regarding old friends gave Mama and me something safe to talk about. I learned that Barbara Dawson had married her boyfriend from Albertsville, where they were now raising four children. Mona Tesch had been an old maid by Bradleyville standards until finally marrying at twenty-five, her knight in shining armor riding into town behind the wheel of a lumber truck. Following in his daddy's footsteps, Gerald Henley had gone off to dental school and was now practicing somewhere in Tennessee. His wife was a nurse. Mama shook her head as she answered my questions about Mary Lee. "Still wild as ever," she said. "Divorced twice, no children. She lives in Lexington."

I thought of Mary Lee and her continuous stream of boyfriends from Albertsville. Apparently, she hadn't changed a bit.

As for Granddad's friends, Jake Lewellyn had died ten years previously at eighty-four. Hank Jenkins had made it to eighty-seven before slipping away in his sleep at the Albertsville Nursing Home.

"Whatever happened to the marble?" I asked.

Mama rolled her eyes. "Can you believe it? Jake willed it to the town as if it was the Mona Lisa. It's matted and framed and hanging in Tull's Drugstore."

A pang of nostalgia shot through me at the name. I turned a sad smile on Daddy. "Perfect place for it, huh?"

"Yaa."

"That silly old marble." Mama ladled more gravy onto Daddy's plate. "Mr. Tull still shows that thing off like it's some jewel from a king's crown."

I looked at her, astounded. "It *is*, Mama."

She scoffed. "It's a piece of glass, Celia. And it was just one more way your granddad sought to exalt himself."

I had determined not to dwell on the past during mealtime, but Mama's caustic remark opened a floodgate. Despite Daddy's presence, I couldn't ignore the hateful comment. Why had she held on to the same old bitterness after all these years?

"The marble brought Granddad joy, Mama," I said evenly. "Just like all his battle stories."

"Don't talk to me of his storytelling!" she retorted. "I didn't mention that."

"You didn't have to."

"Celia, don't you dare—"

Daddy thwacked his right hand on the table, startling us both. "Sstaapuh!"

"Oh, Daddy, I'm sorry." I placed a hand on his arm. "I didn't mean to upset you."

He glared at us. "Paaapuh! Rrrituh!"

"Sure, okay." I pushed back my chair while Mama sat motionless, her cheeks flushed. "It's probably in the living room," I blabbered. "Your pen too. We should think of a way to hang them from your chair so you'll always have them with you." I exited the kitchen as I chattered, irrationally unnerved by Daddy's reaction. Not that Mama and I hadn't deserved it, but this new emphatic side of his personality still sent me scrambling. "Here we go!" I sang as I trotted back to the table.

Mama and I watched in silence as Daddy wrote with purpose. When he held up the paper for us to see, his face was grim.

No more fighting. I won't have it!

"Now, William, we weren't fighting." Mama's tone was patronizing.

"Yaa! Wuhrr!"

"Daddy, we won't argue anymore," I said quickly. "Will we, Mama?" I didn't like the redness in his face, afraid of what stress might do to him. The idea to call John Forkes and ask him about possible consequences flashed through my mind.

"Yyoo." Daddy pointed at me. "Yyoo." His finger moved to Mama. "Taawkuh."

I almost laughed. Insisting that we talk without fighting was like asking a dog and cat to sleep side by side. "We are talking," I replied lightly. "We're talking just fine."

"Nnuuh! Taawkuh. Heer." He hit his chest over his heart. "*Taawkuh!*" As soon as the words exploded from his crooked mouth, his energy began to waver, then rippled away, his expression slackening. His eyelids drooped.

"Oh, Daddy, you're tired." I jumped out of my seat again, placing a hand on his blanching cheek, pulling his chair away from the table while Mama watched worriedly.

"Rest now, William," she crooned as I began to push him. "You've been up a long time." She looked at me, accusation in her eyes. "Need help puttin' him to bed?"

"No, thank you. I'll do it."

My words were as polite as those of Melissa's parents.

chapter 33

On Saturday the rains finally ceased, and under an azure sky I found myself yearning to escape the oppression of the house once more. As Daddy and I pushed through an unusually tiring therapy session, I decided to later venture out for another drive. Dr. Forkes was right—the exercises were gruesome and boring, and it was hard to exude the energy to keep up Daddy's spirits. How easy it would have been to let the second session of the day slide, but I wouldn't allow it. I thought of our deadline, one week now already gone. At some point I had to steal away long enough to go to Albertsville and discuss the untenable situation with Mr. Sledge.

My plans to escape alone were changed by the phone's ringing just before lunch. Jessie Harding was on the line, declaring she'd waited long enough to visit and, my goodness, if I hadn't seen the town yet, she wanted to be the one to show me around. "Such new sights," she added, "all two blocks of 'em."

Miss Jessie turned out to be just what my sodden spirits needed. She was as pretty and trim as she was the day I left Bradleyville, and I told her so. Laughing, she pointed to the crow's-feet around her eyes as testament to her ripe age of fifty-three. Mama appeared from the kitchen and they chatted briefly, Miss Jessie inquiring about Daddy's progress. I watched their exchange with growing curiosity; something wasn't right between them. As far as I knew, they'd always gotten along. I wanted to ask about this and so much more once we were in Miss Jessie's car, but I found myself tongue-tied.

We reached the intersection at Main Street, and the old memories came flooding back. I squeezed my eyes shut.

"So," Miss Jessie said, "you haven't been downtown yet."

I opened my eyes. We had turned the corner. "Well, I went up to the church," I said, hoping I sounded normal. "But that was at night, so I didn't see much."

"Oh, that's right."

I frowned at her profile. "What do you mean, that's right?"

She laughed in embarrassment, as if I'd caught her at something. "You know Bradleyville, Celia; everybody knows what everybody's doin'. I heard you visited the cemetery the night you arrived."

"You heard that? I don't know how anybody other than Mama would know that."

"Oh, don't worry about it." She waved it away. "Someone saw you, that's all, and word got around. You know gossip is hard to avoid in Bradleyville, even though I do my best. I've never been very comfortable around idle talk. But anyway, it's not important. What *is* important is what you're doin' for your daddy."

"Good grief," I breathed, anger stirring in my veins. "I've been gone all this time, and the very night I come back, people start yakking again."

"Look, forget it. You grew up with this. Pay no attention; just go about your business. Now here we are. Let's walk around a bit."

I worked to push down my irritation. "Sure."

She hesitated. "You don't sound like you really want to."

"It's just that I feel like a walking billboard all of a sudden," I burst. "'Here's Celia Matthews, folks!' Merely showing my face in town should give everyone a great topic of conversation at supper tonight."

A hint of a smile graced her lips. "You never let it bother you before."

Touché, Miss Jessie, I thought. *But then I had something to fight for, didn't I?*

Ruefully I smiled back, knowing she was the wrong target for my anger. It was true that she never spread gossip. Unlike her aunt Eva Bellingham. "No. I didn't let it bother me." Firmly I opened the car door.

My grand tour began with her shop, in which four sewing machines whirred. Folks were now coming all the way from Albertsville for their tailoring, due to Miss Jessie's reputation. She introduced me to each employee. I was amazed at how the shop had grown, and told Miss Jessie so. How proud I was of what she'd accomplished.

"I haven't seen your aunt in over a week," I remarked as we left. "I suppose she hasn't gotten out because of the rain."

Miss Jessie paused. "Rain does bother her hands. I'm sure you'll see her eventually."

She wasn't telling me something. I was trying to imagine what it was when I spotted a familiar green awning down the block. The thought vanished. "Oh, Miss Jessie, Tull's Drugstore looks just the same!" I stopped on the sidewalk, gazing at it. "It's late April and no chairs are out."

"No. The soda fountain's gone, so it's not the hangout it used to be. No more booths inside, either. See across the street, where the doctor's office was? That's now a little restaurant. Can you believe it, Bradleyville with its own café. Tammy's. Folks meet there now."

I could almost see Granddad and Jake Lewellyn and Hank Jenkins under that awning, sitting in their chairs. Could almost feel the graininess of the warm sidewalk beneath me as I sat listening to their stories and drinking my strawberry shakes. I swallowed hard, pressed back the images. "Let's go in, Miss Jessie. I want to see the marble."

As soon as we entered the store, Mr. Tull flitted from behind his counter to give me an effusive hug. "Goodness, look who's here; I heard you were back in town!" He was plumper than before, his tufts of hair now gone, but surprisingly his movements were as quick as ever. He beamed at me, clasping his hands. "Came to see the old place, did ya? Well, it looks a bit different from your granddad's day, but I'll bet you remember that." He pointed toward a custom frame next to the large front window.

Drawing close, I gazed at this "piece of glass" that held such significance for the town. The black and silver marble was now artfully suspended in its frame, a little above center.

"Oh, Granddad," I whispered, "I miss you so much."

"Look closer," Mr. Tull encouraged. "Jake's will told us exactly what he wanted us to write."

I leaned in to read the curving script. The words brought tears to my eyes.

Thomas,

    We both won.

Jake

chapter 34

"All right, Daddy, last thing. Lift that leg up from the knee." He sat in his wheelchair in the living room, working diligently. Mama had gone to church and I was glad for our time alone.

"Good!" I praised as his foot rose. "That's the highest you've done it yet!"

"Yup." He grinned at me, and I noticed that the left side of his mouth worked better.

"This is wonderful. See, I told you! We just have to keep at it and suddenly things start to work. You're gonna be running around the house before we know it." I rubbed his cheek affectionately. "Let's do your speech; then we're done. Got your writing stuff for later?"

While downtown with Miss Jessie the previous day, I'd stopped by the dime store and bought a clipboard, some yellow pads of paper, and a small cloth tote bag. Attaching the paper to the clipboard and tying on a pen, I'd placed the whole thing in the bag, which was hanging on the right side of his chair for easy access.

"Yup."

"Good. Okay then, let's get to it. Say 'bell.'"

"Bvvell."

"Okay, let's try to keep that *b*. Make those lips go together."

We practiced various words and sounds for about fifteen minutes. Just as we were finishing, Daddy pointed toward the porch. "Ceela. Daar."

I peered out the window through the sheer curtains. "Oh, it's Dr. Forkes." Surprised, I hurried to open the screen door, running fingers through my hair.

"Hi, Celia."

He smiled at me, eyes lingering, black bag in hand. The coat of his dark Sunday suit was unbuttoned, showing a starched white shirt. I invited him in. "And just why aren't you in church?" I demanded.

"I got paged by another patient." Taking off his coat, he placed it over the back of the couch. "Hi, William. Came to check on you while I was out and about. How are you feeling?" He extracted a stethoscope and blood pressure cuff from his bag.

"Kaaa. Fiine."

"That's good. Let me just listen to your heart now; you know the routine."

"Want something to drink, John?" It was the first time I'd called him by his given name, and he glanced at me. I waited as he moved the stethoscope across Daddy's chest.

"Iced tea would be great," he said, straightening.

I returned with the drink as he finished the examination. "You're looking good, William," he told Daddy, putting his instruments away. "Still taking your medication every day?"

"Yaaa."

"And doing the therapy, I see. She's making you work?"

"Shee tufff."

"Well, the tougher she is, the better you'll be."

"Uh-huh."

John and I laughed at Daddy's sarcasm.

The doctor closed his bag and accepted the glass of tea from me, our fingers touching. "Am I interrupting one of your sessions?"

"Not really. We were just finishing up." He gazed at me and I looked away. "Daddy, what would you like to do now? Are you tired?"

"Naaa." He thought for a minute. "Paaor." His chin pointed toward the porch.

"You sure you want to sit out there by yourself?" He nodded. "Okay. It is a pretty day." I leaned down to unlock the brakes of the wheelchair. John moved to hold the door open for us. "I'd like to take him for walks in his chair," I mentioned as I pushed Daddy through, "but I haven't had the nerve yet to try getting him down the porch steps. There were no stairs at the nursing home where I volunteered. Maybe I'll practice with an empty chair and then put Mama in it, if she's willing to risk her neck."

"You're a very determined person, aren't you?" He bent down to reset the brakes.

"Sometimes."

We made sure Daddy was comfortable, then returned inside to sit at the dining table, John remarking that he'd just finish his tea and be on his way. I sensed the comment was more for Daddy's ears than mine.

"How's he doing?" he asked quietly after we settled ourselves.

"Good. He's progressing slowly but well."

"And how are you handling it?"

"Fine."

He regarded me for a moment, as if wondering whether or not to speak what was on his mind. "I heard you saw the town yesterday. I imagine it brought back a lot of memories."

The gossip mill once more. Plus he was getting personal again. Annoyance compressed my lips. "You know, this really isn't fair. You probably know all about me and I know nothing about you. I don't like that. I came here to help Daddy, not to answer your questions or anyone else's."

He held up both hands. "Whoa, okay, okay! I know when I've been slapped."

"Well," I said half grudgingly, "I wouldn't go quite that far."

"Glad to hear it." He reached for his iced tea. "Let me play doctor for a moment, if I may. You promised me you'd hang in there as long as William needed you. His spirits are so much better now that you're here, and even if the therapy is slow, at least he's working at it. That's because you're the one who's pushing him; it's obvious he'll do anything to be close to you. So what I'm getting at is, I hope you don't get upset at Bradleyville and leave before he's ready."

My defenses rose. "I told you I would stay till the end! And I promised *him* that. Nothing will make me leave; you have no reason to doubt me. I've been working with him twice a day, whether I felt like it or not. Not once have I let a therapy session slide." I stopped, put a hand to my face. "Good grief," I said with a sigh, "it's enough that I argue with Mama; I don't want to argue with you too."

"Then don't." He almost smiled.

"Well. You started it."

"Maybe I did. Okay, I did. Now let's both stop."

I assumed an air of petulance. "Fine then."

"I do understand what you're talking about, though, Celia," he said after a moment. "This is a great place to live, with wonderful people, but it is true that some of them tend to breathe down your neck. That's typical for a small town. I'm pretty sensitive to it myself, after having lived somewhere else. Being the small-town doctor is a two-headed beast, you know. On one side you're revered, but on the other you're watched all the more closely because their lives are in your hands."

A bead of moisture ran slowly down his glass. "Why did you come back?" I asked.

His face softened. "I wanted to be near family after my wife died."

"I was sorry to hear about her; it must have been very hard." I hesitated. "You're engaged now, I hear."

"Yes."

For some reason the mention of his fiancée seemed uncomfortable for us both.

He gazed out the window, watching Daddy wave to a car. Church must have let out. "Sharon's a wonderful woman," he said slowly. "We're getting married in December. But you've probably heard our plans in detail." He gave a light shrug. "Gossip, you know. The nectar of Bradleyville."

"Actually, I haven't. I haven't heard anything about you." I watched him finger his glass.

"How about that. And I thought I was so interesting."

I smiled but did not look up. The air around us glistened.

"Is my glass that intriguing?" he said, breaking the silence.

I forced my eyes to him. "No." Ages ago Danny and I had faced each other like this, a few feet between us, worlds apart. I couldn't think of a thing to say.

Lifting his hand from the glass, John placed it on mine lightly. I felt the icy coolness of his skin. "You're doing a great job with your dad," he said, his eyes warm. "I know he's glad you came. So am I."

"Thank you."

He pulled his hand away. "Well. I'd better be going."

I nodded.

"Your daddy looks content out there," he remarked, pushing back the chair.

I was still feeling his hand on mine.

"I'll check him again on Tuesday."

I walked John to the porch, standing by Daddy as he strode down our sidewalk. Watching him drive off, waving, I pictured the tremulous wings of a moth drawn to flame and understood its fascination.

Blinking hard, I forced the thoughts away. Had I not caused enough heartbreak in Bradleyville? Had my own heart not been broken enough? Sudden fear surged through me. The things that could happen if I stayed . . .

I got to git outta this town. Danny's words from years ago sounded in my ears.

"You still want to stay out here?" I asked Daddy.

"Yaaa."

"Okay."

I reentered the house, the movie screen in my head unrolling itself, beginning to play its pictures. The scene of Danny leaning against a tree on that day years ago when I began to lose him . . .

~ *1978* ~

chapter 35

We were leaning against one of our oak trees down by the river in July when Danny blurted, "Celia, I got to git outta this town."

I turned toward him in hurt surprise. "What do you mean?"

"We're not makin' it—Mama and me and Daddy. The farm ain't hardly payin' for itself. Mama and me's doing all the work; Daddy's doing nothin' but drinking."

"I know."

He bit his lip. "You don't really know, Celia. All you do is hear it. But my mama's livin' it. I'm livin' it. And we can't take much more."

"Well, what are you goin' to do?" My voice tinged with accusation at the mere thought that he would leave me.

He shook his head. "For now, nothin'. Summer's halfway through. When school starts up again, I got one more year; then I'm out."

"You can work at the mill after you graduate, like we talked about."

"I can't, Celia." He pleaded with his eyes for understanding. "I can't work at the mill full-time and care for the farm, too; there ain't that much time in the day. The farm's struggling so much, I can't even keep up with it working all day this summer. If I worked at the mill, I'd earn money, but the farm would really fall apart and we'd have no place to live. If I just keep carin' for the farm, we'll never git anywhere. And then there's Daddy. Most nights I barely sleep. I lie in bed with my muscles stiff, ready to jump up if he starts hurtin' Mama. And she cries all the time. I got you but there's nothin' here for her."

I stared sightlessly across the river. I knew that life in Bradleyville was becoming harder and harder for him and his mama. Lately Anthony Cander was always drinking, even on weekdays. On weekends he'd drive his beat-up truck to Albertsville bars and not return home until all hours of the night.

"Listen, Celia, I ain't talkin' about leaving you. I love you with all my heart. What I'm talkin' about is making a life for myself. I don't know how things'll turn out after I graduate, but I need to find a way to take Mama away from here, away from Daddy. You're only a year behind me in school. We wouldn't have to be apart for very long."

A year without Danny was a lifetime. I lowered my eyes, not wanting him to see the tears that stung them. I respected him for putting his mama first. Wouldn't I do the same for Granddad or Kevy or Daddy? But the thought of staying in Bradleyville without him sent ice through my veins. "Where would you go?"

"I don't know. And I don't know how I'd manage it, either; it may never happen." His tone was tinged with bitterness. "But I been talkin' to Cousin Lee and Miss Jessie. Lee's got a great aunt and uncle that's kept in touch ever since they moved away. He was thinkin' maybe they could help."

"What if your daddy won't let you leave?"

Danny exhaled slowly. "I just don't know."

I didn't want to speak any more of his moving away but could think of little else. Months before, Lee Harding had promised Danny a job at the mill, and when I mentioned it again the following Saturday, Danny soothed me, saying he'd accept it. Somehow the farm situation would work itself out. Perhaps when he wasn't around to do the work, his daddy would straighten up. Or maybe Danny and his mama could rent a little house in town, letting the farm and Anthony Cander go to seed together. His mama could work, too, Danny added as we reached our oak canopy. With two paychecks they would do just fine.

"She could work for Miss Jessie," I said brightly. With more customers coming from Albertsville, Jessie Harding now employed two people. She worked so much that I had baby-sat for the kids almost full-time since school let out. With my pay I'd opened a bank account, which was growing steadily.

"Yeah." Danny caught me around the waist. "And when I ever do leave this town, it'll only be to travel with you."

"To the ocean," I said, grinning.

"And the waves."

"We'll dig our toes in the sand."

"Camp out under the stars."

We plopped down on the grass underneath our trees. I leaned against a trunk, imagining the possibilities. Danny grew pensive. "You've always said you want to go to college."

"I still do. You could stay here for a year, and then when I graduate we can get married and go off to college together."

"Somebody's got to work."

I pondered this. "We'll both work part-time and go to classes part-time."

Danny pulled my head against his shoulder, wrapping his arms around me. We sat for a while in silence.

"Celia, for all my talk, I really may have to leave here and take Mama away," he said quietly. "But I promise you if that happens, I'll wait for you. I'll count the days till we can be together again."

"Things will change and you won't need to go." I raised my head from his shoulder. "Things would be easier on you—and me—if we could be together more. Maybe Mama will let us date this year."

He shook his head. "You're crazy if you think your mama will let you date when you're only sixteen. Even if it was Bobby Delham you wanted to see."

We both guessed Bobby would be Mama's choice for me. Everybody knew he had liked me for a long time. "Well, I'm gonna try anyway," I retorted. "She's lettin' me come here, isn't she? And who would've guessed that? I've got to do something so you can stay here. I'm not lettin' you leave without a fight."

"Well, don't go fightin' with your mama; that's not gonna help us any."

I promised to do my best.

Disaster has a way of striking when you least expect it, like a snake in tall grass. While Danny and I were talking at the river, Granddad collapsed on our couch in dizziness, a blue-veined hand clutching his chest. By the time Kevy and I got home, even Mama was frantic, fanning his gray face while Daddy called Doc Richardson. It took all three of us to get Granddad in his own bed. Meanwhile Kevy set his bucket of fish on the back porch and put his pole in the garage. Then we all paced the living room, waiting as the doctor examined Granddad.

"There's not much we can do, Estelle," the doctor said when he finally emerged from Granddad's room. "His heart's simply wearing down, like the cardiologist told you. Just keep him as quiet as you can."

"Ha! Since when do you keep Thomas Bradley quiet?"

Doc Richardson laid a bony hand on her arm. "Estelle. Your daddy's had a long, good life. He's always been stubborn and he'll enter the gates a heaven that way. Don't try to change him; that's not what I meant. Just . . . enjoy him. While he's still with you."

I stood near Mama's chair, hand on the headrest, feeling the nubby fabric beneath my fingertips. *Such simple words*, I thought as I saw my own dreaded understanding creep across Mama's face. I couldn't remember Mama ever enjoying Granddad while he was vibrant. How was she going to enjoy him now in his decline?

Mama's eyes grew round and bright. Daddy slid a protective arm around her shoulders. "How long?" he asked.

The doctor shook his head. "I can't answer that. It could be a while, unless he has a full-fledged heart attack. Given his circumstances, that is certainly possible."

"I see." Mama's voice was flat. "Thank you for comin'."

Doc Richardson had been dismissed. Daddy walked him out to his car. Kevy and I both ran to Mama, putting our arms around her. She hugged my brother and managed to pat me on the back.

"He'll be all right, Mama," I said. "Granddad always comes through."

She remained silent, her hand warm upon me until she pulled away brusquely, telling Kevy to clean his fish and asking me to look in on Granddad. There was work to be done, she declared; supper needed fixing and she had a load of clothes to iron.

As I walked down the hall, I reflected that she repelled sorrow as well as affection.

chapter 36

After a few weeks Granddad seemed to return to normal. Perhaps his voice was a bit more frail as he regaled us with his war stories at dinner; perhaps he was a touch slower settling into his porch chair for an afternoon with Jake Lewellyn. But a certain determination lit his eyes, even as he would carefully tilt back his head to wash down a pill. "Missy," he said one evening as I dusted his room, "I ain't ready to meet my Maker yet. There's still things I got to do."

He rested on his bed, propped against two pillows. I sat down beside him. "What do you have to do, Granddad?" I asked softly.

He closed his eyes for a moment before answering. "For one thing, I ain't made things right with your mama yet. Lord knows I've tried and tried. I done lots a prayin', and I know the Lord answers prayer. But this one's been a long time comin'."

"What wrong with her, Granddad? Why is she ... the way she is?"

His head shook briefly against the pillow. "Ah, missy, your mama's got hurts that go deep, and I'm to blame for some of 'em. I been askin' her forgiveness for years now, but she just ain't got it in her yet. I suppose when it finally comes, I'll feel I can pass on to the Pearly Gates."

"Granddad, please tell me what you're talking about."

"Not now." He smiled wanly. "The past ain't important anyhow. I'm lookin' toward the future."

"Mama's been like this as long as I can remember, Granddad," I said. "She's never going to change; don't expect her to. It'll only hurt you more. I don't think she *can* change."

"God can change her, missy. If he could change my heart, he can sure do it for her."

"But she's got to be willin', right?"

"Yep. God don't force us. Amazing, but he don't. I just pray he'll soften her heart, help her be ready. But you got to understand, I pray the same thing for myself every day. I always got to watch my pride; the Lord has to help me with that constantly. It gets in the way between me and your mama."

I marveled at his big heart, both tender and tenacious. Then another thought struck me. If he was right, if by some remote chance God did have an answer to my ancient problem with Mama, I was not seeking it. Only for a moment did I consider that thought. Then purposefully I pushed it away.

Granddad interrupted my pondering. "Enough talk about me. How're you and Danny?"

How easily I found myself spilling our problems to him. "And in the midst of everything," I complained finally, "Mama doesn't understand how we feel. She probably keeps thinkin' I'll come to my senses and forget about Danny. But I'm not goin' to care about anyone else. Ever."

Granddad nodded. "He feels the same way about you, don't he?"

"Yes."

He gazed absently at the medals on top of his bookcase, ruminating. "That boy's got the world on his shoulders. He's right, you know, about leavin'. I never thought I'd be advocatin' you shovin' off from your hometown, but I don't see how the two a you can stay here. Anthony's just not stable, and I don't want you put in a dangerous situation."

"But Granddad, I can't stand to think of Danny leavin'."

"Yes, you can." He reached for my hand. "You can if you're sure Danny's the one God wants for you. Make sure a that first. Then one year apart may be hard, but it can give you a lifetime together that'll be blessed. God'll watch over you both in the meantime. So let him get situated somewhere and take care a his mama. But missy"—he squeezed my fingers—"your mama may not understand your havin' to go. Even though you'll be old enough to make your own decisions. She don't like the thought a people leavin' her."

I nodded.

"Just don't judge her too hard. Keep a tender spirit. Keep lovin' her and, above all, keep prayin'. She'll come around in time."

I did not want to return to the subject of Mama. "What about this comin' school year?" I pressed. "Do you think Mama will let Danny and me date?"

He sighed. "Well, that's a difficult situation; you're young yet. We'd have to start slow. But maybe if I worked on her, she'd at least let him come to supper."

School started at the end of August, and once again Danny and I were back to see-but-don't-touch. Granddad and I had been trying to persuade Mama to let Danny come for a meal, with high hopes that one grudging invitation would lead to more and eventually he could come calling. I couldn't imagine Mama finding anything wrong with Danny if she knew him better. The more Danny and I talked about it, the more we began to believe that our very lives depended on such a supper. Daddy posed no problem; for all his quietness, he shared Granddad's understanding and wisdom. Unlike Granddad, however, he did not possess the gall to declare it to Mama.

When Mama finally agreed to invite Danny for supper that coming Thursday "just this one time," Danny and I were ecstatic. I was also scared to death. At long last I would see Danny surrounded by my family. How I longed for Mama to embrace his presence with us. I told Danny to work on his English; Mama wouldn't be impressed with poor grammar. He humbly took my warning to heart, informing me Wednesday at lunch that he was practicing at home as well as at school.

"People are lookin' at me strange," he said, breaking a piece of cornbread in two. "Like I'm trying to be highfalutin or somethin'."

"Well, let 'em," I replied testily, not bothering to correct his use of the word *strange*.

The cornbread stopped halfway to his mouth. "What's wrong with you?"

"It's just people, that's all. Haven't you noticed the way they're lookin' at us this first week back? It's like teachers are all sayin', 'Oh my, are they still together?'"

"So let 'em." The cornbread disappeared into his mouth.

"Just look at ol' Miss Hemington over there givin' us the eye. And I know I saw Mr. Leam watch you sit down across from me, then comment to the principal."

"It don't—doesn't matter, Celia. Leave it alone."

"Except for Mr. Rose. He actually smiled at me when you sat down."

"Celia." Danny cast me an exasperated look. "Will you quit readin' something into everything that goes on around you?"

"Well, you know it's true."

"I don't know nothin'. All's I—"

"Anything."

He tapped a finger against his green plastic tray. "I don't know *anything*. All's I know is that I'm sittin' here with you. And here come Mona and Barbara, and Bart's headed this way; none a them's looking like anything's wrong. Besides that, half a the things you think people're thinking, they're not really thinking at all. You're just gettin' a chip on your shoulder. And that's something you got to watch. I should know; I carried one around for long enough."

Mouth tightening, I studied him, unable to admit he was right. His upbeat attitude was most annoying. For someone who faced my mama's appraisal in little more than twenty-four hours, he seemed as unconcerned as a baby possum crossing the road. I opened my mouth for a retort, then closed it. Fine then. If he was nothing but excited about tomorrow, I'd leave him to it.

I was terrified enough for both of us.

Danny's carefree demeanor did not last. On that inauspicious Thursday evening he arrived late, sweating and nervous. Granddad, Kevy, and Daddy greeted him warmly. "So sorry, Mrs. Matthews," he blurted. "At the last minute Daddy took the truck and I had to walk."

You mean run, I thought. He'd probably sprinted the whole way in the heat.

"That's all right, Danny," Mama said, smiling coolly. "Supper's not quite on the table yet."

Months later I would view that evening as the first drop of fitful rain before a torrent. But at that moment I knew only anticipation. Danny was everything I knew he would be—he was polite, he watched his grammar, he complimented Mama on her food and responded with humility when Daddy thanked him again for saving Kevy. Mama watched Danny carefully with an I'm-boss-here expression. Danny must have been intimidated, but he didn't show it, and I chose to believe I saw grudging respect for his poise in Mama's eyes.

And then came the moment when it all changed. Mama asked him what he wanted to do in the future.

"Cousin Lee's promised me a good job at the mill," he replied innocently. "But eventually I'd like to travel, see the world."

The air chilled.

"Sounds good," Daddy offered a little too jovially.

Disapproval moved across my mama's face like sand blowing off a seashell, and I felt my hopes spin away. Danny glanced at his plate, flustered. My heart ached for him. How hard he was trying to please. And how stupid I'd been, neglecting to warn him about mentioning his dreams of travel.

"How did I do?" he whispered anxiously as we sat later on the back porch steps in the few moments Mama had allowed us before Daddy drove him home.

I smiled reassuringly, longing to promise everything would be all right. "You were wonderful. You *are* wonderful. I'm so proud to be with you."

His hand furtively found mine on the wooden slats between us. "No matter what, I love you, Celia," he said. "With all my heart."

"Thank you, Mama, for lettin' him come."

We stood in the kitchen doing dishes after Daddy left to take Danny home, Kevy riding along. I'd desperately wanted to drive Danny myself; I'd recently gotten my license and ached to be alone with him. But I hadn't dared ask.

"You're welcome." She was busily putting leftovers into containers.

"He's nice, don't you think?"

"Very nice." She sounded troubled.

"And he's already got a job lined up once he graduates."

"Uh-huh."

I pushed a large blue sponge underwater and watched it expand. "Can he come again?"

"He's not content to stay in Bradleyville, Celia."

I slid a plate under the lemony suds, feeling my legs go weak. "Would you, if you were Anthony Cander's son?"

No reply.

"He just wants respect, Mama. And it's a little hard for him to come by here."

"No, Celia, that's not what he wants. What he really wants is to see the world."

"What's the matter with that? Lots of people want to travel."

Firmly she snapped the lid over a plastic bowl. "It's more than that. I see it in his eyes; I know that look all too well. It's a yearnin' so deep, so ... *selfish* ... that it becomes more important than any other thing or any other person. And regardless of who it hurts and how badly it hurts them, it can be rationalized away. With great pride."

"He's not like that, Mama," I whispered, tears biting my eyes.

She came to stand beside me, nudging my chin up with her hand. "I've tried to overlook things," she said quietly. "I've done what I could for you, whether you believe that or not. But this ... He'll break your heart, Celia."

I could not utter a word. Never before had she been so gentle with me. Pain stabbing my heart, I realized how long I'd yearned to see such an expression on her face. After sixteen years, here was the mothering I'd witnessed when Danny sobbed in his mama's arms. But it was all for nothing—for some distant disappointment apparently suffered in her own life, now unfairly projected upon Danny and me.

"I love him, Mama. You can't change that."

She took her hand from beneath my chin, turning away. "I suppose not, Celia. I've never been able to change your mind about anything."

My hands were hot and slick in the soapsuds, steam dampening my forehead. *What do you want from me?* I raged silently at her retreating back. *To throw my arms around you, gush appreciation for a long overdue moment of tenderness? Say, "You're right, Mama" and toss Danny away just because you finally showed me a little love?*

"He hasn't done anything," I said thickly. "Please let him come over again."

She was too busy putting food in the refrigerator to reply.

I couldn't bring myself to tell Danny.

"Your daddy and I got along real well," he told me joyously at school. "I was feelin' so good about everything, I even asked him if I could take you out, can you believe it? He said he'd have to talk to your mama. Kevy was in the backseat, thinkin' the whole thing was right funny." He beamed at me, bouncing a fist off my locker door. "Isn't that great! It's gonna work, Celia. After all this time I think it's really gonna work!"

"Just remember," I countered, "Mama's the hard one."

"But she liked me, too, didn't she?"

I adjusted the books in my arms. "She said you were very nice."

He shot a blissful look toward the heavens.

Mama's warning rose unbidden in my head. "If this does work out, will you think twice about leaving at the end of the year? Will you wait for me here?"

He nodded decisively. "Somehow I'll do it. I don't know how I'll take care a the farm and Mama, but I'll do it. As long as we can be together, I can do anything."

For three weeks we held on to our hopes. "I go to sleep thinkin' about being with you someplace other than here," Danny said after school one Friday as we stood on the sidewalk. "I dream about it. I wake up thinkin' about it."

"We'll be together soon, somehow," I replied. "It's driving me crazy, too. Daddy and Granddad have both talked to Mama about having you over again, but she hasn't made a decision yet. She keeps tellin' me to wait a while longer. I don't know what she's waitin' for. Sometimes I think she believes that if she just pushes it from her mind, it will all go away." I fell into silence as Bart passed us, mumbling hello. "How's your mama?" I asked.

"Anxious. Tryin' not to do anything that'll set Daddy off. And she's worried about all this with us. She wants so much for me to have a better life than she's had."

Life is so unfair, I thought. "And your daddy?"

"Mean as an old goat. Asks me who do I think I am, tryin' to be with you? I have to work hard to keep my temper around him."

"He knows about us?"

"He can't be drunk all the time." Danny scuffed his shoe on the cement. "Celia, I got to see you; it's been a whole month since the river. It's all buildin' up inside me—the worry over what your mama'll say, the watchin' my daddy every minute I'm home. I just can't go through another year a this. I was so happy bein' at your house, so sure it was all gonna work out."

"It will work out," I reassured him. "Somehow. I'll ask Mama if you can come to supper tomorrow night. I'll *beg* her. And if you can come, I'll call you."

He nodded tiredly. "Okay. Otherwise I'll see you Monday."

But Mama said no when I begged her. Not this week. Perhaps the next. I was bitterly disappointed but she'd given me some hope.

And then everything fell apart Saturday afternoon.

chapter 37

The late September weather was nippy that day, trees on the hills turning their brilliant fall colors. Granddad was feeling better than he had for some time, and he asked if I'd drive him to Tull's for a soda. It had been too long, he said; he needed to "git outta the house for a while before people think I done up and died." I was happy to take him. Kevy had just come back from playing at Reid's, his bike carelessly thrown on our front lawn. Mama made him put it away before he could go with us.

It was too cold to sit under the awning. Granddad and his friends slid into one of Mr. Tull's red vinyl-covered booths inside while Kevy and I placed our orders at the counter. People were coming and going through the store, the chilled air swirling at their feet as they stepped inside. Dustin Taylor, Mary Lee's big-bellied, jovial daddy, happened in and chatted amiably with the men for a few minutes before saying he had to be on his way. Mrs. Clangerlee bought some medicine for an early-season cold, and Mr. Henley picked up a prescription for Gerald's little sister's earache. There wasn't enough room in the booth for Kevy and me, so we sat on stools at the counter, watching Mr. Tull's birdlike movements as he made milk shakes. Gazing idly out the big glass window, I was none too pleased to see Mrs. B. pulling up to the curb. "Oh, great."

She clucked about, holding out her freckled hands to display how crooked her knuckles were becoming and calling to a worried Mr. Tull that she'd come for her pain medication. "I think once Frank retires next year," she prattled on, "I may not be far behind him. These fingers a mine just don't want to handle that mail anymore."

"Dustin Taylor was here just a few minutes ago," Granddad told her. "Looks like Lee Harding'll be takin' Frank's place."

"Yes," she laughed. "Nothing like keepin' it in the family."

Wishing she would leave, I rested one elbow on the counter and went back to staring out the window. That's when I saw the Canders' truck rattle up the street and park at the curb beside Mrs. B.'s car. Both Danny and his daddy were inside. *Oh no*, I thought, *not here, not now.* I didn't want the likes of Mrs. B. or the school principal's long-necked wife, who was two aisles away comparing toothpaste prices, watching like hawks to see how Danny and I would greet each other. Danny was probably upset already about not being able to come to our house again for supper. And I dreaded even being in the same building with Mr. Cander; the memory of his chasing Danny's mama sent a shiver between my shoulder blades. But I could only watch helplessly as they crossed the sidewalk, Danny's daddy unsteady on his feet. Danny gestured impatiently for him to wait in the truck. Mr. Cander slurred something back loudly. Although his voice was too muffled for me to hear the words, from the angry expression on his face it was clear he wasn't happy with his son telling him what to do.

Stepping inside ahead of his daddy, Danny saw me frozen on my red stool, one hand around the base of a cherry cola. He pulled to a halt, taking in the back of Mr. Lewellyn's head and meeting the gazes of Hank Jenkins and my granddad. Mrs. B. had been patting back her bun when her hand went still, her elbow hanging in midair. "Oh," she exclaimed under her breath.

"Git on in, boy; what in tarnation you doin'!" Danny's daddy knocked him forward.

Danny regained his footing, remaining in his daddy's way. "Why don't you go back to the truck, sir," he said in a measured tone, his eyes on me. "I won't be long."

"Git on, stupid boy!" Mr. Cander pushed him aside.

I saw the anger skitter across Danny's face, knew in that instant what so easily could happen. *Danny, it's okay*, I pleaded silently. *Hold it in, be strong, don't let him drag you down in front of these people.* Strange how I thought of my mama at that moment. In some ways it would have been worse if she were present. However, in the few seconds' time it took for Anthony Cander to process the scene through his muddled brain, no one did anything but stare—except Granddad, who struggled to slide out of his seat. Mama would have responded more quickly. She'd have thought of something.

"Good afternoon, Danny!" Granddad declared, pasting on a wide smile.

Danny regained his equilibrium. "Good afternoon, sir." Convention demanded that he approach the booth and shake hands with all the men.

"Don't git up. We'll just be a minute here anyway. Afternoon, Mrs. B., Mr. Tull."

"Hi, Danny!" Kevy jumped off his stool to wrap Danny's chest in a bear hug.

"Hey, Kevin." He buffed my brother's head with affection.

"When you comin' to supper again?"

I shot a glance at Mrs. Willoughburn, the principal's wife, thinking it wouldn't be long before the whole town knew Danny had visited our house.

"I don't know." Danny tried to keep his voice light. "Sometime maybe." Untangling himself from Kevy's grasp, he turned toward me. "Hi, Celia."

"Hi."

Mr. Cander ran a black-haired arm under his nose, tasting the sight of me like I was a bottle of his favorite whiskey. "So," he said with a leer, "this's Celia Matthews, is it?"

"Afternoon, Anthony!" Granddad called in an attempt to capture the man's attention as Danny stepped in front of me.

"Sir, let's go. We can come back later."

I couldn't help shrinking away, even with Danny between me and his daddy. I knew that my obvious fear of the man would only feed the town's opinion that the Cander and Matthew families mixed like oil and water. But he was so close to me that I could smell the liquor. How could a man drink so much, I wondered, that the alcohol oozed out through his very pores?

"Aw, don' be so uppity. I jus' wanna git a good look at yer girl, tha's all."

"Daddy!" Danny's voice rose sharply. "We're leavin' *right now*." Hastily he nodded to Granddad and his friends. Maybe things would have turned out all right if he hadn't been trying so hard to be polite in the midst of his daddy's disparagement. But in the second that he turned to take proper leave of Mrs. B., Anthony Cander reached out a beefy hand to feel my hair. I flinched at his touch, petrified.

"Right purty gal here yer shackin' up with, boy."

Air caught in my lungs. I'd never heard the term in my life, but there was no mistaking its meaning, particularly amid the horrified gasps from Mrs. B. and the principal's wife. Anthony Cander might just as well have ripped my clothes off right there in the store. I dropped my eyes in mortification.

Even if anyone could have moved in that instant, no one would have been fast enough to stop Danny's furious reaction. Spinning on his heel, he curled his fingers into a fist and let it fly, smashing Anthony Cander squarely in the jaw. Bellowing, Mr. Cander reeled backward, arms flailing, until he hit the wall near the front window, bouncing his head against the wood and sliding to the floor. Danny leaped to him immediately, grabbed the man under the arms, and lurched him toward the door, ignoring his indignant groans.

"I hope you drink yourself to death," Danny seethed through clenched teeth as he shoved the door open.

We all watched as Danny threw his daddy into the passenger seat of the pickup and slammed the door. Chest heaving, he paused on the sidewalk to run a fumbling hand over his eyes. I watched his face drain of anger, then etch itself in despair. He hesitated, deciding what to do. Then with resolve he straightened his back. Reentered the store and walked over to us. He did not lift his gaze from the floor. "Mr. Bradley." He fought for steady breath, voice trembling. "I'm most sorry, sir, for the shame I caused you. And I deeply—I humbly ask your forgiveness." He shifted his head slightly, eyes still at his feet. "Celia"—he slipped into a whisper—"I'm so sorry."

Pain stabbed through me. It wasn't his fault. He was so willingly taking the shame his daddy had dumped on my head and heaping it on his own. I longed to slide off my stool and hold him, showing the town I didn't care, that Danny was as good and kind as his father was despicable. But I could only nod slightly, lips pressed together.

It was not up to me, however, to absolve Danny. This was up to Granddad, whose lineage and name had been blackened by the disgrace of his only grandgirl. By day's end the whole town would hear about what had happened and Granddad's response. His silence would pronounce that for all Danny's sincerity, he could chance no further dishonor from the Canders. Or he could declare his faith in Danny— despite Anthony Cander's loathsome behavior—by accepting the apology. I turned pleading eyes on him, terrified that I was expecting too much even from the godly man who'd possessed the courage to bring Danny and me together. Deep sadness etched into the laugh lines around his mouth, a slump rounding his shoulders.

Danny had no pride left to wait for a reply. Without another word he started to leave.

Please, Granddad, I begged, weeping inside.

Granddad lifted his eyes to mine, saw the tears there. He made a sound in his throat. Raised his arm an inch off the table. "Son."

Danny stopped, turned back.

Slowly the thin, wool-clad arm reached out, offering a hand.

Danny's eyelids flickered. He hesitated, then brought his own hand forward, stepping to the table to clasp Granddad's bony fingers with his own, strong and brown. Shaking the elder man's hand, he gripped it hard, veins standing out along his wrist. His chin quivered as he held on, gratitude bubbling like water from a hot spring.

Then swiftly Danny was gone, returning to his drunken father, who was holding his jaw and moaning his ills as he slumped in the seat of their truck.

Even Granddad's public stand didn't matter in the end. Mama would have none of his forgiveness. Listening to her rave, I almost believed she'd been waiting for something like this to happen, biding her time until an excuse to break Danny and me apart presented itself. Well, she had it now. No more, she announced as I hid my crumpled face in my hands. Danny could not come here; I could not see him at the river.

Not now.

Not ever.

chapter 38

The word whispered through Bradleyville, its sibilance a shout. At church hands were laid on my shoulder in unspoken condolence, not for my loss of Danny but for my loss of dignity through the vileness of a drunkard.

Danny did not show his face at school all week. Nor did anyone see his mama in town. I went to school aching to see him, barely hearing the voices of teachers. Mr. Rose smiled sadly at me in the hall. Melissa, Barbara, and Mona could not console me. Bobby Delham failed to hide his triumph, as if I'd be making eyes at him in no time.

I did not know what to do; if I defied Mama, folks would blame it on Danny's influence. By Friday afternoon I couldn't stand it and, while Mama was pulling weeds in the backyard, stole a chance to call him. Mrs. Cander answered and with hesitation put him on the phone. "Danny," I whispered, "I love you. Please come back to school. Please graduate so you can leave Bradleyville; I know you have to do that now. And the very first day I can follow, I will."

"Celia, it's no use." His voice sounded dead.

He finally returned to school the following week at his mama's insistence. Everyone whispered and watched. At lunch Melissa and I sat at the table where Danny usually joined us. When he'd filled his tray, he passed us and sat alone. I had trouble blinking back tears. But I had no trouble firmly picking up my tray and walking over to sit across from him. When I looked at him in defiance, he closed his eyes wearily as if to say now I'd done it, I'd made a public statement, and one way or another he'd pay.

"Danny," I declared, "no one will keep me away from you. No one."

Mama was waiting for me on the porch when I arrived home, her eyes simmering heat like white coals. One look at her face and Melissa scurried silently up the street, ponytail bobbing. I drew to a stop, books heavy in my arms, and locked gazes with Mama across the length of our sidewalk. "That didn't take long," I ventured challengingly.

"No, it certainly didn't."

Inside I dropped my books in a heap on the dining table. She put a fist against her hip. "I don't want you seein' him even at school; haven't I made myself plain enough?"

"You can't stop me."

"Yes, I can."

"No, you *can't*. We're not doin' anything, Mama, except eatin' lunch together. What's the big deal? Who cares?"

"I care. Your daddy cares."

I threw my hands in the air. "Daddy doesn't care! Granddad doesn't care! You're the only one who does. And why, just tell me that? Danny hasn't done one thing wrong. He can't help it that his father's the way he is. Danny's not like that and you know it, Mama. But his daddy isn't why you're not lettin' me see him, anyway; that's just an excuse. The real reason's just because he wants to get out of Bradleyville."

"I don't have to explain my reasons to you; I'm your mama! The whole town's talkin'. I won't have shame brought down on all our heads."

"Shame for what? What happened was Mr. Cander's fault, not mine or Danny's."

"Celia, *you* should be ashamed for defying me! What kind of Christian behavior is that? And while your granddad's doin' poorly. I've got to deal with losing him; I don't want to lose you too. Can't you see I'm trying to protect you? I understand your feelings much more than you know. But the longer you carry on with Danny, even just talkin' to him at school, the more it'll hurt when it comes time for a boy to come calling and he can't be it."

My eyes welled with tears. "But he should be, Mama. He's the one I want. And he's tryin' so hard to overcome his life; he's got to work twice as hard as anyone else."

"That's why I gave him a chance. But even with all his tryin', it'll never work. It's his *life* that makes him yearn to be free. That's in him, Celia, and it won't change."

"I don't care."

She gripped my shoulders. "I've done all I can. I've tried more than you know, doin' my best to shrug it off when folks were talking. Yet you think I'm your enemy. I can't keep fighting with you about this; I got too much else to deal with. You see him at lunch, you do it without my blessing. And when he leaves Bradleyville to seek his fame and fortune—which I can assure you he'll do—you'll pay for your disobedience. You understand? What hurt you feel, you'll bring on your own head. As for me, I'm done with it. We've been dealin' with that boy for over a year, and between him and your granddad, I've had about all I can take. I don't even want to hear his name again, you understand? I've *had* it!"

Snatching her hands from my shoulders, she stalked into the kitchen. As I glared at her, a touch of smug satisfaction curled my mouth.

chapter 39

After the incident at Tull's Granddad began to weaken again. Doc Richardson started making house calls twice a month to check his heart. Granddad rested more frequently, taking morning and afternoon naps. Jake Lewellyn would visit from two till four, and then Granddad would rest in his room until supper.

"Missy," he said with a sigh one day in late November as I put clean clothes in his dresser, "I'm afraid I failed at some a the things that matter most."

I turned to him, shaking my head. "Granddad, you've been a hero all your life. The whole town knows it."

"I ain't gettin' along with your mama any better than I ever did, no matter how much I pray about it. And I cain't fix it for you and Danny."

I took his frail hand. "You did all you could for us. You're the only one who's ever understood. Not that long ago you told me I should let him leave Bradleyville and follow him when I'm out of school. That's exactly what we're goin' to do."

"I did tell you that. But you will hurt your mama somethin' terrible. A girl needs to have her mama. Might be it's the most important relationship God made in this world."

The most important relationship in the world. I didn't want to believe that. "Granddad. I've never had my mama."

My statement watered his eyes. "You still love Danny?"

"I need Danny to live."

"Then go, with my blessin'. You'll be eighteen then and a woman. But remember what I tol' you; don't give up on your mama. Just keep puttin' it in God's hands. Maybe in time she'll forgive and you can heal old hurts. Otherwise you go through life thinkin' you always got time, and then one day you realize you ain't."

It was my turn to sigh. "I don't really understand this, you and Mama."

"Well, you're young yet. And you got your own problems. I'd expected to live long enough to see you happy with Danny, with your family's approval. But I'm not sure I'm gonna make it. You may have to manage without me. I done tol' God I need to stay here and help you, but he may have other plans. So whatever happens with me, you just trust him to get you through."

I couldn't imagine life without Granddad. "You're not going anywhere for a long time yet. Jake Lewellyn would be most upset. It's gonna take him at least a year or two to think up some new scam to get his marble back."

"*Try* and get it back, you mean. I'm goin' to my grave with that marble, and I done tol' him so a million times."

"See there? You got plenty of fight left."

"Yep," he said tiredly, his eyes closing. "I think I'll take me a little snooze now."

In public defiance of my mother I continued to see Danny at school. My family and I did not speak his name aloud at home, although from time to time Daddy would quietly ask how he was doing. Mama and I spoke very little but at least we weren't fighting. I spent time with Granddad or in my room, studying and painting pictures. The ocean scenes were back on my wall, often with the silhouettes of two distant figures. Sometimes I painted a scene for Danny, giving it to him between classes.

Danny was constantly morose, as if he were merely going through the motions of living. As much as he wanted to be near me, I could see his thoughts slipping away as he pined desperately for the day he could leave town. He and his mama were now willing to walk away from the farm, he said, but they had no money and no place to go. The Hardings were talking to relatives about jobs for Danny, and they promised something would come through. They seemed to hurt for Danny almost as much as I did, and their coolness toward Mama at church bespoke their attitude toward her decision.

It was nearly Christmas, with six inches of snow on the ground, before I hit on a plan to see Danny. I'd never taken the chance of sneaking out before and knew it wasn't right. But desperation drove me. When my conscience clamored, I told it to be quiet. What else were Danny and I to do? "Mary Lee," I whispered over the phone one Saturday morning, "Danny and I have to see each other. Can you help?"

"Well, well, Celia." Her voice could turn honey to sugar. "What happened to Miss Goody Two-shoes?"

"Mama happened."

"Ah." She fell silent for a moment. "Well, how about tomorrow afternoon? My parents got some Christmas deal. Your mama doesn't have to know they'll be gone."

"Okay." I heard Mama and Daddy pulling into the driveway. "But can you call Danny for me? I may not get another chance to use the phone."

"Ooh. You're goin' to let *me* talk to your guy?"

"Mary Lee. Just . . . call him. That's all."

"Sure thing, Celia. By the way"—she giggled—"you're a lot more fun than you used to be."

I trembled when Mary Lee drove up Sunday afternoon. She looked perfect as usual, with a multicolored jacket open to reveal a soft teal sweater tucked into tight jeans. She'd long since let that crazy perm of hers grow out, and her chestnut hair now fell in soft waves across her shoulders. Her large brown eyes were enhanced with eye shadow and mascara, and her lips were red. I felt keenly envious of the makeup; I wanted to look that way for Danny. "Where do we meet him?" I was breathless.

"He'll be at Route 347, down below town."

"Oh, what do I do?"

"Get down in the backseat, idgit, that's what."

I couldn't believe how easy it was. Within ten minutes Danny had ducked down in Mary Lee's backseat with me, grinning like a Cheshire cat.

"What did you tell your mama?" I whispered.

"That I was goin' for a walk. She's used to me settin' off by myself."

Guilt stabbed at me. Danny had always been so honest; now I was turning him into a liar. "If she finds out, what'll she do?"

"Kill me. After raggin' that I don't need my daddy to shame me anymore; I done did it on my own."

The three of us talked in Mary Lee's game room, where Danny and I had danced forever ago. I didn't like the way Mary Lee made a point of stretching out her long legs as she slouched back against an armchair. Catching my eye, she cleared her throat and rose languidly. "Well, think I'll go upstairs. Don't be too long." Tilting an eyebrow at me, she slunk out of the room.

Danny held me tightly as we sat on Mary Lee's couch, and we talked about our plans, our future. Being with him was so wonderful; neither of us wanted ever to let go. I told myself there was no harm in sneaking behind our parents' backs, not if God had put us together in the first place. Since he hadn't chosen to change my mother, what else was I to do? Then in no time at all, it seemed, Mary Lee was back, saying an hour had passed and her parents would be home soon. We left her house with sinking hearts, vowing we'd sneak out again.

Ten minutes later Danny thanked her profusely before hopping out of her car.

"Anytime," she said, her voice dripping with meaning. She watched him lope away, then headed toward Minton Street, tossing her head. "No wonder you're so crazy about him," she sighed. "He's gorgeous."

I kept silent.

"Celia, don't ever let him out of your sight. Girls in this crazy town may not know what they've got, but if he steps outside Bradleyville, they'll run for him like mice to cheese. I mean, just *look* at him!"

Suddenly I didn't care for her thick chestnut hair and that tight expensive sweater over her tight expensive jeans. "Mary Lee, he's mine."

"Yeah." She blew out air. "But you ever get tired of him, you just let me know."

Lying in bed that night, I thought about Mary Lee's admonition. *Never let him leave Bradleyville.* Yet I was planning on doing just that. For the first time I was scared of what Danny might find after he'd gone.

Danny and I managed to sneak to Mary Lee's house a few more times when her parents were out. After a while my conscience no longer bothered me. Sometimes she brought her own boyfriend along, a tall basketball player named Mike whom she'd been dating for a record four months. They'd wander off while Danny and I remained on the game room couch, savoring every moment we could be together. Sometimes my heart was so full of him, I thought it would burst.

If I'd stopped to think about it, I'd have realized I wasn't praying much anymore. Nor were Danny and I talking about God in our lives. And during Sunday school and church I only pretended to listen. I was too busy planning the next opportunity to see Danny.

In February Danny turned eighteen. Using some hoarded baby-sitting money, I bought him a locket and chain with my picture inside. We had no chance to be together at Mary Lee's as we had hoped, so I gave it to him at school under cover of my locker door. "Don't open it till you get home," I said. "I hope you don't think it's self-serving. It's just that it represents me. And that's what I want to give you most."

"I love it," he told me the following day. "Like I love you. I'll keep it in my pocket always."

A week later Danny had news. Lee Harding's great uncle thought he had a lead on a job for him. "I'm hopin' and prayin', Celia," he said as we stood outside school, shivering in a lightly falling snow. "Things're so bad for us; Mama and I got to leave as soon as I graduate. I'd do it even sooner for her, but she won't hear a me not finishin' my education."

He'd talked so much about leaving Bradleyville that you'd think I'd get used to the idea. I knew he had to go and I still supported it. But it was so hard. I knew life hadn't been fair to him; now life was being unfair to me, forcing me to stay behind while he stepped out into the world. *Danny*, I thought, standing in the snow, *don't leave me*.

"Where would the job be?"

"Well, I don't know what the job is yet."

"But where does Lee's great uncle live?"

He hesitated. "Miami."

The sidewalk dropped away beneath my feet. "Miami. *Florida?*"

He nodded, biting his lip.

"Miami." Miami was a world, a planet, away. It had never occurred to me that he would leave Kentucky. "Miami's on the ocean," I blurted, accusation in my voice. "Miami's got beaches and sand. *Our* beaches."

"Celia, it would be perfect, don't you see? Once you're done with school, you can come, too. I'll save the ocean for you."

"But we were supposed to see it together. You weren't supposed to go see it first, without me."

Hurt painted his words. "You think I want to go without you? You know if there was a way, I'd stay right here. But you and I can't make a life here, plus I got to take Mama away. I'll git everything set up for you. I got to do it, Celia; I got no money now, nothin' to offer you. I can't ask you to leave your family to live in a shack. You don't know what it's like to be without."

"I know what it's like to be without *you*. Anything else I can stand. But I can't be without you."

"It won't be forever."

"It'll be a whole *year*. I can't live without you a whole year. And why is it so easy for you all of a sudden?"

He closed his eyes. "It *ain't* easy. Nothin's ever been easy for me. But Celia, my whole life I done my best and nothin's worked. Don't deny me this. Don't deny me the chance to make somethin' outta myself."

I wanted to throw my books down on the sidewalk and cling to Danny and cry. Why couldn't he find a job in the state? Or Ohio or Tennessee. I could even bear to think of him in Lexington, where Mary Lee would be attending the University of Kentucky. But the ocean. The wild ocean, where seashells rolled in from distant beaches and the endless horizon made you think you owned the world. Between me and it, which had he loved first? Which would he choose if circumstances demanded it?

"Danny, you already are somethin'; you're the one I love. Why isn't that enough?"

Forgetting restraint, he reached out to grip my shoulder. "It is. But we can't love each other the way we want."

"Wait for me, then," I pleaded. "Just one more year. Until we can go together."

His arm fell away. "Celia, I can't. I got my mama to think of. I've got you but she's got nobody. She'll wither up and die if I don't git her outta here."

"That's just an excuse! You just want to travel; you always have. You want to see the ocean. And if you have to leave me to do it, you will!"

He turned his head aside, stung by the words. "No. I want you. I will always want you, always love you. Please understand. If a job comes through, it's gonna be hard enough, tryin' to get Mama away without Daddy finding out and killing her first, trying to scrape money together to even git there." He faced me, his jaw tight. "And if I happen to find a job where I've always dreamed a being, why deny me that? Why not be glad for any little happiness I might find while I'm waitin' for you? It'd be like letting a wild bird out of a cage."

Tears fell, turning icy on my frozen face. "And what do wild birds do? They fly away, Danny. They fly away and they don't come back."

"Celia, I'll never fly away from you. You're the only girl I've ever loved. I love you so deep that nothin' can change that, not miles between us or the ocean or fanciful dreams. If a job opens up, I'll go and I'll wait for you. Then we'll be together forever."

I wiped my cheeks with the back of my hand. "Promise me."

"I promise."

His emerald eyes misted with pleading, the shock of hair across his forehead dusted with snow. He held his books loosely in one hand against his coat, worn and barely enough to keep out the cold. I heard the sounds of youngsters squealing at thrown snowballs, and the door of the school building slamming in syncopated rhythm. Melissa had already left, long ago learning not to wait for me. Mona and Barbara, Randy, Gerald and Lyle and Bobby—they'd all left, too. I hardly talked to any of them anymore. Word was, Bobby couldn't take being near me, knowing I cared not a whit for him. Only Kevy would wait to walk me home. Shivering on the sidewalk, I realized I'd isolated myself from the town almost as much as the town had isolated Danny. And the thought of next year without him left me colder than the air swirling about us.

"Then go," I said, voice catching. "Take care of your mama and wait for me. And when I come, we'll dig our toes in the sand."

He smiled faintly. "Run along the beach. Camp out under the stars."

"Yeah," I replied, managing to smile with him. "We will, Danny. We will."

chapter 40

Three days after Danny told me about Miami, Granddad suffered a heart attack. It struck suddenly after lunch, during which he'd impatiently informed his "overprotective daughter" that he was as healthy as an ox. By the time Kevy and I arrived home, the ambulance from the Albertsville hospital had come and gone, Mama riding in the back with him. She'd left a hasty note taped to the front door, saying she'd call as soon as she could.

Numb with shock, I wandered into Granddad's bedroom, running my fingers over his medals and the German canteen, rolling Jake Lewellyn's marble in its little cup. In the dining area I picked up the phone and dialed Danny's number. His daddy answered. I hung up.

"Celia," Kevy asked, lip quivering, "Granddad's not goin' to die, is he?"

I pulled him down on the couch, putting my arm around him, his head on my shoulder. Poor Kevy. Seeing his hurt only added to my own pain. "No, Kevy, he won't die. We love him too much."

Even if surgery could have helped Granddad, he was too weak to withstand it. So the doctors sent him home after five days, gray, his face stubbly, his legs so unsteady that Daddy and Mama had to practically carry him to bed. I helped prop him up on pillows, refusing to leave him at supper time, feeding him soup. We tiptoed around the house, not wanting to disturb his naps. During lunch at school I'd use the office phone to call Mama, checking on him. After school Danny and I would speak briefly; then I'd rush home with Kevy, afraid of what I might find. In the meantime no further news had come about a job for Danny. Either that or he simply wasn't telling me, knowing how bad the timing would be.

Granddad's body may have been failing but not so his mind. He'd still entertain Kevy and me with long war stories, some of which we'd never heard before. Those I suspected he was making up. Jake Lewellyn came to visit one afternoon and was met with the same temperament Granddad had always bestowed upon his best friend. "Jake, you ol' coot, whatcha doin' in my bedroom?" Granddad struggled to rise a little higher against his pillows. "Celia, go over and hold that marble afore he steals it right out from under me."

I pulled a chair near the bed, supporting Mr. Lewellyn as he sank into it. "Now, Granddad, be nice. Mr. Lewellyn's come to visit; you could at least show him some respect."

"Respect? Since when did he ever show *me* any respect?"

"Oh, hush, Thomas." Mr. Lewellyn shook his head. "I'm here, ain't I?"

"Well, good for you. Can you still play checkers?"

"Can you?"

"'Course, ol' man. I ain't dead yet."

Jake Lewellyn sighed. "Well, that board's an awful long ways away."

"I'll get it," I offered. Fetching the game from the dining table, I stopped to pick up a folding tray. "Here," I sang cheerily, "we'll put the board on top of this and you can play just fine."

Granddad snorted. "No tray's goin' to help Jake Lewellyn's game."

In the following weeks it seemed as if everywhere I turned, emotion roiled. Mama was beside herself, afraid her daddy was going to die. I'd catch her staring sightlessly out the kitchen window, ironing the same spot on a shirt until she'd nearly scorched it, rubbing her forehead as if she could rub away all the wasted years. She'd hover over Granddad, trying to nurse him, only to purposefully flee the room when his talk of battles began. Watching, I was torn between feeling sorry for her and wanting to tell her off. I knew her pain was real. But she could not let go of her stubbornness and give Granddad the one thing he'd always wanted.

"Mama," I burst one night after following as she marched from his room, "can't you just stop a minute and see what he's doing?"

She shot me a disdainful look, as if I had the mentality of a two-year-old. "I see what he's doing." Her voice was edged with bitterness. "He's going to his deathbed hangin' on to empty heroism, that's what he's doing."

"It's not empty, Mama. It's his life."

"His life." She leaned against a wall, eyes closing. "Yes. His war stories. And you. That's been his life. Never me."

Stunned, I touched her arm. "He loves you, Mama. He loved you long before I ever came along. Can't you see how it hurts him, not havin' your respect? The whole town admires Thomas Bradley. And you, his daughter, are the only one who doesn't."

"I can't give him that, not after all he's taken from me. He's got everyone else's admiration; he doesn't need mine."

"Yours is what he *does* need. Hasn't it ever occurred to you why he insists on tellin' his stories in front of you? He keeps thinkin' that if he tells them one more time, maybe you'll *get* it, maybe he'll finally be a hero in your eyes."

"He was a hero to me, Celia," she spat. "And then he went off to war."

Dear God, I cried inside, crossing my arms over my chest, what was I doing here? Why was I between these two adults, trying to fix something I'd never understood? Danny was leaving me, Granddad was leaving me, and Mama, wrapped in her own grievances, didn't understand my pain. I felt as if life were slipping right out from under my feet.

"Mama," I replied evenly, "don't do this. Don't let him die without givin' him what he longs for. All you have to do is tell him you're proud of him. Pick up one medal, hold it to the light. Tell him he's a hero in your eyes."

She pushed away from the wall, straightening her back. "You're still a child. You understand nothin'."

"I am not a child!"

"Don't raise your voice at me! And don't tell me how to treat my own daddy."

I turned away, throat tightening. "No wonder you can't understand my love for Danny," I seethed. "You have none in you at all."

She inhaled sharply, as if I'd kicked her in the stomach. Then without a word she retreated to the kitchen.

I returned to Granddad.

I watched Granddad's demise. Every day I saw it in his labored breathing, his trembling hands. But I couldn't accept it. *He'll get better,* I told myself. *It's just taking longer than we expected.* Granddad had always been the victor, even when death stared him in the face. At the Volturno River, in Korea, Granddad always won.

I should have known from his crying. I'd never seen him do that before. Now tears would trickle down his face onto the white pillow. At first I thought his eyes were simply watering after staring too hard in the afternoons at the checkerboard balanced between him and Jake Lewellyn. But as I brought him a drink of water one evening, I caught his chin trembling.

"Granddad." I placed a palm against his cheek. "What is it?"

He wrapped weakened fingers around my arm. "I'm tired, missy."

"I know. You just need some rest."

"No. I mean your mama and me. I'm givin' up. I'm tired."

"Oh, Granddad, no. She's upset, that's all, and worried about you. She loves you so much, she can't stand to see you like this."

His mouth flickered. "She'll never understand how much I want her forgiveness."

"She doesn't understand a lot of things." Instantly I felt a stab of guilt. Here was Granddad sick and *crying*, for gracious' sake, and I was stewing about my own problems.

"Missy, you keep prayin' for her. She needs to learn to forgive and let go a the past, for her own sake. Her bitterness is squeezin' her soul. I pray she'll finally see that, even if it's after I'm gone."

"You're not goin' anywhere."

"I'm dyin'."

"No, you're not. You're too mean."

He smiled feebly. "I done made a decision. I waited as long as I could, hopin' things'd change. And I prayed and prayed, askin' the Lord's guidance. Now I believe I got his answer, and I'm gonna carry it out, harsh as it may seem."

Pressing my hand against his withered skin, I asked him what it was.

"You'll know soon enough. Just remember the one thing I always taught you."

"Choose your battles carefully," I recited, "then fight like Michael."

"Yep. And you're goin' to have some battles, I'm afraid."

"Oh, Granddad, I already do."

"Guess so." He fell silent for a moment. "Now there's a few items you got to take care of for me."

He told me three things.

First, there was George Quince from Albertsville, who had been Granddad's lawyer for years. When Granddad sold the sawmill, Mr. Quince had drawn up the papers. Now, Granddad said, he had to meet with the man about his will.

I'd never even thought about Granddad's having a will.

My conversation with Granddad was on a Tuesday night in early March. Wednesday morning I called Mr. Quince before leaving for school. When I arrived home that afternoon, he and Granddad were behind closed doors until almost supper time. Mama accosted me with questions; Granddad had made his will years ago, she breathed; what was he doing? It was the first time she'd talked to me in days. I had no idea, I said with a shrug.

"Leave it alone, Estelle," Daddy commanded, surprising us. "It's his business."

Second, incredibly, there was Danny, whom Granddad was summoning to his bedside. I shouldn't pick him up myself; that would be going too far, Granddad had said. Mama was going to have a fit as it was. If Danny couldn't drive over himself, Daddy could fetch him. I told Danny Granddad's request at school. Wide-eyed, he promised to come after chores that evening, around eight.

Granddad must have prayed mighty hard over the decision to see Danny. He knew it would not only anger Mama but hurt her as well, for she would see his action as an alignment of forces against her. But Granddad had insisted it was important. At his suggestion we waited to tell Mama until just before Danny drove over. Her face blanched. "I'll not have it," she stated angrily, "my father goin' against me in my own house."

Daddy held up both hands. "He's not askin' for much, Estelle; how can you deny him? He may not be with us much longer."

"Not askin' for much! He's askin' for *everything*, makin' a statement to our daughter right in front of us; can't you see that?"

Daddy's voice was dead quiet. "I see lots of things. And I say Danny's comin'."

Kevy's mouth formed a perfect, round O as he slid his eyes toward me. Watching Daddy stand with his legs apart, hands low on his hips,

I had the feeling he was enjoying himself, Granddad's request an excuse to pump up his courage. And the way he'd said yes to Granddad so easily made me think he was secretly happy Danny had been invited.

"William, he cannot come here! We can't allow it!"

"Yes, we can. We will."

"No!" Mama flung out an arm toward me. "She defies me enough already. Don't you understand what this will do?"

"Estelle, your father wants a visitor. And I'm goin' to see that he gets it."

Face crumpling, Mama fled to her room, slamming the door behind her. Kevy started to cry. I couldn't hide my vindictiveness.

"Celia," Daddy commanded. "Don't."

Mama didn't come out of her room all evening. When Danny arrived, he solemnly shook hands with Daddy, offered me a brief smile, and hugged Kevy. "What's the matter, Kevin?" he asked, seeing my brother's red eyes.

"Mama and Daddy were fightin'."

The candidness of youth. I could have kicked Kevy, watching the hurt cross Danny's face. "It'll be all right," he soothed, tousling Kevy's hair. "Your mama's just sad right now, with her daddy bein' sick 'n' all."

I could have cried, too, hearing him defend Mama like that. As if she deserved it.

Excusing himself, Danny walked down the hall to Granddad's room. I heard their exchanged greetings; then the door closed.

Daddy pulled Kevy down on the couch to watch TV, a rare treat on a school night. Listlessly I wandered to my room, studying the ocean scenes that lined my walls. Emotions tumbled through me like clothes in a dryer. How I had longed to see Danny once again in my home. How wonderful it was to see him shake Daddy's hand, to hear Granddad greet him warmly. But the circumstances under which he'd been invited were so great a price to pay. "Oh, Granddad," I whispered, running a finger over a blurring picture, "please don't die. Who's goin' to stand up for me when you're gone?"

Over half an hour passed before I heard the click of Granddad's door. I jumped from my bed to meet Danny in the hall. "What happened?" I whispered.

His eyes misted. "You're granddad's a great man. I'll be in his debt forever."

"What did he say?"

Danny dared to take my hands. "He blessed our bein' together, Celia. Your mama never will, he said, and your daddy may not have the courage. So he did it. After making me pledge before God that we'd get through school first and that I'd take care a you. He said it won't be easy. But, he said, you got to choose your battles."

After Danny left, I tiptoed inside Granddad's room. "Hello, missy," he mumbled.

I adjusted the covers over his bony shoulders. "Granddad, thank you."

He managed a smile. "I'm kinda tired; it's been a long day. Think I'll take a snooze."

As I planted a lingering kiss on his forehead, he fell asleep.

For the next four days Granddad had constant visitors pulling a chair to his bedside, quietly reminiscing. Mr. and Mrs. B. came, as did Hank Jenkins and Mr. Tull, the Clangerlees, the Frasiers, the Taylors and Hardings. It was as if they all knew.

"Miss Jessie." I caught her arm Saturday morning after she and Mr. Harding had taken leave of my weary granddad. Mrs. B. was watching the Harding kids, Miss Jessie not wanting to ask me to do it. "Has Lee's great uncle found a job for Danny yet?"

She gave me a curious look. "Hasn't he said anything?"

Fear gathered in my chest. "We haven't had much time to talk," I replied lightly.

"Of course. Well, I'll let him tell you."

I opened my mouth to press her but promptly shut it again. She was right—Danny should tell me. And it was true that we hadn't had much time to talk. All the same, I couldn't help feeling that he was purposely keeping it from me.

Sunday afternoon Jake Lewellyn visited. I asked if the men wanted to play checkers, but Granddad was too tired. "We'll just set a spell, missy," he answered, eyelids drooping. I should have left them alone, but something made me stay, sitting on the floor against his dresser, hugging my knees.

"Thomas," Mr. Lewellyn declared, "I never thought I'd see the day you'd be too tired to beat me at checkers."

Granddad snorted softly. "Finally admittin' I beat you, are ya?"

"You beat me at a lot a things in your day."

"Don't forget Jake's Rock. You made me serenade that ugly girl."

"You always said I cheated at that one."

"You did."

"Did not."

"Did too."

They were silent for a moment. I could hear the air sucking in and out of Granddad's lungs. "Well, Jake"—his voice sounded so tired— "looks like you done beat me for good this time."

"No sir," Mr. Lewellyn replied gruffly, "you ain't gonna die yet, if that's what you're thinkin'. So don't go talking about it and gittin' my hopes up."

"Jake Lewellyn, you always were a mean ol' coot."

"And you're a thief and a liar."

"Yeah. So?"

"So what?"

"So I still got your marble."

Granddad fought his way to a wicked grin.

During lunch Monday Daddy phoned the school, asking Kevy and me to come home. I received the message just as I was sitting down across from Danny, preparing to ask him about the job in Miami. My stomach turned to stone. Danny looked at me with sadness in his eyes. "Try to call me tonight," he said. "I want to know."

I nodded.

Daddy had stayed home from work. When Kevy and I flew into the house, we found him and Mama at Granddad's bedside. "Here they are, Thomas," he said.

I pulled a trembling Kevy across the worn carpet. "Hi, Granddad." The covers barely moved over his chest. One hand lay tucked underneath them. I reached for his other hand, which was resting on his stomach, and was shocked by its coldness. "Here, put it under the blanket," I urged, dropping to my knees.

"Don't matter." His voice was a grated whisper. "Cain't feel it anyway." He swallowed carefully. "Missy, don't forget now what I tol' you. And never take your eyes off the Lord."

My throat closed. "No sir, I never will."

"Kevin."

My brother shot me a terrified look, then eased next to me. "Yes sir."

"You're a wonderful boy. Sweet and generous, like your mama at your age."

Mama, sweet and generous? Granddad was too sick to know what he was saying.

"Take care a your mama, Kevin, hear?"

"I will."

He does know what he's saying, I thought. *He knows I'll be gone.*

"I love you, Estelle. My pretty daughter."

Mama sobbed quietly. "I love you, too, Daddy."

"Granddad," I blurted, *"don't.* Choose your battles. You can win this one."

His fingers rose slightly off the blanket, then sank again. "No, missy. I'm too tired."

That afternoon time swirled in cycles, Granddad mumbling, then sleeping as I stroked his forehead, Mama fetching him water. Daddy sat in a chair near the end of the bed, holding Granddad's thin ankle through the covers. "Thomas, you just rest," he soothed. "Every hero needs his rest."

Mama squeezed her eyes shut but said nothing.

"William," Granddad whispered, "I been so proud to have you in the family. You been a good husband for my girl."

To my horror Daddy's face crumpled. I froze in my chair, watching him cry for the first time in my life, until compassion overcame my disbelief. Rising, I held him lightly by the shoulders. Mama never moved.

Over the next few hours the phone rang occasionally. No one answered it. Kevy sat against the wall, legs splayed, rising again and again to comfort Mama and me at first sight of our tears. I wiped his away. Mostly we kept vigil silently, waiting, knowing in our heads what would follow, while our hearts staunchly denied it. Around four o'clock Granddad fell asleep again, the barest whistle of air from his open mouth affording us reason to hope. None of us spoke.

At five-thirty, when we would normally be eating supper, Granddad cutting his meat while recounting a war story, his eyes suddenly popped open, animation flicking across his face. "Adele!" he exclaimed, his voice hoarse, tremulous. "You're so beautiful!"

In the next instant his cheeks sagged. His mouth relaxed. Light faded from his eyes like the last yellow waning of a spent flashlight. He exhaled once with a shudder.

Then he was gone.

The funeral took place two days later, Wednesday, March 12. School was canceled, the auditorium opened for the service, our church being too small. The whole town came. Flowers, fragrant and lush, covered the casket and the entire stage floor beneath Pastor Frasier's feet. Many people offered eulogies, both funny and poignant. Lee Harding spoke of the lumber mill being Granddad's legacy, still providing work for so many local men. Mr. B. talked about his wisdom. Mrs. Clangerlee said he always had a funny story down at the IGA. Mr. Tull wept for the empty chair under his awning.

Danny and his mama came, slipping into a back row. I longed to have him beside me. Instead I sat down front between Daddy and Kevy, who patted my arm consolingly. There were moments when I could not cry and moments when the tears wouldn't stop. I had never before experienced true grief and was overwhelmed by how greedily it consumed my heart.

Afterward we drove in a long, silent procession to the cemetery beside our little white church to watch the casket being lowered into the ground. Mama threw a handful of dirt upon it first, collapsing in sobs as it fizzled against the brown wood. Daddy threw dirt in next, then Kevy. Scraping up a fist of dust, I brought it to my mouth and kissed it, then dribbled it over the grave. "Choose your battles, Granddad," I whispered.

When it was all over, there was one more thing I had to do. Granddad's third request. Breaking away from my family, I wove through dozens of consoling arms to Jake Lewellyn's side.

"Mr. Lewellyn." I slid a hand into my purse and brought up a small bundle covered in one of Granddad's old hankies. Unwrapped it. "Granddad wanted me to give you this." I held out the cracked play teacup. The marble lay inside, glinting black and silver in the chilly sunlight. "He said to tell you"—my voice broke—"that you win."

Jake Lewellyn bawled like a baby.

chapter 41

Two days after Granddad's funeral our family gathered in Mr. Quince's office to read the will. Mama was fearful, her tension spilling out in dueling bouts of sentimental tears and caustic anger. Mr. Quince read the document matter-of-factly, eyes not leaving the paper. Granddad had dictated letters for each of us, signed and sealed in separate envelopes. We were to read them later.

The rest was short and straightforward. His medals and military insignia Granddad gave to me. To Kevy, his German canteen. His material possessions, clothes and the like, he wanted donated to a veterans organization. And then there was the issue of money, which I didn't know he'd possessed. From his savings account at the Bradleyville Bank, which had been steadily growing with interest ever since he "sold the sawmill for a hefty profit," five thousand dollars was to go into an account for Kevy, and fifteen thousand dollars was to be given to his sweet daughter, whom he dearly loved. The balance, over sixty-five thousand dollars, was left to his grandgirl, Celia Marie Matthews, to be kept in the account until she was eighteen and graduated from high school, then released in total.

Mama moaned. The look she turned on me as I sat in stunned silence dripped with pain and betrayal and bitterness. I knew she believed that Granddad had reached out and slapped her from the grave. I understood none of it until I could retreat to my room, locking the door and sinking onto my bed, his letter in my hand.

Dear Celia,

Now you know what my decision was. I've hoarded the money all these years, planning on giving it to your mama, knowing she in turn would be generous to you and Kevy when it came time for you both to leave home. Things are different now. You and Danny have a life to build and she won't help you. If Danny owned anything, I wouldn't have needed to do this. But he has struggled all his life and has nothing to give you but himself. So take the money with my blessing.

One request, missy. Don't tell him about this yet. You may think it will ease his mind in the coming year while you two are apart. I think it would make things worse. He has his pride. He'll be hesitant to ask you to leave your family once you graduate, afraid that you'll believe he wants you only because of the money. A stupid thing to think, but people can convince themselves of stupid things about those they love the most. So wait till you're together again, then surprise him.

There's something else, very, very important. Always remember what I told you about praying to heal things with your mama. Because God promised me something yesterday after I talked to you. I'm ashamed to admit I was right mad at him, demanding to know why he never answered me about my problems with her. Something inside me told me to pick up my Bible, and it fell open to Matthew 11:28. "Come unto me, all ye that labour and are heavy laden, and I will give you rest." The next verse says it again, even better—"Ye shall find rest unto your souls." God was telling me plain as could be that I can rest now because I've done all I can and he'll take care of it. And then he told me something else, Celia, clear like a bell. He told me that you are the one on this earth who's going to reach your mama, if you'll just follow his leading. You two are going to learn how to love each other. You can imagine I sure felt better after that. It may take a while for you to see this happen. But don't ever give up. Just keep asking the Lord how to go about it and he'll tell you. One thing I know—the Lord don't go back on his promises. If you don't turn to him for help, though, you'll never manage it by yourself.

One more thing. In my letter to your mama I told her that a lot of prayer went into my giving you so much money. I'm praying she'll understand that and not harden her heart. I also told her many, many things that I hope she'll finally begin to hear.

You're the best grandgirl a man could have. It was a blessing to watch you grow. I loved taking walks with you, and fishing and swimming, and most of all going to Tull's.

All my deepest love,
Your Granddad,
Thomas Bradley

P.S. Don't forget to give that old henpecker Jake Lewellyn his marble.

~ 1997 ~

chapter 42

How I wished for my wise granddad's guidance as I struggled with my growing feelings for John Forkes. He had begun to haunt my thoughts. Visions of his hand over mine swirled with my ancient ache for Danny. The visions did not lessen the old loss. But in the midst of living with Mama and cheerleading Daddy through seemingly endless therapy sessions, John's image sent a warmth through me that I had not felt in a long time. I imagined that he was thinking of me as well. Since the day we met, an inexplicable communication had flowed between us. I pictured Carrie talking about Andy and remembered the quickened senses of a woman desired.

But John wasn't free, as Andy was. John was engaged. Planning a wedding. He was Daddy's doctor; that should have been our only connection. And I was no longer a teenager, too self-absorbed to realize the tragedy of poor choices.

Our talk over iced tea happened on a Friday. The following Tuesday John would return. I waited for the day with impatient dread, as I once had waited for Saturday and my next visit to the river after Danny had not shown up.

"Mama," I asked as I set the table for supper Monday, "I was thinking of painting the living room. What do you think?"

She was stirring rice on the stove. "Paintin' it? With us right here?"

"I'd just do a wall at a time, so it wouldn't be too disruptive. It really needs it."

"Well, I know, but—"

"Let me do it for you, Mama," I pressed. "I need a project to keep me busy anyway."

She hemmed and hawed but ultimately acquiesced, even smiling at me briefly. I smiled back. For Daddy's sake we had been trying harder to get along ever since he became so upset at the supper table last week. I knew, however, that solving our differences would not be as simple as painting a room.

After Daddy's therapy Tuesday morning I drove to Albertsville, ostensibly to buy the paint but intent on other business as well. Reaching the south end of town, I followed the familiar streets that led to Sledge's Farm Equipment. Many times when I was a child, I had driven with Granddad to pick Daddy up from work on the days Granddad had needed the car. How Granddad used to fly over the hills, my stomach bouncing into my giggling throat as he trumpeted that we were "streakin' into battle for the Allied Forces."

My mission today was just as important, as far as Daddy was concerned. I had to reverse the damage Mama had done. His boss was not expecting me; I could not have risked Mama's overhearing a phone call. I hoped that the element of surprise would work in my favor.

To my relief, Mr. Sledge greeted me heartily, asking about Daddy and saying how much he was missed. "That's good to hear," I replied, "because I'm here to talk to you about how we can best get him back to work."

He didn't blink an eye. "Of course, of course."

Ushering me into his industrial office, he bid me to sit in an old wooden chair opposite his gray metal desk. Boxes, papers, invoices, and supplies littered the room and the sill of its one grimy window. From the showroom outside filtered the sounds of a salesman testing a tractor motor and another calling for a serviceman to "pick up that doggone phone!" Mr. Sledge nodded to me apologetically. "It's always pretty noisy around here. Your daddy amazed me, the way he could work the books in the middle of all the commotion. He had a knack for filterin' out what he didn't want to hear."

I thought of Daddy when I was a child and found that easy to believe. However, he was no longer so distant from his surroundings. I wondered if that would change his ability to perform here. It had certainly changed his tolerance for my fighting with Mama.

"You told my mother a temp is replacing him right now?"

"That's right. He knows he's most likely got two months here; after that we'll see."

"Mr. Sledge"—I leaned forward in the chair—"I'm handling Daddy's therapy. We work very hard at it twice a day and he's improving. The improvement is slow; it's likely to take all of those two months. It might take longer, though, and that's why I'm here. To ask you early on to grant him some extra time if we need it. He's worked for you a lot of years and I know you value him. So it seems to me that if you have to employ a temporary accountant for a few more weeks, it's worth it for you to wait."

He regarded me indulgently, light from the overhead bulb reflecting off his glasses. "You came from outta state to help your daddy, didn't ya? Left your own job?"

"Yes sir."

He shook his head. "Your daddy sure is lucky to have you. I'd like to think my kids'd do the same for me, but . . ." He shrugged. "I guess you're mighty close to both your folks; that's the way Bradleyville breeds 'em."

"Well, I've been gone a long time. But they needed me, so I came."

"That's what I mean." He leaned back, looking at the ceiling as he plucked absentmindedly at the blue-and-white striped shirt half untucked around his bulging stomach. "Tell you what, Celia. I do want your daddy to return. But the impression I got from your mama was that he may never be able to. So she and I settled on two months as sort of a reassessin' time, know what I mean? Gosh, she told me he couldn't even talk. I figured, 'Who knows if he can ever handle my books again?'"

"He couldn't talk at first but he's learning," I responded. "And his mind is clear. What he can't say, he can write. It's not a matter of being able to think logically; it's merely a matter of his body regaining the strength to function normally. He may never drive himself to work again, for example, but there's no reason Mama couldn't bring him."

"Your mama seemed awful protective; I don't know if she'd go along with this."

My fingers gripped the arms of my chair. "Excuse me, Mr. Sledge, but I don't think it's for her to say. It's up to Daddy. Put yourself in his place—stuck in a wheelchair, working so hard to relearn the simplest things like pulling on your socks. Imagine how depressing that would be, then imagine someone telling you that even if you completely recovered, you could never return here, that your working life was over. Don't you think that would affect how hard you'd work at your therapy? Don't you think you'd say to yourself, 'What's the use?' You know it's true; a man's life is his work. And I know that with all Daddy's been through, this place means a lot to him." I stopped abruptly, aware that my voice had risen. I felt my cheeks flush.

Mr. Sledge slowly tapped his thumb against the desk. "I'll say it again—your daddy's a lucky man to have you fightin' for him. And yes ma'am, I do understand. So let's do this. I told your mama we'd reassess in two months, and I'm gonna stick to that. That's, let's see"—his lips moved as he counted silently—"six weeks away. If William ain't ready to come back by then, you come around and see me. Tell me how much longer you think it'll be, if he can come back at all. You'll be honest with me about that, won't ya?"

"Yes, I will." Relief rushed through me. "Thank you, Mr. Sledge! Thank you so much."

"That's all right." He pushed back his chair, slapping his palms against his knees. "Sounds like you'll be here for however long it takes, huh? Till your daddy can come back."

My smile froze as the impact of his statement hit me. In wheedling extra time out of Mr. Sledge, I had opened the door to an indefinite stay in Bradleyville. How on earth could I not have thought of that before? What if Daddy didn't heal in time and my remaining six weeks stretched to ten, twelve? At what point would I cut it off, admit defeat? How could I just return to Little Rock and leave Daddy forever at home with Mama?

"Well, yes, of course," I replied lamely. "If he's able to come back."

Mr. Sledge was opening his office door, chuckling. "Sounds to me like you won't stop till you git him back; that's what you got your mind set on. And that's fine 'n' dandy. We'll be countin' on ya. Just like your daddy is."

"Yes sir." I forced my lips to curve. "I'll do my best. Thank you again."

In my car I leaned back against the headrest and closed my eyes, keys dropped in my lap, not knowing whether to laugh or cry.

I had planned to call Bobby Delham while in Albertsville, to see if I could meet him after work. I still felt I needed to see him and express my sorrow over Melissa's death, and I thought it might be awkward to visit him at home with his children present. But after my discussion with Mr. Sledge, I no longer had the energy. Driving to the hardware store, I promised myself I would phone Bobby another day.

Another day. Another week? Month? Who knew? After the commitment I'd just made, I could possibly put off seeing Bobby Delham all summer. What in the world was I doing, I railed inwardly. The therapy sessions, difficult as they had been, were not half as draining as the tension between me and Mama. I didn't know how I could be under the same roof with her for more than two months. I worried about being absent so long from the ad agency. And June 30 would come all too soon. I couldn't imagine conducting my annual all-night candle-light vigil in Mama's house.

On cue, the memories began to play in my head.

"No." I fought them as I entered the store. With effort I thrust them away. Paid for the paint supplies. Wheeled my heavy shopping cart outside. As I loaded the items into my car, a quiet, selfish voice in the back of my head grew louder, replacing the memories. It murmured that more time in Bradleyville meant more opportunities to see John Forkes.

chapter 43

I borrowed some old clothes from Mama and got ready to paint the back wall of the living room and dining area, moving out the dining table and telephone stand and spreading tarp. The house soon filled with the smell of paint, and I opened windows and the front door, allowing the warm spring breeze to blow through. Leaving time for Daddy's therapy, late in the afternoon I announced I'd done enough damage for one day, doused the paint splatters with turpentine, and took a bath.

"Luuk guud," Daddy told me at supper, awkwardly holding a chicken breast steady with his left forefinger as he cut it. He couldn't hold a fork in his left hand yet, although movement was improving due to his frequent attempts to squeeze the rubber ball.

"Thanks. Are you talking about me now that I'm cleaned up or the walls?"

"Bvoth."

I squeezed his arm.

Daddy and I had not had another of our long conversations yet, and he'd been bugging me about it. "Letsss tawk," he'd said that morning. I'd promised we would—sometime when Mama was out. He'd cast me a disappointed look and reached for his pen and paper.

What waiting for to make up with M? Armageddon?

Here we go again, I'd thought. "Daddy"—frustration had coated my voice—"how do you make up for a lifetime?"

"The paint does look good," Mama agreed. "Thank you for your work."

"You're welcome; glad to do it."

How civil we were to one another.

As we finished supper, John arrived, taking in the moved furniture and tarp with a glance. His tie was off, shirt collar open. He turned his eyes on me, and I thought of the way Danny used to look when he'd see me at school and we couldn't touch. While John examined Daddy, I hung around, telling him of the various improvements I'd seen. When he was ready to leave, I offered to walk him out. "Just a quick question," I explained.

I waited until we had stepped off the porch, far enough from Mama's listening ears. "I wanted you to know," I said quietly as we walked, "that I saw Daddy's boss yesterday and he granted us extra time for Daddy to return to work if we need it. I haven't told Mama yet."

"For William's sake, that's good to hear." John scanned Minton Street, apparently looking for nosy neighbors. It struck me that he thought this necessary, as if we had something to hide. "Think she'll be glad you did that?" he asked.

"It doesn't really matter. Whether Daddy returns to work is for him to decide, not her."

We stopped halfway to his car. "She's only trying to protect him, Celia. She almost lost him and it really scared her."

"This isn't about protection," I informed him. "It's about control. You don't know her. She's always tried to control our family, and she never wanted people to leave her; that was her big thing. Now she doesn't even want Daddy to leave for a day's work. It's ridiculous."

"Don't you think you're being a little hard on her?"

"Don't talk to me about being hard, John; you don't know the half of it."

"Okay. Sorry."

I closed my eyes, suddenly tired. "No. I'm sorry. I'm just . . . touchy about the subject."

"Don't worry about it." He placed a hand on my arm briefly. My skin tingled.

Suddenly self-conscious, I resumed walking. "When will you be back?"

"Friday. That way I can keep my weekend clear. Unless some old lady calls about her hemorrhoids."

I managed a smile. "A doctor's duty is never done, I suppose."

"Nope." He opened the passenger door and placed his bag on the seat. "See you soon."

"Ceela. Luuk!"

It happened Saturday afternoon. I'd finished my painting, the living room and dining area fresh and clean looking. I had informed Mama that I might as well do the kitchen with the paint I had left. Later she had taken a casserole to a sick church member, saying she wouldn't be long. I was about to call Monica about my house and cats but instead found myself running to the porch at the urgency in Daddy's voice. He beamed lopsidedly with victory, pointing with his chin toward his lap.

"Oh, wow!" I cried. "Look at you! You can touch it!"

The fingers and thumb of his left hand curved around the red rubber ball, brushing it. As I watched, he slowly uncurled his hand, then curled it once more.

"That's wonderful!" I hovered over him like a proud parent. "Can you pick it up?"

"Uuhh." He frowned, concentrating every ounce of energy on bending his fingers just a little more. They moved slightly.

"There! Now try it." I dropped to my knees and we stared at the ball, willing with all our might for it to raise the slightest bit. His fingers trembled. "Come on, come on," I whispered to the ball, "you can do it." Daddy began to raise his arm and the ball slipped through his fingers. "It's okay," I encouraged. "Try again."

Twice more he failed but he was unwilling to give up. "Don't worry about it, Daddy," I said soothingly. "A few more days and you'll have it."

"Nuuh! I doo."

He tried one more time, breathing heavily through his open mouth. The ball began to move. Slowly he raised it a good three inches before it fell.

"Yay!" I shouted. I jumped up to perform a little dance step, then hugged him tightly. His shoulders shook with glee.

That triumph marked the end of our third week and gave way to a rush of improvement in speech as well as physical dexterity. Mama was ecstatic when Daddy demonstrated his new ability. She grabbed his face with both hands and kissed him, then turned to hug me with arms that were warm and real, not stiff like a mannequin's. A wave of childlike emotion splashed over me.

After that our therapy sessions shortened, for Daddy constantly pushed himself throughout the day to raise his leg a little higher, lift his arm a little more, hold the ball tighter. The left side of his face began to firm, his lips dragging less, his smile straighter. We would review all these improvements formally in our sessions, Daddy showing off his latest trick as I pushed him to "do it again, more." Mama still dressed him to his waist, then I would take over, urging him to put on his own shirt. Buttons were still impossible, but even his efforts helped improve the nimbleness of his fingers. His red ball always lay on his lap and he continually worked to press it, the squeezes slowly growing in strength.

"Hey, I've got an idea!" I announced one morning after I'd buttoned his shirt. "Let's see, what we need is a box or something that's not too high." I cast my eyes around the bedroom. "Oh, I got it." I pulled out the paper supply drawer of Mama's dresser and positioned his wheelchair a little to the right of it, about six feet away. "There! Now, what you need to do is, see if you can bounce the ball into the drawer. The exercise will help your strength plus give you hand-eye coordination."

So we had a new game. Daddy was terrible at it, and I kept returning him the ball after it had dribbled to a stop in front of the dresser. "Let's move you closer," I suggested.

"No!" he said stubbornly and continued trying.

A black look crossed Mama's face when she saw that her dresser had been disturbed, but it dissipated when we showed her our game, Daddy's face full of determination.

As Daddy improved during those days, his desire to be out in the sunshine grew. Finally I told him I would take his chair down the porch steps if he was willing to place his life in my hands. "Awlruddy is," he replied. Once we were on the porch, Mama hovered like a nervous hen until I told her to get in front of the chair and help me tip it back as we counted to three and let Daddy down one step at a time, as John had instructed. She concentrated so hard that she forgot to pester me, which is what I'd intended. We made it to the sidewalk without a mishap.

"Awl right," Daddy exclaimed as Mama set out to push him around the block, "letsss go!"

John continued to come twice a week and I began counting the days in between. The expression on his face when he looked at me told me he was counting them as well. We fell into the habit of walking together to his car, surreptitiously on the lookout for neighbors' eyes, a glimmering current of awareness between us. One day as he took Daddy's blood pressure, the sky burst forth in a downpour, and I ended up running him to his car, our bodies pressed together under Mama's green umbrella. When we parted, the desire in his eyes shot right through me, leaving me nearly breathless. From then on, every time we saw each other the feelings intensified, until I knew the only thing keeping us from each other's arms was that we were never alone.

As our anticipation of seeing each other increased, so did my terror of where it would lead. Over and over I told myself this could not be, that John was promised to someone else and I was only encouraging his deceit and mine. How could I even begin to allow myself such thoughts? Hadn't I learned anything after the hurt I'd caused Bobby and Melissa? And I couldn't imagine disappointing Daddy again. Particularly now, when I held so much of his recovery in my hands. How hurt he would be if I made a foolish choice, once again blackening my name and leaving a destroyed relationship in my wake. And how terribly that pain could affect him! What if he became depressed, lost his determination to improve? Just as deeply I worried about Mama, knowing that if she saw the truth in our eyes, she would blame me solely for it.

And even if the situation were different, if John were free, why should I think I could handle a relationship? I'd tried with Roger and Michael, wanting to love them. Yet in the end neither could push aside the much deeper love for Danny still imbedded in my heart.

As the days passed, the conflicting emotions raged inside me until I thought I would burst. Thoughts of John intermingled with memories of Danny, making me ache with loneliness. I fought to maintain my cheerfulness in front of Daddy, digging deeper and deeper within myself to dredge up energy for our therapy sessions. Meanwhile I had to remain on an even keel with Mama while the whirling inside me made me testy and defensive.

One evening at supper, prompted by no one, Mama brought up the subject of John and Sharon's wedding. She spoke of how Miss Jessie would probably be the one to sew the bridal gown and attendants' dresses. How pretty the church would be, all in red and green for a December wedding. How beautiful Sharon would look, and how pleased everybody in town was at the match. Mama's face remained impassive as she spoke, but I could have sworn she was talking just to me. I imagined John's wedding and couldn't eat another bite. When I pushed my plate away, Mama shot me an irritable look at my ungratefulness for her cooking. It was all I could do to be polite. Washing the dishes after supper, I managed to break a glass and cut my finger. And Daddy wasn't as motivated as usual in our evening therapy session, so I had to pull him through it, gritting my teeth and trying to look happy. When it was finally over and Mama put him to bed, I retreated to my room, exhausted from the day and sick at heart.

Falling on my bed, I buried my face in my pillow and sobbed. I couldn't stand another day of this turmoil. Part of me wanted to pack my things and steal away in the night, never to return. I cried and cried until finally, in despair, I did something I hadn't done in years. I began to pray. It was anything but a prayer of meekness. I railed at God, asking why he had brought me back to Bradleyville only to hurt me more than ever. What had happened to his promise that I would find rest for my soul? And what had happened to his promise to Granddad that I would be the one to reach my mother? What a laugh that was!

"Just help me with Mama and John and Daddy," I begged God, my body shaking with sobs. "Please! I don't know how I can do this anymore."

Finally I cried myself to sleep, holding on to the hope that God would do something—anything—to rescue me from the path I found myself on. But as I tossed and turned that night, my fitful dreams were full of John.

In the midst of this upheaval I called Little Rock less and less often. I'd fallen too far out of the loop and could give little help. Surprisingly, it failed to bother me. I was simply too caught up in my current situation. One day Quentin Sammons listened to me proudly recount Daddy's improvements and commented, "You'll have him ready for work in four weeks after all. We'll be happy to have you back." I hung up the phone, not knowing what to feel. *Four weeks.* How could I say good-bye to John in four weeks? I imagined sitting in the silence of my small white house in Little Rock, still loving Danny, missing John, and was filled with a longing that terrified me.

By the time my fifth week in Bradleyville drew to a close, Daddy could stand with support. John ordered him a walker, and on Friday afternoon I drove to a medical supply company in Albertsville to pick it up. I also revisited the hardware store, buying more paint for the house. Having completed the kitchen, I had offered to do the hallway and bathroom, desperate to keep busy.

"Look what I got for you, Daddy!" I exclaimed when I returned, showing him the walker. "We'll start tomorrow morning when you're fresh, okay? Wanna do something now until supper, play our game?"

We laughed like a couple of kids as he tried to bounce the rubber ball into Mama's drawer and failed repeatedly. "That floppy wrist of yours will get better, you'll see." I fell to my knees, fetching the ball once again. He tried another time and the ball bounced weakly and rolled under the bed. "Oh, great," I teased, "now you've done it."

He kept at it diligently for ten more minutes, then gave up. "No more," he said, sighing.

"All right. We'll try again later." I pushed him into the living room. "You haven't been out today; want to go for a walk?"

Mama instantly appeared from the kitchen, drying her hands. "I'll do it."

I was struck by her possessive tone. "Fine."

Seeing Daddy's eyes flick back and forth between us, she softened her expression. "There's chicken baking in the oven," she informed me. "We'll eat when we get back."

Together we bumped Daddy down the porch steps, a chilled silence echoing between us. She made a light comment about the weather as she began to push him down the sidewalk, and I marveled at her unpredictability.

Suddenly alone in the house, I sank onto the couch as depression began to seep through me once more.

After a few minutes a knock sounded at the door. Lifting my head tiredly to see who'd arrived, I froze. *John.* My heart skipped a beat. Somehow I raised myself from the couch.

"You're early," I heard myself say as I opened the screen door.

"Got through quicker than usual." He looked around. "Sounds awful quiet."

My throat went dry. "Mama's taken Daddy on a walk; they won't be long." I hesitated, debating. "Can you wait?"

"Sure."

We looked at each other.

"Do you want some tea?"

"That would be great."

"I'll just ... go get it." Numbly I escaped to the kitchen, feeling the house's emptiness around us. John followed. Hadn't I known he would? Leaning against the counter, he affected nonchalance as he asked me about Daddy and painting the house and was I done yet or did I intend to paint the roof as well? I reached into the refrigerator for the tea, into the cupboard for a glass, extracted ice from a tray, listening to his questions and answering so casually, aware of our aloneness, aware that he was aware. I offered him the glass and was sure he would notice my trembling hand. "Here you go."

"Thank you." He took a drink, watching me. I wandered toward the window, remarking about how long it had been since we'd seen rain. He set the glass down and it clinked against the tile.

"Celia."

I focused on the old oak tree Kevy and I used to swing on. My heart performed an odd little dance.

"Celia."

John stepped in front of me, forcing my eyes up to his. He placed his hands gently on my shoulders and before I knew it, the space between us disappeared and our arms were around each other, his mouth on mine. We clung together, kissing, drinking in the taste of each other, and then he pulled away, his hair thick between my fingers. "I've wanted to do that since the first day I saw you," he breathed, kissing me again, and I was falling as I responded, my loneliness spinning away. "You don't know how much I've wanted it," he murmured. "You don't know."

Yes, I did.

I was shaking. "They could come back anytime."

He cupped my face in his hands. "Promise me we'll find a way to see each other."

"John, I . . . we can't—"

"Yes, we can. We *can.*"

"But—"

"Listen to me, Celia; listen to your heart. I've given up trying to push this away; you're all I think about."

"I'm afraid."

He drew me to him. "Don't be."

I melted against him, remembering how Danny used to hold me so long ago. I couldn't let go of John; I was terrified and I could not let go. I didn't know how long we were there, his hand stroking my head. Only when my parents returned, Mama calling for help to get the wheelchair up the stairs, did we wrench apart, my body on another plane, my feet moving through the living room, my hand opening the screen door as

I remarked that I was just getting Dr. Forkes some tea and did they have a nice walk? John appeared behind me, collected, glass in hand.

"So glad you're getting out, William," he said casually. "You'll have no excuse now; we'll expect to see you in church Sunday."

The actions and words swirled around me. The azure sky, Daddy's exuberance, Mama hovering while John maneuvered the wheelchair up the stairs, the smell of baking chicken permeating the house—everything was the same and nothing was the same as John efficiently conducted his medical examination, chatted with us briefly, then left. As he drove off, I announced to Daddy that we were due for a therapy session, and soon I was urging him to lift his arm, curve his fingers, rotate his ankle, while memories of choices, love, and secret meetings tumbled through my head . . .

~ *1979* ~

chapter 44

"M ary Lee," I begged, "get me out of here. I've got to see Danny."
I'd called her on Saturday, the day after the reading of Grand-dad's will. I could not think, could not study. I couldn't stand to see Grand-dad's empty place at the supper table and so did not eat. Nor could I stand to be near Mama, whose streaming hurt over Granddad's last wishes had funneled into cold indifference toward me. Surely Granddad's prediction about me and Mama would prove to be nothing more than a desperate deathbed wish.

Mary Lee hesitated, saying her parents were home.

"Please. I'll do anything."

So my bad little good-hearted friend picked Danny and me up and drove three miles into the chilled country, where she dropped us off on a dirt road, saying she would return in an hour.

"Where are you going? You can't be seen!" I cried. "I'm supposed to be with you."

She waved me away. "Relax; you underestimate my abilities." And she was off, my beautiful and rich friend who would travel Europe in the summer as a graduation present and drive her fancy car to the University of Kentucky in the fall.

Danny and I perched on a fallen oak stretched across the rutted road. "Tell me now," I said, shivering against his chest, "about your job."

He wrapped his arms around me, stroking my hair. "Cousin Lee's great uncle, Joel Case, found me a job down at the Miami port, where the big cruise ships come in. He says they're as big as buildings, holdin' hundreds of people. They got ballrooms and bars and theaters, bowling alleys and even swimming pools, just like a grand hotel. There's crews that sail with 'em, but when they pull into port, they need extra going over. Cleaning, checking the engines and instruments and all the machinery, making sure the thing's in tip-top shape. Workin' on machinery comes easy to me; what I don't know I'll learn right quick. Mama's got a job, too, cleaning rooms. And we can stay with the Cases until we save enough money to rent a place. It's perfect, Celia."

I was silent. Perfect was having him beside me. Perfect was my mama saying we could date this year. Perfect was anything but being left behind.

"Well, what do you think?"

"I'm glad for you. I know it's what you want."

"It's not what I'd choose, Celia. But it's what must be, under the circumstances."

I buried my face in his neck. "You're excited, I can tell. You're just bein' quiet because it's been such an awful week for me. I know you, Danny. You're thinking about the ocean and beaches, thinking about sailing on one of those ships to other places, other people. I know you love me, but your thoughts aren't here. They've left already."

"That ain't—that's not true. Sure, I think a going. And in a way I can hardly wait, because I'll be gittin' outta this town. You know what I think about? The first night away, when I can really sleep, not having to worry about Daddy beatin' Mama senseless. I think about her being free and happy for once. She's been so good to me. It's time I paid her back."

I dug my fingers into his jacket. "I don't want you to go! I just lost Granddad; I can't lose you too. Daddy's working most of the time, and when he's home, he's not really there. Mama hates me. Kevy's really all I've got and he's only a kid; he's not you. I want you."

"Celia," he said, holding me tightly, "don't do this. Please."

"I can't help it. I *can't*." Clinging to him, I cried and cried. Cried for him, for Granddad, for a mama like his that I never had. I cried for his mama's fear and his stinking daddy touching my hair at Tull's, for Danny's kisses and my lonely nights spent feverishly drawing oceans and beaches. Even as I cried, I knew I was being selfish, that he deserved this lucky chance. I wished desperately for Granddad's money now. So willingly I would give it to Danny so he could buy a house nearby. "Why can't you work at the mill?" I accused, hating myself for asking it. I felt his shoulders slump.

"Celia." His voice was quiet. "I can't stay here. Mama and I got to sneak off without Daddy knowin', to somewhere he can't find us. He'd kill her for sure if he knew she was planning on leaving, and turn a gun on me next. We wouldn't be safe living anywhere around here. You know that."

Yes, I did.

"So you got to keep it real quiet, okay? Nobody else knows we're goin' except Miss Jessie and Cousin Lee. He's gonna lend us money for the bus."

We were unusually quiet when Mary Lee picked us up, her boyfriend, Mike, beside her. She took in my red eyes and Danny's stone face with a glance. "It's been a hard week for you, hasn't it?" she said, patting me on the shoulder.

If she only knew.

April rolled in with a hint of warmth, daffodils blooming. My seventeenth birthday came and went, uncelebrated. Mama was too wrapped up in her own grief; Daddy never remembered dates. Danny was ashamed that he had no money for a present. "Even if you did," I told him, "you should save it for leaving." Kevy spent three weeks of his allowance on a set of watercolors, which he presented me with great pride.

One by one my friends turned seventeen also. Mona was in Danny's class and would be eighteen in October but was distressed that nobody was coming to call. Barbara excitedly awaited her seventeenth birthday in June. Somehow she'd managed to meet an Albertsville boy her parents approved of. Evidently, that town wasn't total Sin City after all.

Bobby Delham worked up his courage to catch me at school one day. "Celia, got a minute?" He had grown to be good-looking—tall and quiet, his generous lips known for their rueful smile. He was dependable and gentle. Well-liked and respected. And I could never love him.

He licked his lips, chocolate brown eyes gazing at me fondly. "I know it's a bad time to visit your folks, so I don't want to do that unless I know you'd ... What I'm tryin' to say is, now that you're seventeen, would you go out with me if they said it was all right?"

My face froze. I didn't want to hurt him, but the thought of Mama gladly accepting his request made me sick inside. "I'm sorry," I replied quietly. "I can't."

"Why?"

"You know why."

He flicked his eyes in frustration. "Celia, that's not goin' to happen; you know that. And meanwhile I'm here. I've always been here. I've liked you since eighth grade."

I've loved you for years. Danny's words floated through my head.

"I know, Bobby. And you're right—it's not fair. But I can't help what I feel."

"You're not as smart as I thought you were, Celia." His voice thickened with hurt. "Go on, then; I'll leave you alone. Someday you'll be sorry. And then you'll come to *me.*"

Within a month he started dating Melissa. Sometimes I'd see him drive by in his daddy's car on the way to her house, slowing down for a glimpse of me.

The days were both quiet and frothing, uneventful and filled with emotion. The whole town missed Granddad. I couldn't go anywhere without hearing about him and his stories. It must have driven Mama crazy, those war tales popping up even after his death. No one could miss him as much as I did. Once my heart had been full. Now there was a hole in it. That was Granddad.

In my grief God seemed very far away. "Why did you take him so soon?" I'd rail at the heavens. "Before Mama could soften to him and when I need him so much? If this is your idea of a plan for us, I don't want any part of it!"

Danny and I stole away when we could, holding each other in a field or on Mary Lee's couch, hanging on to the time we had with quiet desperation. He was studying hard for senior finals and still working at home. "The farm," he said bitterly one day, shrugging, "can burn to the ground for all I care. All that work. All my life. And what has it got me?"

Sometimes his eyes would fill with that faraway look, and I'd know he was thinking about those ships, big as buildings. Jealousy and fear would well within me. *Danny, I know you have to go,* I'd cry inside, *but don't leave me with your heart.*

I had a full-time job for the summer, baby-sitting the Harding kids, and I was glad for it. I didn't care about the money, but I did need something to keep me busy after Danny left.

After Danny left.

It became a finality in my thoughts, a day when time would stop. To think of a summer without him or walking alone through the school hallway next fall. Most of all to think of the look on Mama's face when she heard Danny had gone, fleeing into the night with his mama without a backward glance for me. How smug she would be, how vindictive. "I told you he'd break your heart," I could hear her say. "I told you he'd leave." And I'd have to endure it in silence for a whole year until I could run to him, taking my money—my fortune—which could have been hers.

Then one day in early May Danny didn't come to school. And after that things happened quickly, like a broken clock spinning its hands around and around.

Maybe he's just sick, I told myself when he hadn't shown up after second period. But I knew it was something else. Danny's absence could only signal trouble.

I hung around our living room all evening, desperate for a chance to call his house but finding none. The following day he was absent again. *Dear God, please protect him*, I prayed. After school I told Kevy I had an errand to run and set off downtown to Miss Jessie's sewing shop. "What's wrong with Danny?" I whispered breathlessly, leading her aside. "He hasn't been at school for two days."

Dread rimmed her eyes. "Maybe he's sick."

"Danny's never sick."

Absently she set the pincushion in her hand down on a worktable. "I don't dare go out there if something's wrong. And Lee's at the mill."

"Phone them."

She did but got no answer.

Fear built up inside me. "I'm goin' over there right now."

"No, you're not!"

"Yes, I am, Miss Jessie; he could be in trouble. What if his daddy found out they're leavin'? What if his mama's hurt? What if *he's* hurt?" I tossed my books down and turned to run, not caring about her employees' stares.

"No, Celia!" She caught my arm. "You can't. If something's goin' on, it's too dangerous. You know that. You've seen it."

I couldn't look at her. We'd never spoken of that summer day almost two years ago. "I don't care what that man does to me; I just want to see if Danny's all right."

"Celia! Listen to me. What if nothing's wrong and you show up? You could spoil it all. You could tip off Anthony that Danny's plannin' something. Don't do it."

"Then what do we do?"

"I'll call Lee at the mill. Maybe he can run over."

When Lee finally came to the phone, he said he'd drive to the Canders' right away. I waited for what seemed an eternity, hands clenched. Every time the phone rang, I jumped. Finally Lee called from the Canders' house. He'd been through every room and the barn, he said, fearing at each turn what he might see. But no one was home and the truck was gone. There wasn't a thing we could do.

"It's probably nothing," Miss Jessie consoled. "All this anxiety, and you'll find out they just went into Albertsville. Go home now. Don't worry."

Again there was no chance to try calling Danny from home. Miss Jessie promised me Lee would stop by the Canders' again after work, and if anything had changed, he'd let me know. Mama had plenty of questions, wondering where I'd gone after school and eyeing me suspiciously when I said I'd visited Miss Jessie to talk about baby-sitting. By the time I'd done the supper dishes, I couldn't stand it anymore, pulling Daddy into my bedroom and begging him to let me have the car to check on Danny.

"Celia, I can't let you go to his house alone."

"Then come with me, but I have to see if he's okay. Please. It's the last thing I'll ever ask you!"

Mama rounded the corner at the worst moment, carrying a folded stack of clothes. "Young lady," she announced, glaring accusingly at Daddy, "you're not goin' anywhere."

That night I couldn't sleep. Staring out my window at the streetlight, I begged God for Danny's protection. I just knew something terrible had happened. I *felt* it.

chapter 45

For a long time after that day, Bradleyville would rattle with macabre fascination over the event. But no one else really knew what had taken place. Danny couldn't tell me the details at school with all the eager ears around. Not until we could sneak out again would I finally hear the full story. When we met each other on a Saturday, once again courtesy of Mary Lee, we sat on the log across the dirt road where I'd cried into his jacket. Wearily he told me, his voice streaked with sadness.

"The first morning I didn't come to school," Danny began, scuffing at the ground with his shoe, "we'd gotten a call from Lee's great uncle, needin' to talk about our arrival in Miami. Plus he needed information to fill out papers for us. Daddy was up early for some reason and he overheard Mama talking. He said he'd kill us both.

"So I stayed around the house, not leavin' Mama's side, letting him know that to get to her he'd have to go through me first, and he'd be right sorry for trying. I wasn't goin' to start anything, afraid a what I'd do to finish it and thinking he just wasn't worth ruining my life. But if he made one move, I was ready.

"Something strange settled on me that day and the next, Celia, while I waited, steppin' around Daddy, steppin' in front a Mama. I knew something was going to come of it all, 'cause I sure wasn't about to give up my plans a leaving, and Daddy wasn't about to let us go. Meantime Mama and I prayed a lot and did chores while Daddy drank, swallowin' that whiskey in between shooting his mouth off, cursing and yelling like a crazy fool. By the second day Mama and me was so tired. We hadn't gotten any sleep that night, sitting up behind my locked bedroom door with a chair pushed under the knob. He disappeared the next afternoon, probably sleeping it off in the field, and we left in the truck, catchin' a nap under some bushes way down the riverbank. After supper time had come and gone, we got hungry and slunk home. He still wasn't there. And neither was the shotgun he always kept in the back closet off the kitchen."

Danny fell silent for a moment, his green eyes glinting in the dappled sunlight. "It's hard to explain, thinkin' back on it. But like I said, something strange happened to me. Staring at the empty closet corner where the gun always stood, I told myself this was it, and may God help me. We had the truck. I coulda taken Mama over to Cousin Lee's and fetched Bill Scutch. We coulda hid out for the night. But what then? Another day like that one, and another? Waitin' for my daddy to come busting through the door, drunk and steel-eyed mean, a loaded shotgun in his hands? It was a long minute, Celia, staring at that corner. I remembered so many things right then. I thought a my earliest memories, hearing Daddy holler at Mama. Her soft voice begging him not to wake me. I thought a fights at school, the way the kids looked and whispered. Gerald Henley's nose goin' *crunch*. You and Mr. Rose. And that time I saw you standing in the field, watching my daddy and me fight. I thought I'd die that day. And kissing you the first time, telling you I loved you. Looking for you at school every day, my heart dropping at the sight a you. I thought a the plans Mama and I had for going and what a price I was paying for it, leavin' you behind. And somehow all a that, my whole *life*, came down to staring at that empty corner. I prayed to God for help and wisdom. I had no idea then what I would do."

"Oh, Danny," I whispered, pushing the hair off his forehead. "It's okay."

Danny told his mama to lock herself in his bedroom and slide furniture against the door. "Now listen to me, Mama," he commanded, looking down on her white face. "No matter what you hear, you don't come out unless I tell you. Understand?"

She gazed at him with a mother's fear. "He'll kill you, Danny."

"No, he ain't. Now git on inside."

Mr. Cander came home after dark. He thumped up the steps, bellowing for his son, the shotgun trailing from one hand and a bottle of whiskey in the other. Danny appeared out of a shadow and eased the gun away. "Evenin', sir," he said quietly. "Been waitin' for you."

"Gimme back my gun, boy; I'm gonna need it! Where's that no-good mama a yours?"

"Sleepin'. Come on, Daddy, let's sit on the porch, talk awhile."

Bleary-eyed, his father processed the invitation. "Awright. We'll share the whiskey."

They sat on the porch, Danny's father swigging the bottle hungrily. Danny pretended to take his own sips. He knew he should stop his father; the man had probably drunk enough to near kill himself. But fear for his mama stopped him. He couldn't risk getting his daddy riled up.

Finally the bottle emptied. Danny felt sure his daddy would pass out. Instead the man swayed to his feet. "Le's go get in the truck and head outta town," he slurred. "'Member how fast I used to take those curves when you was little, laughin' when you was scared silly? I'll show ya how fast I can take 'em now."

"No, Daddy," Danny said. "You're too drunk."

His daddy guffawed long and loud. "Ho, boy," he bragged, "you know how good I am at those curves; I could take 'em with my eyes closed, no matter how much I been drinkin'."

"Don't do it, Daddy; not this time."

Mr. Cander started down the steps, using the banister for support. "Come with me, boy. We'll have a good ol' time, roust some chickens right outta their beds."

Danny opened his mouth to protest again. Then closed it.

His daddy thwacked the banister. "Aw, never mind; I'll jus' go by myself."

Danny did not stop him. He stood on the porch, watching his daddy stumble to the truck, open the door, fall in. The engine rumbled. Tires spinning, the truck spun around as his daddy drove away, kicking up dust that swirled in the fingertips of the porch light. The last thing Danny saw was the one unbroken red taillight as the truck skidded onto the road.

Danny couldn't believe what he'd done. As guilt and fear hit him in the chest, he told himself that what happened next was in God's hands. Feigning calm, he walked on shaky legs to knock at his own bedroom door, telling his mama she could come out.

Danny had not allowed himself to think the worst. He never thought his daddy would be hurt badly. Perhaps just enough to need a day or two of doctoring—giving Danny time to send his mama safely to Florida. But the outcome made Danny now believe God would judge him for not saving his father. I insisted that wasn't so. It wasn't Danny's fault; his daddy had brought it all on himself. To the very end Anthony Cander fought for the last word. And in a way he won. You could argue he was too drunk to know what he was doing. Maybe. But he was also mean and small-hearted, hating his son for the goodness he saw in him, blaming the town of Bradleyville for his own wretchedness. For that, I believe, he decided not to turn right at Main Street. Instead he yanked the steering wheel into a rubber-burning left turn, then went flying over the railroad tracks and screaming through town.

The skid marks told the rest of the tale. Flooring the accelerator after bouncing at an angle off the tracks, he managed to straighten out momentarily. Then he lost control. Why did he have to hit Tull's? Danny wondered. I'd guess that was his daddy's final act of rebellion against the town. Tull's, where Danny had sent him reeling in front of the town patriarch. Tull's, the watering hole of Bradleyville.

Maybe in the recesses of his mind Mr. Cander knew. Maybe not. Whatever he was thinking, in that split second he jerked the wheel left again. He careened across the street and smashed up the curb in metal-grinding flight to sail through Tull's front window, smearing medicine, lotions, and tooth powder over the aisles. The truck crashed into the red-cushioned booth where Granddad had sat, and stopped with a jolt at the crushed soda fountain, its broken pipes spraying the felled stools, the truck, and the wasted merchandise. Mr. Cander's head punched through the windshield, his torso slamming against the twisted steering wheel and its horn, sending it braying eerily into the shattered night.

Two deaths in such a short time in Bradleyville. But the town did not mourn the passing of Anthony Cander. There was no funeral, no eulogies. Neither Danny nor his mama wanted that. Instead he was buried by his wife and son in a wooden box out among the daisies of the field in which I once stood, frozen in horror, witnessing his drunken wrath.

"I feel so many different things," Danny said, weeping quietly as we held each other, sitting on the fallen oak. "I killed my daddy as surely as if I'd taken that shotgun to him. I pray for forgiveness but I don't know if God's hearin' me. I feel so tired. And empty. At the same time, the house is peaceful and I feel such relief about that, for Mama and me.

"After the terrible sin I done, that relief is the worst of all."

chapter 46

With less than a month to go before Danny graduated from school, he and his mama put their dilapidated farm up for sale, accepting the first bid that came along, afraid it would be their last. Danny used the proceeds to pay off the mortgage and buy a used Chevrolet Impala. By the time he'd paid Mr. Tull for the damages, apologizing with his head hung and dreaming of the day when he'd never have to face the man again, he had only enough money to drive to Miami. There was no need to keep quiet about leaving now. And throughout the town, people looked at me with a mixture of pity and vindication. "He's runnin' off," I could imagine them whispering. "His daddy shamed her and now he's turnin' tail, him and his quiet mama. That's what happens, you get mixed up with the wrong kind."

Amid all the tumult Danny studied hard to the end. The final day of school he picked up his diploma early, as he'd arranged with the principal. We stood on the sidewalk, staring at the diploma, the June humidity a soggy blanket around our shoulders. For my own piece of paper we'd spend a year apart. He and his mama planned to leave early in the morning. They were packed and had been squeezing into the Hardings' house for the past week. At that moment I was willing to leave my inheritance and all respect behind and run off with them.

Danny was ambivalent about going—excited, terrified, filled with hurt. He didn't want to leave me, but he yearned for freedom from Bradleyville. *The first hill outside of town*, I thought, *and he'll be laughing with giddiness, the caged bird now flying.* I was weeping inside. *Danny, please don't leave me with your heart.*

"I can't say good-bye like this, standin' at school," he told me, ache in his eyes.

"Me either."

We gazed at each other, breathing the hot June air, the jubilant chatter of freed students filtering around us. "Come tonight," I implored, "in your car. I'll meet you at the corner of Main after everyone's gone to bed. I'll slip out. Eleven o'clock."

"Celia, no. I can't leave you shamed like that. Anybody sees us, the whole town'll talk."

"I don't care."

"You don't know what it's like, havin' the whole town against you."

"I don't *care*. Please come. Because if you don't, I'll show up at the Hardings; I'll shame us all."

He slid the diploma into his notebook. "You sure that's what you want?"

"You know I do."

"My mama'd have a fit. What am I supposed to tell her and the Hardings?"

"Wait till they're in bed."

"Mama won't sleep all night; she's too excited."

"Then tell her nothin'. Just leave."

"She won't let me go."

"Yes, she will. She stayed in the bedroom that night, didn't she, while you took care of your daddy? You bear all the guilt yourself, but you think she didn't know what could happen? You're eighteen years old, Danny; she'll let you go. You did that for her. She'll do this for you."

He touched my cheek. "I don't have the strength to fight you. I want to be with you too much."

"Then come."

I took my bath early. Retired to my room, saying good night to Kevy and Daddy. Locked the door, dressed with care. A light blue knit top, tucked into the waistband of a knee-length skirt. Bare legs and sandals. I brushed my hair until it rippled down my back, then waited, palms sweaty. At ten o'clock I turned out my light and sat in the dark, wishing the streetlight wasn't so bright. The next fifty minutes took forever.

Sneaking out at night was a terrible gamble. If people found out, they'd never understand. If God tried to talk me out of it, I couldn't hear him.

Finally my watch read ten-fifty. Cautiously I opened my door, holding my thumb over the lock so it wouldn't snap. The hallway was dark and quiet. Slipping out, I pulled my door closed behind me, releasing the knob with precision and lifting my fingers away. Crept through the living room and kitchen. Eased open the back door and stepped onto the porch. The night was warm, a slight breeze. A half moon hung low, peeking between the leaves of our oak tree and illuminating our swing.

Sneaking down the porch steps was the hardest; they tended to creak. But nothing would stop me, not even my mama discovering me in midstep, hand trailing the banister. I'd simply run.

I made it without a hitch. The soft grass beneath my sandals brought a soundless sigh of relief to my lips. I walked around the far side of the house so as not to pass underneath Mama's window. I flinched at the streetlight, head swiveling, but no one was near. Within a couple minutes I'd walked the block to Main. The stoplight was busily at work, changing from yellow to red to green, commanding cement. At the right corner of the intersection stood the willow tree, its branches a deep, swaying curtsy. I stood beneath it, drawing back from light, and waited.

It wasn't long before I heard Danny's car, its slow glide reverberating between the houses. I appeared from the shadows, waved him to a stop, and slipped into his car. Closed the door as quietly as I could. His eyes traveled my face. "Where to?"

"Our trees."

He turned the car around and headed downtown. I scooted next to him and he put his arm around me. When we were past town and the railroad tracks, he parked on a dark, narrow road and we got out to walk, hand in hand.

"It looks so different at night," I breathed, seeing the familiar spread of leaves shine dimly under the rising moon.

"Come on." He pulled me forward.

The calling of crickets ceased as we picked our way through dark grass, watching our feet. "It's been so long since we've been here," I said. The river was a lazy wide ribbon of silver and black. The colors of Jake Lewellyn's marble.

"Uh-huh. I always liked it after dark."

"You've been here at night?"

"Lots a times. When things got too crazy, I'd come here and think about you."

Another part of Danny I'd known nothing about. How many other things did I not know?

We sank down in the grass and held each other tightly, unable to speak.

"Just think, Celia," Danny said, breaking the silence, "the next time we see each other, we'll be gittin' married. We'll be together the rest of our lives."

"Promise me we'll see a justice that very day. I don't want to wait a minute longer than we have to."

"You won't get to have a wedding." He rubbed my arm as if in comfort. "I thought every girl wanted a wedding."

"Every girl doesn't have you."

I could feel his smile in the darkness.

"We got to get our lives straight," he told me. "We got to pray every day and ask Jesus to get us back on track. I been prayin' a lot lately, and I believe he's heard me, even after all I've done. Your granddad was a wise man. That night he talked to me at your house, he warned me about going out into the world, leaving you behind. 'All kinds of new temptations'll come your way,' he said. But he told me I only had to do one thing: never take my eyes off Jesus. 'It's like walkin' a tightrope,' he said. 'You look at the emptiness around you, you'll be terrified. You look at your feet, you'll fall.' We got to do that, Celia, keep looking at Christ. Not just this year but ever after that. I don't know about you, but I'm afraid that if I look away one more big time, I just won't survive it."

I wondered how I'd survive the year in any circumstance.

"We will, Danny; we'll both keep focused. I can't believe God would let me lose you now. We've come through too much already."

We held each other for hours into the night, talking, planning, dreading the dawn. When he finally urged that we had to go, he lifted my chin and kissed me one last time, darkness flowing around us until the rest of the world fell away and there was only Danny, that moment. I wanted that kiss never to end.

"I love you, Celia," he whispered into my hair. "Remember how much I love you."

"I love you, too, Danny. I love you, too."

Then I burst into tears, clinging to him. "Danny, don't leave me! I can't be here without you, not now. Your daddy's not here anymore; you can stay in Bradleyville this year!"

"Celia, don't." He pulled me to his chest. His crying sounded low in his throat. "Don't do this to me. I love you too much."

We cried together, rocking, until we could cry no more, and we sank against one of the trees, exhausted. Still we were unable to leave, gazing at each other's shadowed faces, tracing a fingertip down a cheek, smoothing hair from a forehead, pledging our love forever.

By the time I woke up in my bed the next morning, trembling and vacant, I knew he had gone.

chapter 47

I thought I'd die of loneliness after Danny left. Bradleyville offered little to console me, save for Kevy and Daddy. Mama remained as indifferent as always, never once so much as mentioning the hurt she knew I felt. I told myself bitterly I should be glad she wasn't overtly gloating. And of course Granddad's room was empty, washing me with grief. Only our letters, so painstakingly written, got me through the days. They skimmed back and forth, passing each other in airplanes and mailrooms and through the arthritic fingers of Mrs. B. at the post office. My letters declared my love. Danny's letters declared his adoration, even while laced with the wonder and fascination of the world we would one day see together.

June 6

Dear Celia,

> *You wouldn't believe the ocean! It's so blue and the waves look so powerful. I like to hear the way they hiss on the sand. The water is beautiful under the moon. The beaches are packed. Kids make sand castles and couples are kissing. I miss you so much!*

All that summer I baby-sat the Harding children, wiping noses and making peanut butter sandwiches while inwardly crying for Danny. My friends called occasionally but we had little to say. How could they understand my torture? Mary Lee I could have talked to. But she was off to Europe, running with the rich and beautiful. Mama and I avoided each other. I spent time with Kevy and went for evening walks with Daddy, who tried his best to assuage my sadness. He took to driving me into Albertsville for lunch every Saturday, pointing out boys my age. Feeling bad about his hurt for me, I almost told him of my plans with Danny numerous times. But I was afraid it would be more than he could keep from Mama and so remained silent.

August 15

Dear Celia,

Mama and I have found a small apartment. It's not in the best part of town, though. We have just enough for rent and food. But she's happy. She even hums while she cleans.

The ships really are big as buildings. My job seems easy after the farm. But life is not easy, because you're not here. The girls here make Mary Lee look like a kitten. Their swimsuits are shameless. Young boys and girls are together and no one cares. Bradleyville may be strict, but now I see the value of those ways.

The pangs of jealousy bit as I thought of Danny surrounded by half-dressed girls. Did they look at him the way Mary Lee had? How many gazed into those emerald eyes, wanting him? *Danny,* I wrote, *there's nothing here for me. I'm counting the months until I can be with you. Wait for me.* Danny answered that he ached for me, too, that the locket with my picture was always in his pocket.

Danny couldn't afford a phone and I had no privacy to talk anyway, so the letters continued to flow. *I'm saving every cent for you,* he wrote. *We can't live in this apartment when you come; you're used to so much better.* I knew we wouldn't have to live there; we'd have my inheritance. But still I did not tell him.

In late August Mr. B. retired, Lee Harding taking his place as mill manager. The church held an outdoor social to celebrate the two men, and most everyone came. Jake Lewellyn attended, sitting tiredly, absently tapping his cane. With no Thomas Bradley to nettle, he was withering away. *Mr. Lewellyn,* I thought, *I'm withering, too.*

Miss Jessie whispered to me of the letters she'd received from Patricia Cander. "She sounds very happy and proud of her son. But he's moody from missin' you." It may have been selfish but I was glad to hear it. He was the one who'd left, after all. Once his daddy was gone, he could have changed his plans, stayed in town with his mama and waited for me.

Mary Lee came with her parents, the bright spot of the day. She was back from Europe and leaving for Lexington the next week. "Look at you," I breathed. Her hair was even longer and her makeup perfect. Rich and beautiful Mary Lee. Was Danny seeing girls like this?

"I met a man in Paris," she gushed. "Ah, such a city!" Pulling at her shirt, she feigned a rapidly beating heart.

We wandered away from the crowd, and I told her about sneaking out to see Danny that last night. I had to tell somebody.

"You mean you managed to sneak out without little ol' me?" Throwing back her head, she laughed at the sun. I laughed with her. It had been a long time since I'd done that.

"When are you leavin' for Lexington?"

"In three days."

"Oh, Mary Lee, I'm so happy for you. But I'll miss talking to you."

"Yeah. I'll miss you, too." She fell silent for a moment. "You sneak a call to Danny every once in a while, don't you?"

"No. He doesn't have a phone."

"Oh, really," she said, the words wrapped in suspicion.

"He doesn't have the money."

"Everyone has the money for a phone. You should be able to get hold of him."

"He's savin' for when we're together."

"Mm. Well. You just keep writing him. Remind him you're here, languishing, while he's chasin' waves."

I didn't like her tone. Mainly because it reflected my own thoughts. *Mary Lee*, I thought, *not everybody is as fickle as you.*

Fall arrived. Leaves turned orange-gold, then skittered in brown crackles along Bradleyville streets. At school I ate lunch with Barbara and Melissa, enviously hearing about their dates, their boys coming to supper. "But I don't know about Bobby," Melissa confided. "His mind seems somewhere else."

I knew where his mind was. Still on me.

He'd arrived at our door the previous Saturday, lips pressed in vulnerability, wondering if I would give him a chance now that Danny had gone. *Poor Bobby*, I thought. Such courage it had taken to come to me again. "Bobby," I said gently as we stood on my porch, "you're calling on Melissa, my best friend. If she was to step outside her door right now and see you here, what would she think?"

He looked at his feet. "It'd be worth it, if you said yes."

"Bobby. Stay with her; she cares for you. You know who I love."

His dreams crumbled from his face. "*Why*, Celia? Why him? I've done everything. Even left you alone. He had nothin' to offer you. Now he's gone and he won't be back."

"He has himself. That's all I want. He's offered that and I'm takin' it."

He stared at me, eyes widening, as understanding seeped into his consciousness. The realization that I would leave Bradleyville to follow Danny shook him to the core. He turned away, holding in his hurt. My heart ached with remorse for him. If it weren't for Danny, maybe I could have loved him.

"I'm not goin' to tell Melissa you came. It would only hurt her."

"Yeah. Well. Be seein' you, Celia." As he crossed the sidewalk, he could not refrain from looking back. Mama drove in from the grocery store as he was leaving and gave me a pointed look.

October 21

Dear Danny,

What do you know, I had a gentleman caller yesterday. Remember good-looking, nice Bobby Delham? Always liked me, hated you. He let me know he'd drop Melissa like a hot potato if I'd just say yes. Mama was all over me about it, telling me I was a fool and that I could learn to love him. First time she'd spoken to me in days . . .

October 26

Dear Celia,

    I punched his prissy friend Gerald Henley in the nose; I suppose I can come back and punch Bobby. You tell him to stay away. I can't stand to think of somebody else talking to you about love. No one could love you like I do.

Ha! I thought, hugging the letter. The wild bird flown knew jealousy, too.

For Christmas Kevy got a new bike, slate blue and shiny. Throwing it on the melted snow of our lawn one Saturday in January, he fell into a porch chair next to me, sweat vaporizing off his head. "Waitin' for the mail?"

I nodded, shivering.

He looked at me pensively. "I miss Danny. You gonna see him again?"

I hesitated. "Sometime."

"When? How?"

"What are you, Mama's little spy?"

Kevy looked hurt. "No. I never told her nothin' before, did I, when y'all were kissin' at the river."

I reared back in my seat. "How would *you* know?"

"Because I peeked one time."

My mouth fell open. "Kevy!"

"Well, it was just once. I sorta got tired a fishin'. All's I did was sneak up and get a good look at y'all, then sneak back."

"I can't believe you did that!"

"Well, I didn't tell anybody. Especially Mama."

She would have killed me. "Kevy, you're sweet for not tellin'. But you never should have sneaked in the first place."

"I was just curious, that's all." He wiggled his shoulders. We were silent for a moment. "I kinda like somebody, too."

"You like a girl, Kevy! Who?"

"Promise you won't tell?" I nodded. "Cindy Halloway."

"Ah," I said, picturing a petite blond with brown eyes. I thought it was cute, Kevy liking a girl. Then it struck me that Kevy was the same age Danny was when he started liking me. Eleven. I stared at my brother. Such a kid. "Well, little brother, you just be nice to her. Maybe she'll like you back."

An exaggerated shrug. "Maybe. Well. I'm gonna ride down to Reid's house."

Watching him race off, I realized with a pang how much I would miss him when I left Bradleyville.

February 16

Dear Celia,

 A new ship came in yesterday, the fanciest yet. It's with Triton Cruise Lines. Mama teased me, saying wouldn't a honeymoon on that be fine. It must cost a fortune.

 Money is real tight and I worry about you coming. It's very hard here, lots of crime, people robbed and killed. Mama and I wanted to be away from Daddy; now we're afraid for her safety all over again. A woman can't even be on the streets alone. Miami may have an ocean but it's far from paradise. I dream about finding our ocean, Celia; my heart is heavy here. Especially without you. I just keep trying to keep my eyes on God, like your granddad said. I love you.

I read the letter over and over, despairing that Danny's dreams of freedom in Miami were slipping through his fingers like sand. Could Mama be right about Danny's wanderlust? About him breaking my heart? *No,* I told myself, *he loves me.* Even so, he had left. *Where next for you, Danny,* I wondered, crying in my room, *while I sit here missing you, the ocean waves mere paintings on my walls?* Many nights I agonized over whether to tell him about my inheritance. But Granddad was right; Danny had his pride. So I wrote only of my love.

Wait for me, Danny, I cried to myself. *Wait for me.*

March 16

The Triton's back again. That same girl was on it—Rachel. I don't know if I told you about her before. Her daddy owns the cruise lines. Anyhow, she says she thinks I could get a job on the ship! Sailing to the Caribbean Islands! And it pays a lot more! I told her I wouldn't leave Mama, but she says maybe Mama can work on board, too. Wouldn't that be something, Celia, me in the islands! When you come, maybe you could work, too, if you didn't mind, and we could all sail on it. The beaches aren't crowded, I hear, and there's a lot less crime. Maybe there I'll find our ocean. Can't wait till you come. I love you.

I hated that letter. My caged bird freed was flying. He'd promised it wouldn't happen, he'd *promised.* Even with our love, how could I compete with endless sand and a glittering horizon? If it weren't the beaches, it might be the girls who'd steal him away. I prayed and prayed at night, begging God not to let that happen. *Don't forget me, Danny,* I wrote him. *We'll be together soon.*

On April 4 he wrote that Rachel was back at port, declaring that the Caribbean was glorious—white beaches and blue water. *I want so much to see it!* he added. *I dream about having you there with me. It's less than three months now. I can't wait!*

A week after my eighteenth birthday Danny wrote that their apartment had been robbed. He'd carelessly left a week's pay in his dresser, and his mama lost a small radio. Danny was glad he'd had my locket with him.

I want to leave here so badly. I hate the place. Crime and noise everywhere. I want lots of quiet beaches. With you.

In mid April he ecstatically informed me that Rachel had returned and had arranged a job for him and his mama.

> *God's really watching over us. We leave in two days, probably by the time you read this. Rachel says we'll stop at lots of beautiful ports. I'll find the beach for us, Celia. Keep writing; I'll read all your letters when I get back in a couple weeks. I love you and miss you.*

Rachel, Rachel, *Rachel*. I pictured a rich girl with Mary Lee's face, long legs, red lips. Balling up the letter, I flung it against my wall.

I told myself it didn't matter, that Rachel was merely to Danny as Bobby was to me—an admirer who would never possess the object of her affection. I told myself Danny loved me more than oceans and that if money weren't a problem, he wouldn't have gone. If he only knew about my inheritance. When he returned to Miami, he could go back to his old job, wait it out until I got there. The extra pay wouldn't be so important. And Rachel could sail on her way.

For two days I agonized over my promise to Granddad. He would understand, I told myself; he'd agree with me under these circumstances. I had to tell Danny about my inheritance. I had to give him a way to leave the higher paying job. Finally I made my choice. I prayed that if Granddad was watching from heaven, he'd forgive me. Then I wrote Danny and told him.

April 27

Dear Celia,

> *My head's about to bust with so many thoughts! The Caribbean trip was incredible. Mama was in heaven. And now to hear you have so much money! Be sure you want me, Celia, before you bring such a fortune. I wouldn't want you to regret it. I'm supposed to provide for you, and now you'll be providing for me. I need your respect, Celia; promise me I'll still have it.*
>
> *One thing, though. I'm not going to go back to my old job like you suggested. If I continue to sail until you come, we'll have even more money. Besides, I like this new job so much better. We go again tomorrow. Back in two weeks. I love you.*

We. Had Danny been thinking of his mama when he used that word? Or Rachel?

Granddad had been right. And my vow to him had been broken for nothing. The words of Danny's letter blurred.

chapter 48

Mama had watched the letters arrive all year in silence. Sometimes I wondered why she let me have them. Perhaps she finally realized she could not control my heart. But when the flow slackened while Danny was at sea, she couldn't keep the smugness from her face. I would flip disconsolately through the mail on the dining room table, her eyes on my back.

"Celia," she demanded one afternoon, "what are you plannin' to do after graduating?"

I shrugged. "Baby-sit again in the summer."

Her mouth pinched. "I don't believe you."

"I don't care what you believe."

She recoiled. "You're a fool, Celia, if you're thinkin' of taking that money to that boy. He'd just squander it traveling around."

I couldn't stand hearing her call my Danny "that boy." "You're the fool, Mama. You don't know anything."

Her face flushed crimson. "How dare you talk to me like that!"

"I dare because you talk to me of Danny, when you don't know him at all!"

"I know what he is, Celia! He's just like your granddad. Independent. Searchin' for adventure. I tried to warn you and you wouldn't listen. Don't give your money to him! That money came from your great-granddad, who built the mill; that's how far back in our family it goes. Don't throw it away."

"I don't plan on throwin' it away."

"Then what are you goin' to do with it?"

"None of your business!"

"Celia!" she exploded. "Go to your room!"

"Mama, I'm eighteen years old now," I hissed. "You can't order me to my room."

Her palm hit the table with a smack. "You're still my daughter and you still live under my roof! I told you to go. Now get out of my sight!"

And I did, raging to myself that soon I'd get out of her sight, all right—get out and never come back.

May 5

Well, I'm back in the Caribbean! This port is just as beautiful the second time around. But I need you so bad, Celia. I sat on the beach last night wishing so much you were here.

But anyway, I want to tell you something really exciting. Triton also has ships that go to the Greek Isles. Rachel says she can get me and Mama on one of those ships soon, plus she can get a job for you. I know you have money but we should save it for a house later. Would you mind working on a ship for a while? Just imagine it, you and me in Greece! We'll find our ocean together after all.

I love you. One more month. Only one more month! I can hardly wait.

Miami. The Caribbean. Now Greece. Danny seemed to have completely forgotten about our plans to work part-time and go to college. Sailing to Greece with him did sound wonderful, but I couldn't even daydream about it. Not when I knew that girl Rachel would be on board. I didn't trust her for a minute. The more I thought about it, the more that fear consumed me. I tried to pray but couldn't, convinced that God was punishing me for my unwillingness to reach out to Mama. What if she had been right all along? Danny wanted me; Danny wanted the world. Which did he want most?

Two days later I received a letter from another port. The letter that would change my life. Clutching it to my chest, I headed for my room, completely unprepared for the words that would pierce my heart.

May 7

Dear Celia,

Writing this is the hardest thing I've ever done. Especially after my promises to your granddad and God and you. But I know it's the right thing to do. I've worn out my knees crying for God's forgiveness. I don't think he'll give it to me until I've asked yours as well. You should know the truth about me, especially since you're bringing so much money. It's only right to give you time to change your mind.

There's no good way to say it. I've been with a girl. Rachel. I never meant to. I don't love her and I want nothing else to do with her, ever. It just happened, Celia, that's all. We were on a beach at night, and I was wishing I was with you, thinking about our wedding night.

I'm dying, telling you this. Only a month to go, and I've gone and shamed myself like my daddy never could. Can you ever forgive me? I pray to God that you will. And will you still come? I'm going crazy waiting for your answer. Please say yes. I love you.

After the third reading I lay staring at the ceiling, Danny's letter having slipped from my hand onto the carpet. At first I felt nothing. Then I shook with rage and jealousy, burying my face in my pillow to cover the racking sobs. How could he? Our love had been so special, so perfect. We'd saved ourselves for our marriage, knowing it was the right thing to do. Now our wedding night could never be the same. *Danny*, I cried, *you've taken what we could have had, white and beautiful, and trashed it, dragging it through the mud.* I thought I would die. I sobbed all night, gasping, until the tears dried up. And I shook my fist at God, long and hard. Where had he been that night on the beach? How could he let this happen?

I did not attend school the next morning, did not venture from my room all day. "I'm sick," I called to Mama from behind my door, picturing her face, thinking surely she'd last seen me with a letter in my hand. *But you were wrong after all, weren't you, Mama?* I raged inwardly. Danny hadn't broken my heart by skipping off to distant lands. He'd broken it in the arms of someone else.

All that day and the next I did not eat. Daddy knocked on my door, begging to come in. "I can't talk, Daddy," I said, choking on tears. "Please." And dear Kevy tried and tried until I finally relented on the second day, sobbing against his thin, boyish arms.

Finally I was spent. I could feel no more, cry no more. I stopped railing at God; I didn't want to talk to him at all. An eerie calm settled over me, spreading like a thick blanket that enveloped me. And from somewhere deep within, somewhere dark and dismal, a new emotion arose. It seeped into my heart and mind; it fisted my hands and stiffened my legs. I didn't even try to push it away; instead I mucked in it until all other thought fled from me. Consciously I swept God aside, telling myself that he'd done little for me anyway. Then, free to do as I pleased, I planned my revenge. Not once did I stop to consider that I would hurt innocent people.

That evening, with purpose, I took a long bath. Naturally, I dressed in what I'd worn my last night with Danny. The blue top, the skirt and sandals. Ignoring my mother's hawklike expression, the curious stares of my brother and daddy, I marched to the phone and dialed Bobby Delham's number. He needed no prompting, this young man of whom my parents approved. "I'm goin' out," I informed them. Mama stared at me, astounded, a cold light dawning in her eyes.

I didn't lead Bobby to the oak tree canopy; that I could not do. I guided him instead to the rutted road where Mary Lee had taken Danny and me forever ago. We sat in the car, waiting for dark, and I watched him watch me with disbelieving anticipation. I did not care that I was about to destroy him, hoping only to destroy the one who had hurt me so much. When night fell, I urged Bobby into the field, where I seduced him, the boyfriend of my best friend. Even as he poured out I-love-you's, I felt nothing.

There is an emptiness worse than being alone.

Within two days a remorse-stricken Bobby would confess his sin to Melissa and stop dating her. "He loves you," she would whisper bitterly. "You ruined him for me. You, of all people."

When I got back home that night, clothes wrinkled and hair disheveled, Mama was still up. She took one look at me, at the blend of defiance and guilt on my face, and knew. I tried to slide past her but she caught my arm. "What have you done?" she hissed.

"Nothin'." My voice was flat.

Her fingers dug into my skin. "Tell me it's not what it looks like, Celia."

Not a word from me.

"*Why?*" she demanded. "How could you? After the way you've been raised!"

I wrenched free.

"What are we supposed to do now? The whole town'll know and you don't even care. Is this what Danny's done to you? Is *this* what he's taught you?"

With a sob I fled to my room, my soul blackened and sick to the core. I could not answer her question. Because the answer was yes.

Behind my locked door, hands shaking, I took paper and pen and told Danny everything.

chapter 49

May 16

Dear Celia,

I am dead inside. I know you did it only to hurt me, as I have hurt you. Now I feel the same pain. Let's forgive each other and go on. I love you with all my heart. Let's not do this to each other. You'll graduate in just two weeks. Come to me, Celia.

Even as I write this, I feel so mad—madder than I ever was at my daddy. Bobby's there with you. You're rich. You two could buy a fancy house, have a good life.

If you choose that, there will be nothing left for me here. I'll take that job on the ship to Greece, and when we get there, Mama and I will stay. There's passage and jobs for us; Rachel has arranged it. There's a job waiting for you too, if only you'll come. The ship leaves in three weeks on June 7. Until then I'll be at port here in Miami. This new job is a chance of a lifetime, and if I don't hear from you, I'm not going to lose it. But I don't want to go without you. I want _you._ Can you hear how bad I feel? God can help us through this if we'll only forgive each other. Will you forgive me, Celia? Will you forgive yourself? Will you come? Please. We had everything.

Wasn't life ironic? Danny and I had made it through three years of Bradleyville's trying to keep us apart. Now we could finally be together forever, and we were wrenching ourselves from each other as the town never had.

Looking down the tunnel of months and years, I saw only blackness without Danny. Even with what we'd done to each other, I still viewed my graduation as the birth of my new life. A life with him. We could not be apart. I loved him; he still loved me. We would go on, forgive, maybe someday forget. I didn't want Bobby. He didn't want Rachel, however beautiful and rich she might be. He didn't want Greece. He wanted me.

May 21

Dearest Danny,

I'm coming to you. You're right; if God can forgive us both, we can surely forgive one another. Please don't go. Please don't choose the world over me, even after what I've done. What you did with Rachel, you hadn't planned. What I did with Bobby was intentional. I was terribly wrong. I love you. I know you love me. Write back. Tell me you'll wait for me, Danny. Tell me exactly where to come. Wait. Please.

The following afternoon I slipped the letter into the slot at the post office. By the time I received his answer, graduation would be close at hand.

At school I could not bear to look Bobby Delham in the eye.

The days were interminable. I waited. People whispered and stared. Mama's outrage I could handle. Daddy's drawn face and grief were too much to bear. "You've disgraced this family and ruined a good boy," Mama spat. "The only thing you can do now is marry him quickly."

"Leave ... me ... *alone*," I warned her, deadly quiet.

Somehow I endured the last two weeks of school. I barely studied for finals. Managed to pass them all. Finally my last day arrived. But I hadn't heard from Danny. Surely with such an important letter, he wouldn't have lost a day in writing back. *Danny, Danny,* I cried to myself, standing on the sidewalk in front of the school building, *a year ago we planned our night together, right here. Where are you, Danny? Why haven't you written?*

I refused to attend my own graduation ceremony. Once again I could not eat. Sleep was beyond my grasp. Some dreadful sense told me that Danny had changed his mind about forgiving me. Unlike his, my sin had been so calculated and vindictive. And surely Rachel was there with him, sweet-talking, with more money than I'd ever have. At night I cried out to Jesus, pleading for him to do something. If he would just put me and Danny back together, I cajoled, I would serve him the rest of my life. I'd never, *never* take my eyes off him again for as long as I lived.

June 6 came. No letter. June 7—the day the ship sailed to Greece. Deep in my heart I knew Danny was on it, but still I clung desperately to hope. I thought of taking off for Miami to find him, just in case he'd stayed. But Miami was a big place. What if I couldn't find him and meanwhile his letter arrived? We could miss each other completely.

I began daily baby-sitting of the Harding children, a smile pasted on my face, my heart brittle, vacant. Finally the letter came. It was sitting on the dining room table when I got home from work, the small white envelope that would seal my life. Mama hovered as I snatched it up, a small gasp parting my lips. Not until I was in my room did I notice there was no return address. With pounding heart and shaking fingers I tore it open.

Celia,

> *We've arrived in Greece, Mama and me. And Rachel.*
> *I'm so sorry. I loved you with my life.*

Danny

chapter 50

In the days that followed I remember only darkness. Scenes of those days flit through my head like phantoms, shadowing despair. Somehow I managed to keep my job at the Hardings', sitting stupefied on their couch while the kids romped. In the evenings I slumped, immobilized, on my bed. Daddy knocked on my door many times but I would not let him in. Kevy grew constantly anxious, upset by the tomblike aura of our home. He tried his best to console me, to calm Mama, and failed at both. As for Mama, I did not think the rift between us could be worse. For in my grief over Danny, I could only lash out at her rebukes, full of my own hatred and spite. Yet if ever I needed her arms around me, it was then. But she offered no consolation, wrapped in her own pain and humiliation over my act with Bobby. I would not have guessed she had a heart to hurt. She seemed no more than a cube of ice, dripping with disdain.

Every moment was plagued with wondering how Danny could have left me. I reeled from blaming myself to blaming Mama to blaming God himself. God had betrayed me—not only with Danny, not only in failing to answer Granddad's biggest prayer, but in my very birth, for he'd placed me in the arms of an indifferent mother. Even Granddad's death seemed a relief to me then, for he would have been so bitterly disappointed in me.

You would think that I had learned enough. That in such grief my rebelliousness finally would have been broken and I would turn to God for rescue. Instead I shook my fist at the heavens, spitting in the very face of God. *Where are your promises to Granddad now?* I stormed. *Where's your healing for Mama and me?*

And then late one afternoon the unthinkable happened. The split-second event that would change our lives forever.

"Everyone's talkin'!" Mama screamed at me that day after I dragged home from work. "I can't take this shame! You must marry Bobby. If he'll still have you."

I slumped into Granddad's chair at the dining room table, full of grief and guilt and incensed that she spoke of this in front of Kevy. "Stop it, Mama!"

"Stop it? You started it! You've shamed us all."

Her piety was more than I could bear. "Nobody shames anybody but themselves, Mama!" I cried, pushing out of my chair. "I shamed me. *Me*, no one else!"

"Yes, you've shamed yourself." Her voice shook. "And Bobby and Melissa and your entire family. There is only one honorable thing now the two of you can do!"

"No!"

"Celia, Mama"—Kevy leaped up from the couch, tears in his eyes—"don't fight."

"Kevy, leave me alone," I spat.

"Please, Celia, don't fight! I can't stand to hear you fight anymore!"

"Kevy, get away from me!" I flung out both arms.

Suppressing a sob, he banged out the door while Mama's face turned purple. I heard the clank of his bicycle as he jerked it from the lawn.

"You got no cause to talk to your brother like that! He's never treated this family the way you have, never!"

"Leave me alone!"

Her voice seethed. "I will not leave you alone; I will *never* leave you alone until you make this right—in heaven and on earth. Get on your knees before God, Celia. Then marry Bobby Delham. And get out of my house."

"I don't have to marry anybody to get out of your house! There's nothin' here for me anyway; I'll just lea—"

I imagine that Kevy's eyes had been blurry from crying. I imagine that he had been too upset to look. But then, he'd often been careless with his bike. We heard the sound—a screeching of tires against pavement, a loud, dull thud. A car door slammed. Somebody screamed. Mama and I froze, scathing retorts dying in our throats as comprehension etched our faces. I was the first to move, running across the living room, flying through the door, down the porch steps, over the sidewalk. People yelled at the Main Street intersection, calling for Doc Richardson.

"Kevy!" I screamed, my feet barely hitting pavement, already knowing what I would find, what my selfishness had done. For a moment I was no longer on Minton Street; I was running over rocks and fallen logs at the riverbank, crying my brother's name, watching Danny Cander swim with all his might to save my brother. It all had started there, Danny and me and Kevy, and here it would end. "Kevy! *Kevy!*" I threw myself on the cement, knocking people away, reaching for him, my brother just turned twelve, who'd covered for me and Danny to Mama, who still had girls to love and fish to catch. I wrapped my arms around his bloody shirt, lifting him up, his head falling back. I held his head with the palm of my hand, cradling him to my chest and rocking, repeating his name. People ran from all directions, stopping cars, gawking at us, and still I rocked my little brother, seeing only my own blurred fingers smoothing hair off his forehead.

Mama arrived, keening like a lone wolf.

I raised my eyes to her, sobbing, and she stared at him, face wild, a hand at her throat, staring, staring at her darling Kevy. Then she turned her gaze on me.

Hatred glittered in her eyes.

~ *1997* ~

chapter 51

As I tried to paint Mama's house, the movie of Kevy's death and my fleeing Bradleyville played and played in my head. I had not even possessed the decency to attend Kevy's funeral. I had lied to Mama and Daddy that I would walk to the service and instead trudged the hot June streets down to our bank. Most of the town was gathering at our church. One lone teller had been left to mind the bank while the other employees attended the funeral. I ignored her stares as I presented her the official documents that would allow me to withdraw all my inheritance from Granddad's account. With the check in my purse, I returned to our empty house, picked up my packed boxes, and called Albertsville for a cab to take me to the bus station there.

Over and over these scenes kept plaguing my thoughts until nothing about my painting went right. I was halfway done with the bathroom only to back clumsily into the wall, leaving a body print in the stickiness and smearing my hair. I had to scrape the wall before I could redo it. In the midst of that, I managed to drip paint on the tile floor, which I didn't discover until it had almost dried. Cleaning it up, I hit the enamel paint on the baseboard and had to do that section over. The day was warm and with each mishap I grew hotter, sweat trickling, making me itch.

The hallway presented its own difficulties. I painted Mama's bedroom door and mine first, putting off the inevitable, but then had to paint Kevy's and Granddad's. I didn't want to look at those doors after yesterday's kisses with John, for the rooms behind them screamed their disfavor. Granddad would have been so terribly upset. Never would he have expected me to take what wasn't mine. I dwelt on that thought as I worked on his door, and then I remembered the feel of John's arms around me. Soon I became lost in the fascination of the memory until once again I realized whose door I was painting, and when my eyes filled with tears, I couldn't wipe them away because my knuckles were covered with paint.

I told myself there was nothing wrong with what I wanted. But I felt no less guilty.

That night I called Carrie, wanting to see how she and Andy were doing. She chattered about how well things were going, saying they'd made a commitment to date exclusively. The more she talked, the more I imagined her pain if she were to learn that he was secretly seeing someone else. I wanted to tell her about my feelings for John, hear her advice, but the honesty of their relationship made me feel so small. I could not bring myself to mention John. "Carrie," I told her, "I am so very happy for you."

Sunday, while Mama took a jubilant Daddy to church, I sat in the empty house, yearning for John to come and scared out of my wits that he would. He could so easily say he had to check on a patient, and yet . . . I pictured his car parked out front, so conspicuous while all Bradleyville knew I was there alone. He dared not be so foolish, I berated myself, listening for his car.

"You should have gone to church with us," Mama scolded when they returned. Daddy was in the bedroom, resting until lunch was ready. "Everyone was so glad to see your daddy, and they were askin' about you."

"I'm so glad he had a good time," I managed, stirring soup at the stove. "He's come so far." Why was I getting teary-eyed? I grasped the spoon harder. "Where's Mrs. B., by the way? She hasn't been here since that first visit."

"Well, she's just been doin' other things, I guess."

Mama was suddenly busy setting the table and pouring tea, and I saw myself in her exaggerated actions. "Are you not talking to her these days?"

She clinked a fork against a plate. "And would that be any of your business?"

My jaw set. I felt too fragile to ignore her suddenly challenging tone. "Of course not, Mama," I said in a tight voice, whisking the spoon through our soup none too gently. "Nothing you do is any of my business."

Her look was withering. "We need to bring your daddy in for lunch now; do you think you can be civil?"

My lips pressed together. "I'll do my best."

After lunch Mama and I watched Daddy slowly cross the living room with his walker, tension still thick between us. Daddy was definitely improving. His first day on the walker, he had crossed the hallway numerous times, his steps methodical but fairly steady. His left arm was strong enough to help support himself, but his right arm still took most of the weight. Gripping the walker proved good exercise for his left fingers.

"You're doing great, Daddy!" I exclaimed, trying to remain upbeat. "You'll be making drawer baskets before you know it. And in a number of weeks," I added without thinking, "we'll be driving you off to work!"

The minute the words were out, I could have kicked myself. This was hardly the time to bring up the subject of work in front of Mama. I looked at her, a silent apology on my face, and was stunned by the instant malevolence of her glare. I blinked. And then suddenly something within me snapped. Maybe my slip of the tongue had been Freudian. Maybe deep inside I'd been aching to fight her, once and for all. Whatever the case, once I saw that expression on her face—a look that rolled seventeen years away in an instant—there was no turning back.

Straightening my shoulders, I swung my gaze to Daddy with purpose. "You want to get back to work, don't you, Daddy?" It was more of a statement than a question.

"Yeah. I do." He focused on his feet, picking them up, setting them down. The wheels of the walker gently squeaked his progress across the worn carpet.

I pressed on. "I know Mr. Sledge will be glad to have you back. Did I tell you I stopped by to see him?" I didn't need to look at Mama to feel the miasma of her anger. "He's got a temporary; I'm sure Mama's told you that. But he's holding your job open and says if you can't come back three weeks from now, I'm to tell him how much longer you need."

Daddy halted, gazing at me, a look of yearning on his face. "I caan go back?"

"If you're able. And I certainly think you will be, don't you?"

"Yyoo bet."

"We just have to keep working hard. I promised him I'd get you back there."

"Yeah. Good!" He beamed until he glanced at Mama. One sight of her crossed arms, her set mouth, her blanched cheeks, and his joy spilled away like water from a cracked pitcher. He looked back at me and I saw the dismay on his face, silent questions replaced by the realization that Mama neither knew about this nor supported it. No one moved for a moment. The three of us stood there, in the present, yet the room swirled back in time to when I was sixteen, a younger Mama controlling our lives and Daddy passively allowing it.

Come on, Daddy, I urged him silently, *you're different now, you're weaker in body but stronger in spirit; don't let her run your life anymore; this is too important.*

Conflicting emotions moved across his face as he lowered his eyes, gazing at his hands, ever so carefully gripping the gray metal of his walker. Nothing he could say would stop my inevitable confrontation with Mama over this issue.

Don't worry about us, Daddy, I wanted to tell him. *Do what you want. This is your work, your life; stand up for it. Stand up!*

Slowly he began to move forward again, one careful step at a time, approaching the back wall of the living room. He watched his hands, his feet, concentrating. "You promus me too?" he said, breaking the silence.

"You mean do I promise that I'll see you back to work?" I asked, fully aware this time of what my answer would mean. "Yes. I promise."

"'Kay. Good." He smiled grimly, shuffled one more step, then began the painstaking process of turning around.

While Daddy took a nap, I wandered into the kitchen under the pretense of getting a drink, welcoming Mama's certain wrath with the bristling indignation of thirty-five years. If she thought she would win this argument, she was mistaken. I'd worked too hard; Daddy had worked too hard. People had to make their own choices, right or wrong. Daddy should not need to be worrying about what Mama thought of his returning to work. Any more than I should be worrying about what she would think about me and John. She simply could not control us anymore.

Mama wasted no time lighting into me.

"How *dare* you go behind my back! You had no right."

I faced her head-on, retorts already welling on my tongue. "No right! I have every right; I'm the one handling his therapy! And I know very well, better than you, how important work is. It keeps you going when everything else in life is tough." I spread my hands. "Knowing he can go back to work will give him the incentive he needs to go the final mile, can't you see that? You expect him to just be happy sitting at home with you the rest of his life?"

"He's not ready to go back to work, Celia; he never will be." Mama shoved a kitchen chair under the table. "He can't handle the stress. Who knows if he can even do the math anymore? Failin' will only depress him."

"He can do it. His mind is clear; it's just his body that needs to heal, and that's happening before your eyes." My voice dropped. "This is not about failing and you know it. This is about you and your fear of being left alone. This is about you controlling him, just like you've controlled the rest of us. Now he's finally strong enough to stand up to you. And I'm glad of it!"

"You're not thinkin' about your daddy at all; you're thinkin' about yourself." Her eyes narrowed. "And as far as controlling you, I never did that your entire life, much as I tried, as any mama would. I tried to raise you like a good Christian girl, but you've fought me since before you could walk. Well, this is one time I won't let you fight, because it'll only hurt your daddy. I'm glad for you helpin' him get better, but that's as far as it goes. You've done a lot a damage today."

I was almost too livid for words. "I come back here to help Daddy after not seeing you for years, and you tell me that's as far as it goes? Do your job, Celia, then get on out of Bradleyville; you're not needed here anymore!"

She tilted her head, eyeing me as a hawk eyes its prey. "Isn't that what you've wanted since the day you came? Pay a debt, then leave?"

Her words hit home but I stood my ground. "Maybe at first but not now. If I wanted to leave as soon as I could, I'd be gone by now; Daddy's a lot better. But I don't dare leave, because if I do, you'll be on him, nagging him every day, fixing it so he'll never return to work. And that'll kill him!"

"How do you know? He might like stayin' home!"

"Come on, Mama, you saw his face! He wants to feel productive; good grief, he's not that old. What would he do every day, go downtown and gossip with the old men?"

"Celia"—she smacked a hand on the counter—"I'm through arguin' with you. I'm tellin' you, don't push this anymore."

"Well, I'm going to, Mama, so you might as well get used to it!" I jabbed a finger against my chest. "I've promised him. And nothing's going to make me go back on that promise."

"Just listen to yourself!" Her cheeks were mottled. "Why do you have to fight with me about everything? Why must you stir up dissension wherever you go?"

Suddenly I was exhausted. I closed my eyes, shoulders slumping, the disappointments of the past whirling through my mind. "I don't stir up dissension," I said, my voice thick. "You do! Everybody in this family got along except you. You were the one who wouldn't let Granddad tell his war stories. You were the only one who wouldn't give Danny and me a chance." Tears filled my eyes, infuriating me all the more, but I could not blink them back. "While Danny tried so hard to prove himself, all you did was tell me how bad he was for me! You say I fought you since before I could walk. The truth is, *you* fought *me*. I colored the sidewalk as a present for you, Mama, remember that? And you wanted to spank me for it! When will you ever color it for me? You haven't wanted me since the day I was born!"

She reeled back, breathless. "That's not true, Celia. I wanted you."

"Then *why*, Mama?" My words choked. "Why didn't you want me to be happy? Why didn't you let me be with Danny? Maybe if you had, he never would have left. I'll never love anyone else like that again, never!"

She swallowed hard, stammering for words. "I . . . I was only tryin' to keep you from bein' hurt."

I laughed scornfully. "Oh, that's great, Mama, that's just great! Because in trying to keep me from being hurt, you hurt me! And all you can say is, you were looking out for me; just like you claim you're looking out for Daddy!"

"Stop yellin' at me, Celia." She gripped the counter, hand shaking. "You don't know how hard it was for me; you have no idea of my own hurts. You were always so busy thinkin' of yourself. But I always tried to do what was best for you."

The pain of my losses, of every time we had fought, of every hug and kiss and I-love-you that never came, injected a bitterness in my voice so caustic that it burned my throat. "Well, guess what, Mama. You *failed*."

I stalked away on shaky legs.

"Celia!" Her call crashed into my arched shoulders. "Come back here!"

"Back, Mama?" I whirled around to her, a lifetime of tears on my face. "Back to what?"

chapter 52

Mama and I could not bring ourselves to speak after our fight. She wasn't about to apologize and, although I wanted to, I couldn't seem to find a way. I'd had the last word but I felt anything but victorious. The longing within me for her love, a longing I'd felt since I was a small child, only deepened. Why had she always been so cold to me? The rest of the afternoon I slumped on my bed, feebly throwing my demands for answers at the heavens. They reached no farther than the ceiling. God was through with me.

In the next few days, amid the acidic atmosphere between Mama and me, Daddy's mood turned fragile, contentious. What's more, his improvement seemed to have peaked. We saw no gains whatsoever in strength or coordination. His eagerness for therapy waned and our sessions became wearisome. I berated myself for ever having mentioned his returning to work, regretting both the argument that had ensued and the bubbling impatience it had placed within him. Nothing Mama or I did was right. He snapped at me when I tried to button his shirt, snapped at Mama for not reading the newspaper loudly enough. Daddy even snapped at John when he arrived Tuesday after supper, informing the doctor, "My haart's fine!" At John's gentle insistence he finally agreed to a quick examination, bristling in his wheelchair all the while.

When he was done, John motioned with his eyes for me to walk him outside. "What's going on?" he demanded as we stood on the sidewalk.

Wearily I told him of my argument with Mama, wishing he could hold me. "I don't know how much Daddy overheard, but he can certainly sense the mood between us, and it's upsetting him. I understand that, but he shouldn't allow it to affect his therapy. In a way he's acting like a child."

"You and Estelle need to get along, Celia," John responded with impatience. "Your daddy doesn't need that kind of stress."

His reaction was far from the understanding I'd expected. Stung, I struggled to remind myself he was Daddy's doctor first. "You think I don't realize that?" I challenged. "Believe me, I'm doing everything I can under the circumstances to keep the house quiet. I'll try to work things out between Mama and me. But it's a little hard, you know, after a lifetime."

His face softened. "You're looking pretty stressed yourself."

My eyes closed. "There are just so many things going on right now, John. In the house. And with you. Sometimes I think I just can't handle it anymore."

He nodded, frowning. It occurred to me how much inner turmoil he must feel as he discussed wedding plans with Sharon, her face lighting up over the details, and plotted how he and I could see each other.

The curtains moved inside the house. I turned away. "Mama's watching."

He took a deep breath. "Listen, Celia." His words were low, hurried. "I have a little hunting cabin about an hour's drive from here. I use it to get away once in a while. Next time I go, I want you to meet me there, even if it's only for an hour or two."

I grew breathless at the thought. "John, I don't know. I want to, but I just—"

"Think about it. Think about us, Celia. I want to be with you, have time to talk to you alone."

My throat tightened. "And I want to be with you."

"Then think about it. We'll discuss it Friday. Okay?"

In the next moment he was gone.

I couldn't stand it any longer. I had to talk to someone. Late that night, in hushed tones over the phone, I told Carrie about John.

"Oh, Celia," she said, sighing. "What are you getting yourself into?"

"I don't know. But I want to go see him so much. Too much." Tears pricked my eyes. "It's very hard here, Carrie, with everything in the present and memories of the past. I'm just so tired of being lonely."

"I know." Her voice was gentle. "I told you someday you'd find someone. But this someone is already taken. And he's being deceitful by being with you. Is that the kind of person you want?"

I closed my eyes, not wanting to hear the words that I knew were so right. "You can't understand. Being here, I miss Danny more than ever.

Some nights I feel him so closely, I ache with it. But he's gone forever, and meanwhile John's here. How can I let this chance go? Maybe John's not supposed to be with his fiancée at all; maybe he's supposed to be with me. Maybe he's the one who will finally help me forget Danny."

"Whoever he's supposed to be with, I can tell you one thing. He should be truthful and so should you. If he's worried about marrying the wrong person, he should postpone the wedding, take time to think about it. But sneaking around—that's no foundation for a relationship."

Her words hit home. How could I even think of being with John when it meant causing his fiancée so much pain? Just like I'd hurt Melissa. Would I never learn from the past? "I don't want to talk about this anymore."

She sighed again. "Okay."

I played with the phone cord. "How's Andy?"

"Still great. We're seeing each other often."

"I'm glad," I said, meaning it. "Don't lose him, Carrie; keep him close."

"Oh, don't you worry."

I could hear the irony in her tone. Here I was, the potential other woman in one man's life, trying to protect Carrie's relationship with another. "Well, guess what," I said, steering away from the subject. "This Saturday I'm finally seeing Bobby Delham. I talked to him today."

"Oh! Was he surprised to hear from you?"

I smiled, remembering the conversation. "He was very glad. Said he'd hoped I would call."

Carrie laughed. "And they say nothing ever happens in small towns. A doctor, now a widowed ex-boyfriend. Wouldn't it be a riot if you two really hit it off after all these years? Imagine ending up with him after all, just like your mother wanted!"

I rolled my eyes. What I could imagine was the gossip. *Poor, nice Bobby Delham. Got her hooks in him again.* "Yeah, Carrie, there'd be a riot all right."

Miss Jessie called Wednesday, inviting me to meet her downtown at Tammy's Café late that afternoon. "It's always a quiet time," she hastened to add. "We'll probably be the only ones there." Nerves frayed, I jumped at the chance to get out of the house.

Seated in a vinyl-covered booth, coffee and Tammy's home-baked oatmeal cookies between us, I spilled to Miss Jessie what was going on at home. I knew she would understand and not judge. She had always been so sweet to me when I was a child. I told her that the rift between Mama and me dated back to when I was very young, and was surprised to hear that Miss Jessie already knew. She had noticed it herself, she told me, particularly beginning the summer Kevy was born. *Of course*, I thought, *the summer I colored the sidewalk*. And finally we spoke of my teenage years, when Mama and I had fought so much over Danny.

Danny.

Miss Jessie grew quiet when his name slipped from me. She had so tactfully avoided any mention of it. The topic suspended between us with the fragility of blown glass as she searched for something to say. All these years, and I'd been so afraid to ask anyone about him. Selfishly, I couldn't bear to hear of his happiness with Rachel. But suddenly I longed for news of him.

"Miss Jessie," I said, plunging in, "how is he?"

Her expression softened. "Oh, Celia, he—" She stopped abruptly, pasted on a quick smile. "He's doing very well. Still works for the cruise lines, although it's a different one. He switched to another company soon after he went to Greece. Now he's risen high in the corporation. Danny's such a hard worker and they noticed him, little by little giving him more responsibilities. Eventually he went to college, taking a few courses at a time as he worked. He's been settled in Greece for a long time now, although he has business in New York three or four times a year."

"That's ... wonderful," I managed. I could hardly breathe. "Danny Cander, world traveler, Bradleyville's biggest success." All the oceans he must have seen. I hoped there was no bitterness in my voice.

"We're very proud of him. We hear from him occasionally, but men aren't that great at writing, you know. He does call when he comes to the States."

"Has he ever come back here?"

"Oh no. As much as he'd like to see Lee and me, nothin' has ever gotten him to set foot in Bradleyville again. Too many bad memories. Most of his news we get in regular letters from Patricia."

I pictured Danny years ago telling his mama about what I'd done with Bobby, and Patricia Cander writing of her shock at the news. What Miss Jessie must have thought of me.

"Patricia's doin' wonderfully," she said. "She married in Greece, a good man that treats her like a princess, and she's so happy."

"I'm really very glad to hear that," I replied, remembering her sad but pretty face, her soft voice. "I always liked her. She took such tender care of Kevy that day . . ." I blinked at Miss Jessie, aware that my words had trailed away.

"She was like that," Miss Jessie said, rescuing me. "But I haven't told you the best part. She had a baby—another boy. She was forty-one at the time but sailed right through it. Patricia always loved children and wanted more; she and her husband were just ecstatic. The boy's name is Gregory Allen; they call him Greg. He's fifteen now and playing in some rock band in Greece. Lucky kid, the way his parents and his big brother dote on him."

I stared at the blue silk flowers in their white vase upon our table, struck with the irony. I felt happy for Danny and his mama, I *did*, even though it seemed he'd gotten everything he wanted in life, while I had lost it.

After coming this far, I told myself I might as well hear it all. "I suppose they've got kids, too." My voice sounded pinched.

Miss Jessie wrinkled her forehead. "Who?"

"Danny." Her name lay acrid on my tongue. "And Rachel."

"Rachel?" Miss Jessie replied blankly. "Who's Rachel?"

chapter 53

The repercussions of my fight with Mama continued to stretch through the week with glaring tensility. She remained cold and unyielding; Daddy was touchy. Thursday afternoon, upset with them both and sick at heart over Danny, I struggled to lead Daddy through a stagnant speech therapy session.

"Say 'long,'" I told him, hearing Miss Jessie's words.

Oh, Rachel. She didn't last long, Celia. Got them to Greece; that was about it. Danny changed jobs and never saw her again, as far as I know. That was . . . a very difficult time for Danny. Patricia was worried about him.

"Okay, Daddy. Try 'news.'"

Mama must have known this news of Danny, yet had never volunteered a word. Her silence had probably been for the best; I could imagine her I-told-you-so's. How could I have been so shocked to receive Danny's final letter? Why had it been so hard to believe he'd changed his mind at the last minute, heeding the ocean's call, his desire to see the world? Hadn't Mama warned me enough?

"Good. Now say 'time.'"

To have assumed for all these years that Danny and Rachel were together, only to learn they'd lasted no time at all. To know now that he'd walked away from a love as deep as ours not because he'd found someone else but merely to fulfill his dreams of traveling. To see now that those dreams were far more important to him than I ever was. But Miss Jessie's last piece of news had been the final straw. Danny had never married, she said, had never even been engaged, although he was finally dating someone steadily now. According to Patricia, it sounded serious.

"Tiimuh," Daddy repeated.

All this time that I'd been alone, *all this time*, he had been also. And why, I moaned to myself as I uttered more practice words. The waste of it, after everything we'd had. I wanted to cry as I sat before Daddy, a plastic smile on my lips; I wanted to scream at the loss of it. We had both lost. If he'd really loved me, he could have tracked me down in Little Rock; he could have given us another chance. I'd have sailed any ocean to be with him. Now he'd found someone else.

"Say 'fine.'"

Fine then, I raged to myself, fighting tears. Just fine. He could have her, whoever she was. As for me, I refused to sit around and hurt over him anymore. I would never read his old letters again, *never.* After seventeen years enough was enough. I'd been an absolute fool, mooning over him for so long. Here I was now, back in Bradleyville, and John Forkes was here. He wanted me. Surely he'd be the one who could finally pull my ancient, stupid love for Danny out of my heart for good.

After all the pain I deserved some happiness.

By Friday morning Daddy was ready for a battle of his own. When I wheeled him back to his bedroom after breakfast and informed him that we needed to begin his therapy session, he responded with a tight-lipped no.

I tried to laugh it off. "What do you mean, no?"

"No thurapy."

"Why, what's wrong? You tired?"

"Yes!" He smacked his hand on the wheelchair. "Tarred a you an' Mama fightin'."

"Come on, Daddy, we're not fighting now."

"Yes. Aare."

I was glad Mama was still in the kitchen. I closed the bedroom door. "Look, I'll work things out with her, I promise, but we can't let that get in the way of your exercises. I know the last five days have been rough. If we keep at it, we'll see improvement again."

"No. No thurapy till you an' Mama taawk."

I stared at him in consternation. "Are you blackmailing me?"

"Yup."

For all the weakness of his limbs, Daddy displayed an inner strength for which I proved no match. He was immovable. I reasoned with him, I cajoled, I told him he was only hurting himself, and asked didn't he want to get back to work? Finally, nearly in tears, I blurted who did he think he was, that he could force us to mend such a broken relationship? "It's never been right, Daddy, you know that! It's going to take time to fix it, and you can't sit around waiting for that, or you may end up waiting forever!"

He shook his head and reached for his tablet and pen. I sat down on the bed and as I watched, his slowly written reply plopped into my heart like fat raindrops falling into a pond.

> *You can only have bitterness against a person you don't under-stand. There is much about Mama you don't know. I spent my life understanding her. You must do the same.*

"What is there to understand?"

> *She must be willing to tell you. You must be willing to listen.*

Why was it so difficult, I wondered, for Mama and me to do that? What was it about mere words that tied the tongue and made sweaty hands fidget?

I plucked at one of the tiny balls of lint that were scattered across the bedspread and let it drop onto the carpet.

"You still luv Danny?"

I looked up in surprise, wondering what had prompted this sudden broaching of a long-taboo subject. Even in our recent talks we had not spoken of Danny. *No,* I wanted to tell him, with the anger of a woman scorned, *that ended years ago.* I opened my mouth to deny it, then saw the look in his eyes. He knew the answer.

"Yes."

He emitted a sigh. "Such a llong tiime."

His voice held a sadness that delved beyond empathy for me. I gazed at him questioningly but he said no more.

When John arrived after supper, Mama immediately accosted him. "Talk to William! He refuses to exercise, hasn't done a thing all day."

"Aask them," Daddy replied tersely when John questioned him. We'd all gathered in the living room, Daddy looking defiant, Mama upset. John spread his hands.

"This is ridiculous, William," Mama declared, swiping hair from her face, "that we should need to bring Dr. Forkes into this." She pointed at me. "I told you, you shouldn't have talked to him about workin'. It's just depressed him."

"This doesn't have anything to do with that, Mama, and you know it," I retorted. "He's just—"

"Sstop!" Daddy threw up a hand. "See?" he exclaimed to John.

"Oh, for heaven's sake!" Mama stalked to her bedroom.

I collapsed onto the couch, jaw set. "John, talk some sense into him"—I glared at Daddy—"so he doesn't lose any of what we've worked so hard to gain."

John looked nonplussed. Briefly I wondered how often he'd been forced to play psychologist with his patients. "Maybe I should talk to him alone for a minute, Celia."

"Fine." Like a dismissed child I flounced from the room. Slumping on my bed, face in both hands, I swore to myself I should go home. Forget all this, forget my promise. The only reason I wanted to stay was John, and that reason was all wrong. Yet in the midst of all the simmering hurt and after hearing about Danny, I wanted John more than ever.

He knocked at my door. Daddy and Mama were in their bedroom trying to talk, their door closed. I led John to the kitchen. "You've *got* to fix it," he commanded in a low voice. "Seeing you and your mama together is far more important to him than his own health."

"Okay!" I trembled. "I want things right for Daddy, whatever the cost. But how am I supposed to fix something that's been broken so long?" I brought a hand to my forehead, tears welling in my eyes.

"Celia, I'm sorry this is so hard for you." John reached for me. "Come here."

"No." I pushed him away. "Mama could come in anytime."

"I told William to give us five minutes to talk. Come here." He pulled me to him, pressing his lips against mine, and amid everything I was falling again, away from Mama and Daddy and therapy sessions and hurt and disappointment. "Listen," he said, "I can get away this weekend while another doctor covers for me. Come see me at the cabin Sunday while they're in church; just tell them you're going out for a drive. Tell me you'll come, Celia."

I took his face in my hands, imagining. Wondering if being with him could drive away the pain. Weighing the possible consequences. I thought of Carrie's warnings. Of her insistence that God had brought me here. What new way would he think of to punish me if I went through with this? What on earth would happen if anyone found out?

What would it do to Daddy? Finally I thought of the pain I'd endured over Danny and my new resolve to put it behind me once and for all.

I looked into John's eyes and the questions melted away.

His hair was mussed on one side and I combed it with my fingers. "I'll need directions."

chapter 54

I could not sleep Friday night with the demons that plagued me, my thoughts skittering like dry autumn leaves. I longed for Sunday with an aching heart. Yet my conscience still railed at me. I knew Mama would not begin to understand; I'd never make peace with her if she found out. And the stress it could cause Daddy! I couldn't bear to think of his paying the price for my impulsive actions. How could I even think of saying yes to John? Had I not cost us enough already?

My mind squalled until night became morning, the gray dawn seeping across my wedding ring quilt and spilling onto the floor. Daddy was quiet at breakfast and Mama was sullen, both of them glancing at the circles beneath my eyes and misunderstanding their reasons. I thought of other girls and their mothers; I thought of Danny and Patricia Cander and wondered for the millionth time what it would be like to feel loved and nurtured by Mama.

I thought of John.

"Daddy," I pleaded, "will you do your exercises today?"

He was caught. Clearly, he did not want to hurt me and feared, based on my appearance, that he had done so, the recalcitrant pupil disappointing the teacher. Neither did he want to give in, for the silence between Mama and me had only grown deeper.

"Okay," he replied, defeat in his voice.

I nodded solemnly. Gathered my nerve. "Mama. Maybe you and I can take a walk together later."

She gave me a look. "We can't leave your daddy alone."

"Oh, right," I said, "I'm not thinking. Well. Maybe we can . . . bake something together this afternoon. Something for Daddy. An apple pie."

"Maybe." Her tone sounded cautious. "I'd need to go to the store, buy some good apples."

It was a small step, yet for Mama a very large one. Maybe it had nothing to do with me; maybe she was reaching out merely for Daddy's sake. Still, she was trying. I managed a slight smile.

"Sure. Or I could go."

"I suppose I have enough cinnamon," she added. "And sugar and flour of course we've got."

The mending of our lives, discussed through the ingredients for pie.

Daddy's therapy went poorly; his heart was not in it.

"I'll talk to Mama this afternoon," I told him as I pulled out her dresser drawer. "I'm really going to try, I promise." He squeezed my arm with his left hand. "Hey," I exclaimed, "I feel some strength there! Maybe you'll make that basket today."

"Maaybe."

He tried ten, fifteen times in a row but still couldn't bounce the ball hard enough. "Ah, well," I said with a shrug. "Guess I'll just have to stick around another day. Come on now, you need to walk some."

The walker's wheels squeaked down the hall, across the living room and back again. I watched them turn and thought of John's arms encircling me.

"Good going, Daddy."

"*He loves you,*" Melissa's voice sounded in my head. "*You ruined him for me. You, of all people.*"

I glanced at the clock. In two hours I had my clandestine appointment with Bobby Delham. Tired as I was, I wish I hadn't scheduled it.

I wondered how it would go. Other than my brief phone call, I hadn't talked to Bobby since that night years ago on the country road. He had tried and tried to talk to me in the following week, even stopped by our house, but I had refused to see him. And after Kevy's death I couldn't bear to see anyone.

Daddy crossed the room another time and announced he was ready to rest. I helped him get settled on the couch.

"Lookin' foward ta that appul pie tunight," he said with a slow wink.

Bobby Delham had given me directions to a coffee shop on the outskirts of Albertsville. I sensed it was a place where he believed we would not be seen. One person from Bradleyville spotting us was all it would take to turn the town on its ear. Bobby, I imagined, could handle that well enough, but his children didn't need to hear any gossip.

I chose the booth farthest from the door.

"Celia!"

I stood to greet him and he gave me a brief, hard hug. "Let me see you," he said, pulling away, his hands on my shoulders. "You look wonderful. Just the same except for your shorter hair. I'd have known you anywhere."

I felt a rush of affection, meeting his gaze. Loyal, kind Bobby. His face was thinner than in the photograph on the Westerdahls' mantel, the curve of his mouth airbrushed with a quiet sadness. His dark hair was still thick, his mouth generous. I found him handsome in a brooding sort of way.

We ordered coffee. He launched into questions about me, and we talked briefly about my life in Little Rock and my therapy with Daddy. "But how are you?" I asked, touching his arm. "I'm so sorry to hear about Melissa. I didn't know she was sick, Bobby. Believe it or not, I didn't even know you two had married."

He accepted my condolences with a nod. "I'm doin' okay."

Melissa fought the cancer hard, he told me; she was courageous and trusted God to the end. Many of the things her parents had said, he now echoed, as though they had become a mantra to soothe his pain. I watched his face as he spoke of her, and reflected on the paths our lives had taken. If I had married him, we would still have each other. Now we were both alone.

"But I'll tell you," he said with a brief smile, "even with everything, it's been worth it. We had sixteen years, each one of them better. Until she got sick."

He looked away at nothing and we were silent.

"You know, Celia," he said slowly, "I want to tell you this. When you left Bradleyville—just up and disappeared—I thought you'd run off to Danny. For a while I hated you—because I cared for you so much, if that makes any sense. I wanted to run, too. I even thought about leaving and looking for you. It was hard here, knowin' I'd hurt Melissa like you'd hurt me. And a course people were talking a blue streak. I kept asking your folks if they'd heard from you, but they always said no.

"Then one day about two months after you left—and they'd been right bad months for me, I'll tell you that—I just sort of woke up. Maybe it's because it hit me that you weren't comin' back. I took a good hard look at my life and my future. I knew God had forgiven me, but what was I supposed to do with that forgiveness? And then I realized that right here in Bradleyville was a wonderful girl who loved me in spite a what I'd done. That if I had any sense at all, I'd go to her on my knees and beg her to take me back. And that's what I did. It was hard at first because I felt so bad inside, wishing she was you. But in time something started changing. God helped change my heart. Your face faded; meantime she was always there. And I fell truly, deeply in love with her."

"I'm glad for you, Bobby," I said quietly, rubbing a small bump on the handle of my coffee cup. "I'm so sorry I broke you two up. I'm happy to hear it wasn't for good."

He waved away the apology. "I was just as much to blame as you." His expression changed. "But enough about me. I never got the chance to tell you how sorry I was about Kevin. I know you must miss him very much."

"Yes."

His empathy for my pain in the midst of his own warmed me. I was surprised to find myself telling him of the argument that had led to Kevy's death, and my final, hateful words to the little brother who had loved me so much. "It's another regret—my heaviest—that I've carried ever since."

He smiled sadly. "I know about guilt, Celia. I also know Jesus can heal all the guilt you carry and more. But let me ask you somethin'. What makes you think the guilt is all yours in the first place?"

The question startled me and I couldn't find a reply.

"Think about it. If you take a hundred percent of the blame for somethin', what you're really sayin' is, you made it happen all on your own. And that's—well, heck, that's a lot of power for one person to have."

I rubbed my cup in silence. His words may have been rational, may even have carried the wisdom of ancient oracles, but they couldn't touch my heart. The tremors of a guilt-ridden conscience could never be quelled by mere logic.

On the drive home I mourned that regardless of what Bobby believed, God could not seem to quell them, either.

chapter 55

After lunch Daddy rested as usual. Mama had bought the apples. We peeled them side by side at the kitchen sink, the pie pan ready, flour out for the crust. I watched the blade of my peeler whisk back and forth, back and forth across the green skin. My actions were methodical, ever so efficient, and my tongue was numb with fear. I sensed the same in Mama as with affected concentration we made small talk, passing observations about the fruits' firmness and the preheating oven. I thought of the hundreds of times we had stood in that kitchen, I washing dishes and she putting away food, our current argument frothing silently between us. How life circled, situations different but meanings the same.

The apples cut and precooking on the stove, Mama's hands dusted with flour, I pushed together the peelings in the sink, collected them, and threw them away. I wondered if John was missing me, alone in his cabin. I wondered where Danny was at that moment. "Mama"—I pulled out a wooden spoon to stir the apples—"I don't want to fight anymore."

"I don't, either. I never wanted to fight."

I glanced at her profile, so absorbed in the making of the dough. Her comment struck me as accusing, and I pushed away the proclivity to defend myself. "I just want to say I'm sorry. I thought work was real important to Daddy, so I . . . did what I did. I guess I shouldn't have."

"No, you shouldn't." She was patting out the dough on a floured cutting board. "But I know you did it out of concern for him."

At least she wasn't intimating I did it for spite.

"So how much longer are you staying?" she asked. The rolling pin glided between her hands, flattening the dough.

"I don't know. I mean, I did promise Daddy I'd get him back to work, however long that takes. If that's what you two decide you want."

"It's up to him."

"You don't mind?"

"I don't mind if he's able. I just don't want him hurt. I'm worried about him."

"There are alternatives these days, you know." The fragrance of cinnamon rose from the pot as I stirred. "He could do a lot of the work from home by computer."

"I don't know about such things. Neither does your daddy."

"He could learn. It would give him something new to try. And it would keep him close to you while he worked, at least part of the time. I'll bet Mr. Sledge would be negotiable."

"Maybe. We'll see." She sent the rolling pin in another direction. The dough began to form a circle.

"Anyway, there can be compromises. It doesn't have to be black and white."

She glanced at me meaningfully. "Few things are."

The comment touched on so many things that I couldn't follow it. I cleared my throat. "How long do you want me to stay?"

"That's up to you."

"You don't care?"

"That's not what I said."

"Well, that's what I'm asking."

The circle was complete. She set down the rolling pin and pulled the pie pan close. "I want you to be happy."

I repressed a laugh. *It's a little late, Mama.* "Here, let me help." We each picked up a side of the dough and placed it over the pie pan, its edges hanging over. She began to tear off the excess, crimping the rest between her fingers. "I'll be happy just to see Daddy's life back to normal."

"And what about you?" she pressed. "Your life?"

I gathered the extra dough lying on the counter. "I'll go back to the ad agency in Little Rock. And my volunteer work."

"Those things don't make you happy."

She was placing the dough in the oven to prebake before adding the apples, her back to me. I stared at her grayed bun, a piece of hair straggling from it. "They keep me busy."

She made no response.

Ten minutes later, the crust lightly browned, we added the apples and returned the pie pan to the oven. It now needed to bake, and cleaning the pot and the few other dishes didn't take long. I poured us both some iced tea and we sat at the kitchen table. Seeing Kevy's empty chair, I thought of how he used to love her pies.

Kevy, get away from me!

"Daddy walked well today," I commented. "And he's talking so well, too."

"You've done a good job with him."

"He's done all the work. I've just coached."

The kitchen was filled with silence and the smell of baking pie. I waited for her to say something and she waited for me, the ice in our glasses shifting as we drank. Apparently, we'd made all the headway we were going to make in one day. We'd need to do far more. If we were ever truly going to reach out to each other, we'd have to gather enough courage to talk about the past. The thought scared me to death. Still, for the little we had accomplished today, I was grateful.

The kitchen clock read 1:15. Less than twenty-four hours until I'd be with John. I wondered what I would wear.

"Well, you can stay here as long as you like, you know," she offered.

"Thank you."

The pie baked and the clock ticked. I examined my fingernails and she brushed at her apron. We discussed the weather, various people in Bradleyville. I mentioned how cute Tammy's Café was. And weren't her cookies delicious?

At supper we each had a piece of our creation, Daddy looking from Mama to me and declaring with fervency that it was the best pie he'd ever tasted. I remarked that it could have been a touch sweeter, and Mama said another apple would have made it complete.

"But it's good," I added hastily, seeing his disappointment.

"Yes," Mama agreed. "It's good."

That night I dreamed of being swept away by a rapid river current toward treacherous rocks. Mama screamed on the bank, afraid to dive in and help. The rushing water grew louder in my ears, turning into ocean waves as I called to her. I sank beneath their force.

With a start I awakened, sweat on my forehead, my chest damp. I kicked back the covers, breathing hard. The green glow of my digital clock read 2:12. Further sleep eluded me. After an hour I arose in frustration, pulling on a light robe and padding softly into the kitchen, where I turned on the light above the stove. I made myself a cup of hot tea, pulled out a chair and sat. It was 3:20. Eight hours or so and I would be with John. I wondered if he was awake, staring at the ceiling and thinking about me.

I'd drunk half my tea when I heard a noise from the hall. Mama appeared in the doorway, dressed in a white gown, her hair in a long, loose braid down her back. "Thought I heard you," she said.

My shoulders lifted. "I tried to be so quiet."

"You hit a squeak in the floor. I was awake anyway."

"Did I disturb Daddy?"

"No. He's snorin' a bit."

We laughed softly.

I surveyed her. "Want some tea? There's hot water left."

"That would be fine. I'll get it."

I watched her drop a tea bag into a cup, pour water over it. She added a spoon of sugar. Her chair rattled gently as she pulled it out from the table, glancing at my mug. "You're about done with yours."

"Maybe I'll get some more in a while."

Our fingers curled around our cup handles. Iced tea in the afternoon, hot tea at night; hadn't we done this before? We appeared no less awkward at it, despite the practice. She looked away, gazing through the window at the black beyond. Her eyes were puffy.

Silence.

And then she blurted it out.

"I was supposed to marry Henry Bellingham."

Henry. Mr. and Mrs. B.'s son, killed in the war. Her words hung above the table, waiting for me to absorb them. I could not.

"God is giving me the strength to tell you now," she said, voice hushed. "Finally. All these years I've been so bound up in my own pain, I just didn't believe he could heal it. And that unwillingness to trust him—I'm afraid I've passed it on to you. But now all this worryin' over your daddy has driven me to my knees. It's a miracle, really. After I admitted to William that you and I hadn't managed to talk much this afternoon, he came down on me hard. Said it was about time I asked God's forgiveness for the way I've been toward you all these years. And finally, *finally*, I found myself ready to do that. I'm just too tired of it all. So I did. Now I need to ask yours."

She took a deep breath. "I'd like to explain everything, if you'll hear me out. Not to try to convince you I was right in the way I've been.

But just so you'll understand a little more. There's a lot to tell you. Probably too much for one night."

"It's okay, Mama." I couldn't take my eyes from her face. I was afraid to move for fear of breaking the spell.

She managed a weak smile. "So. Henry. He was seventeen when we fell in love. I was fifteen. Both of us knew there would never be anyone else. Then the Korean War started. Your granddad, ever ready to fight, signed up and encouraged Henry to 'do his duty.' They went off to war when Henry was eighteen, two proud men, leavin' Mama and me and Eva behind. I was devastated, both for losing Daddy—again—and losing Henry. I blamed Daddy for leaving Mama when he'd promised he was home for good. He'd been back less than four years since World War II. 'You're too old, Thomas; you don't need to go,' Mama cried, but he wouldn't listen. It was bad enough, him walkin' out the door that day, Mama falling to her knees, sobbing. But to see Henry go with him. I hated Daddy for taking him away from me. He promised me Henry would come back safe. Daddy came home after three years, wavin' his third medal. Henry had already come home in a box shortly after my seventeenth birthday. Daddy was heartsick, but nothing like I was. I just wanted to die."

How could I not have known this? I marveled. I tried to imagine Mama at sixteen, loving and losing as I had, and wondered what I could possibly say now. "Was Granddad with him when he died?"

She shook her head. "Henry was sent off to a different troop or whatever. They were stormin' some hill. Hardly any of them made it."

"What about Mr. and Mrs. B.? Did they blame Granddad?"

"No. They were always such good Christian folk. They told your granddad that if Henry hadn't signed up, he'd probably have been drafted anyway." She looked down at her hands. "And maybe so. But maybe not so soon. And maybe he wouldn't have ended up in that battle." Steam rose from her tea. She picked up the cup, put it down again. "Daddy always thought travelin' the world and fightin' was so glorious. He volunteered for service when he was eighteen, and by World War II he was almost forty. He didn't need to go but he did. He left when I was nine and he didn't come back till I was thirteen. Every night I lay in bed wonderin' if my daddy was alive or dead. The nightmares were terrible. I used to be a happy child before that. While he was gone, I counted the days and weeks and months and years, worryin' about him so much that I'd get sick over it. Mama too. I can't tell you how hard those times were. Finally Daddy came back. But the minute somebody else's fight started in a foreign land, he was off, and Mama and I faced it all over again. He just wouldn't see how much he was hurtin' us. All he wanted was more medals. Which he got."

The thought of her pain at so young an age overwhelmed me. "How old were you when Granddad came home from Korea?" I whispered.

"Not quite twenty." She still did not look at me. "I was dead inside with Henry gone. I became the Bradleyville old maid, not courting, just workin' behind the counter in the Albertsville dime store. That's where I eventually met your daddy."

A realization dawned upon me, the cycles of life more enveloping than I could have dreamed. "But you hadn't gotten over Henry."

She looked up at me slowly, sorrow filling the lines on her face. "No."

"And you married Daddy anyway."

"What else was I to do?" She raised her shoulders. "I was twenty-five when I met him, still livin' with my folks. It took me three years to say yes. I'd never have Henry back. I told William everything; I wanted to be honest. He told me he'd take care of me. And that in time maybe I'd forget."

"But you didn't," I said softly.

She sighed deeply. "Time has a way of healing things you never thought could be healed. I'm not sayin' the hurt completely goes away, but life goes on." She gazed at me. "Don't think I don't love your daddy; I do. I've been with him so many years now, I'm scared to death to think of being without him. But Celia—" She hesitated. "There's so much for you to understand. Maybe I should've told you long ago, but you were too young then. Soon after we married, I got pregnant with you. I was still so sad. Henry had been dead eleven years by then, but it was like it was yesterday. Watchin' Daddy and Henry go off to war had changed me. I was determined that nobody was going to make decisions over my head again. Your daddy was always easygoing and quiet. But then you came along, feisty, stubborn, talkin' your own mind practically the day you were born. We just got off on the wrong foot from the very beginning. I prayed and prayed about it; I tried to be the Christian mother that I should. But my prayers just seemed to fall to the ground. I couldn't find much in myself to give; my heart had closed up. By the time you started school, things were set between us."

My tea had grown cold. I had no taste for it now; her story flowed bittersweet. I remembered Mama arguing with me over Danny, and for the first time pictured the scenes in a new light, their shadows dispelled by a warm, amber glow. "You knew how I felt about Danny."

Her smile was sad. "You were the same age I was when I fell in love with Henry. Oh yes. I knew."

"Then why wouldn't you let me be with him?" The question spurted from me, streaked with hurt.

"I tried, don't you see?" She leaned toward me. "That's why I let you see him at the river every Saturday, when I never should have, even with Kevin nearby. That's why I had him over for supper; that's why I gave him a chance when I knew the whole town was talkin'. I saw how much you loved him, and I saw that Danny had grown into a good boy, despite his daddy's drinking. But then he started talking of travel. And when I saw that yearning in his eyes, I knew he'd hurt you. Maybe he wouldn't run off to war and get himself killed, but he was goin' to leave you someday for the world and medals of his own, whatever form they took. I wanted to spare you that. Because I, of all people, knew the pain."

I picked up my mug and swirled the tea. "You fought me so hard. It hurt so much."

"I never meant to hurt you. God forgive me for what I did; I only meant to help!"

Her voice was tinged with desperation, and discernment stunned me as I looked into her soul. She had carried guilt for years, as I had. Seeing this, even so I couldn't quell my bitterness. "You wanted me to marry Bobby when I didn't love him! You were assigning me the same kind of life you had with Daddy."

"And I was heartsick over it. But Celia, after what you'd done, it was the only right thing to do. I could only pray that God would bless that marriage and you'd learn to love him, as I'd learned to love William."

No, I couldn't believe that. "You knew Henry would never come back, Mama, but it was different with Danny! I dreamed of finding him; I dreamed things would change. I had just lost him, Mama; think of it! I was dead inside, like you were dead when you heard about Henry. Could you have married Daddy then? It took you eleven years to get to that point!"

"Celia, believe me, I was tryin' to spare you those years. And I'm so sorry!" Her voice trembled. "You don't know how often I've asked God for a chance to tell you so. I set things in motion and we all paid for it. Most of all Kevin."

"Kevy?" No, no, I thought. She could have her guilt for withholding love from me, for fighting about Danny, but she could not claim the guilt over Kevy's death. That was mine alone and I would not share it.

A tear fell on her cheek. I felt rooted to my chair. I had so rarely seen my mama cry. "If I hadn't been yelling at you," she said, her voice breaking, "if I'd only paid attention to Kevin instead, our whole lives would have been different."

"Mama"—disbelief etched my words—"what are you talking about? *I* did it; I'm the one who yelled at him! You blamed *me* for that; I saw it in your eyes." My own filled with tears. "I had taken Kevy away from you. If anyone had to pay, it should have been me, but it was him. I couldn't face you after that; that's why I left."

Her cheeks blanched. "I thought you blamed me," she said, choking on tears. "I took Kevy from you, and you wanted to punish me for it. So you waited until we were at his funeral, for God's sake! We came home already dressed in black to find our only other child gone, and for six years we didn't even know if you were alive or dead! Maybe I deserved that, but your daddy didn't."

"No, that's not true." I leaned forward with intensity, clasping her arm. "I wasn't even thinking about you when I left; I was in shock. Then the longer I stayed away, the harder it was to pick up the phone. Finally that Christmas I just ... did it. And you sounded so distant, I thought you still hated me."

"Distant?" She snorted a laugh. "I'd just learned my only remaining child was still alive! I can't begin to describe my feelings. I thought that call would never come. I'd blamed God for years for losin' you. But Celia, by the time you did call, you'd hurt me so much, I couldn't let you hurt me all over again. I *had* to hold back."

Hold back. Is that what we had done our entire lives? I from her, she from me, our miscommunications intertwining until they squeezed our very hearts? "Oh, Mama." I slipped from my chair as she rose from hers, and we reached for each other. "I'm sorry," I said, sobbing, and she said it, too, crying. I didn't know all the things she was crying for. I cried for a colored sidewalk and Granddad's medals, for Kevy's abandoned fishing pole, for no more suppers with Danny, for a child's unreturned I-love-you's, and misunderstandings and chilled silences. I cried for her pain, too, for her nightmares while her daddy was off to war, for burying the man she loved and burying her son, for enduring Granddad's tales of the very war that had taken Henry from her, for living one life and dreaming of another, as I had done the past seventeen years.

When we were done crying, we collapsed, exhausted. "Oh, now my head hurts," I moaned and she said, "Mine too." She fetched aspirin from a cupboard and doled out two apiece. We washed them down with cold tea, smiling weakly.

A voice in my head told me very clearly that Mama was right—this was a miracle from God. This time I could not push that voice away.

It was nearly dawn before we trailed off to bed, hoping for a few hours' sleep. I paused in the kitchen doorway, fighting with myself. "Mama, mind if I take a drive while you and Daddy are at church?" I hoped I sounded nonchalant. "I have a lot of things to sort out. Can you get him up the porch steps?"

She smiled at me and my conscience twinged. I told myself that going to see John had nothing to do with the miracle that had happened tonight.

"'Course I can. You go ahead; you've been stuck in this house too long."

"Okay." My hand lay against the doorpost, which still smelled vaguely of fresh paint. A bird hailed the new morning in one of our front yard oak trees. Before I slept, I would thank God for all he had done. "I love you, Mama," I said, feeling the words on my tongue.

"I love you, too, Celia."

chapter 56

Mama had unveiled so much to me that I'd only begun to grasp it as I sank onto my bed that dawn, crooking my arm around Cubby as if I were six years old again. My perceptions of past years shifted inside me as I replayed her words over and over. One revelation after another filled me, until I thought I would burst. One of those revelations was about Granddad. Thoughts of him were painful; he'd always been my hero. To hear he had deep faults that a young granddaughter could never see was hard to accept. His medals, his victories—these were some of the things I cherished most about him, and these were the very things that had hurt Mama most.

Mama.

Thank you, thank you, God, I breathed, *for giving her the strength to come to me. Thank you that we narrowed the gap between us so much with just one conversation.* Mama and I had already wasted so much time. Just as Danny and I had wasted so much. But with Mama, God had given me another chance. *Please don't let anything hurt our new relationship now, Jesus. I couldn't bear it.*

I hadn't talked to Jesus in so long, yet the words seemed to flow from me. I hugged Cubby tighter as I began to see God's plan. In rapid succession the pieces of this plan sifted through my being, each one more awesome than the last. First, that God had been the author of my conversation with Mama. Second, that he had brought me back to Bradleyville for that express purpose, just as Carrie had declared. And third, that God had planned this healing long ago—before my flight from Bradleyville, before Kevy's death, before I lost Danny. Even before those tragedies, God had *known.* Known enough to promise Granddad on his deathbed that he could rest easily, for one day I would heed a call beyond the self-centered, guilt-ridden world I'd built in Little Rock and return to the town of my childhood.

My mind could barely hold these revelations. *How amazing, Jesus*, I prayed, *that you could show me so much in just a few short hours.*

I, who had held a dead brother in my arms, knew all too well that a cataclysmic moment could alter a life forever. But as the sunrise of thirty-five years cast an ever widening ray through my curtains, I felt the impact of an *internal* life-changing event designed by God. At the mere raising of his finger, new meanings, ancient discernments, tucked among the shadows of everyday occurrences, had suddenly revealed themselves, emerging to gleam brilliantly like fragments of gold. Even as I marveled at this discovery as one would hold glimmering ore to the light, I marveled at the planning and time he had taken to create it. The sands of minutes, days, and years, of conversations, events, and choices, funneling, hardening into nuggets of wisdom yet to be revealed until the moment he enabled me to distinguish them from the sediment of dreams gone awry.

Now that you understand, God nudged me, *will you let me lead you?*

What was I going to do with my life now? I asked myself. Continue down the same dark path or allow Christ to light it for me? For some reason God's invitation did not bathe me in emotion. Perhaps I'd been drained of tears already. Instead it was gentle, quiet. Considering it, I saw how hopeless my future would be if I turned him away after the mercy he'd shown me. So ultimately I made my choice. I prayed from the depths of my neediness, giving Jesus Christ my life, asking him to guide me from that moment on. I needed his help in so many areas. Further healing with Mama, energy to help Daddy, release from the guilt I'd borne for so long. I was so *tired* of the guilt. I wanted to just take it off, like taking off a lead coat. But the heart clung to what the mind would shed. *God*, I prayed, *I give the guilt to you. Please heal this too.*

And, most pressing as the sun rose higher, I needed God's help with John. For I knew what I should do, but the right action seemed more than I could bear. "I don't know how to do this, Lord," I whispered. "I'm like a newborn, and you're asking me to make an adult's decision. Please show me another way. Please let John and me be together. Please...."

Finally I fell asleep.

chapter 57

Exhaustion sat as a lump in my chest as I drove out Route 347 toward John's cabin a few hours later. A gentle breeze blew through my open window, like the breeze the night I had returned to Bradleyville. Following the narrow road with one hand on the wheel, I held John's directions, lips moving silently as I read. I turned from 347 onto another Kentucky back road, which looked much the same as it wound through the forested hills. Five more minutes and I should see the private road that led to his cabin. "If you pass a large red barn on your left, you've gone too far," he had written. My veins flowed with a thick, sleep-deprived adrenaline as I thought of seeing him, of what I would say and how he would respond. For the hundredth time since early that morning I asked God for strength. I pictured John waiting for me and felt my arms tremble.

I rolled to a stop underneath dense trees, the shade cool. Turning into John's long gravel driveway, I'd had to close my windows against the dust. He had heard my approach and was standing in front of his small porch, his A-frame cabin of natural wood nearly blending into the forest. He smiled, expectant, clad in jeans and a red knit shirt. I'd never seen him in jeans before and he looked wonderful. I felt my heart turn over.

"Hi," he called, opening my door. "You found me!"

"Yes," I said quickly. "But John, we have to talk."

He paused, studied my face. "Okay."

"I . . . I can't—would you just sit in my car for a while?"

"Sure." He walked around the front, patting the hood, and got in, rolling down his window. "Good thing we're in the shade." He started to reach for me but stopped at my expression. Leaning against the passenger-side door, he rested a hand on each knee, concern creeping across his forehead. "What is it?"

He looked so handsome in his jeans and shirt, arms tanned and strong. I could almost feel him kissing me, his chest filling my arms. *God*, I prayed, *I can't do this*. "I have a lot to say," I began, "and it's not easy. So I just want you to listen. And I hope you'll understand."

"Okay."

I took a long breath. "Something happened last night between Mama and me. We talked deeply for the first time. I . . . don't know where you are with God, John. But I know without a doubt that he made that conversation happen. Now I understand the hurts in my mother's life. And in understanding those hurts, I can finally begin to forgive her past coldness to me.

"After we talked, I lay awake most of the night, thinking about lots of things. And I realized some incredible truths. I realized that all my life I'd judged Mama when I didn't know the whole story. I could only see my little piece of it. Then I thought about my granddad's life, his mistakes. And my choices as a teenager—some of them terrible mistakes that I'm still paying for. And I realized that Granddad's wrong choices and Mama's and mine were all made because we only focused on our little perceptions of what had happened and what was to be done. When we focused on our hurts and wants, we all did foolish, foolish things that caused other people pain. And we all knew better. We all knew that Jesus was there and willing to lead us, but we just didn't want to follow."

I paused, amazed at the words flowing from me. John remained silent.

"What I'm trying to say is that for the first time in years I have finally promised Jesus that I'll listen to him. Because I know if I don't, I'll just mess things up again, and he gave me too much understanding last night for me to want to chance that. So here's the hardest part." My breath caught. "I can't feel at peace about what you and I are doing. Even with my promise to God, I tried to deny that uneasiness. I can't tell you how much I tried. I *want* to see you, John. I want so much to be wanted. But my conscience won't be quiet. It's telling me that the way we're going about it is deceitful and that God's got a better plan for us."

"I see." His voice held a defensive edge. "And just what would you suggest?"

I gathered myself. He wasn't making this easy. "I think we should hold back for now and pray about what to do." *Pray.* The word felt so rusty on my tongue. "There's a lot to consider. I won't be in Bradleyville much longer. It would be hard to see each other once I'm gone. Maybe we're just not meant to be at all. On the other hand, maybe you're not supposed to marry Sharon. But we need to ask God about this, because if we rush ahead, all of us could get hurt. And even if you and I worked out, our relationship would have started in such a negative way."

He gazed at me intently. "Do you want us to work out?"

"So much." My throat tightened. "I'm very needy, John. Maybe too needy for you."

"No. No, you're not," he said gently, taking my hand. "But come inside with me now, out of the heat. We'll talk about this more."

I knew I couldn't. I knew I dared not even get out of the car, because if I did, no matter the sincerity of my promises to God that morning, I wouldn't have the strength to keep them. I wanted John too much. And in my frailty it was all too clear what would happen once we were inside his cabin. "You're not hearing me, John," I replied softly. "We can't do this today."

"I am hearing you, Celia." He gripped my fingers. "And I know you're right; you're not telling me anything I haven't thought about many times over. I know I have to tell Sharon. But just . . . not yet. It'll break her heart."

"It'll break her heart more if she hears it from someone else."

"She's not going to. No one knows you're here today." His words were tinged with disbelief. "It'll probably be the only time we have before you leave; let's not lose our chance."

Lord, help me!

"John, I *can't*. I want to so much, but . . . I just don't feel it's the right thing to do."

"Yes, it is. Of course it is. Because of the way we feel about each other."

I gazed at him sadly. "What we feel doesn't change what's right and wrong. Can't you see you're just rationalizing?"

He dropped my hand and stared at me. "I'm not rationalizing; I just want to be with you. I want to hold you and be near you. I want you and you need me, and that's all that matters at this moment!"

"And forget God and everybody else, right?" My voice grew thick. I couldn't bear to hear how much he wanted me. "That's exactly what I'm talking about."

"I know you want to be here today. Don't deny us this."

"I have to, John. It's not what God wants."

Sudden anger rolled across his face. "How do *you* know what God wants? And what makes you so pious all of a sudden?"

I looked away, heartsick at his defensiveness.

He lowered his head, scrubbed his face. "Why did you come here anyway? Why did you drive all the way out here?"

"Because," I said slowly, praying that he would understand, "I had to face you and make this choice. And I knew we wouldn't have another opportunity to talk like this."

He surveyed me for a long moment. "I don't believe that's the reason," he said finally. "You came because you wanted to see me. Regardless of what you're saying, deep inside you want me to talk you out of it."

"Please don't try." My throat had begun to hurt. "This is hard enough as it is."

He spread his hands. "So what do you want me to do?"

"I want you to think about—pray about—what to do. And if you decide you still want to see me, you'll need to tell Sharon first."

"Yeah, well, by that time you could be gone."

The words were meant to sting and they did. "Maybe," I replied, my head hung. I pictured myself alone again at home in Little Rock and my heart twisted. "But if God wants us together, it can still happen."

He blew out air. "This is all so easy for you to say, Celia," he accused with frustration. "I don't want to tell my fiancée; you don't know how awful that would be!"

God, I cried, *where are you? Who am I to judge him?* "No, I guess I don't. But will cheating on her make you feel any less awful?"

He shook his head, deflated, hurt. "I can't bring myself to let you go."

I can't either, I thought, feeling the pull of him, wanting to lean across the gearshift and throw my arms around him, saying forget what I've said, forget all of it, just hold me. Just take me into your cabin and kiss me, make me feel what I felt with Danny so many years ago. Let me lose myself in you; wash away my pain over him, give me another chance to love. I cried inside at these desires, and then I thought of my talk with Mama and all that God had shown me. I thought of his truths, the nuggets of gold I had discovered, and I imagined the shell of a person I would become if I buried them again. And I pictured the faces of Mama and Daddy should they discover my duplicity with John.

"You're making this so hard," I whispered.

"I don't mean to," he said softly. "And I admire you for everything you've said, really I do. But this afternoon could be so special, Celia." He lifted my chin until our eyes met, and I understood his meaning. "I could so easily fall in love with you."

"Don't, John, *don't*," I pleaded, my voice breaking. "Don't promise me that; I've been without love too long."

"You can have it again. Right here."

"No, I can't." The world grew blurry, a tear dropping onto my cheek. "I can't take what you're offering. I would be turning away from God again. He may never give me another chance. For years I've been in so much pain; I've got to straighten my life out. Please understand. If you care for me, you'll let me go!"

"Let me help you straighten your life out." Now he was pleading, his voice hoarse. "I care about you; I want to have that chance."

"It's not the right thing to do."

"Our hearts make it right."

"No, John." A single sob burst from me. "Hearts don't make *anything* right! Hearts are greedy and selfish; at least mine is. I've followed my heart all my life and I can't do it anymore." I drew in a ragged breath. "I'm begging you to understand. You're shooting arrows right through me."

He exhaled loudly, putting his face in his hands. I waited in silence, unable to stop crying. A minute ticked by.

"Okay," he said finally, raising his head. "All right. If this is what you want, I'll let you go. I don't know how I'm going to get out of this car, but I will."

My chest felt like lead. "It's not what I want, John. It's what must be. At least for now."

He shifted in his seat, letting his head fall back against the headrest. "Okay. That's it then. Okay, fine. Go." He sat up again, resolve in his actions, and groped for the door handle. "I'll be here till about six," he added. "If you should change your mind . . ." He managed a rueful smile.

I nodded, unable to speak.

"Well. Good-bye, Celia. See you for sure on Tuesday."

How would I ever face him in front of Mama and Daddy? How could I ever greet him as if nothing had happened?

"Bye."

He hesitated, then firmly pushed the door open and got out. At that moment all the resolve I'd had drained away.

Please help me, God, I begged silently. *I can't go through with it.*

I swiped at my eyes, waffling. Then somehow, of its own accord, my hand reached out to start the engine. I told myself I would go only if John remained silent. All he had to do was say something, anything. Didn't he realize how little it would take at that moment for me to turn off the key? Just lean down, John, look at me through the window, tell me again you could love me. Tell me we'll work things out, tell me God wants us together today, and I'll believe you. Talk me out of this; I haven't the strength to leave, not really. I can't go through with it. One little move, John Forkes, just one.

He remained motionless.

My shoulders sagged. My left hand found the wheel. I put the car in reverse, backed onto the side of his driveway, and turned around. He had walked to his porch and was watching me, hands on his hips. I looked at him through the rearview mirror, his eyes finding mine, and my heart clutched with one final hope. He raised his fingers in a still wave. I couldn't tear my gaze away, even then willing him to move.

As I drove away, his image slowly faded into the dust.

chapter 58

In the next few days, somehow I found the strength to push Daddy in performing his exercises and talk more to Mama. All the while I ached for John.

Daddy could not contain his joy over the change between Mama and me. Had he been able, he would have leaped from his wheelchair and danced. As it was, I encouraged him to channel his energies into therapy, and he did just that, attacking his exercises with newfound vigor. Then on Tuesday afternoon he made his first basket into Mama's dresser drawer with the rubber ball.

"Aaah!" I yelled. Daddy let loose a bray that brought Mama at a run, fearfully demanding, "What happened, what happened?"

As fortune would have it, Daddy tried and tried to repeat it for her with no success, only to make another basket after she had left the room. "We'll have to see who can get to twenty points first!" I challenged, fetching the ball from the drawer with a flourish. "I'll use my left hand, too, just to be fair. We could even get a little wager going on the side. What do you think we should bet?"

"Appul pie."

Daddy sat in a chair I had brought from the dining table. He rarely used the wheelchair anymore, except when Mama took him around the block. The previous day he had requested, after Mama pushed him back home, that I bring his walker outside, and he and she went slowly up and down our sidewalk.

I continued to pray for God's help but still thought of John constantly. Cars would pass on Minton and I'd find myself glancing through the curtains to see if it was he. Once I even looked up his office number, with a question about Daddy as an excuse to hear his voice. As Tuesday evening approached, I was filled with ambivalence over seeing him. I found myself eating supper quickly, saying I wanted to go to the dime store before it closed. I hurried out and ended up buying a few unnecessary items, lingering over each choice. Even then I was afraid to return too soon, and some masochistic hunger prompted me to drive to the field where Danny and I had parked the night before he left Bradleyville.

I got out of the car, gazing at the path that led to our fishing spot, picturing Danny sitting on a boulder, waiting for me. Hurting over John, filled with my age-old longing for Danny, I almost followed the path but knew I couldn't bear it. I climbed back in my car and turned down Wilder Road, slowing as I passed the Canders' old property, gaping at the large new house built by the current occupants. The farm was immaculate, fresh and green, cows dotting the pasture, a rich field newly planted. *This is what Danny could have made it,* I thought, *had he stayed.*

By the time I returned home, John had come and gone. "He said to tell you he was sorry he missed you," Mama related. She looked at me curiously but did not ask where I had been.

Daddy continued to improve. Thursday at breakfast he spoke openly about returning to work. As he broached the subject, I glanced at Mama but she showed no sign of irritation. "I mentioned to your daddy about the computer and maybe doin' some work at home," she said casually, buttering toast. "He thinks it's a good idea, if Mr. Sledge will agree to it. We talked about drivin' in next Tuesday to see him, if William continues to feel well."

"Haa!" Daddy put in. "I feel graeet!"

I could only silently thank God.

We didn't speak of my leaving, although we were all thinking of it. With Daddy's new rate of improvement the day was fast approaching. I wanted to tell them that even when I returned to Little Rock, we would never be separated as we once were. I'd had estrangement enough for a lifetime. But I couldn't bring myself to mention it, for the thought of the quiet aloneness within my own little house filled me with despair. "Daddy, that's absolutely wonderful," I exclaimed. "I'll drive you to Albertsville next Tuesday, if you like."

"That's all right," Mama responded. "I want to do it."

"Okay."

I calculated my time alone while they would be gone and thought of John.

Daddy and I were playing "twenty points" after supper when I heard Mama answer the phone. He had six points to my ten. To even the contest, I had placed myself farther away from the dresser. The game had been doing wonders for Daddy's strength and coordination.

"Eight!" he declared upon making another basket.

"Humph," I said. "If you beat me, I'm gonna make you back up your chair."

"Celia!" Mama called. "Telephone!"

I returned the ball to Daddy, hoping it was John. "Be right back."

"It's Jessie," Mama whispered, handing me the phone. I managed a smile.

Miss Jessie asked me where I had been Sunday. "Even your daddy was in church," she chided.

"Oh, I was tired, that's all. Just needed some time by myself."

"Well, I suppose you've earned that," she said agreeably. "Anyway, I called to see if you would come to our house next Sunday after church for our family get-together. The kids still haven't seen you and neither has Lee, for that matter."

"I'll be at church for sure," I replied, knowing I did not dare stay home alone. "And I'd love to come to your house afterward." All the same, the thought of seeing Mrs. B. did not thrill me.

"Great! I'll see you Sunday, then. And just in case you decide to sleep in, when your parents get home from church, you just head on over."

"They're not coming?"

She hesitated. "Estelle's not sure William will be up to it after sittin' through one a Pastor's sermons, I guess."

She laughed and I joined in, unconvinced. I wondered what was going on. "All right, I'll be there."

"Good." Her tone changed ever so slightly. "One last thing, Celia. I heard some more news about Danny and thought you might be interested."

Electric current jolted through me. I braced myself. "Oh?" My voice was forced lightness.

"I got a letter from Patricia yesterday. She says he's finally thinkin' about settling down with this girl in Greece—Kathy's her name. He's flying to New York on Monday for business, and he told Patricia he planned to look for a ring."

"That's great," someone said, and I heard my own voice.

The line grew quiet.

"Celia?" Miss Jessie prompted. "Have I upset you? I thought you'd want to know."

"I am glad to know. And I'm glad for Danny, really I am." I gripped the telephone cord until my knuckles whitened.

"Why don't I believe you?" she said quietly, surprise etching her tone.

Maybe I was too raw from the open wound of John. Maybe I was too fearful of soon returning to Little Rock, the reality of that aloneness weighting me. Maybe after all that God had shown me, I just didn't have the need to save face as before. Maybe it was all those things. For whatever reason, at that moment I blurted words that erased seventeen years of silence on the subject. "Miss Jessie"—my tone turned bitter—"you must have talked to him. Why did he leave me?"

She inhaled loudly enough for me to hear. "Celia—" She hesitated, as if searching for words. "I don't know what to say. I mean . . . you left *him*."

A rush of air escaped me. "Did he tell you that?" I replied angrily, as if it had been yesterday. "He's the one who went to Greece."

"Yes, I know, but . . . but that was only after . . ." Her voice trailed away.

Even as I write this, I feel so mad—madder than I ever was at my daddy.

The cord felt slippery in my palm. She didn't need to say it; I knew. After my hateful act of revenge, little wonder Danny had ultimately changed his mind about us forgiving each other.

"Never mind, Miss Jessie," I breathed. "It doesn't matter."

"But Celia, after all these years—" She paused. "That is, since you're asking. I always thought you'd decided on Bobby. That was true, right?" Why was she insisting on explaining this? "And then when Kevin died, you just couldn't face stayin' here. I never thought that now you might still . . ."

She seemed to have trouble finishing her sentences.

"I don't," I insisted. "I don't care, if that's what you're thinking. After all this time? Heavens, no, that was seventeen years ago; we were just kids."

"Celia—"

"*I don't care.* I'm glad he's happy! Thank you for telling me." I had to get off the phone; my voice could no longer hold steady.

"He knows you're in town." Miss Jessie kept at it. "Do you want me to say hello for you if he calls from New York?"

Wouldn't that just do it, I thought. How sociable, after seventeen years. "No, I don't think so."

"Are you sure? He'd be so glad to hear from you. More than you know."

Right, Miss Jessie, so glad. Glad enough to be skipping into a jewelry store as he looked for a ring to put on someone else's finger.

"No, Miss Jessie. Forget it. I mean it."

"Well. Okay. Whatever you say."

I hung up the phone with shaky hands. Only then did I realize Mama was in the kitchen and had heard every word.

chapter 59

The world spun, its centrifugal force pulling my emotions in a thousand directions. Mama. Daddy. John. Danny. God. My thoughts bounced from one to another, from victory to loss, and could find no peace.

Mama apparently couldn't gather the nerve to broach the subject of Danny until the following morning. Daddy had just aced his way through another exercise session while Mama ran some errands. She and I were in the kitchen as he sat in the living room, reading the paper. "Celia," she said quietly, and I knew from her tone what was coming. "I didn't realize how much you still love Danny."

I froze at the sink, dirty dishes from breakfast in each hand. Our relationship was still too new, too fragile, to speak of this.

"Why not?" I challenged, staring at a smear of jelly on a knife. I told myself to watch my tone of voice. "You loved Henry the same way; why is it hard for you to see it in me?"

She sat at the table, a cup of coffee before her. "I guess I didn't want to believe it, because I . . . because there's—" She rubbed a hand across her forehead. "Because I know how unhappy it would make you."

"Well, I've hardly been bouncing up and down."

"No," she said evenly, refusing to argue. "But there were so many other things to weigh you down. I didn't realize how much of your hurt had to do with Danny."

I turned on the faucet. "It doesn't matter now."

"It matters. I want you to be happy."

"Oh, I'll be fine. As always." My voice was tinged with bitterness. "*He* certainly sounds happy."

"Yes. Jessie told me the news." She hesitated, as if deciding how to continue. "Maybe now, after hearing about his plans, you can finally put it all behind you. God can help you find someone else."

If only she knew. But even John could never be Danny.

"There are other things in life, Mama." I scrubbed the knife needlessly. "I have you and Daddy now. Even after I've gone, we'll call each other often. Maybe you two can come visit me sometime. And I'm going to keep working on staying in line with God."

A smile warmed her face. "I'm so glad to hear that. You know I'm tryin' to do the same thing." She sipped her coffee. "When are you going?"

"I don't know." Could she hear my reticence? "I guess when Daddy starts work. My promise to him will be fulfilled then, won't it?"

"I suppose so. You anxious to get back to your job?"

Done with one knife, I picked up another. I held it under a stream of water and watched the jelly melt, unwilling to admit the answer to her question.

At supper I forced away thoughts of John's impending visit and listened as Daddy talked excitedly about the meeting he had scheduled with Mr. Sledge the following Tuesday. A little over a week past that and his eight weeks would be up. His face had almost returned to normal, and just that morning he'd mentioned trying to walk without the walker. I was so happy to see animation in his features, hear it in his voice. He had thanked me many times, often with tears in his eyes, and I could honestly respond by saying how glad I was that I had come.

The doorbell rang and I jumped. "It's Dr. Forkes," Mama said.

Daddy placed a hand on her arm. "Let me go."

Mama and I exchanged a smile as he slowly rose from his chair, holding lightly on to his walker, and headed for the door.

"Whoa!" we heard John declare. "Who might this be?"

"Isn't he somethin'!" Mama called, leaving the table to join them.

My smile unpinned itself and slipped away.

I was gathering the leftovers when John stuck his head through the kitchen door. When he gently spoke my name, I was so busy finding a plastic container for the mashed potatoes that I didn't look up.

"I just wanted to congratulate you," he said. "You really did it. And I thought you'd never see it through."

"Thank you." I pulled out a container, rejected it, and tried another. I could feel his light hazel eyes on my back.

"Does this mean you're leaving soon?"

I shoved back the second container and the whole stack fell from the cupboard. Daddy was asking Mama in the living room if she wanted to go for a walk. *No!* I begged silently. *Don't go now!*

"Why is everybody asking me when I'm leaving?" I said irritably. "I don't know when I'm leaving, okay?"

"Are you sure you're up to gettin' down those steps?" Mama asked, balking.

"I'm up ta anything; just watch me!"

"Fine, then, let me take your walker down first." The front door opened.

Furiously I snatched the containers from the floor and tried to stack them in order, willing Mama and Daddy to stay, wanting them to leave, afraid to turn around.

"You know I'm not trying to run you off," John said.

That was an understatement. I replaced the plastic bowls in the cupboard, knocking down a row of lids. "Drat it!"

"Celia."

"What!" I gathered the lids, still too busy to look at him.

"I just want you to know," he told me quietly, "that I respect what you said at the cabin. As much as I rejected your words at the time, I've been doing a lot of thinking since then. And I need to tell you something. I realize I'm not ready to break things off with Sharon just yet."

The statement shot right through me. I'd never expected him to make such a decision so fast. At the threat of losing him for good, I began to turn around.

"But I still want to see you."

I halted, the plastic slick in my fingers. Fleetingly I visualized a woman betrayed. The woman had Melissa's face.

"Celia, would you just look at me?"

I slid the lids back into the cupboard, leaving out two that I needed. I found the bowls that matched, shut the cupboard door. Hung on to the counter.

"I can't, John."

With resolve I picked up the bowl of mashed potatoes and began scraping them with a rubber spatula into a plastic container, waiting, as I'd done five days before, for him to say something. *Please, God, why is this happening again?* The potatoes done, their lid on, I started on the lima beans. The silence grew longer and I forced myself not to turn around, finishing the beans, snapping on the lid, until I could stand it no more and turned. He was gone.

"John!"

I caught him before he reached the front door. Searched awkwardly for words. "I'm sorry," I blurted, failing to keep enough distance between us. "We may not have another chance to talk."

"I know." His expression turned expectant, pleading.

It hurt, standing so close to him. I swallowed hard, feeling as if everything I'd ever done came down to that one moment. I saw the tragedies of my past, the future years alone in Little Rock. My legs weakened. *God, why?* My mouth opened. I still did not know what I would say.

"You and Sharon." My voice sounded flat. "You'll make it."

Of course they would. Everyone around me did. Bobby and Melissa, Danny and his new love, Carrie and Andy, Roger, Michael.

John's face fell. A moment passed before he could speak. "Well, I . . . hope so." He smiled sadly.

My tears wouldn't blink away. "I'll pray that you will."

chapter 60

G unna beat you this time." Daddy wrapped his fingers around the back of the wooden chair in his bedroom and carefully lifted it, forcing the use of his left arm. Mama had offered to do the supper dishes alone so he and I could play our game. "There," he said, his words still slow. "I'll sit here an' you stand there. Saam distance."

On his first try he made a basket. "Two," he declared.

"Smart aleck." I bounced the ball and it landed inside the drawer. "Ha!"

"You goin' ta Jessie's tamorrow?" he asked as he took his turn. "Four."

I fetched the ball. "Yeah. Why aren't you two coming?"

"I don' know." He shrugged. "Your mama doesn't wanna go."

"Mama hasn't seen Mrs. B. for a long time, and I know she's going to be there. You didn't say you'd be too tired after church?"

"Heck, no, I'm Tarzan."

"Yeah. Well, Tarzan, you just missed and now I'm ahead."

"Not for long."

We fell into silence as we each made two more baskets. I pushed away constant thoughts of Danny and John.

"You know what?" I said after we continued to score. "This is too easy now. We need a narrower space to aim for. Isn't there a box around here somewhere?" I thought a minute. "Let's do this. Let's pile all this paper and stuff in the drawer into two stacks on either side, and we have to get the ball in the middle. If we hit either of the stacks, it'll bounce away."

Daddy screwed up his face. "Mama won't like it. She's particalar."

I shrugged it off. "Don't worry, I'll put everything back where it was." I knelt before the drawer and began moving things aside until there were two even piles of envelopes, cards, and paper. "There."

Daddy took a turn and missed.

"Aha!" I exclaimed. "See, it's harder." For the next three turns I didn't do so well myself.

"You gunna make sure I get ta Sledge's, right?" Daddy said a few minutes later.

"Yes. I promised you, didn't I?" I chased the ball before it could roll under the bed. "You want to go back pretty badly, don't you?"

"Yeah. I'm tired a sittin' here day after day. Need some brain food. Now that I got you and your mama gettin' along, I got nothing ta do."

"Oh, really. Well, you're not exactly swinging from trees yet. Don't think you can let up on your exercises."

"I know, I know. Slave driver." He aimed, closing one eye, and threw.

"Hey, look, you got it! Straight shot in."

I moved to the dresser and bent down to pick up the ball. "What's the score, anyway? I for—"

My eye was caught by the corner of an envelope sticking from the bottom of a stack. Something about the few visible curves of writing looked familiar. I cocked my head and stared at it.

"I got ten; you got eight," Daddy claimed.

"No way," I responded absently, looking at the envelope. "*I've* got ten."

"Uh-uh."

I reached into the drawer, mesmerized by that little corner of white envelope, and for absolutely no reason my hand began to shake. I told myself it was nothing, just some old letter to Mama, but it pulled me. Grasping it, I hesitated, then slid it out the slightest bit, exposing more of the return address. I saw my own handwriting.

My heart began to pound. My eyes burned a hole through the envelope, and I pulled it out further until I could read the entire return address. *101 Minton Street, Bradleyville, Kentucky.* My throat was tightening; I could barely swallow, and somewhere behind me I heard Daddy asking what was taking so long. My heart was hammering in both ears, blood whooshing through my head. I tried to pull the envelope out further and it slipped from my fingers; I tried again, sliding it slowly, hearing it hiss. It was halfway out and I could not breathe. I rotated my head, waiting for the address to appear, and already I knew. A rubber band ran across the writing, and I could bear it no longer. I snatched the envelope up and a smaller one beneath came with it. I held the top one shakily, reading Danny Cander's name, the familiar Miami address, noticing that the envelope was slit open at the top. I ripped off the rubber band and stared at the smaller envelope, seeing the handwriting I would always remember, the envelope addressed to me, a return address in Greece. A cry escaped me and I fell to my knees, slipping my fingers into the first envelope, drawing out the letter, the other papers released and falling white against the blue carpet. I opened the letter as my heart kept pounding, and I sucked in air, little sounds spilling from my lips. Daddy was talking but I couldn't understand what he said; I could only gape at the painstaking, gut-wrenching answer of an eighteen-year-old desperately in love.

May 21

Dearest Danny,

I'm coming to you. You're right; if God can forgive us both, we can surely forgive one another. Please don't go. Please don't choose the world over me, even after what I've done. What you did with Rachel, you hadn't planned. What I did with Bobby was intentional. I was terribly wrong. I love you. I know you love me. Write back. Tell me you'll wait for me, Danny. Tell me exactly where to come. Wait. Please.

A sob wrenched my throat. I snatched up the envelope, searching for a postmark, knowing I wouldn't find it. I reached into the second envelope. His letter trembled in my fingers as I read it.

June 30

Dear Celia,

I can't live like this, without you. Please forgive my last hurtful letter. I've made a terrible mistake by coming here to Greece. I don't want to be anywhere unless you're with me. I should never have gotten on the ship. I should have gone back to Bradleyville and made you want me again, even after all that's happened. Are you with Bobby now? Is that why you didn't write me back? You must have chosen him but I just can't believe that. I know you love me like I love you. I'm begging you again, let's put everything behind us and start over. I've hurt you, you've hurt me, we're even, okay? I don't know how I'll do it, but I'll save every penny and get back home to you, even if it means leaving Mama behind. She already loves it here

anyway and wouldn't want to leave. Just write me. I can't give up
on us. I'm waiting for your letter. I'll come back to you. Do you hear
me pleading, Celia? I love you. I'll always love you. Write, please.
I'm waiting.

I clutched the envelopes and letters, Daddy asking me what was
wrong, my mind flying into a million pieces as I sorted through the
misunderstandings, the *waste* of years. Danny had written to me the
very day Kevy died. It was more than I could bear to think about, his
pain and mine, the love that had crossed continents, unknown and
unreached. My agonizing wait to receive his reply to a letter never read.
The years I longed for him, wondering why he'd left me.

"Oh, Danny, Danny." Hot tears flowed from my eyes as I began to
cry desperately, the thought that he believed I'd left him sending a knife
through my stomach.

"Cela, what . . ."

Daddy's voice thickened with fright but I couldn't answer. I rose,
feeling the carpet beneath my feet, the floor of the hallway, as I ran
into the living room yelling for Mama. Somewhere along the way my
knees buckled and I fell; I pushed myself up again, not stopping, the
envelopes and letters still in my hands. She appeared from the kitchen,
wide-eyed, her face pale.

"What's happened?" She looked past me, thinking it was Daddy.
Then she saw the white of the papers, the black of her deceit. And she
froze.

"Why? Dear God, why?" I held up both hands, shaking the proof at
her, wanting her to tell me it was all a bad joke, a mistake. "Why did
you—how could you do it?"

She searched for an answer, fingers splayed across her throat. "Oh,
Celia, I was going to tell you—"

"But why? Do you understand what you did?" I could barely squeeze
out the words. "He thought I didn't want him! All these years!" Sinking
to my knees, I sobbed wildly. She hurried over to comfort me but I
pushed her away. "No, don't! How could you? You took my *life* away!"

"Celia, listen to me." I heard the intensity in her voice. "I didn't
know how important your letter was when I kept it. I was just tryin' to
keep you from getting hurt. With all those letters flying, I had to see
for myself what was happening. And the very worst thing I feared, I
saw in that letter. The next thing I knew, he was writin' from Greece."

"Mrs. B. helped you, didn't she?" I said, sobbing. "She saw my letter in the post office and gave it to you!"

"She was worried about you, too."

"Worried!" I laughed scornfully. "What about worrying about me all these years I've been alone? All the years I've believed a lie and Danny's believed a lie?"

"Celia, please," she begged, reaching for me again. I wrenched away. "By the time that letter came from Greece and I realized what I'd done, you were gone! I kept thinkin' that as soon as you came back, I'd show you the letters; why else would I keep them? But you never did, and by the time you finally called, six years had passed. I didn't think it would still matter."

"You should have known!" I screamed. "Because you felt the same way about Henry! You just didn't want to admit you were wrong about Danny." I sobbed harder. "I can't believe it now, after all that's happened. After you've supposedly turned back to God. I was amazed how fast you'd changed but now I see the truth. You haven't really changed at all! You were just lying! I just don't understand how you could have done this, and now it's too late, it really is too late!" The sobs hurled from my throat, my chest on fire.

"I tried to tell you, Celia," she said, pleading for my understanding. "I came so close. I *have* changed. But I was afraid you wouldn't be able to forgive me, and I couldn't bear to lose you again. And I didn't know till just yesterday how m—"

"You're so good at closing your eyes when you don't want to see!" My voice was acrid.

"Celia, don't, *please.*" Mama began to cry. "I tried to do what was best."

"Cela, Estelle! What? What?" Daddy stood with his walker at the hall entrance, face drawn.

Mama sucked in a breath. "Oh, William, don't—"

"Daddy!" I flung out my arms. "Tell me you didn't know! She took Danny away from me. She took Danny!"

"Cela, wh—"

Mama cut in harshly. "Leave him out of this, Celia; he never knew a thing, for heaven's sake! William, sit down; your face is gray." I heard the rustle of her clothes as she hastened to him. "Tell him you're all right, Celia," she commanded. "Tell him so he'll sit down; you're worrying him."

"I'm not all right!" I swayed to my feet. "I'll never be all right again! How can I be? And I'll never forgive you for what you've done, you hear me? *Never!*"

"No, Cela—"

"William, sit *down!* Celia—"

Bending over, I swept the papers from the floor, pressing them against my chest as I ran to my bedroom, Danny's letter, his love to me, burning a hole through my heart.

chapter 61

I could not stand the shrinking walls of my bedroom for long and soon slipped out to my car. My eyes blurred with my renewed losses as I drove randomly through the Bradleyville streets. *How could you let this happen, Jesus?* I asked, weeping. *Where were you then? And where are you now? After I've obeyed you and stayed away from John. After you gave me Mama back. Why should I listen to you now?*

After some time I found myself downtown, crossing the railroad tracks. Of their own accord my wheels put me on a winding course, spinning me again toward the field where Danny and I had parked his Impala so long ago. I stopped the car at the field and got out to walk, watching the riverbank draw nearer, drinking in the boulders and water as I approached, imagining the roar of the rapids.

Nothing at the riverbank had changed.

For all its appearance, Danny could have come walking through the daisy field, fishing pole in hand. I could picture him so clearly, could feel his hair sifting through my fingers, smell his sun-drenched skin.

God, why?

I turned up the riverbank, remembering the day it had poured rain and we first ran to our trees. The setting sun fizzled embers of burnt orange upon the water. When I saw the trees in the distance, I broke into a run, stumbling over rocks and onto the deep grass, the canopy wrapping around my shoulders. There stood the trunks; there was where we first sat side by side, hesitant and fearful.

I threw myself down, clutching an exposed tree root, its surface worn smooth, crying until I could cry no more. I hurled more accusations at God until I found myself turning to him out of sheer despair. I couldn't lose the hope I'd found in him, I *couldn't*. But pray as I might, I could find no sense in all this. On my knees, I begged him to help me understand.

I had no recognition of time, looking up suddenly to find darkness engulfing the river. Fear of being drenched in blackness flushed through me, and I heaved myself from the ground and walked away swiftly.

I drove again, my headlights washing over the gloominess of downtown, pulling me up Main Street. On sudden impulse I turned left to the Hardings' house, warm light through their windows beckoning me to their front door. Miss Jessie took one look at my puffy face and pulled me inside, eyes wide. "Is it William?" Lee appeared, still a big bear of a man, his black hair grayed at the temples, his mustache now shaved. I hugged him wordlessly, then pulled the letters out of my pocket.

"Look what they've done," I said thickly, giving them to Miss Jessie. "I found them in Mama's drawer."

She glanced at them, startled, then read, her mouth falling slack. "Aunt *Eva?*"

I nodded, swallowing hard. "I mailed my letter at the post office. She held it back."

She stared, meanings and consequences moving across her face.

"Let me see," Lee broke in, grabbing the letters.

"This is what you meant, wasn't it?" The words poured from me. "When you said I left him? You didn't mean what I did with Bobby; you meant that I never wrote Danny back. But I did! No wonder he was so sad when he first went to Greece! Why didn't you tell me?"

"Celia," she said, her expression still one of astonishment, "how could I have known?"

"Maybe not about the letters, but you must have known how hurt he was over me."

"You disappeared, Celia; nobody knew where you were!" She ran a hand across her cheek. "By the time we heard from you, years had gone by. If I'd known you still cared, I'd have told you long ago."

My knees trembled. "Oh, Miss Jessie, what do I do?"

"Talk to him," Lee said with a shrug, as if it were obvious. "He'll be in New York in a few days."

I laughed hoarsely. "Just like that, after seventeen years. Sure, Lee."

"But you should," Miss Jessie agreed. "He'd want to know."

"He's in love with someone else."

"He's waited all this time," she returned. "I don't think he's ever really wanted to marry anyone but you."

"How can you say that, when he's ready to become engaged? I can't just pick up the phone and tell him this now, after all these years!"

Miss Jessie thought for a moment, her face working. "Maybe not. It's a lot to say over the phone. Maybe you should go see him. I know what hotel he'll be staying in. Go soon, be there when he arrives."

I fell into a chair, dropping my head into my hands. "That's crazy. Absolutely crazy. For all the same reasons. And besides, I can't leave Bradleyville yet; I promised Daddy."

"Promised what? You came to help him get better, and he is."

"No, I've promised I'd see him back to work. Just a few hours ago I told him that again." Had it really been only a few hours? It seemed a lifetime ago. "It's so important to him. I can't go and leave things to Mama; she obviously can't be trusted."

"Celia, I don't mean to belittle your promise, but this is so important to you," Miss Jessie argued. "Your daddy will understand; he'd want you to go. And besides, you can come back. Just talk to Danny, see if you can get things straightened out. I know it's been a long time, and I know his life is about to take another course, but if you don't do it, won't you always wonder?" She dropped to her knees beside me. "Oh, Celia, you'll manage. Go. If you're afraid of surprising him, you can call him in Greece, tell him you're comin'. I know he'd want you to."

I bounced my head against the back of the chair and gazed at the ceiling. "But I promised Daddy. He's got a meeting with his boss Tuesday. If that doesn't go well, I should be here to push things with Mr. Sledge. It may not sound like such a big deal to you, but it is to me. I can't run out on him again, don't you see? I did that once before. He's counting on me. I can't stand to think of hurting him again."

Miss Jessie exchanged a stymied look with Lee. "Why did Estelle ask Aunt Eva to do this?" she wondered aloud.

"She wanted to keep me from getting hurt," I told her. "How's that for laughs?"

"I'll bet that's why they argued," Lee commented.

I frowned at him. "Who?"

"It's nothin', Celia." Miss Jessie waved a hand. "Your mama just had a little tiff with Aunt Eva, that's all."

"What do you mean, that's all? Those two have never argued in their lives. I suppose you know all about that relationship, too." My tone sounded too harsh and I was instantly sorry. Miss Jessie looked at her lap. "What did they argue about?"

"You. When Aunt Eva and Uncle Frank visited, your mama told her not to come back as long as you were there."

I gazed at her in astonishment. "Why?"

She shook her head. "Evidently after they saw you, Aunt Eva made some remark about you still being single, and your mama told her she was in no position to judge."

Mama fighting with Mrs. B. over me. Eva Bellingham, her closest link to Henry. "I can't believe that," I whispered and then thought, *Yes, I can.* Mama felt so guilty over what they'd done that her first instinct had been to defend me, even against her closest friend and cohort. I turned this over in my mind, imagining the instant flare of her temper at Mrs. B.'s offhand comment and seeing in its blaze the illumination of her love for me.

God, help me hang on to this.

"I have to get back," I exclaimed suddenly. "I have to talk to them about Danny. Maybe I *can* go, crazy as it is. Maybe they'll understand." Vacantly I stared through the front window, unable to think clearly. "I would have to pack and figure out ... everything. How to fly there and get to the hotel. I should call Danny first; you're right." I rose from the chair, picking up the letters from the couch. "Thank you both so much; it's good I came. I'll have to call you later. For how to get in touch with Danny. In Greece, I mean. And the hotel. I don't want to take the time right now; I've got to get back."

"All right." Miss Jessie looked nonplussed at my turnabout.

The next thing I remember, I was in my car.

I drove home with anticipation, telling myself this would work, it *had* to. Far-fetched as it was. This must have been another part of what God had planned for me in my return to Bradleyville. He had simply insisted that I turn to him first. How awful it would have been, I realized, if I'd said yes to John. Maybe God would have changed his mind, not allowed me to find the letters. But now, after all the years and pain and lies, I could be with Danny in two days. *Danny.* I imagined catching my first glimpse of him, looking into his eyes. Surely he wouldn't turn me away ...

Then reality rose before me. What of Kathy? Did she love him? How could I do anything to cause her pain? Yet if what Miss Jessie thought about Danny was true, how could he ever really make Kathy happy?

Could Danny and I have another chance? Could we? I had to see for myself.

I rehearsed my words to Mama and Daddy, believing they would understand—Daddy because he yearned for my happiness, and Mama because she was heartsick over what she'd done. I slid from my car in the driveway, crunching over gravel in the dark, hurrying onto the lighted front porch. As I reached for the door handle, I prayed for the right words to say, thinking I had to pack, I had to call about flights; it would be a long drive to the Lexington airport.

I pushed the door open and heard Mama's muffled scream.

chapter 62

Vaguely I heard John's footsteps approach. I was slumped on the couch, forehead pressed into my palms, staring at my feet. Mama had been slowly pacing and drew to a halt when he entered the room. I lifted my head, looking to John for answers, fear and remorse dulling my nerves. He met my eyes, his smile tight.

"Let me tell you what I know." He sank to the edge of Mama's chair. "It looks like he's had the kind of stroke we call a T.I.A.—transient ischemic attack. I know you had a scare there, Estelle, but the good news is, it probably isn't as bad as it looks. It's set him back, that's for sure, but he's not as bad as the first time around, and he'll be able to bounce back much faster. Mainly, a T.I.A. can play a psychological game, especially in William's case because he was fairly near recovery. Now of course he's very depressed. His mind's as clear as ever and he feels trapped again by a body that's not working. It's very important to keep his spirits up and keep him doing his exercises. As long as that occurs, you should find that in a couple of weeks he's returned to the level of recovery he was enjoying before this happened."

"What if it happens again?" Mama demanded.

He shrugged slightly. "We have no guarantee that it won't. On the other hand, just because it happened once doesn't mean it will again. Don't despair. I do believe, because of the progress he's already shown, that he's going to lead a normal life again. Celia, you've got your work cut out for you the next few weeks. I hope you can stay and see it through, because he's going to need you more than ever."

My mind numbed as I stared at John, fingers clenched. "Is he awake?"

"Yes, he's waiting to see you both. Everything I've told you, he already knows."

Mama hurried off to see him. I looked at the floor again, dreading to face Daddy.

"Celia," John said, moving to sit beside me, "he's going to be all right."

I nodded.

"Heck, you pulled miracles out of a hat with him before. After all you've done, this is going to be easy."

"John, I have to ask you," I said to my feet, "could stress have caused it? Mama and I had a bad argument and he was really upset."

He reached for my hand. "Celia, if you're trying to take the blame for this, don't. These things just happen; if I could predict them, I'd be a wealthy man."

Air caught in my throat. "I don't want to see him suffer anymore because of me."

"He's not; you're the one who's helped him so much. You'll help him now."

"I don't have the strength. And I feel so bad for Daddy." I suppressed a sob. "And now I can't *leave.*"

"Are you really that anxious to go?" The hurt in his voice was unmistakable.

I closed my eyes. "I need to get to Daddy now. Thanks for staying with us so late."

"Hey, I'm a small-town doctor; what do you expect? We never sleep."

I squeezed his fingers and released them, seeking the energy to face Daddy with a reassuring smile. Worse, Mama would be beside him. What could I possibly say to her after history had chosen to repeat itself and I once again felt the burden of blame on my shoulders?

"Okay, Daddy. Let's see how high you can lift from the knee."

It seemed so long ago that we had been at this point. I watched his leg move with one-third of the motion he'd had twenty-four hours before. Was it just the previous night we had been shooting baskets? Now, the next morning, he could barely hold the ball. He was back in his wheelchair. I had rehooked the bag that held paper and pen to its right side. Writing seemed easier than talking.

Tears had burst from me the moment I'd seen Daddy's newly sagging mouth the previous night. My planned encouragement whisking away,

I had knelt next to the bed and buried my head in his side. "I'm sorry, Daddy, I did this to you; I'm so sorry," I said, crying as he patted me on the head, intoning, "Nuuh, nuuh." Mama watched silently, her eyes burning into my back. She and I still had not spoken. God had abandoned us both.

Daddy performed the exercises with grim determination, sweat on his forehead. I rubbed his cheek and he took my hand, pressing it. Then he reached for his writing utensils, gesturing for me to sit. Watching him once again write so laboriously cut me to the heart.

Choose your battles.

I stared in surprise at Granddad's old admonition. "I am, Daddy. And you're it. Or I should say, your arms and legs are it. I told you I'd see you back to work and I will. This time we're going to make it."

Only this time it would be too late for me.

He shook his head slowly.

Mama is your battle.

She had been my worst enemy, all right, but this was not what he meant. "Oh, Daddy," I said with a sigh. "You forget something. Mama was the one battle even Granddad couldn't win."

With God you can win.

"Not this time."

He tapped the sentence with the point of his pen.

"It's too late, Daddy; I don't know how to even try now. Everything's too late."

You're trying again with me.

I exhaled in frustration. "You I can mend. But with her it's been a lifetime of problems. What she did with that letter was so intentional."

The result was wrong but her intent was good.

He regarded me with hopeful eyes.

Had I more tears, I would have shed them, because searching Daddy's face, I realized that his disappointment over Mama and me ran deeper than his disappointment over his own body. I didn't know how to rebuild the bridge to Mama, for she had cost me Danny and that was so hard to forgive. And now I had done this to Daddy; how could she ever forgive *me?* Yet now more than ever we needed to get along for his sake.

"I know," I said, forcing the words. "And I'll talk to her, try to straighten things out. Don't worry."

The sweetness of his lopsided smile was heartrending.

I called the Hardings before they left for church. Mama had already phoned Pastor Beekins, who consoled her, telling her that the congregation would be praying. "I can't leave now, of course," I told Miss Jessie in a low voice.

"There's still a chance, Celia," she said, her tone heavy. "I'll give you the number; you can at least call him at his hotel Monday evenin'."

I laughed tiredly. "We've been through this, remember? A phone call after seventeen years? When he's planning to become engaged? It's too late, Miss Jessie. Thank you for trying to help. But it's just too late."

"Sorry for pushin', but I think you're just scared. What have you got to lose?"

"Everything!" I burst. "At least now I know he didn't leave me of his own choice. What if he turned from me now—purposely? I couldn't stand it!"

"Do you want me to call him for you? Or say anything if he calls me?"

"No! Let him be; he's got his own life now."

"What if he asks about you?"

"Tell him the truth. That I'm very busy with Daddy. And that"— my voice faltered—"that I'm glad for him."

Miss Jessie could not seem to let it die. We argued quite a while before she reluctantly agreed not to press me anymore.

Hanging up the phone, I turned, lead in my chest, to see Mama standing in the threshold of the hallway. "You were goin' somewhere?" she asked, surprise in her voice.

Such a pipe dream, my foolhardy plans of flying to New York. Such a fairy tale. Her demand for an answer swelled my feelings of devastation, and I found myself bitterly telling her about my visit to the Hardings'.

"Stupid, huh?" I scorned. "As if appearing on his doorstep at the last minute would change his mind. But it was my only chance, Mama, after everything you've done. I said I'd go."

My accusation cut her to the quick. "And now?"

"I can't go. Daddy needs me."

She swallowed.

"Well, I promised him, didn't I?" My voice thickened with disappointment and anger. "I promised I'd see him back to work! So don't you think I'm going to run off like last time! I may have caused this just like I caused Kevy's death, but I'm not running again, okay? Even for Danny Cander. You can count on me this time, you hear?"

Her face creased and she leaned against the wall. "Oh, Celia." Her eyes closed. "I don't want to be your enemy. I can't bear to lose you now. What's it goin' to take to earn your forgiveness?"

Her meager apology failed to move me; we had fallen back too far. The acidity of my answer nearly closed my throat.

"Turn back time, Mama. Bring Danny back."

She remained still as I brushed against her shoulder on the way to my room.

chapter 63

The clock moved slowly Monday. I pushed Daddy to the breakfast table and pictured Danny on his plane to New York. "Lift a little higher," I encouraged during morning therapy, and wondered if he was thinking about diamonds. While Daddy read the paper, I stared at the phone, thinking I should call Quentin Sammons about the stroke, but I was unable to summon the energy. I considered leaving a message at Danny's hotel. If he didn't call back, well, then I would know. I wanted to ask Miss Jessie for the number but knew she wouldn't have it with her at the shop, so I waited until evening. Then evening arrived and it was supper time and more exercises and no privacy at the phone. John came to check on Daddy and I couldn't take my eyes off him, wanting the comfort of his arms, crazy as that was in the midst of everything else. I felt as if I were falling into a big, black hole and would never climb out. I could no longer pray. Mama ran to the store before it closed, leaving Daddy and me to talk, his paper filling slowly with words of encouragement—the patient becoming the doctor. I found no chance to call the Hardings until Mama returned, looking flushed and murmuring that she hadn't expected to be gone so long. When I finally dialed, Miss Jessie sounded inexplicably hesitant to give me the number, which increased my timidity.

"It's a dumb idea anyway," I told her, "and I probably won't call. But just in case."

I kissed Daddy good night as he and Mama went to bed; then I sat in the living room. I couldn't find the courage to pick up the phone. After a time I realized the hour had grown too late, and forced myself to bed. Where I did not sleep.

Daddy was noticeably better Tuesday morning, his leg and arm rising a bit higher, the red rubber ball clasped just enough to lift.

"John told us things would improve quickly!" I cried, cupping his chin in my hands. "In a few days you'll be throwing it again. I'll find us a box we can bounce it into."

He gazed at me and I wiped at a smudge on the coffee table.

For the next two hours I passed the phone repeatedly, fetching iced tea, placing a dish in the sink, picking up a book on the dining table. I called the ad agency and talked to Quentin but couldn't find the courage to call Danny, even though he was probably in meetings somewhere and I would only have to leave a message. Quentin accepted the news of my postponed return with such understanding that it left me moodily wondering whether I was needed there at all. The clock ticked and Daddy napped, Mama reading in her chair. I wandered in and out of my room, checking the time, thinking of Danny returning to Greece, wedding plans in his head.

And once as I passed, I picked up the receiver.

The number was on a scrap of paper tucked under the phone. I glanced at Mama's profile, pulled it out. Thinking nothing, nothing at all, I dialed the number. My heart began to pound. When the hotel answered I could barely speak.

"Danny Cander's room, please."

"Just a moment."

My knees shook, the receiver wet in my palm. I couldn't believe I was doing this. What if he picked up the phone? What could I possibly say?

"Sorry?" I replied to a distant voice, pulling back from my thoughts. "What?"

"I said Mr. Cander is no longer here," the woman informed me. "He checked out this morning."

chapter 64

*H*ow *does a person win life's hardest battles, Granddad?* I wondered. I wasn't talking about battles between soldiers and countries. Nor was I talking about the strenuous battle for use of a left arm, the ability to walk. I was talking about the most gut-wrenching of all battles, the kind that could forever change a life. *You won three medals in the wars, Granddad,* I thought. *You swam the Volturno River right under the eye of the enemy. You rescued soldiers from certain death in Korea. You were lauded and respected for your courage. But you lost in the end, didn't you? You lost the most important battle you ever faced. What good did God's promise of my victory with Mama do for you? You were left on one side of your chasm, Mama on the other, even the threat of impending death not strong enough to bridge the darkness in between.*

Maybe I had been right after all. There *were* some things even God couldn't handle.

There I sat in the bedroom of my childhood, fingering Granddad's colorful medals in their velvet-lined boxes, remembering how proud I had been of his accomplishments. But at that moment I could only see his disappointment and pain. Like Granddad, I had lost. I had lost my battle for Danny—again.

And I had lost Mama.

Again.

Tell me, Granddad, I asked the ceiling, *what good were your medals when they cost you the ones you loved the most?*

I was tucking the medals away when Mama called from the living room. "You promised to see Mr. Sledge," she reminded me, "if your daddy wasn't ready after eight weeks. Daddy can't keep his appointment with him today, so you have to go."

"Oh, Mama," I begged, "I'm so tired. You've already called him anyway, so he knows Daddy's not coming. Can't I just go tomorrow?"

"No, you can't. I told him you'd be there around two."

My eyes closed involuntarily. "Why did you do that?"

"You want your daddy back at work, don't you?"

"Yes, but—"

"Then go! And on the way back, stop by the store." She handed me a grocery list.

Her excuse to get rid of me was hardly subtle. But there was no use arguing. I couldn't risk another fight in front of Daddy and she knew it. Pushing down my anger, I told myself I should be grateful to get away.

An hour later, exuding energy I did not possess, I met with Mr. Sledge. He proved empathetic, shaking his head over our sudden setback. "But Daddy's getting better fast," I insisted. "I can already see improvement. It shouldn't take more than a few weeks."

"Don't worry, Celia," he replied, smoothing a blue knit shirt over his large belly, "you've kept your end of the deal; I'll keep mine. His job's ready for him when he can take it—in any capacity. These temps are fine in a pinch but they're certainly not William."

Woodenly I drove back to Bradleyville, relieved that at least something was going right. My eyes strayed to the dashboard clock. Two forty-five. Somewhere in New York, within three hours, Danny would probably be winding down his business day. Evidently he was catching a night flight back to Greece. Couldn't wait to take the ring back to Kathy.

At the grocery store I walked the aisles, my heart heavy, checking off Mama's list. Fresh corn. A roast. Eggs. Vanilla ice cream. I imagined an exotic wedding with cascading flowers and beautiful music. As I paid for the groceries, I wondered if Lee and Miss Jessie could manage a trip to Greece to attend.

Back home my tires crunched as I turned into the gravel driveway. With a sigh I slid from the car, gathered a full paper bag in each arm. When I was halfway across the front lawn, a spray of color caught my downcast eyes. Automatically I raised them to our sidewalk.

It was covered with pictures.

I halted. My head tilted, looking. Slowly, skin tingling, I approached the porch and set down the bags. Walked purposely through the grass out to the curb. Then turned around and viewed the length of the sidewalk.

I couldn't believe what I saw. Remaining on the lawn, I began to follow the sidewalk back to the porch, square by square.

The pictures were crudely drawn. She was no artist. I imagined the cautious bending of stiffened knees, the unfamiliar feel of warm, grainy cement under her palms. Her awkward forward shuffles. The stares of those driving by.

In the first square was a baby in a blue shirt. Kevy. A small hand, giving him his bottle. Mine.

In the second square, a fishing pole. A needle and thread mending a torn yellow shirt. A black and silver marble.

I took my time with each multipictured square, pausing, remembering. There was a book I once read to Kevy. Clean dishes draining on a counter. A war medal.

Cubby.

Tull's Drugstore.

A sparkling river.

How her back must have ached by that point.

Next, a wheelchair.

The strain of her shoulders as she reached for yet another piece of chalk.

Daddy's walker.

Apple pie.

By the time I reached the final square, my eyes were blurry. I blinked rapidly, lips moving as I read the words she had printed in large red letters. Read them again. I frowned, read them a third time, but couldn't understand why she had written the message.

At the porch I stopped to stare at the entire sidewalk, drinking in its pastel colors. I could almost hear Melissa's childish voice. Granddad humming the *Pink Panther* theme song.

Look, Mama! We colored the sidewalk for you!

Mama was trying so hard for my forgiveness. I wanted to rejoice but was afraid I would sob. Such a gift she had given me. So very late.

Practicality is a brash interloper. I suddenly remembered the ice cream. Picking up the paper bags, I took them into the kitchen, where I found a brief note.

Took Daddy for a walk.

The pictures flowed through my mind.

Mama and Daddy were gone longer than I had expected. I put the food away, folded the bags. As I stowed them under the sink, I thought I heard the sound of a car door shutting but dismissed it in the ensuing silence. When the doorbell rang loudly, my head jerked, bumping the top of the cabinet.

"Ow!" I pressed the spot with annoyance, rolling my eyes at my own clumsiness. Stood up. "Coming!"

Rounding the corner into the living room, rubbing my head, I looked toward the porch. The screen door meshed gray over the figure of a man in navy slacks and an unbuttoned sport coat. He stood half turned away, hands interlaced, forefingers tapping with impatience, gazing distractedly at the sidewalk. Beyond him was a car I'd never seen. Something about his stance looked familiar and I hesitated, staring at the light brown hair, a stray shock on his forehead, as though he were a figure from an ancient dream. I took another step and he heard my approach, swiveling. Dizziness washed over me as our eyes met. His were a shining, brilliant green.

"Celia."

He said my name in a voice that spoke of fishing and a lazy summer river, of a daisy-laden field and canopied oak trees, of dancing to the Bee Gees and whispered I-love-you's, of disappointments, heartbreaks, elation, and hope. The last time I heard his voice, he was saying he'd wait for me, that space and time could never part us. That he would save me an ocean. And that until then nothing could separate our hearts.

He called me again.

Mama's colored sidewalk; now this. I could not answer. With weak ankles my feet struggled across the worn carpet and halted before the door. The anticipation etching his face faded to uncertainty. I could hear my own heartbeat.

Danny, I pleaded silently, *have you come to torture me?*

He hesitated, a hand against the door. "Can I come in?"

Briefly I nodded.

He stepped across the threshold, easing the screen closed behind him. I watched his unsteady breathing, my own snatched away, his gaze traveling over my face, imploring response. I found none.

"I—" He stumbled. "Your mama called me last night from the Hardings'. I could hardly believe her story at first. Then all I could think about was catching the next plane."

The words refused to gel in my throbbing head. I continued to stare.

"Celia, listen to me." His voice rose with urgency. "No one has ever replaced you. I tried and tried, but . . . 'You're too distant,' they all say. 'Who are you really thinking about?' Kathy won't be surprised when I tell her. In her heart she already knows. I love *you*, Celia. I always have."

I've loved you for years.

Something inside me cracked, the words washing through me like warm current.

"Oh, Danny."

Suddenly his arms encircled me, grasping, my face against his neck. *It's a dream*, I told myself. *It's just a dream, one I want to last forever.*

"I've waited so long," he murmured, "so many years without knowing."

Time fell away like loosened flower petals as I clung to him, throat tightening. I didn't know how long we stood enfolded or what finally quelled my sobs, my head tilting back to drink in the sight of him, his mouth meeting mine. Our breaths long intermingled, his hands in my hair, hearts scudding. Then he pulled away, cupping my face, remarking with awe that I was more beautiful than before. And he was taller, his chest broader, the weight of Bradleyville long erased from his brow.

We found ourselves sinking onto the couch, kissing, smiling at each other, fingers trailing with renewed wonder along a jawline, a shoulder, a neck. Brushing hair from his forehead, I tried to tell him I was sorry for what I had done, but he shushed me abruptly, whispering, "No more apologies, no more past. We've both had enough."

Thoughts swirling, I asked about Greece, and he extolled its beauty.

"I've never seen the ocean," I blurted ridiculously.

He smiled sadly. "Will you let me show it to you?"

I could only nod.

His gaze grew intense and I watched him search for words. "There's so much to talk about, Celia. We have different lives now. Do you think we—can we find a way to start over? Try again?"

Little Rock flashed through my mind, the possibility of leaving it weighted with sentiments that dreams merely skimmed. I couldn't begin to think through details at that moment. But touching Danny again, I did know one thing. My artistic skills and advertising experience were portable, while my grief over him had been so hard to carry.

"You won't get away from me this time," I said.

He squeezed my hand until I thought it would break. "We've both made terrible mistakes, Celia. We didn't do what your granddad told us; we took our eyes off Jesus. After I lost you, I rejected him completely. I told him it was all his fault. But deep inside I knew that wasn't true. Your mother's phone call was a miracle—God's gift to me, when I didn't deserve it. He's given you back to me and I'm not going to blow it this time."

"You won't, Danny," I replied quickly. "Neither will I. Not after all this."

"We could, Celia. Left to our own devices, we'd manage it. So we've got to promise each other that we'll look to Jesus for guidance this time—in everything. He's the only binding that will hold us together."

The seriousness of Danny's tone brought me up short, the brilliance of my sudden happiness momentarily fading. This was no small pledge that Danny demanded. Selfishness and pride had once destroyed our relationship. That may have been years ago, but I knew those same traits still existed within me. Just look at how I had treated Mama in the past few days. Even so, she had responded in tremendous love. God was giving me another chance with both Danny and her after so many years. But this wasn't the end; it was only the beginning. The old hurts and grievances between Mama and me, and Danny and me, were sure to raise their ugly heads. I had much to learn and much to work on within myself before I could completely let go of the past, and some of that process would not be easy.

Of one more thing I was certain. No way could I do it without God's help.

"I promise you," I told Danny, this time understanding the depth of the words. "Before God, I promise!"

"And I promise you."

He took me again in his arms.

Sometime later distant voices meandered through the open window, and before I realized it, I was on my feet. "Mama and Daddy!" Sudden shyness overwhelmed me. There was so much to thank Mama for, so much to say. Helplessly I looked to Danny. "Come with me."

We stepped through the screen door hand in hand, walked down the porch steps to stand on the multicolored sidewalk. Danny's gaze swept the cement. "This is all for you, isn't it?"

"Yes," I said, smiling. "Isn't it beautiful?"

From a half block away Daddy beamed lopsidedly at us, Mama pushing his wheelchair. "Haay, Daannyy!" he cried. "Guud ta see ya!" Leaning forward expectantly, he urged Mama to hurry up.

"Good to see you too, sir!"

"Heaven's sake, William." Mama's voice floated to us, brusque with self-consciousness. "I can't move any faster."

Danny started to tug me across the grass, but my footsteps faltered, a realization dawning. Slowly my eyes traveled from Mama's face to the last square in the sidewalk.

"Wait, Danny." I pulled him back. "This one. She meant it for you."

Aloud Danny read the message in its careful red print and squeezed my hand with joy.

You'll be staying for supper, I expect.

Author's Note

While writing this story, I attended my family's annual reunion at my parents' home in Wilmore, Kentucky. God has blessed our family with a wonderful closeness, even though we're now spread across the country. Mom and Dad, lifetime servants of Jesus Christ, have modeled for their four daughters what it means to trust in him daily. Being with them has always been a special time for us. By that year's reunion, my parents had reached eighty and were still in good health. My sisters and I cherished the time with them even more.

One night after dinner a cousin presented me and my sisters each with a small, thoughtful gift. Mine, God bless him, was a box of sidewalk chalk. Gleefully the four of us went outside to color the sidewalk for Mom and Dad. As cousins and in-laws and children looked on, we each took a square. The youngsters, including mine, giggled at the sight of us adults on our hands and knees, drawing. Soon the walkway was covered with flowers, hearts, messages, a cozy house with smoke curling from its chimney, a star, an exclamation point.

When we were through, I gazed at the colorful designs, explaining to my curious daughter why we had done it. Through the writing of my book, I told her, coloring the sidewalk had come to symbolize a special way to honor someone, to say to that person, "I love you . . . accept you . . . *celebrate* you." It is a way to depict what, through loving that person, you should live every day.

When you're a little older, I added, maybe you'll color the sidewalk for someone you love.

Amberly was only seven but I think she understood.

My mother was joyous at the gift, radiant. Whisking a hot-pink jump rope from the lawn, she began skipping it on the sidewalk. I grabbed a camera. In the picture she is still wearing her green-and-white checked apron, the rope caught sailing over her head. Her arms are flung out, fingers grasping its handles, her mouth open in a wide, unabashed grin.

And spread beneath her skipping feet are the colorful life celebrations of her four beloved children.

Brandilyn, daughter number four
Redwood City, California

We want to hear from you. Please send your comments about this book to us in care of the address below. Thank you.

ZONDERVAN™

GRAND RAPIDS, MICHIGAN 49530

WWW.ZONDERVAN.COM